SHATTERED
A Russian Guns Novel

BETHANY-KRIS

Published by Bethany-Kris

www.bethanykris.com

ISBN 10: 0-9947909-5-8
ISBN 13: 978-0-9947909-5-8
eISBN: 0-9937797-6-3
eISBN 13: 978-0-9937797-6-3

Cover Design © Jay Aheer

DEDICATION

For all the people who believe in second chances.
.

CONTENTS

ACKNOWLEDGMENTS

There are so many people who deserve love, hugs, praise, thanks and cookies in these few paragraphs because without them, *The Russian Guns* would never have gone any further than *The Arrangement*.

To my editors who worked with me on this story, you are invaluable and beautiful people. Elle, my forever girl. And Dixie, my fic wife. My *dushkas*—my *Russian Guns*—always.

Jay Aheer deserves a huge thank you and love for her awesome work with the Guns covers. My pre-reader Tracy who took to *Demyan & Ana* and *Shattered* before their release and didn't hold back. Thank you for being awesome and loving my words even when they hurt. My spouse, who never fails to give me unwavering support in this writing gig of mine. He's the one who tells me I am perfect even when I'm so clearly not.

And to the readers … this is the end of *The Russian Guns*. Thank you for making it what it was for me. Thank you for reading, for giving me time out of your lives, and for loving this series like you have. Thank you.

—Kris

.

PROLOGUE

Claire Braden had spent the majority of her life trying to stay away from the violent lifestyle of the mob and the men within it. Or rather, one particular man, her step-uncle. Liam Dolan didn't—or couldn't—comprehend the word empathy. In all things, he was unfeeling and cruel.

Family was another word her step-uncle didn't have in his vocabulary, unless they could be of use for him in some way. Claire supposed she should count her lucky stars in that regard because he mostly left her alone. But she still knew what his influence on those around her could do and had done.

After all, just because Claire's mother had married into the Irish mob after her first husband's death didn't automatically mean her daughter was married to it, too, right?

Wrong.

The mafia left no one untouched, especially those closest to it through affiliation. Usually those touches came in the form of cuts that left scars behind. The worst kind of scars that were a brutal red, puckered skin, sore to the touch even when healed, and would never fade.

No matter how much time passed, those scars didn't leave.

So, it was surreal to sit across the room from Anton Avdonin, a man in a position of power and dangerous like her uncle, while they talked about Liam as if they were having tea. Dreamlike, even bizarre, because all of her work and effort to stay away from a man like her uncle led her to one who simply shared a different last name.

"You don't sound very …"

"Irish?" Claire offered.

Anton smiled, flashing white teeth. "Yes."

"You don't sound very Russian."

"Point taken, although it's taken me years to lose the accent."

"It still comes out," Viviana Avdonin said from her spot on the couch. "When he's angry, or in the midst of se—"

"*Vine.*"

"Well, it does."

Claire was amused at the two, but she hid it. "My biological

3

father is Irish and my mother is half. My step-father is full, but he didn't think to teach me much and I tried to stay away from a lot of things, if you know what I mean."

"I suppose, yes," Anton said quietly.

"So, no quirks or accent from me. Sorry to disappoint."

"No disappointment here. I am curious as to why you've done all this, though. Come to us, I mean."

"I want to know," Claire said.

"It isn't a pretty story," Anton replied.

"I didn't come here for a fairytale."

"I should hope not," Viviana said. "Because our life sure as hell isn't one."

A ghost of a tender smile shadowed Anton's features as he regarded his wife from the side in silence. Claire decided in that moment, with that one gesture, this Russian man was nothing like her uncle and she had obviously been mistaken in thinking so.

Liam would never smile, and if he did, something awful was sure to follow.

"You've been in the city for how long?" Anton asked.

"A couple of months," Claire said.

"How did you learn of my family?"

Claire glanced away, uncomfortable under the man's scrutiny. "I asked enough of the right questions, I suppose."

"About Cavan."

"Yes."

"Your half-brother," Anton added pointedly.

Claire hated that she had to admit her relation to the dead man at all. "Yes."

"What do you know about what happened?" Anton asked.

"I know you killed him."

"No, my son did."

"Oh," Claire whispered. "I only knew the Russians had their hand in it and I assumed—"

"That the boss does all the work?" Viviana interrupted with a soft laugh.

Claire shrugged. "I guess."

"And you want to know why," Anton said, drawing out the last word slowly.

"I do."

"Do you miss him?" the man asked instead.

That was an easy question to answer. "No."

"Why not?"

"Because he was a monster," Claire said honestly.

Anton hummed under his breath, his fingers pattering to the table in a fast beat. "He raped my daughter, and my son retaliated on him for what he did. Count your blessings that it was a closed coffin, my dear."

Claire shivered. The information she had been trying to find for years was tossed out so fast that she almost missed it. Except she couldn't miss it at all.

And she *knew* ...

Knew before he even said the words why Cavan had died. Not because someone else had told her first, but it wasn't the first time Claire had experienced the backlash of her half-brother's brutal nature.

A learned behavior, her mother said once.

Claire agreed. Cavan, spoiled and indulged by Liam, had grown up to be the man his uncle created. Yes, a monster.

"It didn't end with that, of course," Viviana added when her husband stayed silent.

"Oh?"

"Unfortunately, no," Anton said, resting back in his chair. "Demyan, my son, was expecting his first child—a little girl—with his fiancée."

No.

The word banged around inside Claire's head but miraculously, didn't make its way out.

"Your uncle—"

"Step," Claire corrected quickly. "I share no blood with that man, not even a last name."

"Lucky," Anton murmured. "I would have killed you, otherwise."

Claire didn't even blink. "Really?"

"Yes." Anton waved the statement off, dismissing it altogether. "It's not important. You came here for information, so I will give it to you. Liam had his men kill Gia, my son's fiancée and my former best friend's daughter."

A quiet man in the corner lifted his hand but kept his face down and his attention on the glass of vodka in his hand.

"Ivan, I mean," Anton said, gesturing at the silent man.

"Former friend?" Claire asked.

"Best," Anton corrected.

Ivan chuckled but the sound was hollow. "What a bullet can do to an over thirty year friendship is … amazing."

"Something like that," Anton replied coolly.

"Are we going to start shouting at one another in Russian again?" Viviana asked as she pulled out a yellow buffing file to work on her already manicured nails. "Because if so, I would like to leave before you two get started."

"No, we'll be good," Ivan muttered.

"Something like that," Anton repeated, his gaze leveling on Claire once more. "An apology is right on the tip of your tongue, isn't it?"

"Yes," Claire admitted.

"Don't. I have no interest in hearing it from you, neither does my wife, and I'm sure Ivan would say the same. Neither your apology, nor your blood, will pay for ours that spilled."

Claire shifted in the seat, her fists clenching tightly in her lap. "How did you know I wanted to apologize at all?"

"You have honest eyes," Anton said simply. "They're the kind of eyes that are an opening to your soul. An old soul, which I can understand. My son had eyes like those once, too."

Did that mean he didn't now? Was it possible for everything you were to be shattered and taken away by one man?

"Because of Liam," Claire said.

"Because of Liam," Anton echoed. "And now when we see Demyan, there's nothing staring back. It's hard to watch a man slowly suffocate to death in his own private hell, especially when he doesn't even realize he's dying."

Viviana sighed. "Harder when that man is your son."

Anton nodded, agreeing with his wife. "You also have a look of guilt, Claire. Like maybe you feel you have something to answer for."

She did. She had so much to answer for.

"What it is you have to answer for, Claire?" Anton asked.

"I didn't protect someone once," she said softly.

"Does your family know you've sought us out?" Anton asked.

"No. And my aunt and uncle believe I'm in the city to work, mostly. Since they're the only family I have here and I'm twenty-seven-years-old, they treat me like an adult who doesn't need to be babysat."

"Apparently you should be if you've found your way to my den," Anton replied.

"Maybe."

"You said work. Doing what, exactly?"

"I'm a nurse."

Again, a small smile curved the man's lips upwards at the corners. "So was my mother. ER, mostly."

"I prefer pediatrics," Claire explained.

"Children," Viviana said, giving her husband a look. "Imagine that."

"Vine …" Anton's voice barely contained a hidden warning.

"I didn't say anything, Anton."

"I can hear your wheels turning, baby. Don't start."

"Fine," Viviana replied, huffing before going back to buffing her nails.

Claire was lost, but she didn't bother to ask what she missed between the two. She figured they wouldn't tell her anyway. "I do feel guilty about what happened to your daughter and …" Claire nodded at Ivan in the corner. "His daughter, too."

Anton lifted a single shoulder in response. "We all are. Apologies have gotten us nowhere but cold."

She supposed she couldn't possibly understand these people's pain because hers was not the same and theirs was much worse.

Leaning forward in his chair to rest his arms over his desk, Anton said, "I'm going to kill your uncle." Claire wished she could be surprised, but she wasn't. "And strangely, I have the distinct feeling you don't even care if I do."

"I really don't. I know how he is and the things he's done. His death wouldn't be a loss to this world after everything, but a gift."

"Good, because you're going to help me do it."

Her back straightened like someone had shoved a metal rod up her spine. This was not what she had come here for, but Claire knew by the way Anton Avdonin was staring at her, he wasn't going to give her a choice.

It was yet another thing she wasn't surprised about.

She also didn't care.

"How?" Claire asked, unsettled.

"We'll figure something out. I always do."

Claire fidgeted with the hem of her shirt. "I don't know if I can do that. Help you, I mean."

"Sure you can," Viviana said sweetly, smiling a brilliant sight that looked warm but felt cold.

"Won't that make me just as bad as them? A monster, too?"

"Haven't you realized it, yet?" Anton asked her quietly.

She shook her head. "No."

Viviana smiled from her seat on the couch, still buffing her nails as though the conversation happening wasn't really going on at all. "We're all monsters, sweetheart. Some of us just hide it better than others."

That was the key, wasn't it?

CHAPTER ONE

If there was one particular thing that frightened the Bratva men who worked under Demyan more than anything else, it was his ability to kill and carry on a normal conversation. Sure, his coldness and the disinterested attitude he sported usually kept others at bay, but the cruel factor left them warier than ever.

"What are you doing tonight?"

Koldan shrugged from his spot on the makeshift, plywood counter. "After the party? Whatever Ana wants, you know. Probably chill at your parents' place for a bit and try to stay the fuck out of Anton's way."

Demyan snorted under his breath. "He likes you."

"For the last two years, he's wanted to kill me."

"Nah, for the last *four* years he's wanted to kill you."

"Thanks," Koldan said. "I just have to make it to the wedding."

"Honestly, my father likes you, man. Especially since …" Demyan trailed off, waving a hand at himself like that explained it all. He supposed it did because shit, Anton Avdonin had a son, but he wasn't there anymore.

"Anyway," Demyan drawled, bored with the entire conversation. "He likes you. If he didn't, he'd have killed you by now."

"Maybe," Koldan agreed quietly.

"What did you two get her for tonight?"

"That dollhouse she's been talk—"

The flat end of the hammer came down on the kneecap of a man Demyan had found poking around his territory. The guy screamed into his gag, the stench of urine and vomit emanating from his form. Demyan wasn't sure of the man's name, and he didn't give a fuck, but the shamrock tattoo on the inside of his wrist said enough. That, and the fact he had been toting a gun and tried to go in on one of Demyan's guys.

After what happened to the Avdonin family by the Irish four years ago, none of that scum needed to be in Little Odessa.

Numbness settled in Demyan like it always did when he worked. Well, it never really left.

The hammer came down again. Another muted scream sounded as the guy's eyes flew wide, and his kneecap blew out from the force of the hit. Bone, blood, and matter spilled.

Demyan didn't even flinch.

This was the business. His life.

Welcome to the freak show.

Flipping the hammer around, so the claw was out instead, Demyan swung it down and let it lodge into the cavity of the man's knee.

Yeah, that shit fucking *hurt*.

If the second round of vomit that bubbled around the man's gag as he choked was any indication, he felt it, too.

Apparently, Koldan was just about done with the scene.

"Goddamn, Demyan," Koldan muttered.

Glancing over his shoulder, Demyan chuckled at the sight of Koldan burying his mouth into the side of his arm, poorly hiding his disgust. "You're a pussy, Koldan."

"I am not, but I would have put the bastard out of his misery a couple of hours ago."

So, maybe he'd been at this for a while.

Demyan shrugged in response.

"Irish, I know," Koldan said, filling in the blank Demyan wouldn't.

After what they took from him, they deserved everything they fucking got.

"Good thing you've got a boss position coming to you in the future." Demyan yanked the hammer out of the guy's knee, ignoring the tears streaking down the fool's face. Tired of using the weapon, he tossed it across the room.

"Why is that?" Koldan asked.

"Because then you can just order sorry assholes like me to do this for you instead of doing it yourself. No need for a pakhan to get his hands dirty."

"Hey, your father didn't order you to—"

Demyan turned, flashing his teeth in a wicked sneer. "I know."

Without another word, Demyan turned back to the man he'd been making hurt a whole hell of a lot for the last few hours.

"Christ, you're one stubborn motherfucker, aren't you?" Demyan asked the bound man sitting on the metal chair in the middle of the warehouse. "Just blink twice if you're going to tell me why in the fuck you thought it'd be okay for you to be anywhere near Avdonin territory, not to mention, coming after one of us. When you do that, everything will move a lot faster."

Didn't mean it wouldn't hurt, however.

The man's lips curled back behind the dirty gag in his mouth, but only muffled garbles of nonsense came out. Demyan had tied the bandana tight, so it wasn't a surprise.

"You almost done?" Koldan asked.

"Not yet." Demyan squatted down to the floor, keeping his gaze locked with the Irishman. "Keep looking at these eyes, asshole, because they're the last thing you're ever going to see."

"It's nearly five," Koldan informed. "Party is at six-thirty."

Shit. Demyan would need a good shower and a change of clothes. That was going to eat up some time.

"Yeah, give Kyle a call and tell him he's got a mess to clean in warehouse three," Demyan ordered Koldan without turning around.

"Will do."

Standing, Demyan reached into his back pocket and pulled out a knife. He cut the gag from the man's mouth, careful not to get the fool's vomit on his hands. He didn't need that stench in his SUV.

Immediately, the guy started screaming. Demyan stood stock still with his arms crossed and a cool expression until his captive was all screamed out. It didn't take long. When he was done shouting to no one, he prayed through sobs.

God didn't help men like them.

Demyan pulled the gun from the waistband of his jeans, waving it and the knife in the man's face. "Talk, and you'll get quick and easy with a bullet. Stay quiet, and I'll gut you like a goddamn pig and let you hold your intestines while I cut out your tongue."

"I ... I-I ..."

"I-I-I, what?" Demyan barked. "Speak the fuck up, man. Why was an Irish mobster in our territory? Do you think Detroit cares if we cull a couple of you useless fucks? Trust me, that family doesn't *know* how to feel."

The guy coughed out a bitter laugh. "Us?"

"Yes, you. That's what I said, wasn't it? I hate repeating myself."

"*Us*," the guy spat, but it wasn't a question the second time. "You were in our territory first."

What?

• • •

"Hey," Ana said as Demyan walked into the family room of his parents' large Oceana home.

His sister bumped his hip with hers playfully. Ana was the only person Demyan allowed to act like that with him. Mostly because she left him alone when he wanted her to while everyone else kept demanding more. Like he was supposed to be their personal project to make happy again or some nonsense.

Right.

Demyan rested back to the wall, relaxing for a moment as he watched people mill between the kitchen and family room with plates of food in hand. Balloons and streamers were strategically placed, giving the house a birthday party kind of feel. Demyan wasn't in the mood to party, but it also wasn't his day, he supposed.

"Hey," he said.

"You're a half hour late." His sister nodded at the ornate clock on the far wall.

"Yeah, well ... work."

That usually shut his sister's questions up and this time was no exception.

Ana glanced down at the gift bag dangling from Demyan's fingers. "What did you get her?"

"Something," he replied vaguely, smirking when she huffed at his non-answer. "Koldan get here yet?"

They separated after leaving the warehouse, but he hadn't noticed the guy's car outside.

"Ma needed more pop, so he went to the store for her."

"Ah, I see. Gives him a break from being under Anton's thumb, I guess."

"Papa is—"

"Sometimes an asshole, even to your fiancé, Ana."

"Yeah, well ... not when I'm around."

Yeah, even then, but his sister didn't get to see it because Anton was sly as fuck in that way. Anton didn't want to give away his only daughter for marriage and despite approving of Koldan, felt the need to give the guy shit while he was still in New York. Demyan didn't pretend to understand his father. They were nothing alike. Not anymore.

Demyan pushed away from the wall, ignoring the curious, guarded stares of some of the guests nearby. These people, they didn't know him, not the man he was now, anyway. That or they didn't want to. The ones who did—mostly Bratva—were scared shitless of him, and everyone else always started a conversation with Demyan by apologizing.

Four years after he buried Gia and people were still apologizing for it, like her dying was their fault and the remorse they felt should make it all better. Yeah, Demyan could finally think her name, but nothing accompanied it now. No emotion, rage or pain, just that dull numbness in his fingertips and a deadweight in his stomach.

Like maybe it never even happened, and his memories were simply delusions filled with blood, pain, and horror. Because that's all she was to him, now. A memory.

"I better go find the birthday girl," Demyan said, giving his sister a smile.

It was awkward, he knew it was. It even felt awkward on his face. Demyan didn't like to smile. Sneering, smirking and being an all-around asshole, those were the things he could do. Smiling? Not so much.

"She asked for you," Ana said, shrugging. "Actually, demanded."

Demyan laughed, but even the sound was strained and untrue. "That's my girl."

It didn't take him long to find the princess of the hour. She had been set up at the head of the long kitchen table, surrounded by pink and yellow streamers with helium filled balloons tied to both ends of her chair. Smiling wide and showing off perfect white rows of teeth, Demyan's daughter sat content between her grandfathers as gifts were passed over for her to open.

Demyan took a moment, staying hidden from Vera's sight in the entryway, to take in his child. She was always happy. Unknowing of the tragedy that had come before her and how her

13

mother was gunned down the day Vera Avdonin made her way into the world.

"One more over there, Ivan?" Anton asked.

Ivan handed a sparkly, purple packaged gift to Vera without a word to his former best friend. How the men were even sharing a space, Demyan didn't know. Then again, Vera always had that effect on people. She brought them together whether they wanted to be or not.

Since Gia's murder, the friendship between Ivan and Anton had changed drastically. In fact, a person who didn't know what the two men used to be like wouldn't believe they had ever been friends, really. Ivan blamed Anton. Anton let Ivan have his anger, even if it was misdirected.

And despite the inner conflict it caused for a good year in the Bratva, Anton allowed Ivan to step down from being his Sovietnik—his right-hand man—in their Russian mafia brotherhood. It had been a rule-altering event in the Bratva's history because as Demyan understood it, no man left the Russian Mafia alive.

Ivan had.

Anton, regardless of knowing how his ex-friend now felt about him, protected Ivan when he walked out of the Bratva.

"Open it, *dushka*," Anton said to Vera as he accepted a glass of water from his wife. "Thanks, baby."

"Where's Papa?" Vera asked. "Grandpapa Anton, I want Papa."

"He's coming," Anton replied, reaching over to tap the present with his finger. "Open it, Vera."

"Is Demyan working, then?" Eva asked from where she stood behind Ivan. "He seems to be doing a lot of that lately."

Demyan held back a scoff. Apparently being involved in the Bratva meant he would skip his daughter's birthday. Sure, the first couple years raising Vera had been tough and sometimes she was away from him more than she was with him but shit …

Vera was still *his*.

Christ.

"He's coming," Anton repeated.

"Soon?" Vera asked quietly.

"Soon, baby," Viviana assured.

Vera was a dark-haired, blue-eyed beauty at just four-years-old. She was the one—the only, really—good thing in Demyan's heart. She was serenity in her soul, joy in her smile, and peace in her eyes. She was also her mother through and through. The older Vera got, the more she reminded Demyan of Gia.

He wished he could say it made him sad or angry, but the never-ending numbness of his detachment didn't let him feel a fucking thing. Hell, even pain would be better than nothing at all.

Demyan knew though, somewhere in the black bleakness of his deadened emotions, that if he felt something, he wouldn't have the capability to get through the day; never mind be who he was. The last time he allowed his emotions to win and take over, he spent months in a vacuum of nothingness.

Six months, actually. The first half a year of his daughter's life was devoid of everything but pain, and it was *easy*. He barely made it out of that alive.

Demyan couldn't do it again because he wouldn't survive it a second time.

"Papa!"

Vera must have gotten a peek of Demyan in the entryway of the dining room, so he walked in the rest of the way, his eyes on only his daughter. Demyan was aware how most of these people looked at him. Some, like he was broken. Others, like he was inept at loving and caring for his child. And then there were people like his parents, the ones who knew how cold and unforgiving he could be, that didn't know what to think at all.

They were all right. Every single one of them.

Demyan still didn't care. He managed both his life and his daughter just fine and had for four years. She was happy, safe, and healthy, and that's what mattered most to him.

Vera pushed the present onto the table, her face lighting up with happiness. Demyan's expression didn't change a bit as he crossed the dining room to meet his bouncing daughter.

"*S Dnem Rozhdeniya, dushka,*" Demyan whispered, leaning down to kiss Vera's pink, smiling cheek.

"Happy birthday?"

"A very happy birthday," Demyan repeated in English.

Vera peeked down at the gift bag in her father's hand. "Is that mine, Papa?"

"Maybe. You'll have to wait and see."

"Demyan, give her the gift and let her open it," Anton said.

"It's her day, after all."

Demyan ignored his father. They were going to have enough words later considering the shit he heard from the Irishman.

Vera's tiny hand found her father's at his side and she gave it a squeeze. Silently, Demyan did the same. It was, and would always be, their way of expressing words that weren't said.

I love you, mostly.

"Later?" Vera asked.

"Later," Demyan promised. "Now, where is your cake?"

• • •

Demyan sat his daughter on the edge of the bed in his old room. Vera hugged her father tightly around his neck, giggling. Despite him moving out long ago, his parents didn't change much in the space. He refused to search too deep into the things left sitting out on his desk or even what was hidden in the shoe boxes under the bed. If he did, he would find marks of his past everywhere.

A past he just didn't want to think about anymore.

"Can I see? Can I?" Vera asked, her excitement level rising like the tone of her voice.

"Calm down, princess," Demyan said, chuckling low.

"But, *Papa*!"

Demyan fixed Vera with a stare that silenced her pleading. The birthday party had gone on longer than he anticipated, although he didn't complain. It was Vera's day, not his, so if people wanted to celebrate his little girl until the sun set, they could go at it.

"All right, *dushka*, but be careful. Okay?"

Vera nodded, snatching the pink bag Demyan held out for her to take. "Okay!"

She pulled each piece of pink tissue paper out of the gift bag slowly, placing them to the side of the bed. Reaching inside, she brought out a long cylinder shaped object, tapered at the ends and also wrapped in tissue paper.

"What is it?" Vera asked, feeling the gift with her hands and turning it over.

"Open it up, sweetheart," Demyan urged.

Vera unwrapped the tissue paper, revealing a hand painted, carefully crafted matryoshka doll. The Russian nesting dolls hadn't been made in some shop in China, but instead, specially imported from Russia by a craftsman who had been making them for over forty years. When he put in the order months ago, Demyan simply asked for a specific design on the dolls and gave a size. They turned out perfectly with their striking faces, and the intricate dresses painted on their wooden bodies.

"Oh!" Vera gasped, her fingers ghosting over the painted face and pink cheeks of the largest doll. "She's so beautiful, Papa."

"Open her up," Demyan said. "There's four more inside her. All of them are a little different."

She was so in love with the nesting dolls her cousins had received last Christmas that it was the only thing Demyan knew to get her that no one else would. It was also special because Vera wasn't the kind of kid to act jealous or ask for something someone else had.

So, when she mentioned to her father the very pretty matryoshka dolls her cousins received, Demyan knew it was something she really wanted. Even more so because she told him and not anyone else.

Vera popped open the first doll to reveal a second smaller one nestled inside the bottom. Pulling it out, she admired the smiling face and reddened cheeks of the doll before pulling it out and opening it, too. She took her time with each doll until she had them all out, their bodies back together, and sitting in a row from largest to smallest along the edge of the bed.

"What do you think?" Demyan asked.

"Thank you," Vera whispered.

"You're so welcome, my *dushka*." Demyan reached over and spun each doll so they were facing his girl. "Notice anything about them?"

Vera nodded. "They look like me."

"They sure do."

Each doll sported painted back curls, bright blue eyes, and wore the design of specific dresses Vera loved. They even shared the tiny, pixie-like nose his daughter had.

Vera stared at the dolls.

"What's wrong?" Demyan asked.

"I don't want to break them," Vera explained. "They're pretty."

Demyan chuckled. "They're yours, Vera, so you can do

17

whatever you want with them."

"Really?"

"Absolutely."

"But you said to be careful."

"I wanted you to see them at least once before you went crazy with them. And they're tough, so I don't think you could break them very easily even if you tried."

"I won't try, Papa," Vera said. "I promise I will take care of them."

Oh, Demyan didn't even need to hear his daughter give him the reassurances to know how close she would keep her dolls and how much she would cherish them. She always did with the things he gave her, no matter how small or seemingly insignificant.

A gift from her daddy meant the absolute world to Vera Avdonin.

Demyan picked up the largest doll, pointing at the Cyrillic lettering along the bottom of the painted dress for his daughter to see. Солнышко моё, it read. Vera was an English-first speaking child, but she was learning to read Russian before anything else. That way, speaking the language would come easier to her. It was transliterating Russian words from the Cyrillic alphabet to the Latin one that was difficult.

"Sol ... ko ... mo." Vera nearly got the pronunciation of the words but not quite.

"Close," Demyan murmured. "*Solnyshko moyo.*"

"Sun?" Vera asked, her little nose scrunching up as if she were thinking.

"Yes, that's pretty much it. *My* sun, bright and beautiful."

"Me?"

"You, sweetheart."

Vera grinned up at her father. "Can I show Grandmamma?"

"Grandmamma would love that," said a dark tenor from behind Demyan. "And maybe she can show you the set she has, too, *hmm?*"

Demyan's spine stiffened as he stood. He forgot to close the door and his private moment with his daughter had been intruded on because of it. Even if it was his father, that didn't matter to Demyan. He didn't like for people to see him with Vera when it was just them alone.

"Does she?" Vera asked her grandfather.

"She does," Anton replied. "They're not as pretty as yours, though."

"I bet they are."

Anton laughed. "Well, you'll have to decide for yourself."

Demyan helped Vera tuck the nesting dolls back together quickly before she hugged it to her chest and skipped out of the room with a beaming smile that would melt the coldest of hearts. Demyan's was no exception, but he always managed to hide it well.

"That was sweet of you," Anton said. "Actually, I think that's the first thing I've seen you give that girl."

Demyan's hackles rose as they usually did whenever his father was around. He refused to defend or explain his choice of keeping his daughter at arm's length in the eyes of people beyond him and Vera. There would never come a day when another human being could use what mattered most against him again. He wouldn't allow it.

Even if that meant appearing like a cold, cruel bastard to his own father.

Frankly, it was better this way. At least, that's how Demyan felt about it in regards to Anton. Vera wasn't the only thing Demyan was afraid to lose, and whoever he loved and was the closest to, might suffer for his attachments someday.

Anton wouldn't be one of them.

Turning to face his father, Demyan kept his expression unreadable. "It's her birthday. She deserves something special, I suppose."

"*Mmm*, and one of those big headed dolls with too much makeup and terrible clothing choices would have worked just as well."

"What's your point, Anton?"

Anton flinched when Demyan called him by his name and not Papa or Dad like he always had before. The first time, Anton did a double take of his son as if he'd been unsure of what he heard.

"No point, son, I was just saying," Anton said, sighing heavily. "You were late tonight."

"Work," Demyan replied shortly. "Which you already knew. I don't need a lecture about being on time when I'm cleaning up messes for the Bratva."

Anton nodded. "I did know you were working, and since I'm

the goddamn boss regardless if we're in my home or on the streets, you can cut the fucking attitude and tell me what happened."

It took all the effort Demyan could muster to swallow back his irritation and give his father the respect he deserved. Demyan spent a great deal of his time getting out from under his father's thumb, not that he hadn't liked it there before, but now it only felt like control.

The Bratva and Vera were the only two places in Demyan's life that Anton really got to see. Mostly because he didn't have a choice but to let his father in for those things. Every place else, Demyan kept locked up tight.

It was his goddamn life, and he wasn't stupid. He was well aware that his father didn't feel as though Demyan was living, not truly. But it didn't matter. It wasn't Anton's choice, and he didn't get to make Demyan's for him.

"Yeah, I planned on having words with you about that shit sometime today," Demyan said, somehow managing to keep the heat out of his tone. Barely.

Anton arched a single brow high. "Oh?"

"Yes. Why the fuck were Russians on the Irish's territory, huh?"

Demyan didn't beat around the bush. His father always taught him not to, and there was a hell of a lot of lessons like those that Demyan could remember growing up. Being blunt was one of the best ones. Straight for the throat, right for the kill. It always set a man off balance when he wasn't expecting it.

Unfortunately, Anton Avdonin wasn't like every other man.

Anton's expression didn't change a bit. "I don't know what you're talking about."

"Sure," Demyan said. "The small Irish syndicate has every reason to be fucking around in Brooklyn and Little Odessa because they have all the protection and power in the world here to be doing so. Right?"

"Demyan, count our numbers. There isn't one Bratva man from our family that didn't show up for tribute last week. The Irish were toeing our line for at least a month before that. You can bet your ass that if even one Russian skipped over into the Irish's territory, they would have put him down like a dog. Kind of like we did for theirs today."

"Well, I made him work for it."

Anton's lips drew thin at that omission. "Did you, now?"

"Making a point, that's all."

"They're not all Cavan or Liam, Demyan."

Demyan shrugged. "I'm not going to give one the chance to be, either."

"Nonetheless, I've sent no men to the Irish and I don't plan to."

"I fucking hope not," Demyan replied. "I don't want them anywhere near me or my daughter, Anton. I don't want them to even think they have a reason to be anywhere near us. You better not be planning some stupid shit that will get us all killed."

Demyan worked damn hard to keep his daughter safe from the prospect of Liam Dolan coming back on her after that man killed Vera's mother. He didn't want his father messing with that in some way.

Anton smirked, scoffing. "And what if I was, son? What could you do? You're as cold as ice, Demyan Avdonin, and someday you'll make a damn good boss because of it. But that day is not today. I'm boss, not you. Cold, yes, right down to your bones, but you're not cold enough to take it from me."

CHAPTER TWO

Demyan worked the kinks out of his shoulders as he waited for the familiar apartment door to open. The stress from his father's veiled warning the day before had somehow settled inside his goddamn muscles, and he couldn't get it out.

Anton was right. Demyan wouldn't take his seat as the boss.

Their conversation also left him with the distinct feeling his father was planning something, even if Demyan couldn't prove it yet. Not that it would matter if he could.

For fuck's sake.

Demyan reached up to knock on the thick door again, but he didn't get the chance. It swung wide open, exposing Sofia Vasin dressed in tiny cotton sleep shorts and a yellow beater.

"You could have called first, Demyan," Sofia said, eyeing him from the doorway.

"I was in the fucking neighborhood."

"Oh?"

"Yeah. Don't act like me showing up here bothers you. We both know it doesn't, and I always leave you fucking happy."

Her, anyway. Demyan, on the other hand, left satisfied but as cold as ever.

Sofia lifted a single shoulder in response like she didn't care either way. Knowing her, the girl probably didn't. "True enough."

"You busy?"

"Not really. Just getting some sleep in before I have to make the trek to Jersey for worship tomorrow."

Demyan snorted, knowing damn well how that sounded to mock a God he was supposed to believe in, too. "Are you ever going to tell Adrik to shove that demand up his ass?"

"I indulge my father," she replied simply.

"No, you lie to him. Big difference."

"Not much."

Sofia grinned a sinful sight that would make any man harder than steel. Demyan was the exception to that rule because he wasn't beguiled by Sofia's games and beauty like everyone else seemed to be. She was a good fuck whenever the need arose, but they didn't play in bed together for the promise of something more. There was nothing there to make something of them. Sofia knew it, and so did he. Better to leave them as they were.

"Are you going to invite me in, or what?" Demyan asked, cocking a brow.

"Do I ever refuse your company?"

"Nope."

Because she was easy for him like that, and not in a nasty way, either. Demyan didn't begrudge Sofia her lifestyle or choices as far as men and refusing to settle down went. She didn't judge him whenever he showed up knocking on her door.

Simple. No mess.

Sofia didn't pretend with Demyan, and she never asked him to, either. They were comfortable, an old habit that worked. He wouldn't stay the night. She didn't question his motives. She was also safe in the way she kept quiet about his appearances, didn't say a thing to anyone about their arrangement, and she wouldn't ask him to stay.

When Demyan needed something physical, anything to draw him back from the constant numbness even if it only would last for a short while, Sofia provided him with the drug: her.

Yeah, easy.

• • •

Demyan buttoned his slacks and done up the zipper, watching Sofia out of the corner of his eye as she rubbed lotion into her thighs. She looked like she always did after sex—mussed, fucked, and pleased. Sofia wasn't into soft, slow, and sweet. Demyan didn't have the time or heart to provide that shit, thankfully.

As it was, he already felt like he had spent too much time in her place. Longer than he normally would. Still, when he glanced around her loft, he figured he ought to be respectful to the woman, even if their relationship—if you could call it that—was focused solely on the physical.

"How do you like the new place?" he asked, slipping on his black leather shoes.

Sofia glanced up from her task, surprise flitting across her features. "Pardon?"

"The loft. You've lived here a couple months now. How do you like it?"

The girl was Jersey bred, so he figured Brooklyn was a bit of step out for her, especially since she'd always been under her father's thumb in some way. She moved down for work, which made the trip a hell of a lot shorter if Demyan felt the need for a visit.

"I like it just fine," Sofia said slowly.

"Something wrong?"

"Yes, you. Since when do you ask me about my life, Demyan?"

Demyan chuckled a dull sound. "I don't know."

"Exactly, you don't. So let's not start because it might feel like something different and you don't want or need that." Sofia pushed off the bed, the shirt she pulled on rising high enough to flash her nakedness from the waist down. Standing, she crossed her arms and faced him. "What are we, anyway?"

"Us?"

"That's what I said."

"Friends," Demyan said though it took him a moment to think about it.

"Friends," Sofia echoed. "Okay. Like friends who hang out or friends who just fuck?"

Well, that one was obvious, wasn't it?

"What's your point, Sofia?"

"I'm getting there. Are you seeing anyone else?"

Demyan's air lodged in his throat, choking him. How in the sweet fuck was that any of her business? He didn't question her on that sort of thing, not that he didn't already know. Of course, Sofia had other men she was running with. He didn't give a good goddamn. It was her life to do with as she pleased, and they made sure to be safe when they messed around.

"Excuse me?"

"You know, besides me, are you fucking anyone else, Demyan?"

No. Not because there weren't offers or he couldn't, but more because he didn't give a shit to try.

"Yeah," Sofia continued, nodding once. "You don't even have to answer because I can see it written all over your face. And if we're just friends who have sex, and only one of us is exclusive in this whole thing, it's not just fucking, Demyan."

"It is to me."

"But it isn't to me. What about Vera?"

Demyan's entire body turned to stone at that question. "What about my daughter?"

"Where is she this weekend?"

"With her mother's parents, as she usually is every second weekend."

"I didn't know that," Sofia murmured.

"Because it's not your business."

"Friends, that's what you said. Friends, even if they have benefits, do more than have sex. They hang out, do things ... learn about the other, like Vera. We've been doing this shit for three years and you don't talk about her, I've never even met the girl, and if our families do happen to cross paths, you do good to show up and speak to me. I don't mind being used, Demyan, but only in bed and when I'm agreeable to it."

"So what, you want to meet my daughter?" he asked gruffly.

"No, because you don't want me to, and I think that speaks volumes."

Did it? Demyan wasn't sure how. "Listen, I like you, Sofia, as far as that goes."

"Just not like *that*," she replied pointedly. "And that's fine. But before this might turn into something it's not, I'm going to cut tail and let you fucking run so you won't have to do it later. That way, this whole thing ends on good terms and neither of us gets hurt in the process."

Demyan just stared at Sofia, thrown and unsure. "You're sure that's what you want?"

Because he sure as fuck wouldn't be running back in a week when she called him.

"Absolutely," Sofia said.

"Fine."

Sofia smiled. "Who knows? Maybe you'll even thank me for it someday."

• • •

Demyan pulled his jacket on, ignoring the biting December cold as he locked the front door to his house. The place didn't feel like home, not really, but he supposed it was in a way. The first house he purchased shortly after Gia's death had remained unlived in for over a year. Eight months after Vera was born, he moved them into a three bedroom apartment in the heart of Little Odessa, needing to get away from the constant eyes and concern of those around him.

Back then, everyone watched him like he was a walking fucking disease or something. Or maybe like he was somehow going to hurt his daughter. Apparently depression could lead to that though the thought had never once crossed Demyan's mind. Well, not for Vera.

Demyan would be a goddamn liar if he ever said he never thought about taking his own life. Those first six months were hell, not that he remembered much about them. He knew what they felt like and frankly, that was enough.

Nonetheless, the first house he bought hadn't been a good fit, either. It only took Demyan one walk through after closing to realize he hadn't bought the house for him, but instead, bought it for a woman who no longer lived.

The wide wall-to-wall windows on the bottom floor wasn't safe for a man of his status in the Russian mafia. It would make his family far too big of a target, but Gia would have loved the openness and the sunlight. The ground floor of the home was eye-level when it came to the other windows and doors, which also wasn't safe, but it was a style Gia had preferred. The house's location was barricaded in by other houses in the tidy, expensive suburb with little chance for a proper fence or security. Not to mention, Demyan would have been given little to no warning if a raid were about to happen as he couldn't see past the neighbors.

So yeah, the house hadn't even been bought for Demyan, but Gia. He couldn't help but think it a little ironic that even after she was gone, he was still trying to please a dead woman by pretending he wasn't born and bred Russian mafia.

Well, Demyan had no one to blame for that but himself. He allowed them both to go on like that for years, ignoring what was right in front of their faces until the gun finally blew, and he faced the consequences for it.

He sold the damn house four months after he moved into the apartment. Shortly after, he bought a smaller home. It had a big back yard for Vera, an open floor plan so he could see from one end to the other, and windows that couldn't be broken in to.

Simple. Perfect for Demyan and his child, which was most important.

Just as Demyan unlocked his white Mercedes, the phone in his other hand began to vibrate. He didn't bother to check the caller ID, as it could be anyone, and picked up the call with his usual aloofness. "Demyan speaking."

"Good morning, Demyan."

Demyan damn near tripped over his own two feet at the sound of Ivan Lavrov greeting him. Mostly their phone calls were short, succinct and done before Demyan blinked. The relationship he had with his Godfather was nonexistent and not because Ivan didn't try to make an effort. Eventually, like most people, the man just gave up trying.

One thing that never happened when they did manage to talk was friendliness. Demyan was as detached and frigid as ever while Ivan kept his distance. Vera was the only thing that kept them coming back together ever since Ivan left the Bratva. Ivan loved his granddaughter, and while Demyan disliked some of the comments Gia's sisters made about his lifestyle and parenting choices, he didn't keep Vera from them.

"You there?" Ivan asked.

Demyan decided to play his stunned silence off like he hadn't missed a beat of time. Opening the driver's door, he said, "*Ello*, Ivan. Just heading over your way to get Vera. What's up?"

"That's why I'm calling. Chrissy had a last minute emergency today, so Eva ran over there to watch the kids. I got a goddamn call from a client that I can't leave until tomorrow, so I took Vera over to your mother's bookstore and dropped her off with Vine until you could pick her up. She's been there for a half hour or so."

"Fine, whatever." As long as Vera was with someone Demyan trusted, he didn't mind the change in plans. "See you in two weeks, yeah?"

"Sure," Ivan replied. "Or Vera, anyway."

"Yeah, basically." No point in lying to the man.

Demyan hung up the call without another word.

• • •

The first thing Demyan noticed when he pulled up to his mother's bookshop was the fact her car wasn't parked out front like usual, but the open sign still hung in doorway window. There was another car parked there, a tiny blue Toyota, but he didn't recognize it. As far as he knew, his mother only kept the shop open on weekends and two days during the week now. She didn't have any employees when it was more of a hobby than an actual business.

Confused, Demyan shut his Mercedes off and got out, locking the vehicle. Not that anyone in Little Odessa would be stupid enough to steal the damned thing. Everyone with breathing lungs and a beating heart around these fucking parts knew who he was on sight.

No one would steal from a Bratva man. And even if he wasn't a Vor, no one would *ever* steal from an Avdonin.

Demyan entered his mother's bookstore and immediately took note of the fact she wasn't behind the counter reading like any other time he came in to visit. Which if he thought about it, wasn't all that often, lately.

"Ma?" he called quietly.

Despite calling his father by his first name, Viviana would always be Demyan's Ma. He couldn't imagine addressing her as anything else, and he knew if he did, the woman was liable to ignore him until he gave her what she wanted.

No one answered his call, but quiet, childish, and familiar giggles echoed from the back of the shop. New laughter— feminine, soft, and light—followed right behind.

'This one!" Demyan heard Vera say excitedly.

"You're sure? It looks pretty ... catty, if you know what I mean."

Vera's laughter filled the bookstore again. "Yes, this one. Please?"

"Sure, sweet girl. Up, up."

Demyan wasted no time weaving through the maze of bookshelves toward the sound of his daughter's joy and the stranger's voice. Clearly they hadn't heard him come in, or his call for his mother. That, or they were too distracted by whatever they were doing.

Either way, Demyan didn't like the feeling welling in his gut. Something foreign balled hard in his middle—a sensation that he worked to repress for so long, refusing to feed it because it suffocated him.

Anxiety.

Fear.

And that shit was colder than even he was.

Because no matter what, Demyan never left his daughter with someone he didn't know and trust inexplicably. In fact, she hadn't once stayed with anyone who didn't share the same blood as her.

Where in the fuck was his mother and why had she left Vera with some goddamn woman he didn't—

Demyan's thought process cut off as he rounded a corner to find his daughter on the lap of a woman he had never seen before. He froze in place, unsure of what to do. Vera was still and quiet as a pretty woman—maybe his age—grinned widely, as if sitting with his daughter was the one and only place she wanted to be.

Reddish-brown curls framed her delicate features, the apples of her cheeks pinked in her happiness. She was pixie-like in appearance, and he bet if she stood, the top of her head might only reach his chin. The black wool, knee-length dress she wore was accented by a wide belt cinched at the curve of her waist and below the swell of her breasts. Her black suede boots, heeled thick enough to be safe for walking on the slush outside, tapped to the floor as she flipped the first few pages in the book over.

She was beautiful and the way her green eyes, framed by dark, thick lashes, lit up as she met Vera's gaze only seemed to accentuate that fact for Demyan.

That thought alone was enough to knock Demyan out of his stupor. He saw beautiful women every day. None made him stop and take note of them, however. There wasn't a single woman whose beauty attracted his attention enough to be important and stand out in his mind, not since Gia died.

For some reason, Demyan's mouth suddenly stopped working, a lot like his ability to walk. He couldn't move from his spot that kept him slightly hidden by the tall bookcase.

"Okay, ready?" the woman asked Vera.

"Yep."

"This is my ..."

Vera's eyes squinted down at the book the woman was holding up. "Cat?"

"Yes! Great job. This is my cat. This cat likes ..."

"H ..." Vera sounded out the 'h', following it with an 'ah'

sound before settling on, "Hats."

"Perfect, Vera. This cat likes hats," the woman read.

"This cat likes hats," Vera mimicked perfectly.

Demyan's heart stopped for a split second. While his daughter was learning to read Russian, they had barely broached reading English words and here this woman was *teaching* his child. And he knew how much Vera loved learning. She was a little sponge taking everything around her in.

"See that cat?" the woman continued to read. "That ..."

"Cat," Vera filled in without prompting.

"Likes my ..."

Vera struggled with whatever word she was trying to decipher in the book.

"What sound do the words cat and hat end with, sweetheart? They sound the same, right? It means they *rhyme*. Like peel, heel, meal. So, cat and hat are rhyming words, too. What is the sound at the end of each word?"

"At?" Vera asked, her lips pursing.

"Yes, at." The woman pointed at the page. "And that right there is a ...?"

"M."

"Right. What sound does it make, Vera?"

"*Mmm*," his daughter hummed.

"So, *mmm* and at make what when you put them together?"

"*Mmm* ... at." Vera tried it over and over, but it wasn't clicking for his daughter. Sometimes all she needed was to be told once and like the sponge she was, the girl wouldn't forget again.

Somehow, Demyan's mouth finally decided to catch the fuck up with his brain.

"Mat," he said quietly.

Vera's head popped up from the book at the same time the woman's did. Something flashed in her green eyes and he almost missed it, but he didn't have the first clue what it was.

"Hi there," she said softly.

"Hello," Demyan said.

While he wasn't entirely comfortable with his daughter spending alone time with someone he didn't know personally, Demyan was pretty sure this woman wasn't out to hurt his child.

Vera slid off the woman's lap without a word, coming over to hug her father around his legs. "I missed you, Papa."

"Did you?" he asked.

"Yes!"

"You should have got Grandpapa Ivan to call me, *dushka*. I would have come and picked you up if you wanted to be with me for the weekend."

Vera glanced up, smiling. "Yeah?"

"Of course."

Sure, Demyan did a lot of work on the weekends while his daughter rotated those days between her mutual grandparents, but he would drop whatever he was doing in a heartbeat for this girl.

A throat cleared from the chair, and Demyan caught the woman's eye again. She tried standing from her seat, but his hand raised, stopping her.

"You can continue if you'd like," he told her.

Demyan's tone was cool and his posture rigid. The habit of giving off the impression he was wholly unapproachable was hard to break, even if he didn't mean to come off as harsh.

Clearly, he failed this time.

"You don't sound like you want me to keep going," the woman replied. "I don't mean to make you uncomfortable, Demyan."

"How do you know my name?"

Shit.

Even he could hear the thinly veiled warning in his own words.

The woman blinked, passing a glance between him and Vera. "She talks about you sometimes, and so does your mother."

"And you talk as though you've spent more time with my daughter than just today." Demyan patted Vera gently on the top of her head, reminding himself that she was there, and he needed to keep his attitude in check. She had yet to let him go. "No one thought to tell me my child had a new friend. I was enjoying seeing her learn. She reads Russian with me, but this is the first time I've heard her with English."

"She's very smart."

"I am!" Vera said, grinning in that sweet way of hers up at Demyan. "You tell me that a lot, Papa."

"Because you are, princess."

Demyan tried to relax his stance because given the way Vera wouldn't let him go, she was picking up on his silent concerns. The child didn't just soak up knowledge, she also pulled in the things her father felt. She always saw right through his bullshit.

"Your name?" Demyan asked.

"Her name is Claire," Vera said.

"Claire, huh?" Demyan passed the sitting woman another look. "Claire who doesn't have a last name?"

"Braden," Claire told him. "Claire Braden."

Demyan didn't recognize the last name. No immediate warning bells rang about it either, and he wasn't one to forget a surname if it might cause him issues. Not after the whole Dolan mess.

"Do you live around here?" he asked.

Claire lifted a single shoulder. "Not far, maybe twenty minutes away."

"I haven't seen you around before."

"I don't do much besides work and read. This happens to be my favorite place to relax after a difficult day."

Demyan understood that, in a way. "Where do you work?"

"The General."

"Huh." Demyan hid his surprise at her answer. The hospital she mentioned was the same one his grandmother Sasha had worked at for many years before she retired. "Doing what, exactly?"

"I'm a pediatric nurse."

Well, he hadn't expected that, either.

"And you've worked there for how long?" he asked.

"A few months," Claire answered.

She didn't offer any information about where she hailed from, but Demyan could tell by the lack of a New Yorker's drawl that she hadn't grown up anywhere in the state. Not that all New Yorkers sounded the same, but they did have their common quirks.

He decided not to push Claire for more information on where she came from only because he didn't think it was the right time to do so with Vera standing right there. Plus, he planned on having a thorough discussion with his mother once she returned from wherever she was.

Viviana owed him an explanation.

Demyan squatted down in front of his daughter, unwinding her grip as he did. "And you like Claire?"

"Yes," Vera whispered.

"Why didn't you tell me she was teaching you to read English?"

"You didn't ask."

That right there was four-year-old logic at its best.

Demyan cocked a brow. "I didn't know I had to, Vera."

"Claire is teaching me to read English, Papa."

Better late than never, he thought.

"Can I finish the book about the cat with Claire before we go?" Vera asked.

Demyan nodded, standing. "Sure."

"Thank you, Demyan," Claire said.

He stared the woman head-on, still unsure of his next move. She watched him with a sort of tenderness that put him on edge, something else he wasn't accustomed to. What he did know was that he still didn't like the fact he knew nothing about her, but his daughter looked at her like she did.

Demyan supposed that mattered more than whatever the hell he thought.

For the moment.

• • •

Claire watched from the window of the bookshop's front door as Demyan closed the back driver's side door and turned to face his mother with anger clouding his features. He had just buckled a smiling Vera into the car.

When she first started visiting Viviana Avdonin's bookshop at the older woman's request a couple of times a week for the last two months, she assumed Demyan was aware she spent time with his child. It seemed like whenever she did go there, Vera showed up, too.

And that was so okay with Claire.

Vera was the sweetest, most polite and happy child Claire ever had the pleasure of meeting. Her job as a pediatric nurse gave her a front row seat to all kinds of children. Those who sometimes experienced nothing but sadness and pain. Vera had become almost a breath of fresh air and a way to relieve her stress after a particularly difficult work day.

Viviana hadn't called Claire today, but after a twelve hour shift that was anything but easy, she needed some down time.

Reading gave her that, and she knew the bookstore would be open. It was just luck that Vera showed up with Ivan shortly after she arrived.

Demyan gestured at the bookshop, and Claire flinched, seeing the darkness in his blue eyes. Claire knew she shouldn't eavesdrop, but she couldn't help it. Using the toe of her boot, she pushed the door open a couple of inches. Just enough to hear the voices outside.

"Who in the hell is she, Ma?" Demyan asked.

"A friend, that's all."

"And you couldn't tell me she's been spending time with my child on the weekends Vera is with you and Anton?"

"Dad."

"What?"

"He's your father."

Demyan barked a laugh that was bitingly bitter. "Fucking Christ, are we going to do that again, Ma?"

"Well, since when is he Anton to you, Demyan? He was always your Papa or Dad."

"Since he became a lot more than just my father. Like my goddamn boss, for one. You've been bitching about this for four years and it hasn't changed yet. Chances are, history says it's still not going to soon."

"Why are you so angry?" Viviana asked. "And quit cussing at me like that. I am not your father, Demyan Anton, and you won't treat me like it. He might put up with that crap, but I sure as hell will not. You owe me the respect I deserve as your mother and I expect you to show it."

Demyan straightened, taking a step backward. "I'm sorry, you're right."

"Thank you." Viviana sighed loudly. "She is just a friend. A girl I met a few months ago who came into my shop and needed a break from the outside world. Vera happened to be here one Saturday when she was browsing some books, and they hit it off. There's nothing wrong with Vera having female company, Demyan."

"She *does*. You, Eva, her aunts. And you know it has nothing to do with her being a female. I don't know that woman, Ma. I know nothing about her and that makes me really fucking uncomfortable to think Vera is around her when I'm not. Not to mention you let that woman watch her while you ran an errand!"

"Claire," Viviana interrupted sharply. "Her name is Claire."

"Fine, *Claire*," Demyan growled.

Claire couldn't have stopped the shiver that worked its way up her spine if she tried. There was no denying Demyan was a handsome man with his chiseled features that barely fluctuated with any emotion. He was tall and built like a runner beneath his opened leather jacket and dark slacks. His posture screamed he was unsociable, but it also spoke of a quiet confidence.

Most men spent years trying to obtain the gift of being mysterious, perfecting their distance and aloofness to draw women in with their bad boy persona. Demyan stood there twenty feet away from Claire and separated by a glass window looking like he had been born that way.

It was … sexy.

He was obviously pissed off about her, and the way he said her name was a mixture of heat and hate though he couldn't possibly dislike her if he didn't know her. She still wanted to know him. But once he did know her because obviously he wasn't aware of who she truly was, he would probably hate her a whole lot more than what he did right now.

Even so, she thought his voice matched his eyes. Claire remembered the first meeting she had with Anton and Viviana Avdonin and how they told her that looking into their son's eyes was like staring into nothingness—death. Suffocating in his own personal hell, they said.

Claire didn't think they saw Demyan Avdonin clearly at all. Sure, he wore a damn good mask, but it had cracks, too.

"I'm sorry," Viviana said softly, bringing Claire's attention back to the conversation still going on outside. "I honestly didn't think it would be a problem. I just wanted to go grab a new receipt book from the office store before it closed. I had forgotten I needed a new one."

Demyan softened his defensive stance, but barely. "You couldn't have taken Vera with you?"

"Your father put her booster seat into his SUV. I didn't know Ivan was going to drop her off today when I came to work."

Glancing away from his mother, a tick showed in Demyan's jaw. "All right. Is this … Claire and Vera reading, I mean … is it a regular thing?"

"She's a nice girl, Demyan. Vera adores her. What's the problem with them reading together?"

"You know what the damned problem is, Ma."

"No, I don't. Try me."

"I told you, I'm not familiar with her. How am I supposed to trust her? It's all fine and great you do, but I would also like to. And for some reason, it feels like you've gone behind my back with this. You know how protective and cautious I am about the people in Vera's life."

"For good reason," Viviana replied. "I can promise you Claire would never do anything to hurt your daughter. She's practically in love with her."

Guessing by the way Demyan's gaze narrowed at his mother, her choice of words were the wrong things to say. "Great, so if I don't approve of this little friendship, I'm hurting people. Right? That's what you're saying."

Viviana laughed drily. "Demyan, since when do you care about hurting people?"

"Don't, Ma."

"Well."

"Don't," he repeated firmly.

"She's not trying to be Vera's mother, okay? It isn't like that."

"Jesus. It always comes down to that shit with every single one of you. The goddamn mother thing." Demyan threw his hands into the air, shaking his head. "I'm done with this conversation, Ma. It's over. And until I spend some time with that woman—"

"Claire."

"—she won't be spending any fucking more time with Vera."

"Fine," Viviana snapped. "Next weekend on Saturday."

Demyan's brow furrowed. "Excuse me?"

"We have Vera next weekend, right?"

"Depends on how I feel after this one, Ma, and right now, it isn't looking very good."

"Don't threaten me, Demyan."

"It's not a threat."

"It damn well is and the next time you stand in front of me, I suggest you correct that attitude. You might be twenty-nine-years-old and your father's right-hand man, but you don't scare me, Demyan. I stand next to a man just like you, son. I've slept beside him in the same bed and have for three decades. I have his last name, I've given him two children, and I share my life with him. He doesn't frighten me, either, and we both know the things he's done. I've seen who you are underneath that vacant façade and your nastiness. I raised you. Don't try to fool me. I am not everyone else and it won't work."

"Ma—"

"Saturday," Viviana cut in. "Claire has next weekend off given she worked this one, so I will invite her over as well as Ana and Koldan for a dinner. I expect you to be at my home by five and do not be late."

"Ma—"

"Don't be late, Demyan. With Vera," she added.

Demyan's jaw clenched. "Fine."

"Fine. I'll see you then because God knows you don't make your way over otherwise."

CHAPTER THREE

Claire wasn't able to hear the muttered response Demyan gave his mother before he yanked open the driver's door and jumped into a white Mercedes SUV. The vehicle door slammed shut so loudly she cringed.

Viviana stood unruffled at her son's show of fury as he backed out, spun his tires on the wet pavement until they shrieked and took off. Once the vehicle was out of sight, Viviana's shoulders relaxed, and she rubbed at her temples.

Claire felt terrible for putting Viviana in a bad situation with Demyan. Had she known how he would react at someone spending time with his daughter who he didn't approve of, she would have tried to keep her distance from the little girl.

She was so sure he had known.

Viviana turned in Claire's direction. "Claire, you can come out now. I think it's safe enough."

Claire laughed under her breath. She hadn't taken her foot out of the door to let it close, and she guessed she probably wasn't obscured standing there in the window. Tightening her messenger bag filled with her scrubs and shoes from work around her shoulder, she pushed the door open the rest of the way and walked out into the cold morning air.

"Viviana—"

"How many times do I have to tell you to call me Vine before you actually do?"

Claire shrugged. "Maybe a few more."

"Well, quit it. I've gone by Vine my whole life. I prefer it."

"Vine, then." Claire smiled, but it didn't feel true. "He's very angry with me."

"No, sweetheart, he's angry with me," Viviana replied simply. "And rightfully so, perhaps, but considering how much fun Vera has with you and how much joy you get from her, I don't see the problem."

"Other than the fact he killed my half-brother and would probably hate my guts just because I'm related to Cavan?"

SHATTERED

Viviana waved the statement off. "You are not your brother, Claire. I have spent more than enough time with you, and so has my husband to know it."

"Demyan might not feel the same way."

"He will, eventually. Give him time. Besides, Vera isn't the only one who could use someone like you in their life."

Claire stilled, confused. "What do you mean by that?"

Viviana smiled. "Nothing. Just thinking out loud. I assume you heard what I said about dinner next Saturday?"

"I did."

"And?"

"I don't have to work; you were right. I can come."

"Good," Viviana said.

"Can I ask you a question?" Claire asked.

"Shoot."

"Why didn't he know that I was spending time with Vera?"

Viviana laughed faintly. "After meeting my son, do you need an answer?"

"Well, obviously he's protective of her."

"Very," Viviana replied.

"I thought you said when you looked at him, there was nothing staring back."

Claire wished she could make the words disappear the moment they left her mouth, but it was impossible. Viviana turned on her heel slowly, eyeing her companion with a contemplative expression.

"Sometimes, it feels that way," Viviana admitted. "You didn't see it?"

"Not when he looks at Vera."

And really, not when he looked at her, either.

Nothing implied blankness—the unaffected slate of a colorless void.

Demyan's eyes were anything but void.

"No, I suppose he's not like that when it comes to Vera, although if you ask other people, they would say differently." The corner of Viviana's mouth lifted into the ghost of a smirk as she said, "He uses his hostile demeanor as a shield to keep people away, and it almost always works. Don't be one of those people, Claire."

Claire cleared her throat, uncomfortable. Once again,

Viviana was talking in vague circles. "Anyway, Saturday, you said."

"Absolutely. Are you leaving? Because you don't have to."

"It's all right. I should get some sleep in before my next shift."

Viviana started walking toward the bookstore, reaching out to squeeze Claire's hand as she passed. "Yes, get some sleep. I think I'll close up early, too. God knows after dealing with Demyan when he's in one of his moods, we all deserve a break."

Claire could hear Viviana's humor, but a sadness remained all the same. "I am sorry for causing you any problems with him, Vine."

As she opened the bookstore door, Viviana glanced over her shoulder with a cocked eyebrow. "Claire, today was the first time I've seen my son have a reaction to anything in longer than I want to admit. Do not be sorry for that, sweetheart."

"Why? I upset him."

"All it takes is one tiny crack in the strongest dam for the floodgates to break."

"Is that what you're trying to do to him?"

Viviana's expression didn't change a bit as she said, "No, but I don't have to."

Claire didn't have the opportunity to press Viviana on the subject further. Viviana slipped into the bookstore without saying more. Turning toward her Toyota Camry, something in the backseat of Viviana's Bentley caught Claire's eye.

Vera's car seat.

· · ·

Vera covered her eyes as Demyan poured water over her hair to wash the soap out.

"Are you mad, Papa?" his little girl asked, wiping at her face.

"At you?"

"No."

Demyan's brow furrowed as he filled the cup with bathwater again. "Good, because I could never be mad at you, *dushka*."

Vera grinned a toothy smile. "Someday you might."

"No, I don't think so. What makes you think I'm mad?"

"You weren't very nice to Claire."

Demyan coughed to hide his surprise. There was something

about the way his daughter just picked up on shit that he didn't understand. "I wasn't mean to her, Vera."

"You don't have to be mean not to be nice. You says that to me before, Papa."

True enough.

"Said," Demyan corrected.

"Okay."

The fact was, Vera rarely saw Demyan with other people and those she did see him with, he always handed out his respect. Usually, in any case. Finding out his daughter was spending time with someone without his permission had been a kick in his gut. Vera was the only good thing Demyan had left. Protecting her was his utmost priority.

He assumed everyone else around him knew it, too.

"I wasn't mean to her," he repeated quietly.

"I like her, Papa. She reads to me a lot like you do."

"And that's why you like her?"

Vera shrugged her little shoulders. "She talks to me, too. I like that."

"I talk to you, baby. And your grandparents, aunts, uncles, and cousins. What's the difference, Vera?"

"I like the way Claire talks to me."

That just didn't make sense.

"How?" he asked.

"She lets me talk about you."

Demyan stilled, the cup he was holding above Vera's head freezing in just enough time to keep the water from dumping out before she could cover her eyes. "About me?"

"Yes."

"Other people don't let you talk about me?"

"They don't ask, Papa." Vera pushed the bubblegum scented bubbles around in circles. "I like talking about you. You're mine."

"And you like Claire," he said, repeating what he already knew.

"Yep."

Shit.

• • •

"An hour to dinner," Koldan informed.

41

Demyan grit his teeth, pushed on the crowbar with more force and felt the wood break under his strength. "Yeah, got it."

"Who is this chick, anyway?"

"I don't fucking know."

Koldan made a sound under his breath. "Ouch. That's the problem, isn't it?"

"Kind of."

After having a shittier week than normal, Demyan decided to take Koldan along to check out a shipment of guns that had come into port the night before. Usually, the Avdonins would simply send the crates to the second destination with the next ship and not check out the load, but Demyan needed something to do.

Running the streets was one thing. It was the best place to let his numbness settle in so he could do his goddamn job. Unfortunately, he was way off his game and had little to no interest in babysitting a bunch of men for his father.

Boris or Erik could handle that shit. Demyan wasn't.

With the first crate opened, Demyan went about pulling the filler out for the shipment. Just below the surface of the dry filler, the shined metal barrels and black butts met his hands. Assault weapons and high-powered rifles were a major seller for any arms dealer and weapons trafficker. Handguns typically did well, too.

"Shit, that's nice," Koldan praised, glancing over the assault rifle Demyan pulled out to inspect. "Not a nick, either."

"Gunrunners always take care of their product," Demyan replied, grinning wickedly. Lifting the butt of the gun to his shoulder, he set the weapon straight and checked the scopes. "And they always deliver."

"They do. Speaking of guns, your father doesn't celebrate Hanukkah, does he?"

"Nope."

"Or Christmas, I suppose."

"He's only Jewish enough to ignore Christian holidays but not Jewish enough to celebrate those holidays."

"Shit."

"Why?" Demyan asked, dropping the weapon and putting it back in the crate.

Koldan shrugged. "Picked up this great vintage revolver. Six hundred made and sold in the United States. I figured he'd appreciate it more than me."

"He would. Are you trying to sweeten him up, or what?"

"Right, because that would work," Koldan barked, laughing bitterly. "No, but he's the one with the gun collection."

"Give it to him on New Year's Day," Demyan said. "He celebrates that."

"Does he?"

"Yeah, with vodka like any good Russian. It's a reason to drink."

"Not like we need one."

"Truth," Demyan muttered. "Yeah, give it to him then."

Koldan chuckled. "Will do, thanks."

"No problem."

"Not much longer to the wedding, man. Nearly three months."

Demyan nodded, turning to lean against the crate and crossing his arms over his chest. "Ana's taking Vera to shop for her flower girl dress after the holiday rush, I think. Vera likes anything girly, so that should be fun."

Fun was one way to put it. Somehow, he was going to figure a way out of tagging along.

Koldan sighed. "My request is still open, by the way."

"My answer is still no," Demyan replied.

"Demyan—"

"Listen, being a best man just isn't my thing, Koldan."

"You're an awfully shitty friend sometimes."

Demyan shrugged. "Yeah, I get that a lot."

It wasn't like Demyan had a bunch of friends because he didn't, but Koldan was the closest thing to it. He was even Vera's Godfather. Ana was her Godmother.

"Offer is still open," Koldan repeated.

"Answer is still no, man."

Not wanting to argue further, Demyan turned his back to his soon-to-be brother-in-law and made quick work of closing the crate back up. There were five more in the warehouse with guns hidden inside of a similar caliber, but he figured they were probably just as good.

"So, about this woman we're meeting tonight," Koldan said.

"What about her?"

"You said her name was Claire?"

"Yep," Demyan confirmed, hammering the last nail into the

43

crate.

"And she's not from New York, right?"

"Doesn't sound like a New Yorker, but she didn't have any defining ticks in her speech for somewhere else, either."

"Huh. Get a last name?"

"Brandon, I think?" Demyan tossed the hammer to a metal table as he faced Koldan. "No, never mind, it was Braden."

Demyan couldn't forget the way Claire said her surname quietly like she didn't want to admit it at all.

"Yeah, Braden," he said with a nod.

"Sounds familiar," Koldan murmured.

"I didn't recognize it at all."

Then again, Koldan was crazy weird with names. Demyan didn't know where the guy picked up that little talent of his. Sometimes it was freaky as hell.

Koldan hummed. "I'll think of where I know it eventually. It's odd your mother didn't think to mention Vera was hanging around this Claire. Did your father know?"

"Not sure," Demyan said. "I'd have to talk nicely with Anton to get that information. The last time we tried talking at all, he challenged me to take his seat."

"You're kidding, right?"

"No. He didn't like me accusing him of planning something on the Irish and telling him to back off."

"It's not your place to question a Pakhan, Demyan. What the hell were you thinking?"

"I don't give a shit if he's my boss or not. I don't want problems, man. Simple as that. Anton is sneaky as fuck and doesn't give a damn what I say. It makes me …"

"Nervous?" Koldan supplied.

"Shut up, asshole. I don't get nervous. It puts me on edge; that's all. Like I have to look over my shoulder again. Liam Dolan has a lot of power behind him, and if he wants my daughter dead, she will be in a grave next to her mother within a week. I will not give that waste of breath a reason to come down on me again. I learned my lesson the first goddamn time."

"That wasn't a lesson, Demyan. It was—"

"A lesson I needed to learn," Demyan interrupted, his tone as sharp as a knife blade. "A mistake I paid for by burying the mother of my child. One I hope you and my sister never have to experience for yourselves. You can't fucking blame me for making sure it won't ever happen again."

Koldan shifted on his feet. "Do you really think Anton is planning something for the Irish?"

"Liam, specifically, but yes."

"Damn."

Demyan cocked a brow. "You sound impressed. If he's planning some crazy shit, this is not the time to be swayed by his nonsense, Koldan. It's more likely to cause a lot of problems. Don't forget, my father nearly spent his life behind bars because of his fucking need to draw blood for revenge. Sometimes, we have to let shit go."

"I get that."

"Considering Ma and Ana are still in the city and Anton is as calm as he ever is, I'd say if he is planning something, it's not going to happen soon. He always protects his family, and he prepares for that shit weeks ahead of time. I would know if that were the case. It's not something he would keep from me if it were close, not with Vera in the picture."

"Anton never goes back on his word, right?" Koldan asked.

"An *Avdonin* never goes back on their word," Demyan replied. "Not just Anton."

A man's word was sometimes all he had. Especially men like them. It was one lesson from his father Demyan would never forget.

"Yeah, well, you remember what he said at that dinner with Liam."

Demyan's feet suddenly felt like cement stuck to the floor. Just talking about that sit-down and thinking about that day led his mind into dangerous territory. He couldn't control it, and while he was perfectly capable of hiding how it made him feel, there was no possible way for him to ignore it.

Like a wave, it crashed into his insides with deadly force, threating to take him under with the pain. It was the only time, other than when he was with Vera, that Demyan felt something. It was awful and suffocating, but he felt it which was more than he could say for most other things. On the outside, Demyan remained as calm as ever. One death was all it took for him to finally gain control. One death too many.

"You were outside," he said. "How do you know what he

told Liam?"

"I got the info later," Koldan explained.

"I don't remember a lot about that day."

Liar, his mind taunted.

It was after that Demyan couldn't remember, once he stared at a line making a straight path across a monitor. He had waited for three entire minutes before a doctor called Gia's time of death. Once that moment came, his memories were mostly flickers and sensations of time passing but nothing solid, nothing pure.

"Sure you don't," Koldan muttered low.

Demyan shrugged his shoulders like it didn't make a damn difference. He knew how cruel it was to dismiss what had happened to him, his family, and his child—to ignore the life that had been ripped from them and the justice they were owed for it.

He didn't know how to do anything else without putting his daughter in danger. He thought about killing Liam a lot, of course, but he didn't have the means to do it without risking Vera just yet.

But if he ever got the chance, even if it meant sacrificing his own life, he would do it.

"It doesn't matter what he said, Koldan."

"It does and you know it."

"No—"

"He promised to kill that man and you won't stop him, Demyan."

CHAPTER FOUR

"And you like that kind of work?" Ana asked from across the table.

Demyan watched Claire out of the corner of his eye, taking her in as she conversed with his family as though they were all old friends. The woman didn't seem the least bit nervous, she usually wore a smile, and despite how it made him feel to see it, Claire was very attentive toward Vera. She indulged his daughter's questions, chatter, and childish antics without any issue.

He had been surprised to find Claire already at his parents and helping his mother cook the meal. The very first thing Claire did after saying hello to him was squat down to Vera's level and then she proceeded to let his daughter talk about her entire week at pre-school.

While Demyan was still pissed at his mother, he apologized for his behavior the week before. Viviana waved it off, but it had to have hurt her.

"I do," Claire replied. "We rotate floors, so it's not like every single day is a sad one. Between the newborn babies, the toddlers, and the older kids, it's always something new. And for the ones who are really sick, you'd be surprised at how joyful they are."

"Grateful," Demyan murmured.

Claire turned to stare at him from where she sat two seats away. Vera was between them at the table, picking all of the mini tomatoes out of her salad and giving them to her father but pretending like she wasn't.

"Pardon?" Claire asked.

"The terminally ill, I bet they're grateful to have time to be happy at all."

Claire smiled softly. "Seems that way."

"And we take too much for granted," Anton put in from the head of the table.

"I think it's better to live without worry or fear, which is something some of those kids never get the chance to do. Some of them don't even get to leave the hospital after they go in. Maybe that's something we take for granted."

"Living without fear," Anton echoed. "I can't say I know what that's like."

Ana laughed. "Since when are you afraid of anything, Papa?"

"Grandpapa doesn't like mice," Vera said out of the blue, taking the opportunity to shove another small red tomato over to her father's plate while she thought no one was watching. "He shouted at one in the garage."

Laughter rung out down the table.

"Vera," Anton chided. "It's not nice to tell on people."

"Well, you *did*, Grandpapa."

Koldan snorted under his breath. "Mice, really?"

"They carry disease," Anton grumbled, ignoring the gazes on him.

"Rats, maybe," Viviana said from the far end. "Mice are just—"

"Baby rats, Vine. With smaller bodies and shorter tails. Disgusting rodents that bite and spread their diseases."

"You considered shooting the poor mouse, didn't you?" Viviana asked.

Anton wouldn't meet his wife's stare. "Vera was there and obviously I didn't have a gun on me to kill it with. So, I yelled at it instead. Haven't seen it since."

"Christ," Demyan said under his breath.

"Bad words." Vera looked up at her father, frowning. "Papa, you should eat your tomatoes."

"*Your* tomatoes, you mean."

"No, yours, Papa."

Silence covered the table. Demyan didn't discipline his daughter in front of other people, not that he had to punish Vera frequently. She was typically a good kid and occasionally had her moments where he needed to reel her back in. The one thing he wouldn't stand for was Vera lying for any reason. It was something he didn't mind correcting her for with others around.

"Vera, what did I say about lying?" Demyan asked.

"Not to," his daughter replied.

"Exactly. And these are yours." He waved at the four baby tomatoes on the edge of his plate. "They're not mine."

"I'm not lying. They are yours. I gave them to you. Eat them, Papa."

• • •

Claire couldn't help herself, a laugh bubbled its way out of her chest before she could stop it. Instantly, she clapped a hand over her mouth, tipping her head down at the table to hide her face from Vera's view. She didn't want the girl thinking her father's chastising could be ignored simply because Claire found Vera's comeback smart.

Cute didn't mean right, after all.

Peeking to the side, Claire could see Demyan staring at her with his usual bored expression planted firmly in place. It was a lie, nothing more than a deflection she was sure everyone else took at face value. His eyes, however, spoke entirely of amusement. She didn't think he minded her quick laugh, but she still sobered and sat straight in her chair once more.

"Vera," Demyan said, waving a fork over the baby tomatoes in question, "... these aren't mine, *dushka*."

"They are *now*."

"Vera."

The girl full on pouted up at her father. "I don't like them."

"Why?" Claire asked before she thought better of it.

"She only likes green vegetables, currently," Demyan informed, his tone dry. "One day she just woke up deciding this and arguing gets us nowhere."

"You did the same thing for potatoes, Demyan," Anton said.

"*Mmhmm*, it's a kid thing," Viviana agreed. "Ana wouldn't eat anything for almost two years unless she believed her father picked it especially for her. That had little to do with enjoying the food and everything to do with the fact she was spoiled rotten."

"Thanks, Ma," Ana said, laughing.

"Well, you were," Anton replied. "I did that, though, so ... no one to blame."

Viviana gave her husband a wink. "Exactly."

Claire glanced down at her plate. "But ..."

"What?" Demyan asked.

Claire shrugged, stabbing her fork into one of her own baby tomatoes. "Vera, you like fruit, don't you?"

"Yes. Remember, we had strawberries at Grandmamma's bookstore," Vera said, turning to face Claire with a beaming smile.

"I don't know why no one has told you this yet, but tomatoes aren't a vegetable, sweetheart."

Vera's little brow furrowed. "No?"

"Nope, they're a fruit."

"But they don't look like fruit," Vera pointed out, watching Claire intently.

"Do bananas and apples look the same?"

"No."

"Do they taste the same?"

"No," Vera whispered, eyeing the tomato on Claire's fork.

"So, you can't not like them because they're a vegetable, Vera," Claire continued, lowering her fork enough to be in Vera's reach. "They're not. Try it if you don't believe me."

"Do you like tomatoes?" Vera asked.

"I do," Claire said, being honest. "They're very good, especially little ones. They're sweet but not quite as sweet as strawberries. Still just as good. If you don't like them, it has to be for a different reason than the one you're giving."

"Don't give her an excuse—" Demyan's words cut off when Vera snatched the tomato off Claire's fork and popped it into her mouth.

"Well, then," Anton said, chuckling. "There's that."

Claire wondered if she stepped over her limits. Vera chewed happily away on the tomato, already reaching for another one she'd put on her father's plate earlier. Even so, Demyan's features were still an undecipherable passiveness.

"I'm—"

"Don't apologize," Demyan interjected. "I know that's what you're about to do. I've been trying to get her to eat tomatoes for two months now. Thank you."

Claire shrugged, smiling. "No problem."

"Vera, I told you a tomato was a fruit on your birthday," Viviana said.

Vera acted as though her grandmother hadn't spoken at all.

"Good?" Demyan asked his daughter.

"Not as good as strawberries," Vera answered.

"But almost," Claire said.

Vera nodded. "Almost."

Conversation flowed for a while though Claire noticed Demyan was mostly silent except for when his daughter spoke to him, or his sister addressed him. Other than those times, he

50

focused on his food and little else.

Claire offered to help Viviana serve the second dish but was told to act like a guest, so she did. Ana decided to take the break in eating to question Claire more. While she knew this dinner had a purpose for Anton and Viviana, mostly consisting of getting Demyan comfortable with having her around, Claire got nervous about answering certain things.

Viviana had been clear. They didn't want Ana or Demyan to know who she was just yet. It was something they wanted to work into, which she could understand to some degree.

Nonetheless, as she sat across from Ana, Claire couldn't help but wonder how much Cavan had hurt her and if she was healed from his awfulness now that he was gone. Clearly Ana was in love with the man at her side—Koldan—and he doted on her shamelessly as if she were his queen.

Still, Claire's half-brother had brutally attacked Ana. And she knew Ana was not the only one of Cavan's victims.

Ana took the plate of meat and potatoes her mother offered before her attention was back on Claire. "So, you're not from New York right?"

"No, out of state," Claire said, hoping her vague answer would be enough.

"God, your parents didn't have a fit about you moving away?" Ana asked. "My father is on the verge of a nervous breakdown and I'm only going to Jersey."

"I am not," Anton said, looking offended.

"You are," Viviana replied, setting a plate in front of her husband.

Anton scowled.

Viviana disappeared back into the kitchen and returned with three more plates balanced precariously between two hands. Demyan took his and Vera's plates. Claire turned in her seat to take the one Viviana offered her before resuming with the conversation at the table.

"My mother actually thought it would be a good thing for me to get away and my father passed away when I was young. My step-father was a lot like my mother and didn't mind me leaving."

Claire didn't miss how Demyan straightened in his chair as she spoke about her family.

"I'm sorry about your father," Ana said quietly.

Claire smiled, but she imagined the sight was as sad as she felt on the topic. "I was only a few months old. I don't have any memories of him."

"What happened?" Demyan asked, surprising Claire.

"Car accident on his way home from work."

Hoping to end the discussion, Claire leaned forward to stab a potato with her fork. As she did, the only piece of jewelry she ever wore slipped from its hidden spot under the neckline of her long-sleeved shirt. The small Celtic cross was a shiny gold, interwoven with knots. It hung off a medium sized chain, and Claire mistakenly assumed it would stay under her shirt for the evening because it never fell out of her scrubs when she worked.

She probably should have taken it off before coming to the Avdonin residence, but it hadn't left the spot around her neck since her now deceased grandmother gave it to her. While most people wouldn't recognize the jewelry as Celtic, Claire didn't want to take the chance someone at the table might. Quickly, she slipped the necklace back under her shirt. Her actions did not go unnoticed.

Steel blue eyes from across the table surveyed the spot where Claire's pendant had swung. Koldan Vasin's gaze narrowed, his mouth opening like he was going to speak before it snapped shut again.

"Braden, you said?" Koldan asked.

Something in the lilt of the man's tone felt threatening. All evening, Koldan had been quiet at the table. Claire recognized him as the kind of person who liked to observe people more than he enjoyed interacting. When he did speak to her, Koldan was respectful and polite. This didn't feel the same at all.

Claire passed a glance to Viviana, praying it was subtle. The woman gave her nothing in return. What could she give, really?

"Yes," Claire finally replied.

Koldan cleared his throat, tossing his napkin on the table. "Demyan, could I speak with you—"

"We're eating, Koldan," Anton said.

Claire wondered if the Russian boss was oblivious to the sudden tension thickening the room, but given the way his shoulders squared and his hands curled into fists on the table … probably not.

Koldan ignored the warning, pushed back his chair, and stood from the table. "Demyan?"

"Koldan," Anton said again.

Ana's brow dipped in her confusion as she stared back and forth between her fiancé and her father. Demyan stood as well, giving his daughter a passing pat on the head as he left the dining room with Koldan on his heels and no words.

"I think—"

Viviana's words were cut off by Anton's low cuss. "Ana, take Vera upstairs to play."

"What's wrong?" Ana demanded.

"Just … take her and go, please," Viviana said quickly.

Claire stayed silent as Ana left her uneaten plate of food where it was, ushered Vera from the table and left the dining room through the opposite entrance from where the men had gone.

"What should we do?" Viviana asked after a moment.

"Nothing," Anton muttered. "There's nothing we can do. Koldan is loyal to Ana, his father, and Demyan. I come after those people, Vine. You can't blame him for it. He respects me, but he doesn't have to listen to me if it doesn't benefit him to do so."

Claire didn't need to ask what they were going on about to get the gist. Koldan, like Anton and Demyan, was Russian mafia, too. Just not from the Avdonin clan. Claire had known that from Viviana's explanations before everyone arrived for dinner. While Koldan did business with the Avdonin Bratva, he wasn't in with their family but for his connections with Ana and Demyan.

Those were his loyalties. Anton's didn't matter.

"Should I go?" Claire asked.

"No, stay," Anton replied. "With Vera in the house, he's liable to take it better, anyway. It's high time I let him in on my plans. Who knows? Maybe once he considers it, Demyan will be just fine."

Claire wasn't so sure about that. Viviana didn't believe it, either.

"Right," Viviana said sarcastically. "You keep telling yourself that. I love you, Anton, but God, sometimes you are just so … *frustrating.*"

Anton waved a hand in the air. "Yeah, thirty years, baby. I know. Nothing new to see here."

• • •

"What is up with you?" Demyan asked, following Koldan down the hallway that led to the front of the house. Koldan didn't answer, but once they were in the privacy of the living room, his friend turned fast on his heel, raking a hand through his hair. "Wasn't it you who told me a couple of hours ago that it's not my place to question a boss, man? Christ, you basically just told my father to go fuck himself by ignoring him like that. If you're looking for a way to slip out of his good graces, that's a great place to start."

"Shut up," Koldan snapped, glaring at Demyan.

Demyan sneered, unable to stop the reaction to retaliate. "What did you just say to me?"

"Just shut up and listen to me for a second, man." Koldan paced a short line back and forth, gesturing at Demyan. "He's sneaky, you said that. And we both know he'll play dirty if he has to, but this, really? I mean, Anton wouldn't do that, right? Bring somebody into his home like that? Right here in his fucking home with his family. Would he do that?"

"What are you going on about?"

Demyan was far too annoyed to pick his friend's rambling apart. Koldan had also pissed him off by being a smartass.

"Hey!" Demyan reached out and grabbed Koldan's arm, yanking hard enough to stop the man's pacing. "Talk to me, Koldan. I don't have all fucking night here."

"Have you been paying attention to that woman at all?" his friend asked.

It probably seemed like he wasn't given his lack of conversation, but that was far from the case. Demyan tended to learn more about people by staying quiet, watching from the sidelines, and seeing them interact.

Claire was nice, as far as that went. She was soft-spoken but not timid, and she didn't insert herself into others' conversations unless invited. Respectful, kind-hearted, and honestly bright. She enjoyed her job, obviously she liked to read, and she didn't appear to have much interest in drawing attention to herself.

She was … human.

Demyan didn't know why that stunned him like it did, but he spent so much time with people wearing their own masks to keep up appearances that Claire was truly interesting for him. She felt like what she gave was who she was. She enjoyed Vera's company, which he appreciated. And as he first thought when he saw her at the bookstore, she was beautiful.

Frankly, he didn't know what to do with any of that, so he was just going to leave it alone.

Simple. Except it wasn't. Christ.

"Demyan!"

Demyan blinked out of his thoughts, agitated even more because it wasn't like him to zone out. "What, Koldan? Spit it the fuck out, okay. Whatever it is, just say it so I can get this goddamn night over with and take my daughter home."

Koldan shifted on his feet, cringing up at the ceiling. "Have you not heard a word I said in the last two minutes?"

Not really.

"No," Demyan answered honestly. "I'm not in the mood to play any more games tonight. I've already played the good little son enough."

"Good, right." Koldan scoffed. "You've barely said a word to anyone and you're supposed to be getting to know that woman for your daughter's sake."

Demyan shrugged. "Not saying anything is me being good."

Because when he started talking, it usually ended badly. Demyan didn't like pleasantries and he didn't have time for bullshit.

"Besides, you haven't been talking all that much, either," Demyan added.

"Not the point. Fuck, don't bite my head off, Demyan."

"So far, I haven't. I'm considering it. Seriously, what's got you worked up?"

Koldan sighed harshly. "Her last name, I knew I recognized it, but I couldn't pinpoint where or *why*. Didn't you see the pendant she's wearing?"

"No."

"You're sitting two seats down from her!"

"So she wears jewelry. Who gives a fuck?"

"It's a Celtic piece," Koldan growled out. "And she hid it the moment it fell out of her shirt. Why would she want to hide it, Demyan?"

Demyan froze on the spot. "You're wrong, man."

"And her last name, yeah, that's Irish. Not directly related to the Detroit family as far as I know. I've picked apart the families working under the Dolans, and I could probably go through it again only to find the same shit, but that doesn't mean anything. Her biological father is deceased. That's what she said. Her mother could have remarried and then they might not share a last name. But it is Irish, Demyan. Brennon, Brannon, Braden. All Irish surnames."

"He wouldn't do that, Koldan. My father wouldn't bring——"

"She's Irish. I'm sorry, but she is." Koldan gestured in the direction they came. "And her eyes, didn't you notice anything about them?"

"They're green."

"They're *familiar*," Koldan argued.

Demyan blinked, unsure. The memory slammed into his mind like a wrecking ball, crushing the air right out of his chest in the process. Green, bloodshot eyes with the pupils dilated thick from pain and terror as a knife sliced through flesh. Demyan hadn't been able to hear the screams after the vocal cords were cut, but the eyes spoke of agony and that was enough.

Cavan's eyes.

Familiar.

Rage flooded Demyan. Right behind the heated wave came the chill of fear gripping his spine. He hadn't wanted to be right in his assumption that Anton was planning something on the Detroit family. Inside he knew, but he *didn't want to*.

And this shit here? Bringing Irish blood into their home … their private, safe folds that had always been untainted by outsiders and protected so fiercely. This was how his father did that?

Demyan didn't give a single fuck what she was doing, what she could do to help his father or any of that nonsense. No, the girl was Irish. She would always be loyal to those bastards regardless if Anton trusted her or not.

How could his father be so damned stupid?

God.

Betrayal left a disgusting taste in the back of Demyan's mouth. A hard ball of sickness punched him straight in the stomach, knocking him back into reality. Vera spent time with that woman. They knew who she was, and his parents let Vera spend time with someone who Demyan would never trust to be around his child. Christ, he didn't even want Claire knowing Vera's name.

Why would they do that to him?

"Hey," Koldan said, forcing Demyan out of his thoughts. "You okay?"

Demyan managed a tight nod of his head. "Yes."

Lies. Koldan knew.

"Really, because you seem like a fucking stone right now. That's not a good thing, Demyan. When you go quiet and still, bad shit usually follows."

The odd sensations continued to ravage Demyan's insides, throwing him into inner chaos and turmoil. He wasn't accustomed to being bombarded with such intense emotions, not when he could usually slip into the numbness he preferred. Lately, he didn't have a choice.

Only on the inside, however. Outside, he was still the same. Blank, uncaring, and distant. Keeping everyone outside of his personal space and never letting them close enough to try and crack his mask. All except for Vera.

Vera. Vera. Vera.

Vera.

"Fuck," Demyan snarled.

Turning fast on his heel, Demyan headed back for the dining room. Koldan was right behind him, silent. It didn't take him long to shadow the entryway, angry but hiding it. His mother, father, and Claire hadn't moved from their spots. Someone must have done something because the table was cleared of food and Ana was gone along with Vera.

"Where is my daughter?" Demyan asked.

"Sit," Anton demanded.

"No. I don't think so. Where is Vera?"

"Upstairs with Ana."

Demyan was ready for a fight. "I only have two questions and I would really like it if you were honest for once."

Anton sighed, gazing down the table at his wife. "Go ahead, then."

"Is she Irish?" Demyan asked, gesturing at Claire.

"Yes," his father said.

"Is she related to the Dolan family?"

"I am," Claire said when Anton stayed quiet.

"Great. Fucking perfect," Demyan muttered.

"Demyan—"

"I have nothing to say to you, Anton."

"Demyan!" Viviana barked. "In this house—"

Demyan choked out a bitter laugh, pointing at the quiet brunette sitting a seat down from his mother. "In this house, Ma? Look at what you've brought into this house."

Claire flinched, but she didn't say a thing. Demyan almost wished the woman would. She played her fucking part well; he had to give her credit for that. She could make one hell of an actress.

"That's enough," Anton warned, standing from the table.

"What, are you going to say you planned on telling me eventually that you lied to me when I asked about the Irish? Or how about the fact you've been going behind my back knowing how I feel about the entire thing? Are you going to tell me how you let my daughter be near someone who could very possibly cause her to be killed?"

Anger flashed across Anton's features. "Listen to me, son."

"I'm only going to listen if you feel like giving me the truth. Come on, tell me. Lie to me again even. Go on, do it."

Demyan's words came out sharp, hateful, and bitter, but his tone was deadly calm. He hadn't even raised his voice once.

"I would never hurt Vera," Claire said softly, meeting Demyan's stare.

"Yeah, well, I find that hard to fucking believe given the shit that happened the last time my family mixed with the Irish."

"Demyan, that's enough," Anton repeated firmly. "Your mother and I invited Claire here knowing who she was and—"

"Obviously, because otherwise, you'd just be a goddamn idiot. And I never knew you to be stupid, but you're proving me all kinds of wrong tonight."

Viviana sucked in a hard breath at the same time Anton moved toward Demyan. It wouldn't be the first time he and his father went toe to toe on something, but his mother had never been privy to it.

Koldan stepped around Demyan, stopping Anton. "Hey, *uspokoit'sya*. Take a minute, Demyan, and think about the way you sound. It's fucking shameful."

"Don't tell me to calm down, asshole."

Anton's jaw was tight, his eyes blazing with anger. "He's right. Think about what you're saying and doing right now. Listen to your friend, son."

"Right, because I have so many of those," Demyan said,

scoffing. "Hell, I can't even trust my own family anymore to do what's right and safe for me, let alone my daughter. Vera, you know? Yeah, her. The innocent one. The child with no mother. The little girl I raise alone because of mistakes I made. And here you are bringing the danger into our home all over again knowing—*knowing*—how it could affect us. I never want to do that again. *Ever.*

"The only thing I have for that man to take away from me is my child. All Vera has is me, and whatever stunt you're thinking about pulling with—" Demyan waved at Claire who was still staring at him with a frown. "—her, could very well put one of us in the graveyard. Think about what I'm doing, really? Go to hell."

Anton clenched his teeth. Demyan tried to ignore his mother's tearful stare and Claire's bowed head at the other end of the room, but since his overwhelming anger was focused on that Irish woman, he couldn't.

Then, as quickly as his father had stood from the table, Anton sat back down. He pulled in his chair and rested his arms on the table as though he was waiting for a meal to be served and not like his son had just ripped into him.

"Are you finished?" Anton asked.

"No, but I think we can safely assume I'm going to leave the rest for another day. Like maybe when she's not sitting right there, and this house doesn't feel like a fucking death trap ready to kill me."

Viviana laughed bleakly. "Shut up, Demyan. You're so goddamn stubborn, you always think you're right about everything. No one else could possibly have your best interests at heart here. We're selfish and stupid. We're awful for lying. Yes, we know. Now shut up and let us talk."

Even Koldan's head whipped to the side at that statement, shock registering on his features. Viviana rarely spoke out like that when guests were in her home.

"I beg your pardon?" Demyan asked.

"Shut up, for God's sake. Just … let us speak. That's all."

"I don't want to hear what any of you have to say."

"Don't you fucking get it?" Anton asked, his tone tired and stressed.

Demyan waved his arms wide. "Get what? How you lied to me?"

"No, son, what I'm doing for you."

"What you're doing for—"

"Yes," Anton cut in darkly. "What I am doing for you—for Vera. I am sick and tired of watching you suffer. Oh, you hide it well, sure. No one even knows. And that's the worst part. Because you look over your shoulder, constantly. You are never at peace. You never will be until that man in Detroit is gone."

"You don't understand. I'm not scared of Liam Dolan. Not anymore."

"No, but you refuse to give him a reason to be scared of you, Demyan. And for that reason, a part of you will always wonder if he's going to finish what he started." Anton pointed at Claire, shrugging his broad shoulders almost flippantly. "She's my best chance of getting to him in a way he least expects. The man doesn't know fear, but he will."

Demyan eyed the quiet, pretty girl fingering the cross at her neck before glancing back at his father. "Why would you do this to me? *Anything*, you could have done anything but this. If you want to start a war with the Irish, go for it. Get Ma, Ana, and you killed in the process—all of us."

Koldan made a painful noise. No doubt his soon-to-be brother-in-law didn't like the sound of Ana being thrown into the middle of this situation. Demyan refused to let up just because someone didn't like what he had to say. It was fact whether they wanted to hear it or not.

"What the hell can I say to stop you, huh?" Demyan asked, walking far enough into the room so that he could place his hands on the table. Leaning over the top, he stared his father head-on, unabashed, letting Anton see what was behind Demyan's composed demeanor.

Fury.

Violence.

Hatred.

Demyan wished he was feeling those things for his father and what he had done, but he wasn't. His revulsion and resentment had somehow directed itself at the woman who kept watching him under her lashes, unruffled and still. Maybe she didn't deserve it, he really didn't know.

"Vera though, she's not the same as anybody else, Anton. She's mine, and you could have gone and did whatever the hell you wanted in regards to the Irish. I'm done trying to make you understand my side, but you should have left her out of it."

"I have," his father said calmly.

"How can you even say that when everything you have done is the exact opposite?" Demyan said, his tone finally starting to heat with his bubbling rage.

"Please stop."

Demyan froze at the soft, kind voice. Claire. He met her stare from across the table, seeing the life of her soul swimming there. Without knowing Claire, Demyan had the distinct feeling her eyes were the window to everything inside her. She'd been quiet during his tirade, and he hadn't expected her to speak up at all once she realized how pissed off he was.

The woman was either stupid or incredibly brave.

Demyan figured it was the latter of the two.

And he hated how something inside of him liked that.

"Please," Claire repeated. "Just stop."

CHAPTER FIVE

Claire could plainly see the hatred glimmering in Demyan's gaze leveling on her like a one-hundred-ton weight. His face was passive, stony even, but his eyes were burning.

After what her step-uncle did to this man and his family, she didn't begrudge him the anger he must have felt. He didn't know her, but she imagined he didn't have to, either. Everything about her probably screamed bad luck to him. Something that would surely bring hell down on him again.

Demyan had loved Gia from the time he was two-years-old. That's what his mother told Claire when they talked about the pain the Avdonins experienced four years ago. Demyan and Gia grew up together, and while they had separated a couple of times as teenagers, they always managed to find their way back together.

Soul mates, Claire had said, the only thought that made sense to her.

Viviana didn't think so, but she didn't explain why.

Nonetheless, a life was just beginning for the two when Liam stepped in to take it away. Nothing would ever be the same for Demyan or his daughter left without a mother. How could he trust someone like her when she was a direct link, an unforgettable reminder, of what had happened to him?

Yes, Claire understood his reluctance and disdain. He could have it, too, because he more than earned it. If only he would stop and listen to her first. She didn't want to cause this man more heartache, even if he did hide his incredibly well. The only thing she wanted to do was help his family and stop hers from doing the same thing again.

Liam was a monster. The kind of monster who molded his own nephew into the same vile, awful creature as him for the sake of an heir and the enjoyment he got from being cruel. In Liam Dolan's world, there was no fun if there was no pain.

"Do *you* have something to say?" Demyan asked, the words coming out sharp like a razor's edge. He openly stared Claire down, the muscles under his thin V-neck gray T-shirt tight like a coiled spring. "Not that I give a damn to hear anything from you, but please, go on ahead and make my night even better."

"Demyan," Viviana said, sighing. "Claire wanted us to tell you and Ana who she was, and for a long time, we simply led her to believe you did know she was spending time with Vera. It was only after the bookstore that she realized you didn't know. We asked her to leave it alone until your father and I could tell you. Claire didn't want you to feel uncomfortable or—"

"Too late, Ma," Demyan cut in. "I felt uncomfortable the moment I found out my child was spending time with someone I didn't know behind my back. You made me even more uncomfortable by forcing me into this dinner and now ... now I find out this? Way too fucking late. I am far beyond uncomfortable."

Yeah, Claire could tell.

Demyan turned to stare at Claire again, weighing her down with his attention. She wished she could say she didn't like it or that it bothered her, but it would be a lie. Something in his eyes drew her in and caught her like a goddamn deer in the headlights and she didn't know what to do with that. It stuck in her chest, like tar in her lungs, making breathing difficult and her heart unsettled. Claire didn't know anything about Demyan, not in a real way. The things she learned from others were just that—*things*.

She bet he had an entirely different story to tell.

He looked at her like he hated her.

So, why did she still want to know him?

"Nothing, huh?" Demyan asked darkly. "Are you speechless, or do you only know how to talk when someone tells you to?"

Claire straightened in her chair, unaccustomed to someone being so blatantly rude. "I'm not sure if you want to hear anything I have to say."

"Demyan, why don't you just get Vera and go," Koldan suggested, reaching out to clasp a hand over his friend's shoulder. "Maybe before she comes back down here looking for you and figures out something is wrong, yeah?"

Demyan shrugged the man off, waving at Claire. "Who are you?"

Claire understood his question, but she didn't know how to answer it anymore.

"Claire is—"

"I asked *her*," Demyan said, interrupting his father.

Anton scowled in his seat, shaking his head.

"My mother is Mary Dolan," Claire said, somehow managing to keep the nervousness she felt out of her words. "She married Dylan—"

"Dylan Dolan." Demyan choked on air, a disbelieving laugh cracking from his lips. "Liam Dolan's brother. Your uncle is Liam?"

"Step," Claire corrected.

It had long become an automatic reaction for her.

"After my father died, my mother met Dylan through her sister—Aileen's—husband, Brian MacBride."

This time, it was Koldan who spoke. "The Irish boss who runs the small New York syndicate for the Irish?"

"Yes."

"Holy shit," Koldan said in a grunt. "That's fucking …"

"Insane," Demyan filled in.

Koldan rubbed at his right temple with two fingers. "No, so wait. That makes you Cavan's half-sister. Cavan Dolan, the piece of shit who raped my fiancée."

"I'm sorry," Claire said instantly. "I'm sorry that he hurt her."

Koldan turned on his heel, glaring openly at Anton. "You asked Ana here tonight so she could meet the sister of the man who attacked her? And you couldn't even be decent enough to tell her the truth of who she would be meeting."

Anton frowned. "Claire is not her brother, Koldan."

"I don't give a damn!"

"And you're not Ana!" Anton shouted back.

Koldan stepped back, appearing stunned. "This is unbelievable."

"Claire found us, not the other way around," Anton informed dryly. "I know you and Demyan must think Vine and I are so horrible for bringing this woman here, breaking bread with her, and treating her respectfully in our home, but you have it wrong."

"Really? I would love to know how," Demyan replied.

"Your father already told you how," Viviana stated, flicking a wrist in her husband's direction. "Claire found us, Demyan. She purposely came to New York wanting to know the truth behind Cavan's death and what led to it. Eventually, that took her to your father's doorstep. Claire made the choice to get involved with our family, including your father's plans for Liam. You're the one who doesn't want to know those plans, Demyan. She's taking major risks by being involved with us at all, and I refuse to treat her badly while she's here simply because you don't approve."

"She shouldn't be here at all, Ma."

"Why not?" his mother shot back. "Because she has Irish ancestry she's not good enough to sit at our table?"

"Because she's related to the Dolans! And she'll get us all killed!"

That was the first time Claire heard Demyan raise his voice and the sound of it shocked her. Deep, heated, and tough enough to cut steel. Even the blue of his irises darkened in his fury. All over again, Claire found her heart racing and her air sticking in her throat.

She was attracted to this man.

This angry, pained, and dark in his soul man.

God, what was wrong with her?

"I only want to help," Claire said, gaining Demyan's heady attention on her again. The unease he created inside her burrowed in, but strangely, it wasn't a bad feeling. "I don't want what happened to you—"

"Don't," he growled.

Claire blinked. "What?"

"You don't know a goddamn thing about me, my daughter, or what happened to us. Whatever they've told you," Demyan said, waving at his parents, "… is nothing compared to what really took place the day I met your uncle. And your brother? Oh my God, that piece of shit. He was a rapist, sociopathic, useless excuse of breath. I did the world a favor by killing him."

"I agree."

It hurt to admit she felt that way because Claire never thought it was possible for her believe in such violence, but she did. Cavan absolutely deserved what he got. Maybe in his last moments, her brother finally understood his actions had consequences.

But he wasn't the only guilty one.

Demyan pushed away from the table. "I'm done with this."

Anton stood. "Demyan, please just give me more time to explain everything."

"No, I'm done. I'm taking my daughter out of here, and I'm going home. Until you clean this house of the trash you brought into it, don't ask me back. You can safely assume my position is the same for Vera. And since I am her father and primary caregiver, I make all the calls for her."

Ouch. Anger filled Claire like someone had poured hot lava into her veins.

"Trash?" she asked.

Without realizing it, she'd been fingering the Celtic cross at her throat. Her hand clenched around the pendant so tightly it bit into her skin.

"Is that all I am to you, Demyan Avdonin? Trash. Garbage. Filth." Claire swallowed the bitter taste of disgust on her tongue. "If I get too close, will I make you dirty, too? Is that what you're afraid of?"

Demyan didn't give a thing away as he said, "Stay the fuck away from my daughter."

Hadn't he heard her earlier? "I would never hurt that little girl."

"Stay the fuck away or you won't like what happens."

• • •

"You're very pretty."

Claire cleared her throat to hide her surprise at the random statement. "Thank you."

Ana Avdonin smiled from the other end of the couch. "How old are you again?"

"Twenty-seven."

"So, two years older than he was."

"He?" Claire asked.

She should have known better.

"Cavan," Ana said.

Claire stiffened, suddenly uncomfortable in her seat. It was the first time her half-brother's name had come up in the conversation after Ana had been told who Claire really was. Once Demyan left the house with a crying Vera, who didn't understand why she couldn't stay, Ana invited Claire into the living room so the two women could speak.

Who was Claire to deny Ana? She had questions, probably.

66

Maybe Claire could provide some answers. At least, that's what Claire thought.

Ana had mostly asked Claire about what Detroit was like, more on her job, and how she had found Anton and Viviana. She didn't touch the topic of the Dolan family, the mob, or even Cavan. Until now.

"Yes," Claire finally replied to her question about Cavan's age before his death. "He was almost two years younger than me."

"Were you close?" Ana asked.

"Ana," Koldan said, his tone soft but still warning at the same time.

He sat on a recliner by the bay window that overlooked the front of the house. Claire didn't think he was entirely agreeable to Ana talking with her about anything at all, but clearly his fiancée didn't give him a choice in the matter. Ana was more than capable of making her own decisions and had plainly told Koldan to sit down and shut up or leave earlier.

Claire decided right then and there that she liked Ana Avdonin. Actually, Ana kind of reminded Claire a lot of Viviana.

"What?" Ana asked Koldan, gracing him with a cocked brow.

"What are you trying to do here, babe?"

Ana didn't bat a lash. "You need to be a little more clear, Koldan."

"Asking about him, I mean. What are you trying to do, humanize him? Find something out about him that will excuse what he did to you and explain it all away? He was a fucking monster who didn't know how to feel, care about others, or have remorse for the things he did. What else do you need to know? Come on, Ana."

"I don't excuse you," Ana said.

Koldan stilled. "What the hell, Ana?"

"Well, I don't. You do things I don't agree with all the time. I've never put on a fake smile and pretended like I didn't know exactly who you are underneath your nice clothes and charming attitude."

"I am not charming," Koldan said.

"You are to me and to anyone else who needs to see a certain side of you to hide what you don't want them to find. Even so, I don't make excuses for you, Koldan. I don't have to like the things you do or how you made the money to build our home. I don't have to like any of it, but I love you, so I accept it."

"It's not the same thing, babe."

Ana shrugged. "I didn't say it was, but I'm not looking to excuse Cavan's attack on me, either. I just … want to know who he was and if that leads to a why, then so be it. Others can excuse him all they want, I'm not trying to."

Koldan nodded. "All right. I'm sorry."

Turning in her seat to face Claire, Ana asked, "Were you close with him?"

"No," Claire said.

"Why did everyone say that Cavan was Liam's only heir when you were obviously in the picture, too?"

"My step-father isn't in with the mob; he didn't want anything to do with it. That's what my mother always said. Not that it mattered. Liam held some affection for Cavan and no one had a choice in the matter when it came to his involvement in my brother's life. That's the impression I was given."

"Like he spoiled him?"

Claire made a face, unsure if that was the right word to use. "Groomed him might be a better way to put it. I guess you could say Cavan was brought up in an environment where he could have whatever he wanted, do whatever, and hurt whoever because he was led to believe he was a king. Or would be. Liam liked being cruel; he got off on causing other people pain. Cavan picked up the same behavior.

"But," Claire continued, sighing, "Liam never gave a damn about me, not that it bothered me. My step-father didn't bring attention to me when his brother was around, too. Then again, he didn't do a whole lot when Liam was in the picture. It could be why Liam never tried to go after Dylan, I don't really know."

"Liam is known for killing anyone who could possibly take any kind of power from him," Koldan explained when Ana looked over at him.

Claire thought it was sweet that Ana could ask a question without saying a word, and Koldan just knew what his lover wanted. If that wasn't love, she didn't know what was.

"Huh," Ana said under her breath. "And what, Liam practically raised Cavan?"

"Essentially," Claire said.

"Your mother didn't care?"

"After a certain point, there was nothing she could do. Liam doesn't give a damn about his closest men, never mind what a woman has to say."

"That's awful," Ana murmured.

"You're right though, Ana," Claire added. "What you said before, I mean. There is no excuse for Cavan and the things he did to you or anyone else. Liam made him believe he was untouchable and for a long time, he was."

"Don't."

Ana's one word froze the blood in Claire's veins.

"Pardon me?" Claire asked gently.

"I can see it in your face. You want to apologize to me. Please don't."

"Of course, I do."

"I don't need or want it," Ana said, tipping her chin down. "I don't blame you and you're not him. Please don't feel like you have to apologize for his misdeeds simply because he's your half-brother. I would never accept it."

Claire blinked, dazed. "That's not why I would, though."

Ana glanced up from her lap, lips pursing as she contemplated Claire's statement. "Why, then?"

"Because I knew what he was. We all did, and we did nothing. And for that, I am sorry, Ana."

There was so much more to the story, but Claire didn't think it was the right time to go into it all.

"The more people apologized to me after it happened, the more I felt like a victim," Ana confessed. "And that was probably one of the most difficult parts for me when it came to healing and moving on. I constantly tried to move beyond this broken person my rapist made me feel like I was. Everyone else didn't even realize that by shoveling apologies my way, they only left me right back at the beginning."

"Why?" Claire dared to ask.

"I couldn't get past the identity of a victim. Everyone kept seeing me as a victim instead of a survivor and that was hard." Ana smiled tightly, gesturing in Claire's direction before saying, "So, when I ask for no apologies, no matter how you feel, please listen to what I need. I'm not a victim. I don't want to be made feel like one anymore."

Claire could understand that. "Okay, I'm sorry."

Ana laughed lightly, the sound echoing in the room. "There you go again. No, I'm kidding. I get it."

"Are you okay with me being involved with your family?" Claire asked.

"I don't get much of a say in that, and even if I did, I probably wouldn't want to know why you're here," Ana said honestly.

"You really don't," Koldan muttered. "I wish I didn't fucking know, too."

Ana sighed. "*Anyway,* no, I don't mind. I wish my parents had been up front with me about you from the start, but I can understand their reluctance. Especially with Demyan and all. He …"

"Hates anyone directly or indirectly related to the Irish?" Claire filled in.

Koldan laughed a dark sound. "Give him a bit of credit; he was taken off guard tonight. Sure, he's got some issues, but mostly Demyan is just careful about who he lets in. Particularly where Vera is concerned."

"For good reason," Claire said.

Koldan lifted a shoulder in response. "Yeah, well, I guess you'll have to make him understand you realize it, too."

"What's in the bag?" Ana asked, pointing down at the gift bag at Claire's feet.

"Oh, nothing big. I missed Vera's birthday a couple of weeks ago. Since I know she doesn't celebrate Christmas, I wanted to give her this tonight, so she knew it was for her birthday." Claire couldn't hide the sadness in her voice even if she tried. "I suppose it doesn't matter now, right?"

"Maybe not," Ana said, humming the words out with a sly grin.

Confused, Claire glanced down at the gift bag. "Really, it's nothing big. I know how much she likes to read, and it's just a couple of books she might find easier to learn."

Ana grinned. "That's sweet of you."

"I like Vera."

It was the truth.

"You truly do, huh?" Ana asked almost tenderly.

Even Koldan had turned in his spot to stare at Claire.

Claire felt uncomfortable under their scrutiny. "Is that so

hard to believe? She's a great kid and spending time with her was always a bright part in my day when I was able."

"God, Ma should have told Demyan, and then he could have worked his shit out a long time ago," Ana said to Koldan.

Koldan nodded. "I know."

"What did I miss?"

Ana waved the question off. "Nothing. I just think it's going to be harder for you, now."

Claire still didn't know what in the hell they were going on about.

"I don't think Demyan wants very much to do with me. He'd probably like to forget he even knows me, Ana."

"But you don't want to forget you know him, right?" Ana asked. "After all, he's a part of Vera's package."

Claire fidgeted with her nails. "Listen, I get he's got some issues."

"More than some," Ana said, lifting her brow.

"But I'm not interested in fixing him. I'm not familiar enough with him to know how to apologize in a way that he would accept or understand. I'm also not interested *in* him. Okay?"

Ana's blank expression gave nothing away as she said, "Sure."

Claire would be a liar if she tried to say Demyan didn't peak her curiosity and interest. He was crazy attractive, but there was more to people, men especially, than their appearance. Obviously there was a hell of a lot more to Demyan than what was on his surface, too.

Maybe she wanted to find what it was. Shit.

Claire blew out a heavy breath, knowing she didn't hide things well. Emotions, most importantly. "I have a feeling if that man let me anywhere near him or his daughter again, it's going to hurt a hell of a lot for me."

"It could," Ana agreed. "You know, when I was upstairs with Vera, she couldn't stop chattering away about you. She's a pretty quiet kid, which makes her super easy to take care of and simple to please. I think she gets that from Demyan."

Claire had noticed that about Vera, too. "You think?"

"Well, he's not easy to please, but the quietness, the desire to be private and out of the eyes of others, and her gentle temperament. He wasn't always like this, Claire. And tonight was the first time in a long time that I've actually seen my brother have a public reaction to anything."

"I don't understand," Claire admitted.

"Demyan's ice inside," Koldan said. "Colder on the outside."

Claire felt offended just hearing that though she didn't know why. It wasn't her responsibility to defend Demyan, but they couldn't possibly believe that nonsense. "That can't be true. Look at how he is with Vera."

"We do," Ana said, her face drawn. "And most times, it's like he isn't there at all."

Well, that was absolute crap, too.

Sure, Claire had noticed how Demyan tended to stay silent and he didn't show a lot of outwardly affection toward his child when others were near, but Christ, all people had to do was dig below the surface. In his eyes, it was clearer than day that he loved Vera with everything.

"Two years," Ana murmured, bringing Claire out of her thoughts.

"Two years, what?"

"That's how long it took before my brother decided to be a full-time father, or something resembling it, in any case."

"That can't be true."

Ana made a noise under her breath. "Sure seemed like it to us. That kid spent weeks with my mother before he showed up for a day or two. Then, he would go again and maybe Eva and Ivan would take her for a while until Demyan came back."

"Ana, I explained to you what was going on a lot of the time," Koldan said.

"That doesn't mean it wasn't wrong, Koldan. We were all so worried about him and Vera. Mostly, we were concerned about her and how she would see him for being as distant as he was. Obviously she loves him, he's her father, but it still feels like sometimes they're not as connected as they should be. I can't help but wonder if that's because of those first two years."

"That doesn't make sense," Claire said.

"For you, I suppose it wouldn't. You haven't been around our family for the last four years."

"No, I didn't have to be. I don't know what you're talking about, Ana, but that kid adores her father to the moon and back. He's all she ever talks about and maybe you don't get to see it from her because you haven't asked. Whenever I spent time with Vera, her father was the first and last thing on her mind. If we picked up a book that reminded her of something about him, she just had to tell me. She loves him and guessing by the way she talks, Demyan loves her, too.

"No child who is ignored or uncared for would be that amazed by a father who didn't love her totally," Claire finished sharply.

Ana's mouth fell slack. Claire instantly felt bad. It wasn't her place to say what she just had.

"I'm sorry, I shouldn't have said that. You're right, I don't know your family that well or the problems you have."

"She talks about him with you?" Ana asked quietly.

"Yes."

"Oh."

"She doesn't with you?" Claire asked.

Ana looked guilty, her attention down on her hands in her lap. "I thought asking her things might make her feel bad and I didn't want Demyan to think I was questioning his parenting more than I already have."

"Maybe you should try something different next time," Claire suggested. "Vera always gets so animated when she talks about her father. It's cute."

"Maybe I will." Ana eyed Claire with a little more intensity than before. "Our family, we're a little odd, you know?"

Claire shook her head. "Everyone—minus Demyan, but I don't blame him—has been great to me, Ana. I don't see anything odd about any of you."

Ana laughed low. "Look a little deeper, I guess. The eyes are the window to the soul, after all. It's what my father always told me. Old souls, and all that crazy nonsense."

"Doesn't sound all that crazy," Claire replied.

She had been given a clear glimpse into Demyan's earlier. Even if he hadn't meant for her to.

"I didn't say that I never believed in it," Ana said. "You have the same eyes as him, you know."

"Who?"

"Cavan."

Claire's chest constricted with a force that was painful.

"But, they're also different," Ana added.

Claire wished she could have controlled the emotion in her tone when she asked, "How so?"

"In his eyes, there was nothing looking back. In yours, everything stares back."

CHAPTER SIX

"Hey."

Demyan forced back his scowl at his sister's voice. Instead of greeting her, he continued pulling boxes of different kinds of electronics out of the back of the stolen carrier truck.

"What are you doing?" Ana asked.

"Working," Demyan muttered, tossing another box onto the loading dock of his father's warehouse. "How the fuck did you know where I was today?"

"Koldan."

"Bastard. Someone needs to super glue his fucking mouth shut and teach him a lesson about keeping quiet for once."

Ana didn't respond to that, thankfully.

The only reason Koldan knew where he was working today was because Demyan needed to let his father know what his value had been on the take his guys stole. Ana's fiancé was with Anton when Demyan called about the hot goods.

Demyan was still pissed off like nothing else about his family keeping shit from him that seriously affected his daughter's life and safety. Maybe Ana hadn't been directly involved, but giving her attention and time meant his mother would surely dig it out of her if she wanted to. Then, his father would get the information, too.

So yeah, Demyan had spent the last two weeks ignoring the shit out of his family as a whole, even Koldan. Because that stupid fucker would tell Ana anything she asked about Demyan.

Vicious fucking circles. Nobody knew how to leave someone be or mind their own goddamn business. Right now, he needed time alone, and he was taking it.

"Seriously, what is this stuff?" Ana asked.

"Ana, listen. I only have forty-five minutes to get this truck unloaded before it needs to disappear forever. What I don't have time for is to sit here and have whatever fucking chitchat you feel the need to force on me because I haven't been around. I'm fine, alive or whatever, now leave."

"Nope," Ana replied sweetly.

Demyan blew out a harsh breath. "Christ, you're still just as annoying as you ever were."

"Most people find me charming."

"I'm not most people. I grew up with your spoiled ass."

"I am not—" Ana's words cut off as she grinned wickedly. "Yeah, maybe I am a little."

"God, what do you want?"

Demyan pulled off the gloves he wore and slapped them down to the back of the truck. "Hurry up, I was serious about the truck."

"What is this, anyway?"

Wasn't it obvious?

"Electronics, Ana."

"Since when does Daddy—"

"Don't ask questions, okay. The less you know, the better it is for everyone involved."

Ana's brow furrowed. "It's *hot*? Like, stolen hot?"

"Fuck, Koldan never should have told you where I was knowing what I was doing today. I'm going to kick his ass for that."

"Demyan!"

"Seriously, how's he ever going to make it as a boss when he can't keep his mouth shut, and he lets you know everything he does? All that's going to earn him is a private room with one window and door of bars, Ana. If he's lucky, he'll have a roommate that prefers the bottom bunk."

Ana openly glared at her brother. "Just because he does things differently than you doesn't mean he's worth less as a future boss, Demyan. Look at Dad—he never hid things from Ma and he did just fine."

"There's a difference, Ana. Ma doesn't mind Anton doing whatever the hell he wants to do business-wise. You, on the other hand, hate the Bratva and how we make our living. So, maybe he shouldn't feed into that resentment of yours. That's all I'm trying to say here."

"Like how you didn't feed into Gia's resentment?" Ana asked sharply. "Or the way she pretended for years that you were just a regular guy instead of seeing who you really were just so you two could live in some happily ever after of your own making? And you let that happen, you fed into that bullshit. Is that what you mean, that he should act like you did for her?"

Demyan froze. "What did you just say?"

Guilt flashed brightly in Ana's dimming gaze. "I didn't mean it like that, Demyan."

"I think you did."

Ana whined under her breath. "Can we just forget I said anything at all?"

Shit, he'd sure like to, but she put it out there.

"No. Is that how you looked at me and Gia?" he asked.

"I liked Gia, you know I did."

"Sure." Ana had always been close to Gia, as far as Demyan could remember. "But that's not what I'm asking here, Ana."

"I saw you trying to please her and I saw her ignoring things that were right in front her face. And fine, maybe you two were doing just great that way. Who am I to say? I don't have to like the shit Koldan does, or even you and Papa, for that matter. But I accept you. I don't pretend you're somebody else. Sure, it took me longer than I want to admit to realize that, too.

"Because I remember what happened when you were seventeen the first time she wasn't able to turn cheek to some of the stuff going on in your life. Do you remember that, too?"

Demyan did. He had ended up killing a gang member who tried to attack him and Gia after a football game at his high school. Gia left him because of what he did that night and shortly after, met a man who would become her fiancé for a while. Well, until she came running back to Demyan. Of course, he took her in with open arms and a mended heart. After that, they just didn't talk about the Bratva or anything relating to the mafia unless there was no way around it.

Just because he remembered it didn't mean he had to grace his sister with a response.

Ana waved her hands, clearly exasperated by Demyan's silence. "What would have happened down the line when Gia wasn't able to pretend anymore, Demyan? What, when you were stuck married and with a child, huh?"

Demyan didn't have an answer for that. "I guess we don't have to worry about finding out, right?"

"Doesn't it bother you at all to think maybe her love only reached as far as your ability to be who she—"

"Yeah," Demyan said, cutting off whatever crap Ana was

about to say. His tone turned dark in a flash, warning her to back off. "I don't want to do that, Ana. Not hear it or listen to it. Don't go there. It's not your place."

"Fine," Ana said, huffing. "But you asked."

"Not for that."

"Same thing," his sister retorted hotly.

More frustrated than ever, Demyan tugged his gloves back on and began pulling more electronic boxes from the truck. He hated the fact that despite his composed exterior, inside he was raging like a forest fire out of control.

Demyan preferred the perpetual numbness he usually slipped into, especially when dealing with topics like Gia. Unfortunately, lately the only thing he did was fucking feel. Constantly, like a disease inside his heart, pumping the sickness through his veins to the rest of his goddamn body.

He didn't want to deal with this shit.

"What do you want, Ana?"

"To talk a little," his sister said.

"I'm kind of busy today."

"Yeah, well, you were supposed to bring Vera over yesterday after her preschool because New Years is done, and I can finally take her dress shopping."

Demyan hid his scowl by tossing another box to the dock. "So?"

"So, when are you bringing her over?"

"When I think I can trust my family to take care of her when I'm not around. Right now, I can't fucking do that, Ana. Christ."

"God, you're really angry about this," Ana said, seeming surprised.

"Of course, I am."

"No, I mean … you're angry, Demyan. Usually, you're like a statue, silent and hard. And at this moment, you're not. I mean, I've seen you and Papa go at it over the last couple of years quite a few times, but you don't even yell. This is new, and I'm just surprised, I guess."

Demyan was surprised, too. What he needed to do was get a goddamn handle on himself before it started to bleed over elsewhere. As his father's right-hand man next to Erik, and as an acting Brigadier in the Bratva, Demyan was known for his sharp exterior and ruthlessness when it was called for.

SHATTERED

Which could be anytime someone crossed a line, invisible or not. Frankly, Demyan never gave a man the chance to realize he did something wrong before he bled for it. The mafia business was vicious and Demyan was the most brutal of them all.

Reputation was everything.

Demyan wasn't about to lose his simply because he was having a rough month.

"I need to take some fucking time to myself," Demyan tried to explain, still working on unloading the truck as he spoke. "And I need you and the rest of our family to respect that, Ana."

"Because of Claire."

Demyan's back tightened and his teeth clenched at the woman's name. Rage skipped over his skin and nerves, lighting his body up like a fire. Then, green eyes filled his vision, and her soft-spoken voice flooded his thoughts. While he considered who she was related to, the way Claire treated his daughter jumped in line demanding to be noticed, too.

Fuck, he wished he could get that woman out of his thoughts.

Easier said than done.

For two weeks, that was all he did—think about her. Demyan wasn't entirely sure why, but it didn't help that even Vera chattered on and on about Claire like the woman was her new favorite person. He couldn't be awful and tell his child to forget about the woman, but he was honest when Vera asked if she could see Claire again.

No way. Absolutely not going to happen.

Vera didn't like that answer.

Claire had even started to invade Demyan's dreams, which was more unusual. He kept falling back to the fact he found her beautiful the first time he encountered her and his body wasn't letting that go. She was the first woman to catch his attention in a long damn time but no matter what, he did not want to feed into that craziness.

Apparently it was possible to dislike someone and be attracted to them at the same time.

Who knew?

"Demyan?" Ana asked, forcing him out of his thoughts.

"What, Ana?"

"She's a really nice girl."

Demyan grabbed the handle on the box of a sixty-inch flat screen, yanking it toward him. "Who?"

"Claire."

Yeah, he should have known that.

"Don't care, Ana. She's—"

"More than just Irish and more than a relative of the Dolan family. Stop being a goddamn asshole here. She had a good connection with Vera and—"

"And, what?" Demyan demanded, dropping the TV harder than he should have. Jumping down from the back of the truck to the pavement, he faced his sister with an expression he hoped gave her the hint to fuck off and leave him alone. "Because my kid likes somebody, I should, too?"

"No, but you could at least give her and Dad the chance to explain themselves. Ma, too, I guess. You're being a stubborn prick, Demyan."

"I'm always a prick, Ana."

"We both know that's not true. You just hide behind that mask like it's going to keep everyone away from you. That's a damn shame. *You're* a damn shame, Demyan."

"Go away, Ana."

"Oh, I plan on, don't you worry." Ana crossed her arms, a gift bag in her hand catching his attention for the first time. "I'm not saying you have to like or get to know her just because Vera has, but the least you could do is give your daughter what's good for her. A woman role model, someone who isn't her direct family, is something she might benefit from."

Demyan's jaw ached from clenching so hard. "I am not going to let my child play pretend with some woman just because she doesn't have a mother."

"I didn't say that!"

"You didn't have to. Vera is doing just fine, Ana. She is perfect, healthy and happy. And she didn't need a mother to get that way, either."

"What bothers you more, that Gia couldn't raise her with you and you're left trying to ensure she doesn't forget a woman she never met, or that someone else might take a mother's place for Vera?"

"You just jumped over a big line, Ana. A *huge* one."

"Yeah, I'm not surprised. When the feelings come out,

Demyan runs. *Shocker.*"

Demyan had taken just about all he could of his sister. "Ana, do whatever you came to do, or say whatever you came to say, and leave. I told you I had shit to do and you're putting me way behind with this fucking nonsense."

"*Mudak*," she cursed at him.

"So I've been told."

Ana thrust the gift bag in his direction with a glower. "Here, this was what I came for. It's a birthday gift for Vera."

"Her birthday was a month ago." Demyan took the bag, setting it on the back of the truck. "And didn't you and Koldan give her that humongous dollhouse that took me four hours to put together?"

"Yeah, I know when her birthday was, but since you've made it your first priority to avoid all of us, I had no other choice but get it to you when I got the chance. It's not from us, okay. Just make sure she gets it."

"Who—"

"Hey, Boss, we're—whoa, hey there, *seksual'nyy.*"

Demyan turned fast on his heel to face one of his men who had been working in the warehouse to make room for the stolen goods. A leering grin split the fucking fool's face from ear to ear as he looked Ana over like he wanted to take a bite out of her.

And he called her sexy, for Christ's sake.

Demyan did not want to hear his sister being called sexy.

"Kyle!"

"Yeah, Boss?"

"Remove your eyes from my sister, *durak*, or I will cut them out."

Kyle swallowed audibly, likely knowing Demyan didn't toss out idle threats. His stare dropped from Ana in a heartbeat, and he tipped his chin down to Demyan as a sign of respect. Not that it mattered. The line was crossed, and it was too late to fix it, now.

"Sorry," Kyle muttered.

"Get out of my face and when I go inside, make sure you have a space cleared for this shit. Understood?"

"Yeah, Boss."

"Get gone."

Kyle let the metal door he was holding open close without another word.

81

"Thought Dad was the boss," Ana mused.

"Mine, but I'm theirs. Trust me, there's a distinction. Like the fact they never meet him. Thanks for the gift, Ana, but I need to get back to work. I'll pass it on to Vera."

"Whatever."

Ana spun in her high boots and walked away. Demyan couldn't even feel bad about arguing with his sister or for acting like an ass.

He had enough crap to be pissed off about as it was without letting her add to it.

Like Claire.

"Fuck."

Leaning back against the fender of the truck, Demyan raked his gloved hand through his hair. Frustration and tiredness ran rampant through his nervous system. He wasn't sleeping well at all, and the confusion he felt over Claire didn't help. He didn't want to be attracted to that woman. He didn't want to admit there was a small part of him that maybe wanted to know her and had from the moment he caught her reading to his child.

Because everything led back to Vera for Demyan. If someone wanted to get to him, no matter if they meant to or not, his daughter was the best place to start. The irritation rolling through his insides wouldn't let his racing thoughts slow, either. Nothing could ever be simple in his life.

Demyan wasn't ready for this shit.

It just fucking sucked that Claire had got to him without even realizing she did.

Yeah.

Fuck was right.

Pushing off the back of the truck, Demyan jumped onto the loading dock in one fluid movement. He yanked open the metal door beside the one loading bay, needing to do something else. The other guys could finish unloading the truck for all he cared.

"Hey, Boss," came a chorus of greetings when Demyan stepped into the small warehouse.

The boys had obviously been doing nothing but chatting instead of working. His annoyance jumped a notch. He didn't have time for this today.

"Are we gonna get a pick from—"

"Why are the bay doors not open yet and why the fuck aren't

you fools out there bringing in that shit I've just spent the last hour unloading? What are you doing in here other than dog-fucking around? I can replace my crew in a week if this is what you're going to pull every time we have work to do."

"On it, Boss," one of the younger guys muttered, passing by Demyan to lift the bay doors.

Kyle slid in beside Demyan, grinning like he had before when he noticed Ana outside. "So, your sister, huh? That makes her Koldan's woman, right?"

"Knock it off, Kyle," Demyan warned.

"Just saying, Boss. He's Jersey bred, you know. A girl like Ana might do better with—"

Demyan didn't even think about it. He turned fast, the only warning Kyle got, and punched the idiot in the face. All of Demyan's strength had been behind the hit and the sound of bones crunching under his knuckles was pretty goddamn satisfying.

Anton taught Demyan to only use physical action if necessary because scaring people in other ways was far more effective. Sure, that was true enough.

Sometimes hitting people felt better.

Especially when they deserved it.

"Knock it off, Kyle," Demyan repeated calmly to the bleeding man on the ground.

• • •

Aileen MacBride was typically an outgoing woman with her flaming red hair and striking green eyes. Even at her older age, she didn't lack attention wherever she went because the woman knew how to get it.

Claire didn't have many memories involving Aileen from her childhood, but the ones she did have were loud with some family event involved and most certainly alcohol. Aileen had a taste for red wine and beer, as odd of a combination as that was.

Being as outrageous as she was sometimes, Claire couldn't help but wonder how the woman was related to her mother at all, never mind being the older sister of the two.

Maybe that was why Claire found it so surprising when her aunt greeted her with a somber expression and a quiet tone earlier, something far out of the ordinary.

"What do you think of it?" Aileen asked from where she sat on the chaise.

Claire swirled the thirty-year-old red wine in its glass, sniffing the aroma it let off. "I like the smell, but I could do without the bitterness it leaves behind."

"Maybe it was aged too much."

"I thought you said wine couldn't be aged too much?" Claire asked, lifting a brow. "The older, the finer. That's what you've always told me."

Aileen's high laughter rung out in the near silent home before she slapped a hand over mouth and glanced upwards. "Damn, I hope he didn't hear that. He's been in such an awful mood lately."

"Brian?"

Her aunt nodded but waved a hand as if to dismiss Claire's concerns. "Yes, but we shouldn't talk about it."

"Is something wrong?" Claire dared to ask.

This was, after all, her point of being here today. Anton Avdonin wanted to know if there was any unrest inside the MacBride household. He didn't tell Claire why there would be any problems, but he did say the family might be down a man or two.

Claire didn't know what to make of that, but she figured it was pretty self-explanatory. Sometimes, with Anton, it was better to just not ask for the little details at all. That man had no shame and he wasn't the slightest bit bothered by telling Claire the things he did or planned to do if she outright asked.

She found she liked it better if she didn't know.

Claire tried to make it to her aunt and uncle's home at least once every two weeks for a dinner or even just a chat. It let them know she was doing fine in the city and at the same time, kept her uncle from sending his dogs out to watch her every move. She couldn't let them think for even one second that she had any contact with the Russians.

If she did, it would be a signed death warrant.

Claire loved her aunt, and even her uncle Brian, in some ways. They had always been good to her as far as that went. Her issues with her family went deeper than what was on the exterior. From the outside, they certainly appeared beautiful and good, but on the inside, they were all poison in one way or another.

Even her aunt was no exception to that.

Turning on the chaise, Aileen set her wine glass to the small table and clapped her hands loudly. "Kissa!"

Without making a single sound, a young girl who was maybe eighteen emerged from the shadowed corner of the room with her head down and her hands clasped below her waist.

She didn't make eye contact with Claire or Aileen as she asked, "Yes, Ma'am?"

"Get us some water, would you? Something to wash this back. Claire doesn't like the taste, but I think she just needs a better palate."

Kissa nodded. "Yes, Ma'am."

Claire barely held her disgust in as Kissa scattered from the room as quickly as she'd shown herself. That child—because, at her age, that's exactly what she should be called—was one of the things that turned Claire's stomach inside out when she thought about her family ... and even Liam.

Slaves.

Modern day *slaves*.

Claire didn't know where they came from. She didn't know how they were taken or what came of them when they disappeared. She was never allowed to ask. Voicing an opinion on the men, women, and sometimes young children who showed up on her family's doorstep over the years looking tattered, malnourished, and sometimes beaten only earned her a thrashing, too.

After a while, Claire learned to stop questioning and just pretend like it wasn't happening.

It was impossible. She couldn't pretend, but she learned to be more observant about her family when she helped the people or talked to them in private. While she couldn't make the situation better for people like Kissa in her own home growing up, she had given them a friend and a confidant to talk to.

Claire never hurt them, not once. If she could, she took the blame for certain things that had been a slave's fault so they wouldn't have to face the consequences.

It was not okay.

It was not right.

She didn't know what more to do for them without getting everyone killed and that made her even guiltier.

Her heart broke knowing the people she was related to sold humans like they were nothing more than commodities to be traded and bartered on. Souls—living, breathing, bleeding people.

And they were treated like livestock.

Claire took a small sense of comfort in knowing Aileen in particular took good care of whoever came into her home. Some, like Kissa, were simply more skittish than others because Aileen wasn't their first owner and the last likely didn't treat them well at all.

Not that it made it any better.

Claire didn't excuse or justify her aunt, uncle, or the rest of her family. There was nothing worthy of use to defend them. Not that they deserved for her to try.

She couldn't help but think of the Avdonins, too. She knew they didn't deal in human trafficking, not even prostitution. They also weren't good people with one hand in the drug trade and another in arms trafficking.

It wasn't as though she thought one family was better than the other, but she respected Anton for his position on the fact that in no way was it acceptable for his Russian family to dabble in the trafficking of souls. He also didn't give rationalizations for why he did do the things he did with substance and weapons. Instead, he said if he didn't, someone else would.

Without a doubt, Claire knew he was right.

Unfortunately, the same thing could be said for the Dolan and MacBride families. She knew that if Anton succeeded in his goal of killing Liam, someone else would take the man's place and continue with this way of life. Stealing lives and selling them for others to use and abuse however they saw fit.

This wasn't going to fix that. It would take a hell of a lot more than just one woman to correct that and make it go away— maybe it never would, according to some. But at least one more monster would die.

Claire figured that made the rest worth it.

It wouldn't ease Claire's guilt for the person she had failed to protect from those closest to her, but it might help someone else. Somehow, hopefully. That's all she wished for.

"She's doing so much better," Aileen said under her breath, drawing Claire from her troubled thoughts.

"*Hmm*, who?"

"Kissa."

Claire did flinch that time. "You know I don't approve—"

"Yes, yes. I know. I was just observing, that's all. Anyway, she is. And thank God, because you're uncle has been in a rage for a good month."

Claire knew if she pressed the right buttons on her aunt, she would get some of the info needed to please Anton. "About what?"

"Nothing for you to concern yourself with, dear. But if it keeps up, I'm afraid Liam might make a trip to New York to settle things out himself."

A shiver worked its way up Claire's spine, chilling her to the bone. "Oh?"

"Well, maybe Brian can get it worked out without Liam's help."

"Should I be extra careful, or something?"

When it came to women and the mafia … well, they weren't supposed to know a thing. Claire was mindful about how she posed the question to her aunt. It seemed like she was asking if someone might come after her, but what she would gather from her aunt's answer would be a tell if her family knew the Russians were slowly working in on them to draw Liam out from safety.

"*Mmm*, no, I don't think so." Aileen smiled tightly. "Besides, Brian is gathering everyone for a meeting of some sort."

"Everyone?"

"Not us, of course," her aunt responded. "I'm sure whatever this is will pass. We haven't had any problems since Cavan, you know."

Claire tried to seem surprised. "No, I don't know. What happened?"

Aileen made a face. "Nothing, dear. He just found himself in some trouble and Liam took care of it."

Apparently trouble meant death.

God, it was sickening how her family still swept Cavan's brutal, awful nature under the rug even with him dead. Like they had to continue protecting him, for whatever reason.

Something fell over up above them, followed by the sound of Brian's heavy cursing.

"Oh, bloody *hell*," her aunt muttered. "He needs to lay off the whiskey, the fool."

Claire decided that was her cue to make a hasty exit. Standing from the couch, she made a point of glancing at her watch. "I should go."

"You don't have—"

"No, I should. I have a shift tomorrow."

Aileen frowned. "You and work. At least you're staying out of trouble, Claire. Next week?"

"Sure." Claire gestured in the direction where Kissa had gone to get them water. "Apologize to her for me running out without cleaning up my mess?"

"God, why? She doesn't need your apologies, dear. It's her job."

No, it was her sentence imposed by someone else. One the poor girl hadn't asked for and certainly didn't deserve. Kissa was human, too, regardless of how the people around her acted. Claire wouldn't see her as something to be owned like the rest of her family did.

Claire forced herself not to snap back at her aunt when she said, "Just tell her, okay."

"Whatever you need, Claire, but she won't care."

Yeah, she doubted that.

• • •

Claire had driven at least ten minutes away from her aunt and uncle's home before she pulled her Toyota to the side of the road. She figured it was a safe enough distance. It wasn't the first time she used this particular spot.

Dialing a number that had become familiar to her over the last few months, the call only rang twice before it was picked up.

"*Ello*, Claire."

"Hey, Anton," she replied.

"How is your day going, sweetheart?"

Claire smiled, knowing Anton's question was genuine and honest. There was something about the man that gave off an air of authenticity. If he didn't care, it was apparent. If he did, a person knew that, too. It was the one thing she liked and appreciated the most about him.

Somehow over the last couple of months, both Anton and Viviana had become friends to Claire. Despite the fact they had years on her, she still connected with them on a level she hadn't expected to.

She knew who they were, what they did, and the things they

were capable of, but she trusted them.

"It's been okay," Claire finally said. "Long, though."

"They all are," Anton mused. "Viviana said she hasn't seen you around the bookstore in a while."

Claire cringed, glancing out the window at the passing cars and wishing he hadn't brought that up. "Yeah, about that …"

"If this is about my son—"

"You know it is, Anton."

"He will get over his issues eventually, Claire. If you want to go to the bookstore, feel free to make your way over. I highly doubt he'll be bringing Vera around there for a while, anyway." Anton laughed, adding, "And before you even say it, because I know you want to, don't apologize for that. It's not your fault that Demyan's got shit to work through."

"Maybe so, but he was here first, you know."

Anton scoffed. "If he could manage to make himself feel like he's actually here, then I might agree with that."

"Ouch."

"My apologies. It was … uncalled for. My son is one of the most important people to me, but for the last long while, he's not felt like mine at all, Claire."

She had a sneaking suspicion they would get Demyan back someday, but he might not be the same as what he was before everything. Life could have that effect on a person.

"Still," Claire said, "I don't think he'd appreciate showing up there with Vera only to find me hanging around. If he did bring her over to visit, I mean."

"I understand, I just don't agree," Anton replied. "But do what feels right for you, sweetheart."

"I am."

"Yes, you have a quiet stubbornness about you, huh?"

Claire laughed. "Figuring that out now, are you?"

"Stubbornness makes for a good woman, though others might not agree. It's one of the things I like best about my wife. She doesn't take any of my shit and trust me when I say it's kept me humble over the years. Why the call?"

"I was visiting with my aunt today."

Claire swore she could hear the interest in Anton's voice when he hummed out, "Oh?"

"You wanted to know if anything was happening or if there

was talk."

"I am. Did you hear anything unusual?" he asked.

"A few things that might interest you, actually."

"Great. Let me have it, then."

"Brian has been having an awful couple of months according to my aunt," Claire informed.

"How so?"

"She didn't really say, but she mentioned Liam might have to make a trip here to clean up whatever issues Brian can't."

"I hoped to hear that," Anton murmured. "Doesn't mean he will, of course. I might need to push harder, but I don't want to let them know it's me just yet. Keep going, Claire."

"Something about a meeting, too?"

"What kind?"

"Not for me."

"Good," Anton said quietly. "That's telling."

"I thought so," Claire replied.

Having done this same thing with Anton more than once, Claire knew what information would be useful to the man's plans.

"Did you get a date for this ... meeting?" Anton asked.

"No."

Anton grunted, clearly unhappy. "Next time you're there, maybe try on that. How close are you to your uncle, Claire?"

Claire understood his unspoken words right along with the ones he did say. "I wouldn't lose myself over grief if something happened, if that's what you're asking."

"It was."

"There's something else ..."

"What's that?" he asked.

"A girl—in their home, I mean. She's only maybe eighteen and—"

"Trafficked?"

"Yeah."

Anton fell silent for longer than Claire liked. "You can't save them all, sweetheart."

"Maybe I could for her, though."

"Not today, but I'll see what I can do later."

"Thank you."

CHAPTER SEVEN

"Oh, look at you with your eyes wide open," Claire cooed into the porthole of a baby girl's incubator. "And no breathing tube today, pretty girl."

The name marked on the card in black Sharpie said the infant was called Sara. She had been born three days before in a rushed delivery due to unexpected complications, and her lungs were filled with meconium. This was the first shift Claire had seen the baby awake and without some intervention helping her lungs to breathe.

"Claire, it's eight," came a voice from the NICU doorway.

Sighing, Claire pulled away from the incubator and closed the porthole. Turning to face her younger co-worker, Mina, she asked, "Does the mother know baby Sara is awake?"

Mina nodded but frowned. "PPD signs, and she's not asking a thing about the baby."

Something painful sliced through Claire's heart. Post-Partum Depression wasn't uncommon in traumatic births or early births. Even some fathers were known to show signs of the debilitating depression, almost mirroring their spouse.

"It's important she feels her mother," Claire said. "Where's the father? It'd be great for the baby to bond with him."

Mina shrugged. "She came in alone and she's had no visitors."

"None at all?"

"Sorry," Mina said.

Damn.

Claire smiled at the wide-eyed baby over her shoulder. "I'd stay just to rock her for a while, but ..."

"Yeah, I know, they're difficult about overtime."

"Spend a little extra time with her if you get the chance?" Claire asked.

Mina smiled. "Sure. I've only got her and the Robertson baby on my chart today."

"Thanks."

"By the way," Mina said, drawing Claire's attention away

from the baby.

"What's that?"

Mina tipped her head in the direction of the NICU windows that allowed family and friends to see the babies inside without entering the safe, sterile room. "You've had a visitor waiting for the last hour. He asked me not to disturb you, but he just took a walk a little while ago. Said he'd be back around the end of your shift."

"Oh?"

"Very handsome," Mina noted. "Well, as handsome as ice can be, I guess."

"Ice?" Claire asked.

"I don't know if he meant to come off as frigid and an asshole, but he kind of does without even trying."

There was only one person who Claire thought matched that description, but surely he wouldn't be seeking her out. Right?

"Did he mention a name?"

"Nope," Mina said. "Sorry, and I did ask."

"Huh. Thanks, though."

Mina waved at the door behind her. "Get going before someone starts barking at you about overtime again. What level are you on tomorrow?"

"Off tomorrow, back on Monday. Third level and a night shift this time."

"Yikes, get some good rest, yeah?"

"That's the plan," Claire replied.

With one more goodbye to baby Sara, Claire quickly made her way to the front station where she disappeared into the back room reserved for the nurses and doctor working the unit. After scanning her time card out, she slipped into the private bathroom, washed her face and hands, and then changed into clothes that weren't a pair of scrubs.

A lot of nurses didn't mind wearing their scrubs for half the day after their shift was over. Claire needed to take hers off. Sometimes her work days were spent in a private hell worrying, grieving, and constantly moving in a high-stress environment. She loved her job, but when it was over, she needed to separate who she was inside the hospital walls to the person she was outside of them.

The only way she found to do that was by taking off the scrubs and dressing into her normal clothes. The skinny jeans, suede boots, blouse and tweed coat didn't make her feel like the superhero her scrubs seemed to let everyone else think she was, but they allowed her to be just human until the next shift.

Claire made her way out of the back room, slinging her messenger bag over her shoulder as she closed the door behind her. She said goodbye to the other nurses at the station and as she turned to leave, promptly froze in place.

He stood leaning against the wall in an almost relaxed pose, if the man could be relaxed. Silent, like usual, and stoic in his state. His booted right foot rested over his left ankle while his fingers on his one hand drummed to the wall. His other was clenched into a tight ball at his stomach, dangling a familiar gift bag.

She hadn't seen this man or his daughter for three weeks.

Demyan's blue eyes looked her up and down, but for once, Claire couldn't help but feel as though his stare wasn't the dismissive glance he tended to give out. Oddly, a heat simmered through her bloodstream under his attention, making her mouth dry and her nerves burn.

She didn't understand how someone who clearly hated her could turn her on. It had to be the worst fucking crush she ever had.

Claire cleared her throat, willing the thickness there to leave. "Demyan."

"Evening," he said, the baritone of his tenor washing over Claire slowly. "I hope me showing up here doesn't get you in any kind of trouble."

"Not in the kind of way you're thinking. They use a different hospital and no one's visited me at this one since I started working here."

Demyan's expression didn't change in the slightest. "Good."

"What are you doing here, Demyan?"

"I didn't want to come, believe me."

Claire's gaze narrowed. "Then feel free to leave. The last thing I want to sit through is another one of your rants about how lowly you think of me. I'm aware, no need to go another round."

Something wicked curved his mouth at the edge, twisting it up in what Claire thought might have been a smile. It was hard to tell with this man, considering she never saw him smile. Sneer, yes. Smirk, sure. Smile, absolutely not.

No matter what it was, Claire's stomach curled into a tight

knot at the sight. Demyan was incredibly sexy with his blasé attitude and off-putting demeanor. Claire never thought she would be the type of woman who got caught up in the cliché of crushing on the mysterious bad boy with his shady dealings and dark past, but obviously she was mistaken.

She was not immune to that sickness.

Fucking wonderful, she thought.

This was going to lead nowhere good, Claire was sure of it.

"No," Demyan said, softer than Claire expected him to. "I meant here at this hospital. I didn't want to come here, but since my father refused to tell me where you lived and said there was no way you would come over—"

"I wouldn't have, you asked me to stay away and I was respecting that."

"Actually, I demanded and threatened you, but asking works, too." Demyan swallowed hard, nodding. "Yeah, and that was a dickish move on my part, but you did listen, huh?"

Claire shrugged. "Hey, if you don't think I'm healthy for Vera as a friend, then I understand, Demyan. So no, I haven't been around."

"I apologize for being an asshole."

Claire froze on the spot, unsure if she heard him correctly or not. "Could you say that louder?"

"I don't typically say it at all, so once is going to have to suffice, Claire."

"But you don't like me, Demyan. You made that perfectly clear."

"I'm not entirely sure what I think of you. I do know everything about you and the people surrounding you sends off all the warning bells inside my head. I can't stop the first instinct to protect myself and my child just because you have good intentions and seem innocent. Don't fault me for doing what comes naturally to me."

"I would never hurt your daughter."

"You might have to say that a few more times before it registers to me as truth."

"Okay," Claire said, still unsettled at his random appearance and apology.

Demyan glanced around under his lashes. "I do hate this hospital. I hate every hospital, really, but I manage with others.

This one in particular makes me fucking sick to my stomach."

"It's a good hospital."

"Sure, they saved my daughter's life."

Claire's heart dropped at that statement. Demyan didn't give her the time to recover.

"And failed to save her mother's the same day," he added quieter. "So, maybe being here makes me itch like somebody shot morphine straight inside my goddamn brain."

"I wasn't aware this was the unit Vera had been in."

"People who know me well don't typically discuss that day or the events of it all. Once was enough, I suppose." Demyan turned to face the NICU unit's windows, pointing at the far corner where baby Sara was resting in her incubator. "There's where I saw Vera for the first time. I then puked in the garbage can while a nurse barked at me to get out. That bitch is still around, I noticed her earlier."

"Which one?"

"I don't know her name and I don't care to learn it," Demyan admitted. "My mother probably does considering she was going to have her fired, but Anton convinced her to let it go. Older, tall, a little on the big side, short dark hair."

"Linda?"

That wouldn't surprise Claire. For a pediatric nurse who exclusively worked the neonatal intensive care unit, Linda didn't have the best people skills. She figured her age gave her a right to act however she wanted, even if that meant being rude to parents and family of very sick newborns.

Claire had only been in this hospital for a few months, six to be exact, and it took her one week to pick out the asshole on the floor. Linda, that was. Unfortunately, Linda's head nurse status gave her a bit too much leg room. How that woman still had a job, Claire didn't know.

"Like I said, I don't know her name and don't want to," Demyan muttered. "When I noticed her earlier, I just ignored her. Better for her I did, frankly. I couldn't even be bothered to look at her name tag. I didn't care to find out her name four years ago when she got kicked off the floor for the entire duration of Vera's hospital stay, either."

"Anton should have let your mother get her fired," Claire said under her breath. "It wouldn't have been a loss, let me just say."

Demyan chuckled. It was a deep echo from somewhere inside his chest and reverberated outward. Even his shoulders shook with the weight of his amusement. The sound struck Claire straight in the chest, making her breath catch in her throat.

How often did this beautifully sad man laugh? If she had to guess, not a lot.

She wondered if it were possible to make him do it more often. Because his laughter sounded positively lovely, sexy and immoral all at the same time.

God, there was clearly something wrong with her.

"Two floors down," Demyan said.

The statement was far too vague for Claire to understand. "I'm sorry?"

Demyan spun around, and there wasn't a lick of emotion on his face, but his eyes dimmed. "Two floors down was where they lost Gia's brain function. It was never quite clear whether it was the bullet she took to the side of the head that did it or the stroke she suffered on the table during the operation. Maybe a bit of both."

"That must have been hard."

"I think the worst part was being told the entire time that this hospital was the best place for her to be, especially for a traumatic head injury. It was like they were trying to give us some kind of hope she would make it through alive, and I get that, but no one really sat us down and gave us an honest opinion. She wasn't coming out of there, but the doctors and nurses didn't want to admit it."

"Sometimes hope is the best thing for a family," Claire murmured.

"No, the best thing is being prepared and knowing what's coming. Because I was ready to hear she was gone and when they told me she wasn't, I grabbed onto that and held tight. So tight, that when they came out and said she was brain dead, it was like I shattered all over again. I needed honesty and all I got was bullshit."

Claire didn't know how to respond to that.

"I didn't come here today to get into all that," Demyan said.

"What did you come here for, then? Because you made your position with me clear and I've listened. The least you could do is give me the respect of leaving me alone. I care for Vera, but I won't go through another round of your abuse, Demyan."

"I apologized for that."

"Maybe so, but it doesn't erase it."

"True enough," he conceded quietly. "Nonetheless, I came here because of this."

Demyan held up the small gift bag Claire had left with Ana three weeks earlier after that disastrous dinner at the Avdonin family home.

"Ana passed my gift along to Vera, and you had a fit, I assume," Claire said, trying to remain passive but hurting on the inside. "I didn't mean any harm. The gift was innocent, and I had it for a while but didn't get the chance to give it to her after her birthday. I meant for her to have it that night at dinner."

Demyan nodded. "I'm aware. And no, I didn't have a fit. Ana dropped it off to me last week while I was working, and I only looked inside this morning when I realized I'd forgotten it in my car. When I noticed the books, I immediately thought it was probably from you. Your scribbles on the inside of the title page wishing Vera a happy birthday said I was correct."

Claire crossed her arms, still feeling defensive about his show at her workplace. "Why didn't you just give her the gift, Demyan? You didn't have to come here and give me it back if you don't want her to have it. You could have thrown it out or whatever."

"Listen, I get I can be a prick, but tone down the attitude, huh?"

"You're right, you can be a prick."

"Sure, but what's your excuse?" Demyan asked.

Claire glared. "You're really asking me that right now?"

"I'm being … nice, I suppose … at the moment. I'm trying, which I didn't before."

"Demyan, why in the hell are you here?"

Demyan sighed. "Vera's not stopped asking about you for the last three weeks. I'm running out of excuses, and I can't stand for my daughter to be upset about something. I'm not going to pretend like I'm okay with some of the things I know about you, because I'm not. I don't think you're a bad person; I just have issues with the danger you might pose for my daughter's safety."

"Don't you think if I were such a huge risk, Anton wouldn't be working with—"

"Yeah, you don't know my father as well as you think you

do. Anton Avdonin would do anything to get retribution for his family, even bringing in an innocent no one would suspect to get the job done."

Claire was far from innocent.

"*You're* his family," Claire pointed out. "And you don't have the first clue why I chose to do this, either."

Demyan shrugged. "I don't want to know. I also don't want to be a part of it. If you can manage to keep from being noticed in our lives by your family, I wouldn't mind having you spend time with Vera. It's my only request. She would love to see you again and I don't know how to deny that child anything."

Claire was thunderstruck. "Seriously?"

"Yeah. That's why I came here with this gift of yours tonight. I have to pick Vera up from Ivan's later, but I thought maybe you'd like to come over and give her the books yourself. If you're okay with it, I mean."

Why did he even think he had to ask?

"Of course, I'm okay with it."

• • •

Demayn watched a silent Claire where she sat across from him at his kitchen table. Her meeting with Vera had gone off spectacularly, not that he was surprised. Vera adored this woman, and Demyan was still trying to figure out why.

What bothered Demyan even more was the fact he put Vera down to sleep over an hour ago, but he had yet to ask Claire to leave. Instead, they sat in a mostly silent state, drinking coffee he had made, and occasionally sharing a sentence or two with one another.

It wasn't exactly awkward, but he wasn't sure what to make of it, either.

"Do you want Liam dead?" Claire asked, the question coming straight out of the blue.

They'd been careful to avoid those topics. Clearly she dropped that pretense with a mighty bang.

Demyan considered her question carefully before saying, "Yes, I do."

"Why fight against your father's plans, then?"

"Because starting a war with the Irish puts my daughter front

SHATTERED

row and center to Liam's wrath. While I don't doubt for a second
that with the right planning, time, and care he could be dead, that
doesn't mean we won't suffer some kind of backlash for it."

"I'm sorry for what he took from you."

"It wasn't you who put her in the ground. I don't need or
want your apology."

In fact, it only pissed him off more to hear her say those
words, as if her remorse should be the one thing that took away the
perpetually cold indifference inside him.

"But we both know you still blame me."

"I do not."

"Sure you do. You need someone you feel is deserving of it
to throw your anger at and I'm the closest target that measures up."

"See, that's where you're wrong."

"Oh?"

"You have to feel to be angry. I don't feel at all."

Claire arched a single brow, leaning back in the kitchen chair.
"Really?"

"Nothing," Demyan confirmed.

"That's hard to believe."

"Ask anyone, they'll all tell you the same thing. I'm dead
inside—there's nothing here to see."

"Maybe they're not looking hard enough," Claire said quietly.

"Looking hard enough?" Irritation churned inside Demyan.
"Listen, I don't need a fucking shrink."

"Is that what you think I'm trying to do?"

"Well, you're awfully interested in whatever goes on inside
my head."

"No," Claire replied, unaffected by his heated tone. He hated
how much he liked the fact this woman could be completely
indifferent to his unfriendly nature and harsh attitude when
everyone else always got burned by it. "I'm interested in why you
lie."

Demyan's spine cracked as he straightened in the chair.
"Excuse me?"

"For someone who claims not to feel, you're pretty pissed off
right now, Demyan. Your jaw is tight, your hands are clenched on
the table. Even the way you're staring at me says you think I'm like
dirt on your shoe."

"I do—"

99

"So," she interrupted softly. "You absolutely do and I get it. I just want to know why you're lying about it."

Demyan didn't know what to say. Claire was right, and he hated it. Not about the lying part, but everything else she had nailed bang on. He was pissed, and he hadn't been this angry in a long time. Actually, he couldn't remember the last time rage burned through his gut and spilled into his veins like it was right now.

There had been so many times over the last four years that Demyan should have been angry. Things had happened that would have irritated him to no end if he were a normal person, not to mention his business as his father's right-hand man in the Bratva certainly added to his stress.

But ... nothing.

Not until now.

Demyan stared at the green-eyed, brunette girl across the table from him and soaked it in. She didn't deserve his anger. What her brother and uncle did to his family wasn't her fault and he didn't blame her for it, not really.

But he was still so fucking angry with her.

Searing hot, like a white light was coursing through his senses.

Christ, it felt *good*.

Demyan swallowed thickly, still unsure of what to say.

"Demyan?" Claire asked.

"I didn't lie."

"You're angry, though."

"I am," he admitted.

"At me?"

"I'm not sure if it's at you or because of you, not really. I don't know how to separate who you are from what I know. I told you that earlier, and it still stands. I'm trying, it's the best I can offer at the moment."

"So you do feel?" Claire asked.

"Now."

Silence saturated the kitchen, blanketing Demyan in a sense of awkwardness. Another thing he hadn't experienced in a while. Claire fidgeted with her fingernails as she watched him curiously from the other end of the table like they were old friends or something.

Vera, quiet and sleepy, interrupted their reverie from the

entryway. "Papa?"

Demyan snapped back to the present with a bang. "Yeah, *dushka*?"

"Is Claire going to stay the night?"

Clearing his throat, Demyan shook his head. "No, Vera."

"Oh."

Just like that, Vera's pretty face fell with her displeasure. Like her father, she was usually a blank slate, and when she was feeling something, it was only a few spectrum of things. Happiness, anger, sadness, fear, or boredom. She didn't have many in-betweens. Demyan figured she learned that from watching him. Or rather, learned to give things at face value because he did.

Demyan wondered what he should do. In his soul, he didn't want this woman around. She meant danger and maybe more bloodshed. Her presence could bring the one thing back to New York that could take Vera from him: Liam Dolan.

Claire Braden was everything he needed to keep away from Vera.

But there his daughter was, standing in that entryway with her pink princess nightie on, looking like her father just took the only thing she truly wanted away from her. He supposed in a way he had. Vera didn't have a mother, and he hadn't tried to replace the one his daughter didn't get the chance to know.

Vera attached herself to women much easier than she did men. She craved that female attention; needed a womanly figure in her life to give her what Demyan couldn't. If his daughter and Claire had been spending time with one another on and off for a few months without him knowing like he was told, it wasn't a surprise Vera felt something for the woman.

Vera would be so hurt if he took Claire away from her again. Demyan couldn't have that.

"But she'll be back to read with you again at Grandmamma's shop tomorrow, *dushka*," Demyan said, all but forcing the words out.

Vera's head popped up instantly, a wide smile lighting up her features. Demyan matched it with his own. The first smile he had in a long time that was honest and true. The sight of his daughter's genuine happiness for something he had done warmed him from the inside out.

He knew he made Vera happy just by being her father, but

sometimes, it was hard to tell.

"Promise?" Vera asked.

"Do I ever lie to you?"

Vera's black curls bounced as she tittered on the spot. "No."

"Exactly, no."

"Could she read me one of the stories she brought before she leaves?"

Demyan shrugged. "Ask her, sweetheart."

"Would you read me a story, Claire?"

"I sure will," Claire replied with a grin.

"There you go," Demyan said. "Go back to bed and Claire will be up shortly."

Vera left without needing to be told again.

Sighing, Demyan sat back in the kitchen chair, regarding Claire again. "This is only because she likes you."

"Sure," Claire murmured like she could see straight through him.

Just for Vera. Right.

And it had absolutely nothing to do with the fact Claire made him *feel*.

Claire crossed her arms over her chest, glancing down at the table. "I didn't lie before and I didn't say it just to be nice, Demyan."

"About what?"

"Liam and what took from you. I am sorry."

Demyan's jaw ticked on its own accord. "What he took from me had a name."

"I—"

"And it was Gia."

"I know and I'm still sorry."

• • •

Claire closed the children's book that described a wonderland and placed it to the bedside table. Vera pulled the blanket up to her chin, grinning happily.

"One more, please?" Vera asked sweetly.

"I think your father wants you to sleep, Vera."

"Papa sometimes reads to me until I fall asleep, so he can't tell me I can't do something with you when he lets me do it with him."

Claire laughed quietly. This child was too smart for her own good. "I will read you a dozen more books at your grandmamma's shop tomorrow."

Vera eyed her companion curiously. "How many is a dozen?"

"Twelve."

"That's a lot," Vera said, nodding once like she approved. "I like a dozen."

"It's a deal," Claire replied. "But I'm going to ask your father if you went right to sleep after I leave, and if he says no, we'll only read a half of a dozen."

Vera's little brow furrowed, and her lips moved silently. "Is that six?"

"Yep, that's six."

"I like a dozen better."

"Me, too, sweetheart, so you better close those pretty eyes of yours and sleep."

Vera did as she was told, whispering, "I think my papa likes you, Claire."

Claire forced herself not to laugh. Vera couldn't possibly understand how little Demyan cared for Claire, never mind why he didn't like her. "Why would you say that?"

"Because he doesn't talk to anyone, not a lot."

"Huh."

"He talks to you."

• • •

Claire pulled her coat on, unable to ignore the heavy laden stare Demyan was leveling on her down the hall. Demyan's mask of boredom rarely fell, even his words were spoken in monotone. She knew there was more behind this man than he gave. Face value went a lot deeper than most people realized.

Demyan Avdonin was the perfect example of that.

The man she met before was nothing like the one she saw tonight. There was pain in him, so much of it, even if he didn't let others see it or refused to let himself feel it. Pain shouldn't be hidden. She had witnessed first-hand what could happen when someone held that kind of grief inside.

It could eat a person alive.

This man deserved so much more than that.

"Would you tell me about her?" she asked quietly.

"Who?"

"Gia."

"What's there to know?" Demyan shrugged, leaning against the wall. "You've been hanging around my mother and feeding my father information when he needs it. Surely they've told you the story."

"I know how she died, if that's what you mean. I know she was housed in a hotel for safety, left it after getting a call for work, and was shot in the head by Liam's men."

"Isn't that what you're asking me for?" Demyan asked.

"No, I'm asking you to tell me who she was before."

Briefly, so fast someone might have missed it if they didn't know what to look for, his mask fell. It was the simple twist of his mouth into a frown, the baring of his teeth before his expression changed to indifference all over again.

"Tell you who she was before," he echoed.

"Yes."

"She was …"

"What?" she asked.

"Just Gia."

Claire let her arms fall to her sides as she sighed. "You're lying again."

"No, I'm not," Demyan replied frankly. "Gia was a lot of things. She was beautiful and intelligent. She had a deep passion for the things she cared about. For twenty-five years, that girl was everything to me. I grew up at her side. I can count on one hand the amount of memories I have from my childhood that don't involve her in some way. So, I can't sum her up with anything else other than the fact that she was just Gia because, to me, that's what Gia was."

"Oh."

Demyan cleared his throat. "I'm not very good at talking about her, I suppose."

"Don't you tell Vera about her?"

"Sure, she's her mother."

"What kinds of things do you tell her?" Claire asked.

Demyan's expression turned distant, like he was lost in some kind of memory Claire would never be able to reach. "I tell my daughter how much her mother adored her from the very first second she knew Vera was there; that Gia had picked her name—even though I wasn't agreeable at first—before we knew she was a girl; and I tell her how much she reminds me of her mother."

"She must look like her," Claire said.

"It's more than appearance. Vera has a swagger to her walk that matches her mother's and even the way she tips her chin down when she's thinking about something, or how she cocks her brow when she's angry. That's Gia all over."

"She's a lot like you, too," Claire pointed out.

"How so?"

"She's strong in a quiet way and when she looks at you …"

"What?"

"It's like she's looking into you."

Demyan blinked, his posture softening.

"Just like you," Claire added.

CHAPTER EIGHT

Aileen's words slurred together when Claire asked a simple question about a dinner her aunt wanted to have in a couple of weeks. She wasn't entirely sure what had brought on this drunken episode, or the one last week, but apparently Brian MacBride wasn't the only one tipping back the liquor bottles to deal with his stress.

"I'll clean up my mess and get going," Claire told her aunt, tired of the woman's nonsensical ramblings.

Aileen waved a hand wildly from where she was sprawled over the couch. "Why bother? I told you, Kissa will do it. It's the poor girl's job. If I didn't keep her busy, Brian would send her on to someone else. My Lord, don't you understand that? We're the better choice here, Claire."

Claire ignored her aunt, picked up the saucer with her half-eaten sandwich and the wine glass still three-quarters full, and left a drunk Aileen in the living room alone. Still rambling, likely.

She found Kissa washing dishes in the large kitchen. The girl wore a drab gray cotton dress with a white lace collar and black shoes. Claire suspected that was her aunt's way of making Kissa look more like an actual housekeeper on the payroll than a slave whose life was determined by how quiet and well-behaved she could be.

"Hi there," Claire said, sliding up beside the young girl.

Kissa stayed silent, but she offered Claire a nod. Claire made quick work of getting rid of the sandwich from her plate and dumping her wine out before putting it and the glass into the sink. She then grabbed a dishcloth and began drying the dishes Kissa already had washed.

"Miss, you don't have to do that," Kissa said softly.

The girl's voice was so low Claire strained to hear.

"Of course, I do," Claire replied, offering no other explanation. She figured it was self-explanatory. "How old are you, Kissa?"

Kissa visibly tensed. "Sir said I shouldn't—"

"Sir?"

"Mr. Brian, Miss."

Brian told her to call him Sir? What?

Claire shook off the troubling sensation settling in her gut. "Please don't call me Miss, Kissa. I'm just Claire, not some debutant in need of a proper title."

Kissa frowned and whispered, "I'm not supposed to call you anything else, Miss."

"It's just us here, Kissa."

The girl shook her head. "I can't."

"How old are you?" Claire asked again.

Kissa kept her eyes on her work and muttered, "Seventeen, Miss."

Claire's heart felt like it had fallen from her chest and broke into a million and one pieces on the hardwood floor beneath her feet.

Seventeen.

Seventeen-years-old.

Younger than Claire had previously thought, not that it hurt any less.

Claire couldn't breathe. Her chest ached. "Kissa—"

"They treat me well, Miss," Kissa interjected quickly. "I've heard some things you said before when you visit. They do treat me well, better than the ones before."

It took Claire an entire minute to realize she was clenching the plate in her hand so fiercely that the dish shook.

"Does he touch you?" Claire managed to ask through her fury. "Brian, I mean."

Kissa's eyes widened. "Miss—"

Being treated well didn't mean the girl still wasn't being abused. It simply meant one man was nicer about it than the next.

"Tell me."

"They treat me well," Kissa repeated, but the sadness remained.

"I want to help—"

"Claire," came a deep voice from behind her.

Somehow, Claire didn't flinch at her uncle's voice. She placed the dried plate to the side and turned to face the man standing the entryway. He sported a severe expression as his green eyes looked her and Kissa over, but Claire didn't let it bother her.

Ignorance to these people was bliss.

"Brain. I didn't know you were home earlier when I stopped in to chat with Aunt Aileen."

"Work," Brain replied flippantly. "I see you're getting to know Kissa."

"Well, helping her with the mess I made," Claire replied.

"She doesn't need help, sweetheart."

Disgust curled in Claire's gut. "Maybe not, but I don't like to feel as though I'm doing nothing. Aileen is a little distracted."

"Drunk, you mean."

Claire shrugged. He said it, not her. "Anyway, I—"

Her words were out off by the high-pitch ring of a cell phone. Brian pulled the phone from his pocket and put it to his ear as he turned his back to Claire.

"Yeah, MacBride speaking." Brian began walking away without a backward glance or word to Claire, but she heard the tail end of his conversation just the same. "Yes, a month and a half. Make sure you've got a man or two down here that you want included in on the meeting, so you know what's going down, Liam. I'm using the usual restaurant for it. And no, we don't have a fuckin' clue."

Claire couldn't get out of the house quick enough.

• • •

Demyan separated the stacks of money on the desk into piles based on who it came from. Tribute was typically his father's responsibility, but Anton had taken Viviana out of town for a late anniversary gift or something of that nature. Demyan chose not to ask the details. When it came to his parents, sometimes less was better.

Sliding a stack into a money counter, Demyan watched as the bills were flipped, tallied, and spat out on the other side. The number on the screen for the first pile was on par for what it should be. The second pile that went through, however, was short at least five grand.

A few hundred could be overlooked. A few thousand was nothing more than a problem.

Or a thief.

"Van," Demyan said quietly.

The man in question barely gave Demyan an acknowledgment over the glass of free vodka he was downing. While Demyan had gained the respect of most of the men in his father's office for one reason or another—usually fear was a factor—there were a few like Van Yolkov who still tested his patience and position every chance they got.

"Van," Demyan repeated slightly louder and firmer the second time.

Nothing.

The brigadier in question continued talking to the other captains in the corner like Demyan didn't even exist. Irritation swelled in Demyan's gut swift and fast, threatening to send his anger spinning out of control. Demyan didn't know what in the fuck was wrong with him, but he was barely managing to keep himself steady most days.

Well, part of that was a lie. Demyan knew exactly why he felt so off centered lately.

Claire.

Goddamn it.

That woman got under his skin, and he didn't understand how or why. It was more than the simple attraction he felt for her because Demyan could brush that shit off. Lust was lust, you either fed the fucking need or you didn't. He wasn't. Clearly something else about her just wouldn't get the hell out of his system.

"I'm going to break that man's face if he ignores me one more time," Demyan warned no one in particular.

He figured whoever was listening deserved a little heads up.

Erik cleared his throat. "Just be nice about it, prince."

Demyan's jaw ticked. "Yeah, nice."

Boris chuckled from his perch on the corner of the desk, giving the thickly smoking cigar all of his attention. "Boy, you're more like your father than you realize."

Demyan let that comment go, too.

"Don't go acting like a *bychit*," Erik added. "It'll lead to nowhere good given the club's open for business tonight."

Acting like a bull, he meant. It was a Russian phrase for someone who had a certain attitude. Demyan let his bubbling fury with the shunning simmer for a moment, not that it did much good.

"Van," Demyan said one more time, loud enough that the

brigadier couldn't pretend as though the man in charge for the evening wasn't speaking to him.

Once again, Van ignored Demyan's call.

Any patience Demyan had was gone. He picked up the closest thing he felt was good enough to throw, which just happened to be his own tumbler still full of vodka. Demyan didn't like to drink when business was going down, a habit he picked up from his father over the years.

The tumbler went flying from Demyan's hand without warning. Considering his history with football, he had one fucking hell of an aim. The glass shattered against the side of Van's skull, sending the man to the floor with a shout. Vodka splashed over his head and face. Glass tinkered to the floor as blood began to fall from a cut on the side of Van's head.

Van cursed loudly in Russian, pawing at the bleeding slice and still on his knees.

Demyan was surprised the glass hadn't knocked him out. He kind of wished it had.

Silence covered the room as all eyes turned on Demyan behind the desk.

"Well, shit, would you look at that," Erik muttered around the rim of his glass.

"Nice shot, prince," Boris commended.

Demyan didn't respond to either of the men. Instead, he waited for Van to gather his bearings and get his stupid ass off the floor like a real man. When he did, Demyan stepped out from behind the desk, keeping quiet.

Van openly glared as Demyan took a few steps toward him. Blood continued dripping from Van's injury at a rapid pace to the floor. "What the fuck—"

"Shut up," Demyan said calmly. "I called your name three times and don't even start with some ridiculous bullshit about you not hearing me. You can fucking hear me, Van. You've got ears that work just fine, even if they are attached to your dumbass head."

Not giving the brigadier a chance to respond, Demyan reached out and grabbed Van's ear on the injured side, making sure to pull hard enough for it to hurt. Van shouted, instantly falling to his knees again. Demyan was nice enough to lean down so he didn't have to shout.

Demyan didn't shout. Ever.

A good boss didn't need to.

"And if you ever ignore me again, Van, I'll make sure to give you a good reason to the next time by cutting both of your ears off. Do you understand that?"

"Yes," Van gasped, his hands balled into fists at his sides. Guessing by the way they twitched, Demyan suspected he was holding back from hitting him. Maybe the fool did have a brain, after all.

"Yes, what?" Demyan asked.

"Ex-excuse me?"

"Yes, *what?*"

"I—"

"The answer you're looking for is *Boss*," came a voice from the crowd.

Demyan recognized the man as Rory. He had once been a bull for Demyan and Viviana a long time ago, but the man eventually was made a brigadier. He deserved it.

"Thank you, Rory." Demyan tugged firmer on Van's ear. "Yes, what, *suka?*"

"Boss," Van ground out through clenched teeth.

"Might as well get used to saying that to me, *mudak*," Demyan said.

Demyan released Van and wiped the bloodstains on his hand to his pant legs. Damn, now those would have to be thrown out. Blood didn't come out in the wash no matter how hard a person tried.

Standing straight, Demyan said, "You're five-k short. You've got three hours to remedy that, Van."

Van nodded, clearly having realized it was better not to argue. "Okay."

"Time starts now."

• • •

"Hey, hey. That's a no-go zone, pretty lady."

Claire glowered at the butch of a man blocking her path to the back offices. She had tried repeatedly to call Anton's cell phone only to get his voicemail. The information she heard tonight at her aunt and uncle's was important, and she needed to tell him immediately. Anton would want to know.

Anton had let Claire know once that if she couldn't get ahold of him by calling his home and cell, he would be at the office in his popular Brooklyn club. It was where most of his Bratva business went down, apparently.

She figured that would have been his club in Brighton Beach. For whatever reason, Anton said they didn't use that club for most things anymore, except for Anton's private business that he handled alone.

"I need to talk to—"

"No one back there, girl," the man interrupted firmly.

"Back off," Claire snapped when the man's hands came up to push her backward from the hallway. "Touch me again and I'll make sure you know what your balls taste like, asshole."

The man bust out laughing like she was joking.

Claire wished she was. These Russians all thought they were ten feet tall and bulletproof. There wasn't a single one of them who scared Claire. She'd looked the devil in the face more than once in her life—none of these men were it.

"Listen, cutie—"

"My name is not cutie and I need to speak with Anton ... *immediately.*"

The man finally paid her a little more attention with those words. "Who?"

"Anton Avdonin."

"Why do you need to speak to the boss, girl?"

Claire didn't get the chance to respond. A door opened somewhere in the back hallway, letting out the sounds of several loud voices as someone came stumbling out. The man held his hand to the side of his head where blood seeped from a wound, dripping and soaking into the arm of his dress shirt.

"Oh my—"

"Okay, now you really need to leave, cutie," the man said in a grunt.

"Go to hell!"

Claire ducked under the man's beefy arm. Clearly being huge meant nothing for nimbleness because this tool wasn't quick enough to catch little old her. She slipped under his grabbing arm, ignored the derogatory term he called her and ran down the hallway before he could try to catch her again.

"Hey!" the bleeding man shouted as Claire brushed past him. "Anton—"

Claire's ability to speak was lost as she darkened the office doorway. At least a dozen men stood in various spots in the room, all silent and staring straight at her. None of them were Anton. Claire immediately noticed Demyan in the middle of the room standing over a pool of blood. Probably belonging to the man who just left.

Glass littered the floor and despite Demyan's calm demeanor, Claire could see the tension in his shoulders and the rage swimming in his stare.

Oh, shit.

"Who in the fuck let her back here?"

• • •

No one answered Demyan, but a young bull who worked with Rory's crew took a step toward Claire in the doorway. Instantly, Demyan's blood heated to a fever, anger balling fast and hard in his gut like a poison. He didn't have the first clue what the feeling was, but he didn't like that bull anywhere near Claire.

And he certainly didn't like the way the man was looking at her.

Strange women who were unspoken for by a Vor were nothing more than fodder to a lot of these men. It didn't matter if they had wives and babies at home, or if the girl was as innocent as an angel. Their mindset was simple: she should know better.

Demyan hadn't been raised that way.

"Kos, back off," Demyan warned when the bull moved closer to a frozen Claire.

"Why, Boss, you know the girl or something?" Kos asked, glancing over his shoulder.

Demyan tried to keep his face blank but it was mighty fucking difficult given the ball in his gut tightened harder, threatening to send him straight at Kos with fists flying. What in the hell was wrong with him?

"Something like that," Demyan said. "Just leave the girl alone. Claire, get out of here."

Claire didn't move. "I need to talk to you."

"Not right now."

113

"Where is your father?" Claire asked.

Good God, the girl was stubborn and brave as fuck. Demyan would appreciate that if it were any other time and there weren't a dozen men watching the exchange with rapt attention. He knew his father had taken a special care to keep Claire out of the eyes of the Bratva. It was Anton's way of ensuring Claire's safety while also making sure his plans weren't leaked out.

"Claire, enough," Demyan said shortly, hoping his tone made her shut her goddamn mouth.

"Hey, you were told not to come back here," said Alik, the bull who was supposed to be watching the halls.

At the moment Alik's hand fisted the back of Claire's shirt, Demyan lurched forward. Alik pulled her backward roughly and without warning, causing Claire to stumble in the heeled boots she wore. Her cry of shock sliced Demyan across his chest, but he couldn't afford to dwell on it.

Apparently, Demyan didn't need to do a thing.

Claire caught her balance quickly enough, spun on her heel, and slapped the bull with enough force to send his head whipping to the side. She practically screamed under her breath at him, not even realizing she had quieted an entire room of men with that one action.

"Don't you ever put your fucking hands on me again," Claire spat.

Alik stood straight, glaring. "You little bitch."

"Watch it," Demyan barked, grabbing Claire's arm and urging her to move behind him. "The next words out of your mouth better be an apology, Alik, or so help me fucking God you will bleed it to the floor for her to see."

Alik glanced between Demyan and Claire behind him, silently gauging the situation. "Boss—"

"She's not to be hurt, ever. Apologize, Alik."

Demyan felt Claire's hand find his lower back, fisting into the material of his silk dress shirt. He didn't know if it was for her benefit or his, but he didn't mind either way. Whatever kept her quiet.

"Sorry," the man muttered, hands flying up in a submissive posture.

"Do not thank him," Demyan said, giving Claire a look over his shoulder. The girl was predictable, but it wasn't the time for her politeness. "His actions demand appropriate remorse and it is not your responsibility to offer forgiveness for something he knows is wrong without being told."

"Okay," Claire murmured.

Well, at least she listened to something.

"Everyone out," Demyan ordered.

"Prince, tribute's not over," Erik noted from his spot by the desk. The man hadn't moved during the entire show.

"Doesn't matter. You can wait outside the office until this is taken care of. Out, now. I hate repeating myself."

Demyan didn't move out of the way as men cleared from the office. Once the door was closed, he stepped forward and locked the damn thing to keep anyone from interrupting. Turning on his heel, Demyan faced a somber Claire.

"What in the fuck were you thinking barging in here like that?" Demyan asked.

Claire stared at the floor. "Where is your father, Demyan?"

"Out of town for the night with my mother."

"Don't you have Vera on any weekends?"

Demyan shrugged. "I let her mother's family take turns on the Saturdays and Sundays when she's not with my parents for their weekends. Otherwise, her weekdays are pretty busy, and she wouldn't get to see them much. She's with Gia's sister Chrissy. And none of this has anything to do what I asked you, Claire."

"I needed to talk to him; that's all."

"Didn't he explain the rules of this shit to you?"

"No," Claire said softly. "Well, he said to call first. I did. This is important."

"You're mighty brave or really stupid. I can't decide which one right now."

Claire's head snapped up, her green eyes blazing into his. "I am not stupid!"

"Interrupting a Bratva tribute and slapping a bull who could break you in half in front a room full of Russian mafia men is a little stupid, Claire."

"You know what, Demyan, I am so done trying with you."

Claire tried to stomp on past Demyan toward the door, but he didn't let her get far. His hand snapped out and snagged her wrist in his palm, turning her fast to face him again.

"But I'm going to go with brave," Demyan muttered under

his breath.

CHAPTER NINE

Claire's gaze flittered back and forth between where Demyan was holding her and his face. "Demyan …"

He wasn't entirely sure why, but she needed to know something was bothering him inside.

"You worried me showing up like that. Please don't do it again because the next time, I might not be here to stop someone from doing worse, Claire."

"Would they?" she asked faintly.

"Some might."

"You're shaking."

Was he?

Demyan didn't even realize, but he still didn't want to let her go. A battle warred through his mind, the warning bells clanging louder than ever while he tried to figure out what it was he needed. He wasn't supposed to feel—he liked being numb.

How had this one girl—someone he should hate and sometimes did—turn his world completely on axis just by existing?

"What was so important?" Demyan asked.

"You don't want to know about those things, remember?"

Demyan nodded. "I need you to talk, though."

Claire's brow furrowed. "Why?"

"Because I think better when you do."

He could ignore his opinions and assumptions that were based solely on the things surrounding Claire instead of what was good about her. Demyan didn't want to focus on those things, either. He couldn't be something with someone and certainly not Claire. He didn't know how to be something to someone anymore.

"I know the date of the meeting," Claire whispered.

"What meeting?"

"The Irish, my uncle's meeting. It's in a month and a half."

Demyan's spine straightened. "Why does Anton want to know that?"

"I don't know for sure, but I think we can both guess, and if they're not correct, they'll be pretty damn close."

Yeah, he agreed.

Fuck.

"Was there anything else?"

Claire lifted a single shoulder like she didn't want to answer that question. Demyan's hand around her wrist tightened before he tugged, drawing her a couple of inches closer to him.

"Tell me," he said.

"There's a girl in their home."

"A girl. Is that all?"

"A slave," she said. "I need to help her. She's only seventeen and ... and she didn't ask for whatever she's living through, okay. So yeah, I need to help that girl somehow, Demyan."

Demyan blinked, unsettled inside all over again. "You're doing this."

"Huh?"

"This—my father, his plans. You're on board all the way."

"I thought you knew that, Demyan."

Evidently he didn't know anything. Not like he thought he did.

"What's the difference, Claire?" he asked.

"Between what?"

"Us and them. There's got to be some major difference that justifies this for you. Tell me what it is."

"There's no justifying anything, Demyan. I just picked the evil I understand, the one I can help, and I don't have to explain or excuse it."

"No, I suppose you don't."

Claire cleared her throat. "You're still holding onto me."

"I know."

"You're still shaking," she added quieter.

Yeah.

Claire finally looked up at him with an honest vulnerability. Demyan didn't know how to show in his own anymore but he understood it in others. Something else drew his attention in as well, like the way her teeth caught her bottom lip and how she glanced away from his mouth the moment her stare landed on it.

Oh, shit.

Demyan obviously wasn't alone in the odd attraction he felt for this woman. He wasn't sure if that made the situation worse, or not.

"I need you to let me go now," Claire said. "You don't like me and I know it. You're making it really hard for me to tell right now, though."

"Claire—"

"And I'm not stupid," she interjected. "But I'm not brave, either."

He disagreed.

Demyan pointed at her, circling his finger over her chest. "There's good all through you. I didn't expect that. It might be a little misguided, but it's there."

"Please don't say things like that, Demyan."

He couldn't help it.

Staring at Claire, the only thing Demyan could think was how entirely overwhelmed this woman made him. He might not have been showing it, but he was sure as fuck feeling it. Demyan didn't want to feel anything at all but around Claire, he didn't get the choice.

It was ... strange, addictive, and *bad*.

Demyan never pretended to be good.

"There is blood on the floor," Claire said like it was an afterthought.

"Yes."

"From the man who rushed out bleeding." It wasn't even a question.

"Yes."

"Huh. Someone should clean that up or it'll stain the hardwood."

Something inside of him reacted to the fact she wasn't all that bothered by the blood, the violence of it, or even him, for that matter. She didn't question him, demand anything, and she had yet to panic.

That was far too appealing to Demyan.

Yes, he liked that a lot.

Christ.

"Claire?"

"Yeah?"

Demyan hadn't been with someone since Sofia over a month ago. He hadn't even considered it, really. Between life and business, he didn't have the time to find someone to sleep with, never mind be attracted to.

He knew exactly why he didn't like Kos being near Claire earlier. It was jealousy. White-hot and like a kick to his gut.

Dangerous.

"What, Demyan?" Claire asked, bringing him out of his head.

Demyan swallowed back the rising lust that had materialized out of practically nothing at all. He couldn't begin to explain it. "You should go."

Claire blinked. "But—"

"No, you should go. I'll let my father know you were here."

He was still holding onto her wrist, but Demyan didn't let go. Without warning, Claire stepped closer to his body until her forehead was just a tilt of his lips away. The pressure in his chest increased at her proximity.

Lifting her head, Claire watched him under dark, thick lashes. "What's wrong?"

"Nothing."

"You look like nothing is wrong, but that's not what I see."

"You need to stop looking," Demyan said.

Fuck, did she ever need to stop looking for things in him. Nobody ever looked beyond Demyan's surface and he liked it that way.

"I shouldn't want anything to do with you," Demyan said.

Why the words escaped the privacy of his mind, he wasn't sure.

"Do I scare you, Demyan?"

The innocent question burned his nerves. Something else to add onto the pile of things Demyan found attractive about this woman was her subtle confidence.

"Do I unsettle you?" Claire asked when Demyan didn't answer her first question.

"Yes," he admitted.

"Is that a good thing?"

"I don't know."

Yes, because no one else could. No, because he didn't know how to handle it.

Claire's teeth found her bottom lip, drawing the plump flesh in with a suck of air. She reached up and tapped his chest with one finger. Sparks lit up across the place she touched.

"I'm going to take a chance here and do something stupid that I usually wouldn't," Claire informed.

Demyan cocked a brow, unsure. "Oh?"

Claire rattled off an address in Brooklyn. He recognized it as an apartment building in a decent neighborhood close to the hospital where she worked.

"What's that?" Demyan asked, pretty damn sure he knew.

Claire stood a little straighter, patting his chest with her finger again. "The address for my apartment. After I leave here, I'm going to be there all night."

Demyan released the breath he'd been holding. "It's awfully bold of you to invite me to your place."

"Take it however you want, Demyan. I'm just putting it out there, and you can choose to follow through or leave it alone."

"I've not given one reason for you to believe I'm interested in that as far as you and I are concerned," he said.

But he was. Demyan had never been a liar and saying he felt nothing in the way of attraction for Claire would be total bullshit. She turned him on and pissed him off at the same fucking time. It wasn't really her fault when it came to his anger, though. The lust shooting from his palm locked around her wrist, through his arm, and straight down to his cock, however, was a whole different story.

He wondered how many people had told his woman she was beautiful.

Probably not nearly enough.

Claire continued watching him in that way of hers, setting him on edge further. "You don't have to. I know."

Demyan almost laughed, but held back. Fact was, Claire had him nailed down without even trying. "Do you?"

"You still haven't let me go, Demyan. And your eyes … everything important about you, anything I need to know, is all in your eyes."

Any control Demyan had snapped in that one second. Because he knew better; he knew he shouldn't want Claire, and he certainly shouldn't feel anything for the woman. But he did, and he had spent four years under his own suffocating control.

The chain broke and, she was the cause.

Before Demyan could overthink his next move, he caught Claire's fingers still touching his chest with his free hand. He closed what little gap there was between them, but like the smart girl Claire was, she took a step back. Then, she took another and another. Demyan followed each one until she was back against the office window.

The blinds covering the glass crunched under Claire's weight as Demyan pushed against her. He forced her hands up on either side of her head, thoroughly enjoying the feel of her fingernails scoring into his palms.

"You don't even know what you're inviting in, Claire."

"Follow through or don't," she said simply.

Claire was always so soft-spoken, even if her tone was firm or there was anger in her eyes. Demyan tried to remember if she had ever once yelled at him before. He couldn't think of a time when it happened. She seemed sweet but it had to be a lie. The way her legs opened when he stepped in between her thighs and how she pressed her lower half into his growing erection spoke nothing of innocence.

Christ, he was hot all fucking over.

Demyan released his hold on Claire's wrists just long enough to grab her face in his hands. Sex was a need, something to be fulfilled and then it was done with. That's all this was. If he could satisfy whatever fucking crazy craving he had for this woman, it would go away. So, that's what he planned on doing.

His mouth crashed down on hers and he swallowed the gasp she let out at the surprise move. Claire's mouth was hot satin on his and the moment her lips parted, his tongue speared into her heat. She let him dominate the kiss, her fingers locking tightly around his wrists to hold him in place. His teeth scraped along her bottom lip, and he forced her harder into the blinds of the window.

The more Demyan kissed Claire, the harder the pressure grew in his chest. Sensations he didn't understand curled around his nerves, threatening to suffocate what numbness remained in his system.

It was like waking up all over again.

How long had it felt like he was sleeping?

Demyan pulled away before those thoughts could go any further.

Nothing good could come of this.

God, he wished he cared.

"I have work to do and it's going to take a while."

"I'll be there all night," she repeated.

• • •

Claire fidgeted with her key ring for the fifth time since she sat down on her couch after changing into something more comfortable. One key was missing off the ring because she'd given the spare one to get inside the building to Demyan before leaving the club.

Clearly, she had gone insane.

That was the only possible explanation for why she had invited Demyan Avdonin to her apartment and then let him kiss her like he had.

Not that Claire didn't enjoy it because she sure as hell did. She also meant for him to take her up on the offer of sex, but she didn't have the first clue why she put it out there at all.

Okay, that was a lie.

Claire knew.

When he looked at her, Demyan stared straight into her. Something inside wanted more of that, and she would be a goddamn liar if she said that man didn't get her hot and bothered. Did she like that he was a cold asshole on his good days? No. There had to be more to him than that façade.

Claire glanced out the small living room window that overlooked the top of a smaller apartment building. It was well after two in the morning, and self-doubt had begun to settle into her heart.

It would take a while, he said. Claire wasn't sure if he meant this long.

She had been honest when she told Demyan this wasn't her style. Claire didn't randomly hook up with men and she certainly didn't invite them to her place. It wasn't like she was a saint as far as that went, but a casual thing had never been her preference when it came to sex and relationships.

There had not been one man who prickled and fueled the flames of her dormant desires like Demyan Avdonin did. So yeah, maybe she wanted to be a little stupid and see what it all meant, even if would end in the morning and that was it. She just hoped it didn't screw everything up.

Claire sat in the darkness, silent, for a while longer. The ringing of her cell phone broke the daze. She answered it on the second ring. "Hello?"

"Evening, Claire."

"Anton. I heard you were out of town with Vine."

"I am," he replied, a smile in his voice. "It isn't often I get to take my wife away from the nonsense of life, but it's always great when I do. Speaking of hearing things, I happened to hear you were looking for me."

"I was."

"I'm listening."

"It's a little late for you to be calling, isn't it?" Claire asked.

"I don't sleep well when I have things on my mind. Tell me what you know, Claire."

"That dinner, it's happening in a month and a half. I don't have an exact date, sorry."

Anton chuckled. "Oh I think I can find that out for myself, don't worry. There are snakes in every man's grass, believe me. The Irish are no exception. Anything else?"

"It's going to happen at the usual restaurant, or that's what Brian said. I don't know where that is, either."

"I do. Instead of running his business and men from multiple places, Brian likes one in particular. And what about your little friend, Claire?"

Claire sighed, rubbing at her forehead. She figured he would ask about Kissa, given their last conversation about the girl ended with him saying he would help. "She's younger than I thought she was."

"That's unfortunate, but at the same time, good for her."

"Why would say that?"

"Because it's true. The younger she is, the less time she's spent in that situation, Claire. Younger people have an incredible ability to adapt to new changes and grow from their experiences. I need time to figure out a plan for her, but I will have one."

Claire couldn't help but ask, "What makes you want to help her at all? She doesn't have anything to do with your plans for Liam."

Anton hummed a sad sound. "Maybe not, but you asked me to help and I agreed."

"I think there's more to it than that."

"I think you have an uncanny ability to read people, Claire."

She smiled. "So I've been told."

"There is more to it; you're right. My step-grandfather came across a woman once who was in a similar situation to your friend's, but she was older and barely remembered what came before. Clarissa didn't know anything else but what it felt like to be owned. Nicoli made the deal with a fellow family that he would purchase her—"

Claire sucked in a hard breath. "He owned a slave?"

The disgust in her words couldn't be hidden.

"You should let me finish," Anton replied, unbothered. "The only way he could help her was to buy her, so he did. And then when he could do it without causing issues, he gave her freedom in the form of identity and a future as whoever she wanted to be, but Clarissa never took it."

Claire didn't understand. "She didn't take it? God, why?"

"No, she stayed with him because she loved him, I suppose. Nicoli was quite adamant against trafficking souls and Clarissa was the biggest reason why."

"Did he love her, too?"

"Yes, though they were very private and from the outside, it would have been hard to tell he felt anything at all," Anton answered.

"Oh."

"Thinking about it, Demyan reminds me a great deal of Nicoli, especially now."

"Does he?" Claire asked.

"Yes, he's quite private, too. He rarely lets anyone in."

Claire wondered if she might have one foot in the door with Demyan, or if he was two steps away from slamming it in her face.

"Anyway," Anton continued, "My children called Clarissa their grandmamma because, for all purposes, she was. Even after Nicoli passed, she remained with me and she helped us to raise our kids for most of their lives. Her ashes are on the fireplace in Viviana's library along with her picture. Maybe my wife can show you the next time you're over."

"I would like that," Claire said honestly. "I'll make sure to ask."

The Avdonin's family history continued to fascinate her. There was always something new to learn. They had so much depth. Claire was pretty sure she barely scratched the surface.

A knock sounded on the front door of Claire's apartment. No one but Demyan would be at her place considering the time and the fact she had no friends in the city.

"I should let you go," Claire said, wanting to end the call before it turned awkward.

"Sure, but there was something else I wanted to ask you about."

"Oh, what's that?"

Another knock echoed through her apartment. Claire pushed off the couch and crossed the room. Despite her earlier worries about inviting Demyan over, she didn't want him to leave now that he was there.

"Yes, Demyan called to say you had information for me, but someone else called, too."

Claire opened the front door at the same time Anton finished his sentence. Demyan darkened her doorway in his leather jacket. His body was rigid with tension. He looked like a coil ready to spring.

Without saying a word, Claire put her finger up to her lips to ask Demyan to stay quiet. Thankfully, he did.

"What does the other call have to do with me, Anton?" Claire asked.

"Someone thought I should know my son was awfully interested in the woman who showed up during tribute asking for me," Anton said, his tone far too blasé to be true.

"I don't know what you mean," Claire replied.

"I think you do, sweetheart."

Claire took a step backward, allowing Demyan to make the choice if he wanted to come inside her place or not. He didn't move from his spot in the hallway, but his gaze never left hers, either.

"No, actually, I don't," Claire said, turning her back to Demyan so she could focus on ending the call. "You know how he feels about me."

"Well, I know you put my son on edge. That's a dangerous place for a man like Demyan to be. Sometimes it's better to keep a distance. And I would hate to see you get hurt, Claire. Demyan isn't the person he used to be and making him unsettled isn't the best way to repair something that's broken."

"I'm not trying to fix him."

But that didn't mean it wasn't going to hurt.

• • •

Demyan stayed outside the apartment door as Claire ended her phone call. A phone call that had obviously been a conversation with his father. He wasn't sure how he felt about that. Well, he knew how he felt regarding her involvement with his family and Anton's plans, but that conversation sounded laced with something else entirely.

Him, mostly.

"Are you a vampire, or something?" Claire asked, turning to face him.

Demyan didn't move. "Excuse me?"

"The lore of vampires, you know. They can't come inside unless you invite them in. The door is open, Demyan, come in."

"I don't know what I'm doing here," he said.

It was the truth. Partly.

Claire chewed on her lower lip and for a brief moment, Demyan's mind flashed back to earlier when he'd kissed her in the office. "Demyan—"

"I probably shouldn't be here for a number of reasons."

"I invited you here. We're adults. What's the problem?"

He was going to end up hurting this girl.

He'd probably use her for his own gain, too.

Even if he didn't agree with his father's plans, Demyan couldn't deny there was a part of him that understood Claire's involvement was liable to draw Liam out in the end. That man was going to have to die. Demyan might just be that much of a monster to use Claire to do it.

And he wanted to fuck her. That little bit was undeniable, too. It was like a hunger beating through his insides, a beast rattling in a fucking cage. Maybe if he fed the need, it would go away. That was his piss poor plan.

Other than Sofia, there hadn't been a woman Demyan was involved with since Gia's death. But, even Sofia hadn't caused the strange white-hot lust coursing through Demyan's system. He disliked everything that surrounded Claire, but he still wanted her.

"You're one giant mind-fuck for me," Demyan said under his breath.

Claire swallowed audibly, shifting on her feet. "I don't know how you want me to take that."

"Just giving you a heads up."

"Thanks."

Demyan stepped into the apartment and shrugged off his suit jacket, hanging it on a wall hook. The apartment was small but homey. Claire wore an over-sized T-shirt but little else. His cock perked to life all over again.

"Were you heading to bed?" he asked, nodding at her attire.

Claire crossed her arms, which drew the shirt she wore up and showcased cotton panties underneath. "No, I was sitting on the couch, thinking."

"You're dressed for bed."

"I didn't know if you were coming."

"I wasn't going to." Demyan couldn't help but notice how Claire eyed him up and down, and she wasn't the least bit subtle about it. Just the fact she didn't hide her interest made him hotter and more confused. She shouldn't want him, either. "I'm not into the soft and sweet thing, Claire."

"Another heads up?" she asked.

"Basically."

"All right." Claire wet her lips under her tongue, catching all of Demyan's attention again. "You good?"

"Perfect."

Or as close as he was ever going to get.

"Good, then shut the damn door. My neighbors don't need an open invitation to what's about to happen next."

Demyan laughed at her dark humor, turning to shut the door. When he faced her again, Claire had moved to stand only a foot away from his form. He could feel the fucking heat of her body radiating off her in waves. She smelled like honeyed vanilla, and her hair fell in loose, unmanaged waves over her shoulders.

His mind went to earlier again.

"How many men have told you how beautiful you are?"

Claire's chin dipped down. "Why?"

"I suspect it's not nearly been enough, so let me be one of the ones who do. You are exceptionally beautiful and every part of me sees it."

Demyan stepped forward, cupped her jaw in his hands, and kissed her without warning. She tasted just the same, and her tongue felt sublime stroking along his. Claire's fingers found the buttons on his shirt as Demyan turned her around and backed her into the apartment door.

She worked the buttons through the loops, undoing them all but never breaking their kiss. His growing erection ground into her stomach, making him aware of how painfully hard he already was and how much his body wanted this. He threaded his fingers into her hair, kissing her harder until she was gasping his name.

Claire pushed the shirt over his shoulders and down his arms until it fell to the floor. It was only then that she pulled away from his mouth, her fingertips fluttering around the black rose tattooed on his pec before tracing the Cyrillic lettering curving above his navel across his stomach.

Князь, it spelled.

"*Knyaz,*" Demyan said, pronouncing the Russian word before she could ask. "Prince."

Claire's lashes fanned her cheeks as she watched him through hooded eyes. The sight alone had his dick throbbing. Her lips were a bitten red and swollen from his kiss. "Why a prince?"

Because he'd always been the Russian prince.

"It's me," he said simply. Demyan turned, showcasing the Cyrillic letting across his shoulders. Авдонин, it read. "Avdonin."

"They're … beautiful."

Demyan spun back, his hands finding her trim waist to grip tight. Beautiful was not the word he would use to describe his tattoos, but he wasn't this woman, either. "Something like that."

Claire didn't say another thing. Her hands worked at the zipper and button of his pants until she was pushing them down over his muscled hips.

"Condom in my left pocket," Demyan told her.

Claire's hand slid into his pocket, finding the foil packet as her fingers grazed his growing cock through the fabric. Hot blood flooded his member all over again. "Good to know."

Without asking, she lowered until his bobbing cock was eye-level with her pink, plump lips. Demyan swallowed hard, his fingers tightening in her hair. When her silken mouth engulfed his cock, Demyan was lost.

Wet, soft warmth rolled over his length, coating his nerves as her tongue flicked against the underside of his pulsing cock. Claire's hands slipped beneath his pants and boxer-briefs, shoving them down further to free his balls. She cupped his sack as her tongue circled the circumcised head of his cock, driving him fucking insane. With every suck, a hum built in her throat, vibrating the base of his dick. Her teeth scraped lightly over his sensitive skin, pushing him closer to the edge.

Christ, this girl had a wicked mouth.

Demyan couldn't take that, not when his need was pounding at his insides like it was. He was going to blow his load down her throat when what he really wanted was to be buried between her thighs, hearing her scream his name. He tugged hard on her hair, earning him a sharp whine as when she released his cock and stood.

"Wh—"

He silenced whatever question she was about to ask with another burning, hard kiss. Her mouth had the salty taste of his precum. He kicked his pants off the rest of the way, letting Claire help him shove down his boxer-briefs until he could step out of them as well.

Demyan broke the kiss long enough to pull that godforsaken shirt she wore over her head before lifting her into his arms. Claire's legs wrapped around his waist when Demyan turned, needing to find the closest flat surface to put her on. The couch was too goddamn small as far as he was concerned. The table a few steps back in the kitchen was more than big enough.

"If I break your table, I'll fucking pay for it," Demyan muttered against Claire's lips.

Her breathless laughter was permission enough for him.

Demyan crossed the space in the kitchen, thoroughly enjoying the way her body grinded on his cock as he walked. Claire's back met the kitchen table hard, her hair fanning out over the wood top. Immediately, her legs were opening for him, inviting him in again. She was wet all over, so fucking ready for him. A slight tremor rocked her thighs as her teeth cut into her lip.

"Last chance to back out," he said.

Claire shook her head as he snatched the condom she offered, opening it, and rolled it down his length. "Don't stop."

"That's not in the plans."

"Good. Fuck me."

Demyan spread her thighs wider, hooking her one leg over his shoulder. Her heel dug in, holding him in place as he rolled the tip of his cock through the lips of her sex. When he came to her entrance, he pushed in just enough to let her feel the head of his cock starting to fill her. He could feel her tight core hug the tip of his length while her hips canted upwards, seeking more of him. By the end of the night, she'd be fucking begging for him.

Claire moaned the sweetest, sexiest sound. Her eyes squeezed shut as her hands balled into fists against the table. "Oh my God, please don't fucking tease me. Not tonight."

When her hips lifted from the table again, Demyan let his cock slide into her clenching pussy. If her mouth was good, her sex was something else entirely. Blazing hot, drenched for him, and holding him so fucking tight he couldn't breathe.

"*Oh.*"

The quiet whisper of the word washed over his senses like a drug. Claire stilled and he just felt her—all of her. His hands found hers on the table, intertwining their fingers before he pulled her arms straight and flat. There was no pause between his first and second thrust. The third came faster, deeper. Her fluids coated his length, the scent of her sex saturating his lungs already.

His breaths came out in huffed pants, his teeth clenching behind his jaw. Fucking her was like a dream. Her body fit his perfectly and she didn't shy away from the roughness of his desire. Instead, she met every crack of his groin meeting her hips, her back arching off the table.

Claire's body was on perfect display for him. He had the best view of his cock sinking into her wet pussy and the creamy expanse of her skin. She was petite, but the curve in her waist and the swell of her breasts fit his hands perfectly. Her first orgasm crashed down on her when she hadn't been expecting it to. Demyan took in the sight of her face contorting with bliss and his name in her mouth. The walls of her sex gripped him tighter through the waves. He didn't relent in the pace or force of his fucking for a second.

"Christ, look at you," Demyan forced out between his gritting teeth.

"Harder," Claire whispered.

Demyan obliged.

CHAPTER TEN

Claire listened with a smile as Vera read from one of the books she had given her for her birthday. According to Vera, the girl's father had read her the book about the wonderland over and over until her heart was content. She had it memorized though she did recognize the words.

"That was awesome," Claire said, hugging Vera close to her.

"Papa says I'm very smart," Vera replied, grinning widely.

"You are."

"Demyan was like that at her age, too," Viviana said. Claire still came to the bookshop on the weekends to spend time with Vera when she was with Viviana and Anton. "He never stopped and he always wanted to learn. I felt like my head was going in a million directions with him."

"He seems so ... calm, or maybe cool, now."

Certainly not like the hyperactive child Viviana described.

"He does," Viviana agreed.

"Is Grandpapa Ivan coming to get me later?" Vera asked.

Viviana smiled. "Yep. Her cousin's birthday is tomorrow, so we're handing her over for Sunday."

"Demyan won't be going, too?"

"He doesn't spend a lot of time with Gia's family. Especially her sisters. They've ..." Viviana trailed off, wincing in Vera's direction. Lower, Viviana said, "Sometimes, their opinions on how he raises you-know-who are a little harsh. He chooses to keep them at a distance for his own mental health."

"Oh."

Claire felt awkward discussing Demyan given the fact he hadn't spoken to her since their hookup a month ago. He didn't seem to have any issue with her spending time around Vera, but it was clear he was avoiding her for whatever reason.

She didn't want to admit how that hurt her. Waking up alone a month ago was bad enough.

"How is Demyan?" Claire asked, hoping she was discreet.

Apparently, she wasn't.

SHATTERED

Viviana eyed her in a way that put Claire on edge. "Fine, why?"

Claire shrugged. "Just wondering."

"Sure. Did something happen between you two that I don't know about?"

"No!"

Vera's little head popped up from the book, but she went right back to reading.

"No," Claire repeated, softer the second time. "I was just curious; that's all."

"He's at his father's club tonight, working," Viviana said almost offhandedly.

"Oh?"

"Yes. Sometimes a push isn't good enough. Men like Demyan need a good shove."

Claire glanced away from Viviana. "I didn't say a thing."

"You don't have to."

• • •

"What's the plan, Boss?" Rory asked.

Other men in the office echoed the questioning sentiment.

"Two weeks, the Irish have a meeting planned. I've got a bit of information as to times and location …"

Demyan didn't want to hear anymore. He slipped out of the office, thankfully without anyone noticing. Anton could have his plans for the Irish, Demyan wanted to stay the hell out of it. For now, anyway.

Liam was an entirely different story, but for Demyan, that was nothing more than a waiting game. Anton's plans would surely start the ball rolling, but it might take a while to get where it needed to go. Claire's involvement was another matter altogether.

Demyan sighed harshly, making his way to the bar through the crowd of people. It'd been a month since he found himself in Claire's apartment. He thought once would be enough. They'd fuck, he'd get the strange attraction out of his system, and that would be the end of it. Instead, he couldn't get her out of his goddamn head.

She was everywhere.

Demyan didn't like that at all. It made him feel loopy—

fucking stupid. Like he didn't have control. So, he refused to feed into it again and kept his distance. Vera liked spending time with the woman, so Demyan didn't prevent that from happening. He just stayed away while they did it.

"Vodka, dirty," Demyan ordered when the bartender came. He snatched up the tumbler the moment the man pushed it across the bar. "Thanks."

"No problem, Prince."

Demyan turned his back to the bar and sipped on the liquor, letting it roll over his tongue and saturate his taste buds before swallowing. All good Russians liked their vodka, after all, though his father was the odd exception to that rule. Anton liked his bourbon.

Downing the rest of the vodka, Demyan turned to put the glass back on the bar and promptly froze where he stood. Claire stood three feet to his right, a black body-con style dress tight to her form and showcasing off all her curves. The matching pumps she wore had his throat closing and his cock waking up. Her dark makeup and red lips gave her a demure air mixed heavily with sexuality. While he knew she wasn't innocent, the look she sported now shattered what assumptions he might have had remaining.

"Demyan," Claire said, smiling just a little. "We should talk."

Demyan pushed his glass further across the bar, finally snapping back into reality. He faced her, trying to tamper the lust flooding his bloodstream and thickening his dick. What in the hell was wrong with him?

"What are you doing here?" he asked.

"Hottest club in Brighton, right?"

Demyan wet his lips, unsure if she was playing a game with him or not. "I didn't realize you frequent clubs."

"I don't, not often. But you left me in bed to wake up alone, ignored me for a month, I decided I wanted to know why, and here I am."

"Why," Demyan repeated.

It wasn't even a fucking question.

"That's what I said. Figured if I was coming to a club, I might as well dress the part."

"We have nothing to talk about, Claire."

"Don't we?" she asked.

"No. We hooked up. That's all."

"Can't you be like every other man and be civil when you see someone the next day, or is that why you ran? Why ignore me, then?"

"I'm not," he muttered.

"You are," she challenged.

Demyan's patience left. "You shouldn't be here. This is Russian territory, and the last thing you need is someone recognizing you here and running back to tell your uncle."

Claire scoffed. "Haven't you figured it out yet? I don't care."

"Leave, Claire."

"What is wrong with you?" she asked.

Demyan felt his spine straighten at the question. "Excuse me?"

"You. What is wrong with you, Demyan? Everyone else gets the cold side of you, the side that doesn't give a damn. You see me, and suddenly you turn into a raging fucking asshole. Do I bother you that much, is that it?"

"You don't know what you're talking about."

Claire's frown cut him to the bone. "What is it about me that bothers you so much?"

"You make me feel," he said before he could stop himself.

"I make you—"

"Yes. Now leave."

• • •

Demyan knocked on the apartment door, feeling more awkward than he ever had before. He heard the shuffle of feet behind the thick wood before the sound of a metal chain sliding through a track resounded. When the door opened, green eyes regarded him in a way that said he was the last person they wanted to see.

"Okay, now it's my turn to ask," Claire said, huffing under her breath. "What are you doing here?"

So, maybe he'd been an asshole earlier at the club.

"I came to tell you—"

"The next words out of your mouth better be an apology, Demyan, or you can turn around before you even get started."

"It was, but thank you for saving me the time."

Claire glared. "You're impossible."

Demyan nodded. "Yeah, I know."

135

He looked her over, noticing she had lost the tight dress and heels, cleaned her face of the makeup, and was wearing a loose T-shirt and sleep shorts. Guessing by the way her arms were crossed over her perky chest, and the hard peaks of her nipples poked against the fabric, she wasn't wearing a bra.

Fuck.

Why did he have to go there right now?

Why did his mind have to fucking go *there*?

"I didn't mean to corner you tonight, but I did want to talk," Claire said softly. "I didn't know another place where Vera might not be involved and I didn't think that conversation would be the kind you would want her to hear. I knew she was going to be with her mother's family tonight."

Demyan snapped out of his stupor. "You're right. I was an asshole and you caught me at a bad time."

"Do you want to come in?"

"I shouldn't," he replied.

Claire's brow furrowed. "Why not?"

Because if he did, he was liable to land right back in her bed.

"I don't want to be an asshole again," Demyan admitted.

Claire shrugged. "Yeah, well, I'm not exactly dressed for guests, either."

"I think you look fine—better without all that nonsense on your face, anyway."

"Seriously?"

"I'm not a fan of makeup, even if it did, uh … never mind."

Claire grinned. "You're such a man."

"I am. I also don't like how being around you sometimes fucks with my head."

"Are we talking now?" Claire asked.

"Yes. Coming here is a bad idea."

"Why?"

"Because I am ridiculously fucking attracted to you, and I don't know why. I figured once would be enough, but it's not. If it happens again, I might not like what comes next. *You* might not like what comes next."

"I'm a big girl, Demyan. I think I can handle you and your craziness."

"I don't know about that."

She stepped back from the doorway, opening the crack wider

in obvious invitation. "Don't leave before I wake up this time. Okay?"

A pressure built in Demyan's chest, rooting him to the spot. "Don't ask for promises."

"I won't."

Demyan followed her into the apartment and the moment the door closed, he was on her. It was like he couldn't fucking control it. His irritation from earlier, the confusing way his body reacted to her, and the strange effect she had on him all clashed together.

Claire didn't say a word, simply let his tongue war with hers as she pulled at his clothes. She tasted like sin, and her skin felt like silk under his hands. They left a trail of fabric from the apartment door to the bedroom. By the time her back hit the bed, he had her naked and was already spreading her thighs.

"Condom," Demyan hissed, grinding his bare erection into her sex. "Need one."

Needed her, too.

So fucking badly.

Claire's fingernails scored lines over his chest as she arched into him beautifully. Her heels dug into his lower back. "Nightstand … drawer … hurry."

Demyan left the heat of her body just long enough to find the unopened box of condoms in the nightstand. Once he had the latex covering his length, he fitted himself back between her widened thighs, spreading them open further until he knew she would feel the ache in her muscles for days.

"God," Claire moaned.

"Demyan," he corrected.

Claire laughed, breathless and teasing at the same time. The sound melted into a sharp gasp in the very next second as his cock found heaven and slid home. Her body took him into her wet, hot channel without resistance. He reveled in the feeling of her silken walls contracting around him, engulfing his length in bliss.

Fuck.

Demyan let his need take over, losing his control as he began pounding into her sex. Claire met every thrust with a cant of her hips, her heels pressing hard into his back as her fingernails found purchase in his shoulders. The bite of pain mingling with the pleasure of her was overwhelming.

It was more than sensation. More than just sex.

He hadn't felt something like that in a long fucking time.

"I missed this—feeling like this."

Claire's gaze found his the moment the admission left his lips.

She said nothing.

Fuck was right.

• • •

Demyan watched Claire hum under her breath as she grabbed items from the refrigerator and placed them on the counter. Music from her stereo floated through the small space. Dancing in his T-shirt did little to hide the fact she wore nothing but cotton panties underneath as the fabric kept riding up her ass. She didn't notice Demyan's presence, so he stayed quiet in the kitchen entryway, enjoying her little show.

When Claire turned around, shutting the fridge door, she stumbled backward into the appliance with wide eyes meeting Demyan's form. The thick package of bacon she held fell to the floor.

"Jesus Christ, Demyan. Make some noise, would you?"

Demyan chuckled. "Maybe you should be more observant of your surroundings."

"Maybe you shouldn't act like a mouse." Claire huffed. "How long have you been standing there?"

"Long enough to know if your life depended on your ability to shake your ass, you would die."

"That's an awful thing to say."

"If it helps, even though you can't dance, your ass still looks fucking gorgeous. Even better because you're wearing my shirt."

"Thanks, Demyan. You're a real winner in the morning."

"So I've been told," he murmured.

"It's hard to believe you're the father of a little girl sometimes, Demyan."

"My daughter has nothing to do with whether or not I find you attractive. I do, obviously."

"Don't you worry she might hear you spouting off like that?"

"No, because Vera doesn't see women coming and going from my bed or standing at my side. She never has. She had a

138

mother, and she doesn't need the confusion."

Claire frowned but said nothing to that. Instead, she asked, "Want some breakfast?"

"Do you have pickles?"

Claire's canted her head to the side. "Pickles for breakfast?"

"I don't judge you, so don't judge me."

Well, he didn't judge her a lot, now.

"Is this another black shoe thing?"

This time, it was Demyan's turn to be confused. "What?"

"Like your father only owns black shoes and mostly black suits. I asked why once … he said it was a Russian thing. Is it like that?"

Demyan never really thought about it before. But, yes, he supposed it was considering there had always been pickled cucumbers on their table at every meal. "Basically. Again, don't judge me."

"I'll try." Claire made a face, her nose scrunching up in the cutest way.

Cute? Cute, Demyan, really? Fucking get a grip.

He had no idea what this female was doing to him.

"It's kind of gross," she added, winking teasingly. "Pickles, I mean."

"You don't have any, I take it?"

"Gherkins."

"I don't eat those things."

"Fantastic. Go without." Claire bent down to pick up the package of bacon. "I'll still cook you food but only because you said I had a nice ass."

Demyan took a step into the kitchen, deciding he was hungry. "I'll buy some proper fucking pickles for you, that way, I'll have them here."

She raised up a hell of a lot slower than she had gone down. It took Demyan two seconds to realize the words he had said and what they meant. It struck him straight in the chest, leaving a blunt pain behind.

Instinctively, Demyan took a step backward. As if he were trying to get away from the words that had just slipped out of his mouth. Suddenly, he needed to leave Claire's space, especially because the softness she regarded him with said she *knew*.

Something was happening to him, and it was because of her.

139

He was letting it happen because he liked the way she got under his skin, made him think, and forced him to feel. Even if it wasn't always fucking pretty.

Demyan wasn't sure how he felt about that other than the fact he didn't want to think about it at all. Hooking up was one thing, but acting cozy was completely different and not what he should want.

"Demyan—"

"Don't," he forced out.

"But—"

Demyan turned on his heel, a hand flying up in the air to stop her from saying another thing. He made a swift beeline for the front door, grabbing his jacket off the back of the couch where he tossed it the night before.

"Demyan!"

At the front door, he tugged on his coat before yanking on his shoes.

"Demyan, please just wait a second," Claire pleaded. "*Please!*"

Her cry sliced him straight down to the fucking bone. Like it ached in his heart because he was the one making her hurt. She was just feet away from him. Christ, he could reach out and touch her, soothe her if he wanted, but he *couldn't*.

"Don't do that," Demyan said sharply, standing straight and trying to force back the rising anxiety and anger.

Claire snapped away from him as if he'd stuck out at her with his hand. "Do what?"

"That."

"I don't understand wh—"

Demyan waved at her. "That right there. This can't be something. We can't be something. Don't do that."

"Demyan, you're freaking out over nothing."

No, he wasn't.

There were tears in her eyes. They weren't falling, but they were there. She was hurt by his rejection, and he didn't know how to handle what was going on inside his head and heart. So, it was pretty goddamn simple for Demyan. He needed to stop whatever this was before it went any further. Straight for the kill, like any good monster would do.

"Don't fall in love with me. I ruin beautiful things."

Claire flinched. "Why would you say that?"

"You can't fall in love with someone like me and you certainly can't afford to believe there's something here or that you can make me better again. I am broken—unobtainable and unfixable. I don't need a fucking martyr in my life. I've got enough of those as it is."

"Ouch."

"Just ... don't."

"Fall in love with you."

"Exactly," Demyan muttered.

"Why would you say that?" she repeated.

Wasn't it obvious?

"Claire—"

"Why would you tell me not to fall in love with you and then in the next sentence, call me beautiful?"

Because she was.

• • •

Demyan slammed the door open to his father's office at Seven Lights, fury rolling over every inch of his body like a drug.

The door crashed into the wall with a loud bang from the force of Demyan's hand pushing it open. The men inside Anton's office stood at the sudden intrusion into their space. It wasn't like Demyan to barge into his father's office like that, even if he was Anton's right-hand man. It was disrespectful and truthfully, worth a bullet if he were any other man.

Demyan recognized the men inside the office as his father's closest comrades. Captains for the Bratva. Men, who frankly, Demyan didn't give a shit about right then.

"You need to stop this," Demyan said, pointing at his father and all but snarling the words out. "This is done and I want you to leave it alone!"

"I beg your pardon?"

"You fucking heard me, Anton."

Demyan knew he was treading thin ice, but he still couldn't stop himself. "Whatever goddamn plans you've got for the Irish, I want you to back off. I don't want that bastard's family coming back here again. I've done everything I could to protect my daughter from that man."

"Yes, including acting like you weren't her father at all for

141

nearly two damned years, Demyan," Anton spat.

"You don't know a fucking thing!" Demyan shouted right back. "How hard it was for me to look at her, to hold her, and love her when I grieved. And I'm so fucking sorry if the way I raise and care for my child isn't the way you approve but it isn't your choice, Anton! She's not your daughter, she's mine."

"Demyan!"

"And I want Claire out of this city immediately. I don't care what you have to do to get her gone, but she needs to go. Stop using her for your crazy games. All you're going to do is end up getting her killed. And if you think putting her in my path is going to help or fix me, I've got a newsflash for you—it *won't*."

Anton's jaw ticked, and Demyan's mouth snapped shut, finally realizing he'd crossed not one, or even two, but several lines. Hell, he might as well have jumped over them with a bang and a big fuck you to his father.

"I'm sor—"

"Too little, too fucking late," Anton said through clenched teeth. "Sit the hell down."

Demyan's fists balled at his sides. "I'm not ten-years-old. Don't order me around like a child."

"Not a child, a Bratva man who just seriously disrespected his boss on more levels that I care to count. You will sit your stupid ass down, or I will force you to, Demyan Avdonin. I have not reached an age where I am afraid of you just yet, son. Do not test me, you've already pushed your limits enough today."

Demyan found the closest chair and sat.

"You're mighty lucky it's us in this office today," Boris said.

Erik jerked his thumb in his Boris's direction. "Truth."

"Oh, I don't think he's lucky at all," Anton put in with a dangerous edge to his tone.

Demyan held back his cringe, but the shame compounded deep in his chest all the same. Never had he acted so completely insolent and awful to his father—certainly not when Anton acted as his boss.

"Four years are just catching right up to you, aren't they?" Anton asked quietly.

Demyan didn't know what to say. His father didn't give him the chance to figure it out.

"You've been quiet for four long years, doing what you

needed to do, following orders and throwing out your own when you needed to, but it's finally catching up, huh? All that shit you've swallowed, the coldness burning you alive, it's bleeding right out. It's about goddamn time, I think."

"Fuck you," Demyan whispered.

He couldn't have stopped the words if he tried.

"Out of my office, now," Anton ordered shortly.

Demyan stood instantly.

"Not you. Boris, Erik, out."

The men didn't question their boss; they simply did as he asked. Once the door shut, Demyan turned his shoulder to his father, not wanting to stare the man head-on for the moment. Breathing room, that's what he needed.

He shouldn't have come here. Not being as angry and confused as he was.

"Christ," Anton grumbled.

Demyan shot a glance at his father, noting Anton's grimace as he rubbed his jaw with one hand and his chest with the other.

"I feel like shit as it is today, and then you come in here pulling nonsense like that. What in the fuck were you thinking, Demyan?"

"I'm sorry."

"If you want to act like a boss, son, you better be damn well ready to take over the spot. You can't rush into my office challenging me like that in front of people, especially other Bratva. It makes you look like you're making a move on my seat, even if they are my friends. Do you understand that, or are you still an eighteen-year-old kid playing with guns?

"I taught you respect and rules first, Demyan, always," Anton finished sharply.

Demyan hadn't realized how his actions could be construed as him rebelling against his father's authority, but it really was. "It won't happen again."

"Like I said, too late, Demyan." Anton blew out a harsh breath, still appearing like he was in pain.

A flicker of concern shot through Demyan. "What's wrong?"

"Nothing," Anton replied. "I'm just tired."

Right. Demyan didn't believe that for a second.

"Is your chest bothering you or something?"

"No."

"Dad—"

Anton's head snapped up, his gaze cutting into Demyan's. "Look at that. I haven't heard you call me that in four years, Demyan. It's boss, Anton, or asshole, right?"

Demyan swallowed hard, his fingernails cutting into his palms as he let the emotions take him under at the sight of his father's sadness. "I don't know what's wrong with me."

"You spent the night with her, didn't you?"

"I don't want to talk about it."

"Too bad, we're going to."

"No—"

"Yes, and since I have a bull who follows her around to watch after her, don't bother to deny where you were last night. At her apartment. Yeah?"

Demyan sighed, nodding.

"How many times?" Anton asked quietly.

"Twice."

"The only other girl you've messed around with since Gia died was Sofia, right?"

"Yeah," Demyan confirmed.

"What's the difference between the two?"

Demyan didn't have to ask what his father meant, he goddamn well knew.

"Why does that matter?"

"To me, it doesn't," Anton said, shrugging. "To you, it's everything. What's the difference?"

"To feel."

"Excuse me?"

"I fucked around with Sofia to give me something to feel."

"Physically, you mean?"

"Yes."

"And Claire?"

"Because she made me feel something without doing a thing."

Anton rested back in his chair, still rubbing at the middle of his chest and eyeing his son curiously. "Beyond sex."

"I really don't want to talk about this with you."

"I don't care."

Jesus, why did his father have to be so fucking frustrating?

"Aren't you the man who knows everything about

everybody? Why are you asking me?" Demyan asked, annoyed.

Anton smiled. "I want you to confirm what I believe, that's all."

Great.

Demyan didn't want to play his father's head games. Anton could do that shit with whoever the hell else he wanted, but not with Demyan today. He wasn't in the mood after earlier.

"Listen, this is my life we're talking about here, not some sport for your amusement, Dad."

"Is that what you think; your pain amuses me?"

The question was posed so quietly Demyan almost missed it. Almost.

"No, of course not."

"Poor choice of words, son." Anton pushed away from his desk, standing from his chair. "And you're right, this is your life. A life you've simply been existing in for the last four years, but little else. You breathe, blink, and act human, but you refused to feel anything to make you actually be human. So, when someone steps in your path and she makes you open your eyes, even if it isn't necessarily in a good way, you can safely assume I'm going to be interested."

"I'm going to hurt her," Demyan spat, irritated again. "I know it."

"Maybe she can take the pain. Have you considered that?"

"I don't know much about her at all."

Anton lifted a single shoulder in response. "I think it's time for you to start learning, then. Claire is more than her name and blood, Demyan. She's more than her half-brother and uncle, for that matter."

Demyan stayed silent, absorbing his father's words but still feeling unsure.

"And I can't help but wonder ..." Anton trailed off, grimacing again as his fingers rolled circles over the middle of his chest.

"Seriously, is your chest bothering you, or what?"

Anton was a healthy man, as far as that went, but Demyan didn't like the symptoms his father was sporting.

"Do you want me to call Ma or take you to the hospital, or something?"

"It's nothing; I just need to lay down for a while," Anton

dismissed with a wave. "About Claire ..."

"What about her?"

"I can't help but wonder if this is your chance to move on, Demyan."

"I don't want to move on with—"

"Not necessarily with someone, but from what happened. It's taken this long for you to finally blink back awake, son, and she's the person who did it. So, even if nothing comes of it, something already did. Stop fighting that."

"I don't know if I can do that," Demyan admitted.

How could he?

Gia's death had been one of the most defining moments of his entire life. It created a vortex of black space surrounding him. One that constantly sucked him in and drowned him in the expanse of the void. Maybe Demyan had even become comfortable in that place. Claire's presence in the emptiness that had become his life was coloring it with her little by little.

It was so overwhelming.

"Move on, I mean," Demyan said, feeling his throat close around the words. "I don't know if I *want* to do that."

"Again, you're too late."

Anton's hand came to rest on the desk, his breathing turning shallower than before. Just the way his father's face drained of color was enough to send Demyan rushing forward. He didn't make it in time. Anton hit the floor with a dull thud, and so did Demyan's heart.

"*Papa!*"

Demyan's hands trembled when he reached his father, his knees hitting the floor hard. He turned Anton to his back. Agony marred Anton's features while his hand clenched at his chest.

A heart attack was Demyan's first thought. He recognized the symptoms, and he should have demanded his father stop brushing them off earlier, but he'd been too caught up in his own self-loathing and issues to care.

God, what kind of son was he? A terrible one.

At that moment, it didn't matter. Only getting help for his father did. They could deal with the rest later.

Demyan heard Boris and Erik rush the office behind him. They must have heard his shout when Anton fell.

"I'm sorry," Demyan mumbled, a burning sting radiating

over his eyes. The tears fought to fall. "I'm so sorry, Papa."

"Don't be," Anton whispered. "Christ, Vine is going to be so pissed off at me."

Yeah, because that was the one thing he needed to be the most afraid of at the moment.

"Call nine-one-one," Demyan demanded to no one in particular.

"On it," Boris said.

CHAPTER ELEVEN

Claire stared at the plate of food in front of her with little interest. She had been watching it like it might eat itself for the last hour ever since Demyan stormed out of her apartment.

If she hadn't cooked breakfast, she would have cried herself into a complete mess of a human being. Why she kept letting that man reject her like he did and push her away every time one of his walls got hit, Claire didn't understand.

She didn't want to fix him like he thought; she wanted *know* him.

To her, that meant all the parts of him. Especially the ones he kept protecting with his cold exterior and sometimes harsh attitude. There was more to Demyan Avdonin than what was on his surface. Claire had seen it even if he hadn't meant for her to.

It would probably help if she'd stop inviting him into her bed.

Right.

Thinking it was a hell of a lot easier than actually doing it, considering the way her body and mind felt. Her back still ached from the way he fucked her the night before, so hard and good. The memories alone were enough to threaten to send her into the shower for a cold dunk. She hadn't washed the scent of him off her and she could smell his spiced cologne on her skin.

Demyan was passionate, she felt it. Sometimes the way he looked at her made Claire think he hated her and in a blink, something entirely different would take over—something she didn't recognize. If he continued trying to find her faults and secrets, she would bleed every single one of them out for him.

How could she not?

Claire was guilty of knowing certain things, too. Things that would surely give Demyan a reason to blame her for what had happened to him and his family. Cavan had left no one in his life untouched by his foulness. Demyan just didn't know it, yet.

When he did find out—if really didn't exist anymore, it was just a matter of time—there would be no doubting his hatred of her. She didn't want him to hate her at all, the thought killed her inside. Demyan hurt enough in his life because of her family. Claire didn't want to add to his pain but the reality was, she probably would.

Glancing around her small kitchen, Claire's thoughts wandered back to earlier when Demyan surprised her. He'd seemed so comfortable in her kitchen, almost relaxed. Her embarrassment at having been caught dancing to the music quickly faded when she saw how amused he was. Demyan was rarely entertained by anything, but she had made him happy for a split second.

His smile had been honest. It was kind of brilliant and beautiful.

So, maybe she wanted to see that again. And maybe she wanted to be the reason why.

Claire didn't intend to make emotional attachments with the beautifully tortured man, but it felt like it was out of her control, now. Vera had been one string between them and then they had made more by letting it go beyond the child. Claire had always let her heart talk first and then she followed what it wanted.

She wasn't about to start ignoring it now.

A faint ringing snapped Claire out of her daze. She didn't recognize the sound, not at first, and she didn't know where it was coming from. It didn't take her long to figure out it was a cell phone, but she still didn't know whose, or where, it was.

Claire left the kitchen, following the noise until she found a thin, black touchscreen phone on the floor of her bedroom. It was lying on the carpet on the side of the bed Demyan had slept on, so maybe it fell out of his slack pockets the night before when—

She refused to go back to thinking about that again. It certainly wouldn't do anything good for her at the moment.

Unfortunately, by the time she found the damn thing and picked it up, the phone had stopped ringing and the screen was locked when she tried to turn it on. Not that Claire would go through Demyan's phone, but she needed to get it to him and guessing by the way he left her place, the man didn't plan on coming back anytime soon.

When the phone lit up with a call, Claire nearly dropped it. A familiar name flashed across the screen along with the number calling. Wincing because she knew it was going to be an uncomfortable conversation, Claire picked up Ana Avdonin's call.

She didn't even get the chance to say hello.

"Oh my God, Demyan! Ma just called me about Papa. Why didn't you answer my call?"

"Um, hello," Claire said quietly.

Silence answered her back.

Yeah, awkward.

It was bad enough Claire's half-brother had attacked Demyan's sister. Even worse was the fact Ana was as sweet as sugar and acted like she liked Claire the times they interacted, but still … Every time Ana looked at Claire, did she see Cavan again? Did she remember him raping her? Was Claire just a reminder of her assault and nothing more?

She didn't want to cause Ana unnecessary heartache.

"This isn't my brother," Ana said.

"No, it's Claire. Hi, Ana."

"Hello. You have my brother's phone."

Again with stating the obvious, Claire thought.

Claire cringed, knowing what was coming. "Yes."

"He's not with you."

It wasn't even a question, but Claire didn't know how Ana could possibly be aware of that.

"No," Claire replied. "He must have dropped his phone."

"When he *was* with you," Ana clarified.

"Yes."

"Where was he when he was with you? Because Vera is at Ivan and Eva's place for the weekend, so obviously you weren't reading with her at my mother's bookstore and that's the only time you two hang out, right?"

Jesus Christ.

This girl wasted no time beating around bushes. Usually Claire appreciated that trait in others. Today, not so much.

Claire sucked in a breath before saying, "My apartment."

Again, the girl on the other end of the line went quiet.

Finally, Ana asked, "Like, he spent the night with you?"

"I don't know if this is something your brother wants people knowing, Ana."

"Oh, my father probably already knows. You have met him, haven't you?"

Claire laughed, but it came out strained and tired. "Yeah, I've met him."

"There you go. He knows, trust me. So, are you a *thing*?"

"A thing?" Claire asked, confused.

"Together, I mean. A thing. Because my brother hasn't had a girlfriend since—"

"No. Seriously, Demyan's pissed off at me as it is, Ana. Can you drop it? I'd appreciate it."

"Sure," Ana said slowly. "For now."

Perfect.

"Thanks, I guess. When you see Demyan, could you tell him I have his phone?"

"My mother said he was at the hospital, that's why I called him." Ana made a sad noise. "I have to go, but sure, I can let him know."

"At the hospital?" Claire asked.

Something painful sliced through her heart while the air in her lungs just … disappeared.

"My father collapsed at his office in Brighton Beach and Demyan was with him. They think it was a heart attack, and I'm on route there now with Koldan."

Claire didn't even hesitate. "Which hospital, Ana?"

• • •

Claire found herself sitting in a hard, uncomfortable chair in the waiting room of an ICU wing for hours. Slowly, she watched the room fill with men and women, some speaking Russian and others not talking at all. Like her, they waited, but were given no answers when they approached the nurses' station with questions on the state of the Avdonin who had been brought in earlier.

None of them approached her to speak and honestly, Claire didn't give them a reason to.

She did recognize a few of the men, but one face in the crowd stood out: Ivan Lavrov.

The man simply tipped his chin to Claire in acknowledgment when he arrived, little else. She didn't blame him, really. From what she understood, Ivan wasn't good friends with Anton after what happened to the man's daughter. They only communicated now because of Anton's plans for Claire's uncle in Detroit and occasionally Vera.

Nonetheless, no one noticed Ivan's quiet greeting to her.

Anton had made it clear to Claire he didn't want many of his men let in on his plans unless needed, especially her involvement of getting him information when she could. The Avdonin Bratva had practically no trust for the Irish and her being a woman wouldn't make a damn difference to them. Not that they would know she was Irish or related to the Dolan clan in any way.

A tiny figure bouncing through the waiting room doors caught Claire's attention. Vera's dark curls were done up in pigtails with blue barrettes that matched the color of her wool dress and leggings. Her blue eyes searched the space as if she were looking for someone she recognized. Immediately, she found Claire, who was sitting silently in the corner.

"Claire!"

The woman behind Vera reached out to stop the child from running ahead of her in the quiet waiting room, but she wasn't quick enough. Vera shot like a bullet straight to Claire's outstretched arms. She could have brushed the child off to save having attention placed on them, but she wouldn't do that to little Vera. Regardless of what anyone else thought, Vera was just a child, and she was innocent to their opinions and choices.

Hadn't losing her mother—one she never had the chance to know—bad enough for the girl? Claire thought so. For some reason, this child wanted to be near her. Vera enjoyed her and the time they spent together. Claire liked being near her, too.

Vera climbed into Claire's lap without asking or prompting. Claire helped to pull the small backpack she wore off, setting it to the tiled floor as Vera beamed with a brilliant smile. Unfortunately, that happiness didn't last long.

"Grandmamma Eva said Grandpapa Anton is sick," Vera whispered.

"I know, and I'm sorry," Claire replied at the same level. "I'm sure he's okay, Vera."

"I wanted to talk to Papa, but he didn't answer when Grandmamma called."

Claire frowned. Those must have been the calls ringing through to Demyan's phone when she made her way to the hospital. "That's because he doesn't have his phone, but I'm sure he'll be around soon."

Well, she knew Demyan was already here at the hospital. Likely in through the ICU passcode locked doors with the rest of

Anton's immediate family.

"What did you do this weekend at your grandparents?" Claire asked, wanting to ward off the worry Vera was clearly feeling.

The deflection worked. Vera rattled off about an indoor play park, her aunts, and her cousins she played with. Claire took the girl's chattering in stride, happy to see her trick had worked for the moment.

Little kids didn't need the stress of adult problems.

Then, very quietly, Vera said, "I love Grandpapa Anton."

Claire swallowed back her sadness. "I know you do."

Of course, Claire knew how much Vera adored that man. He was one of her constant topics of conversations. She had limitless stories about Anton and Viviana. It was quite sweet, actually, considering the image Anton projected was not particularly warm and friendly most times. Obviously, he was an entirely different man to his family and those he cared about.

"So does Papa," Vera said. "Love him, I mean."

"Of course, he does."

Well, Claire suspected Demyan loved his father in his own way. Most of the interactions she had witnessed between the two were either heated or uncomfortable. It was obvious to her that Demyan had put up walls between him and Anton, maybe to protect himself or just keep his father out. On the other hand, Anton pushed against those walls as often as he could but only if he believed it wouldn't push his son away.

Yeah, Claire had a knack for noticing things about people. It was also the way she stayed out of people's view.

"You only come to the hospital when you have a bad booboo, Claire," Vera said seriously.

"Yes, but the doctors fix it right up, sweetheart."

Vera's brow puckered. "They better fix him."

If the situation weren't disheartening, Claire would have laughed at Vera's indignant, veiled threat for a doctor she didn't even know. Good God, she was her father through and through. Demyan probably didn't even realize it. Hell, Claire had spent very little time with Demyan really, but she could see it.

Claire couldn't help but notice how a lot of people in the waiting room were now watching the exchange between her and the girl in her lap. There was no doubt in her mind that they all knew who Vera was, but they were watching her as if she might bite the child.

The woman who had followed in behind Vera—Claire suspected she was Ivan's wife, Eva—was now sitting with Ivan and chatting quietly. They didn't seem to mind that Vera was with her, so she decided to ignore the curious gawkers and give Vera the attention and time she deserved while they had it.

For the next thirty minutes, Claire played a game of I Spy with the four-year-old. Unsurprisingly, Vera was quick with finding whatever Claire chose to be the target. The girl was smart, and Claire loved it. Vera was also, like she always had been when she spent time with Claire, well-behaved and sweet natured. It was no wonder Demyan had her in a private preschool to keep her mind fully engaged and learning. Anything less would be a shame and waste.

"I spy with my little eye some—"

"Papa!"

Claire's head snapped up at Vera's excited shout. Everyone who had been staring at them before was now looking toward the waiting room doorway of the ICU. Demyan stood just beyond the entrance, stoic and silent. It seemed as though he were surveying the crowd with disinterest, but Claire could see a war raging in his stare.

Anyone else probably wouldn't notice, but she had come to learn Demyan's emotions manifested differently than other people. Like the way his fists clenched at his sides—maybe to hide his pain but to Claire, it showcased his worry—even if his shoulders were loose and his arms were lax. Or even how his stance was almost unbothered, yet his back was still as straight as a rod.

Unlike before when Vera had rushed to meet Claire, the little girl didn't for her father. She stayed on Claire's lap while Demyan made his way across the waiting room. Some of the men stood as Demyan passed them by. They probably wanted an update on Anton's current situation, but Demyan didn't stop to talk.

When Demyan came to stand in front of Claire, he held out a hand and cupped his quiet daughter's face. He used his thumb to sweep along the apple of her cheek for a split second before he dropped his arm back to his side. Nonetheless, that brief glimpse of his intimate, private love for Vera was so obvious to Claire.

Vera's tiny hand snuck out from where she had tucked it into her side and grasped tightly onto her father's pinky, before she let him go as well.

"Is Grandpapa Anton all better now?" Vera asked her father.

"He's doing okay," Demyan responded. "Just fine, Vera."

Claire tried not to feel uncomfortable under the heavy stare Demyan was leveling on her, but it was damn near impossible. Not to mention, she could practically feel the dozen and one questions burning on his tongue.

"Vera," Claire said, gaining the girl's attention and her sweet smile. "Could you go sit with Grandpapa Ivan while I talk to your dad?"

"Okay!"

Vera jumped down from Claire's lap, picked up her little backpack at the same time and skipped over to a waiting Ivan and Eva.

"Outside?" Claire asked Demyan, knowing she didn't need to go into further detail.

"Anywhere but here," he agreed quietly.

"Sure."

Claire let Demyan lead the way out of the waiting room and hospital unit. She pretended like she didn't notice the stares that followed behind them. Despite asking him if he wanted to go outside, Demyan took three turns before coming to a set of elevators. He hit the button, waited for the door to open, and when it did, he checked the inside to make sure it was empty.

Demyan stepped into the elevator and turned around, his hand resting on what Claire suspected to be the button to stop the doors from closing. She didn't understand why he was leading her further into the hospital when he clearly wanted to talk to her. They weren't likely to find a private spot to chat inside the walls of this busy place.

"Are you coming?" he asked.

"I thought you wanted to talk."

"I do," Demyan replied. "And if you don't want to come along, that's fine, but I'm going either way. I need to do something else for a few minutes."

She couldn't help but feel as though his confession left a lot unsaid.

"And?" Claire asked softly.

"And I would like it if you came with me while I did it."

That's what she was waiting for. Claire took his proverbial

olive branch and stepped inside without further prompting. The moment she stood at his side, Demyan released the button he'd been holding, pressed the very top floor, and waited for the doors to close.

"Unless someone wants to go to a higher floor, it's not going to stop," Demyan informed.

"Okay."

Demyan stood rigid with his hands clenched into tight fists at his sides as the elevator moved up a floor. "I can't even go outside because someone out there might see me—Bratva, you know."

"Why would that matter if they saw you?"

"Because now … particularly now … I can't be seen as vulnerable or inadequate for any reason. I know you might not understand, but the world I live in thrives on the strength of a man's character, on his honor and dignity, especially at times like these."

Claire sighed, hating that for him because he shouldn't have to hide behind a mask of indifference when he was hurting. Demyan already hid too much. "How is your father?"

"Better. Stable, which is most important."

"Ana said something about a heart attack?" Claire asked.

Demyan nodded. "Seems so."

"And you, Demyan?"

"What about me?" His tone was gruff, thickened with emotions weighing it down.

"How are you?"

"Scared for my father, over the things I had to do today, and the time I spent pushing him away from me," he admitted. "I haven't been this terrified in a long time."

Claire believed she already knew the answer, but still asked, "How long?"

Demyan shrugged. "Four years, two months and three days."

She didn't have to do the math to realize two months and three days ago had been Vera's birthday. Tack four years onto that and …

"When Gia was shot," she said.

"Well, when I heard her voice on the phone and realized she wasn't safe and sound in that hotel like I left her. The numbness started settling in after that, and I can't really remember how I felt once I dropped the phone. So tormented and already gone like she was. Dead inside in a blink. It just ..."

Demyan trailed off, and Claire caught the sight of his knuckles turning white as they clenched harder. Silently, she snagged his hand in her own, slipping her thumb under his fingers to pry them out of his palms. His hand shook, but the tremors didn't go further up his arm.

"Just what?" Claire pressed.

"It just felt like pieces of me were everywhere," Demyan murmured so low she strained to hear. "Not where they should have been."

"Was that how you felt today?"

"The closest I've ever been, I guess."

The elevator climbed the last two floors without them saying another word. When the doors opened, a group of five people walked in, pressed their floor choices, and down the elevator went again. It dropped all the way down to the ground floor before it emptied of souls again.

A woman with a bag of take-out tried to climb in, but Claire stepped forward, hit the button to close the doors and said, "Take the next one."

Claire kept her finger on the button as she pressed the highest floor.

"What are you doing?" Demyan asked.

She shrugged. "Police use this trick. The elevator will go all the way to the floor I picked without stopping. It's how they get to apartments faster if they need to."

"I didn't know that."

"It's not important. I'm not letting go of this button until you're ready for me to."

The iciness in Demyan's blue eyes vanished in a heartbeat.

"Why did you come here today?" he asked.

"You must have dropped your phone last night and when your sister called it, I decided to come."

"That's not what I asked."

"I know," she said.

"I'd like an answer. After this morning, you shouldn't want to be anywhere near me."

"Maybe you're right, Demyan."

"So why?" Demyan demanded. "I'm not looking for someone to fix what's wrong with me. I don't have something to offer you. I'm an asshole on my good days. I am way too messed up to be letting someone like you get hurt by someone like me."

"You can't hurt me because I'm not trying to make this into something it isn't. You're not going to scare me away with your warnings, either. I get sometimes you're going to push against me or run away altogether. I get that, okay. I don't want to fix you, Demyan."

"Then, what do you want from me?"

"To know you," Claire said honestly. "That's all."

"You're looking at everything I am."

"But you keep saying I'm trying to fix you."

"It sure fucking feels like it whenever you're near," Demyan said, his tone turning harsh.

Maybe that was because who she was made him question the things he thought he knew.

"I've never thought you needed to be fixed."

"Oh, no?" Demyan scoffed, loud and rude. "Take a good look at me and where we are right now, Claire. Take a good, hard look at how entirely fucked up my life is."

"I am."

"And?"

"You have to be broken to be fixed. I don't think you are."

Claire didn't have to make something out of whatever was going on between them because it already *was*. It existed. She wished she could care that he was probably going to break her heart and not even know he was doing it.

"Not broken," he echoed.

"As far as I can see, no."

"You're clearly seeing the wrong man, then."

"No, I don't think so. I think I'm staring straight through you, Demyan. Beyond your sharp as glass exterior and your perpetual silence. Past the coldness you put out to ward people off and the confusion and sadness in your heart. Yeah, I see right through you."

"You don't even know me, not really."

"I don't have to," Claire said quietly. "I'm interested in more than what made you like this, Demyan. I want to know who you were before."

"A naive man."

"I don't believe that. You're going to be someone after this, too. Don't you realize that? You have to want it."

"I'm stuck like this; I'm a guilty man," Demyan said, almost like he was trying to warn her off again.

"We're all monsters."

"You're just you, Claire."

"No, I'm a lot more than just me. And maybe if you tell me about you, I would let you see my monsters, too."

• • •

Vera bear-hugged Claire's midsection and neck like she was a tiny koala refusing to let go. Claire didn't mind. The girl was on her way to falling asleep, but the hospital chairs were uncomfortable, not to mention the noise level of the waiting people. No one noticed that little Vera had stayed at the hospital all day, just like them. She sat quietly and on her best behavior as news traveled in about her grandfather's condition while she played with her doll and listened to Claire read the books she brought along in her backpack.

None of the Bratva even blinked at the child, not in a compassionate or sympathetic way. Claire couldn't understand why that was. Surely Vera was treasured and prized in their Russian family, wasn't she? Her father was their prince after all, and her grandfather their boss. Even her dead mother's father had a place in these people's lives. Or he had, once.

It just didn't make sense why none of them gave Vera any passing concern or attention.

Once most of the waiting people had left for the night, she took the chance to get Vera out of the waiting room to hopefully walk her to sleep.

"My papa loves me," Vera whispered into Claire's neck.

Claire nearly stumbled in her walk, but somehow managed to keep going. "Of course, he does, sweetheart."

Who wouldn't love this child? It certainly wasn't taking Claire any effort to fall in love with Vera's innocence and sweetness. She was nothing but good in her heart and soul.

"He doesn't say it a lot," Vera said.

A heavy weight pressed down on Claire's shoulders. "Some daddies don't, but that doesn't mean he loves you any less."

"That's what he said, too." Vera shrugged in Claire's embrace. "Papa doesn't have to say it, though."

"Oh, why is that, Vera?"

"Because he doesn't. I know. And he holds my hand, too. I always know he loves me when he holds my hand."

Claire's mind went back to earlier when she saw Demyan touch his daughter's face before accepting her tiny hand in his.

"Is that why you hold his hand, too?" Claire asked.

"Yes. To say it back," Vera explained. "He knows."

Claire smiled. "No one else has to understand the way your daddy loves you, Vera. As long as you know, that's the only thing that matters."

Then, even quieter than before, Vera asked, "Does Papa hold your hand, too?"

CHAPTER TWELVE

Claire jolted awake as something warm cupped her cheek. Her eyes flew wide instantly at the same time her arm tightened around the sleeping child snuggled into her side on the cushioned bench.

Demyan kneeled down, his hand dropping away from Claire as he brushed his palm over Vera's black curls. "Thank you for keeping her entertained today. I know she probably wasn't easy to handle, or whatever."

"She was perfect," Claire said truthfully.

"Yeah, she usually is." Demyan sighed, glancing around the empty waiting room. "Took long enough for everyone to clear out of here."

"What time is it?"

"Ten."

Claire's brow furrowed. "Visiting hours were over a while ago. I shouldn't be here."

"As far as the nurses' station understands, you're Vera's caretaker alongside me. Since she's Anton's only grandchild, they're not putting up a fuss about you staying here to watch her. She hasn't caused any problems for them to want her gone, anyway."

"She's a great kid, Demyan."

"I got lucky with her, that's all," he said, chuckling.

Claire was pretty damn sure that was the second time she ever heard this man amused in a way that wasn't sardonic, rude, or unkind. It was just simply genuine.

And it was for Vera.

She wasn't surprised.

"I have a question," Claire said, willing the nerves to leave. She didn't think he would like her probing into the Russian Bratva he was so thoroughly immersed in. "But only if you're going to answer."

Demyan's gaze snapped from Vera's sleeping form to Claire's face. "What's that?"

"While we waited around here, nobody wanted anything to do with Vera. Yours and your father's men, I mean. They weren't outright offensive or anything to her, but they didn't pay her any attention, either. I mean, besides being your daughter, isn't she a little like Ana or you to them, too? Shouldn't they, I don't know, be concerned for her or something? Like her or maybe talk to her?"

"What do you mean, like Ana or me?"

"I heard some of them today and how they talk about you two like you're royalty or something."

"Oh." Demyan rocked back on his heels, and Claire wasn't sure if she crossed a line with him or not. There were things that mafia outsiders shouldn't ask. Maybe that was one of them. "We are, in a way. Ana and me, you know. I grew up being the little prince, and I always knew where I was going. So did my father's men.

"Ana was a perfect angel with no interest in connecting herself to the Russian mafia and then when she met Koldan, it was like … boom. They were a huge thing for all sides and still are."

"I don't understand."

"Two kids from influential, rival mafia families getting married. The daughter of a Bratva boss and the son of another. It's like fucking gold to those people. Even better that they're both Russian with fathers who have big names in the crime world."

Ah. Claire got it.

"Growing up, Ana wanted nothing to do with men like our father or the things he's affiliated with. Koldan slipping into her life was a huge surprise for everyone, including Ana. She was always considered a Bratva princess, but it wasn't until him that she dropped her opinions and attitude toward the mafia lifestyle. I suppose he's okay, too. I've never wanted to kill him like I have with almost every other man who sniffed around my sister, so there's that."

Claire assumed he was joking, but since Demyan always kept his impassive mask on, it was hard to tell.

"You still didn't answer my question," she pointed out.

He offered her a smile, but it barely lifted the corner of his mouth. "I like it better this way."

Claire's confusion and irritation climbed a notch. Would he ever trust her? "Keeping me ignorant of everything about you?"

Demyan's lips cracked with a smile, flashing a row of white teeth in the process. It was only a beat of time before his laughter filled the waiting room, low and gravely. Unlike his earlier chuckles that had been thick with compassion and centered for his daughter, his vocal amusement now was … freeing. Like he'd been waiting to laugh for years.

Claire wondered if he had.

She couldn't help herself but stare at him, watching the way his shoulders shook and a smirk curved his mouth wickedly. Sure, she had taken him to bed and let him have her, but the sexiness in that was nothing compared to his laughter.

Nothing.

"No," Demyan finally said, oblivious to the way Claire stared at him entranced or how her mouth was open and dry. "Not you, *krasivyy*. Vera."

"Did you just call me crazy?" Claire asked, defenses slamming up.

Again, Demyan's echoing laughter filled the space. "How did you get crazy from krasivyy?"

"I don't know; it sounds the same or similar. Is that not what it means?"

Demyan cocked a brow, his humor fading. "Not even close. It means beautiful."

God. "Oh."

"Vera," Demyan repeated.

Instinctively, Claire draped her arm across the sleeping child at her side. A white, thin hospital blanket covered Vera's lower half. "What about her?"

"I prefer the men around me, those who work for my father and me, don't have personal or emotional connection to my daughter in any way. I have tried my hardest ever since she was born to keep a distance between her and them because who they are is not who she needs to see."

"You're one of those men," Claire replied.

"I am, but not with her. She's already paid her dues for being the daughter of a Bratva man, I won't make her pay more."

"But they don't treat Ana badly."

In fact, Ana was treated like the crème de la crème of women. Or so it seemed.

"It's not about how they might treat her," Demyan explained with a shrug. "It's what might happen if they see how important she is to me or how much I care for her. Vera is my everything, the only good thing in my days most times. The last thing I need is for someone to immediately find my one weakness to use to hurt me."

"Vera is that weakness."

Demyan nodded. "Once upon a time, it was her mother. I made it obvious, I could never control myself or my emotions when it came to her, and look at where it got me, Claire. In this business, you can't trust anyone but yourself. Most of the men in the Avdonin Bratva watched me grow up, but that doesn't make a goddamn difference to me."

"Why not?" Claire asked.

"Because it didn't make a difference to my father after his grandfather died, and Anton stepped up for the man's seat. Do you want to know how many men who watched him grow up and treated him like their king in waiting that he had to kill for his seat because they were coming in on him?"

Claire didn't. She understood his point.

"Don't you feel close to any of the men?"

"Some, maybe. In certain ways."

"Wouldn't you trust them with your daughter's life?"

Demyan smiled, but it wasn't a pleasant sight like before. No, his grin was callous and cruel. "As long as they're afraid of me and believe there is nothing they can use to hurt me, then yes, I absolutely trust them with my daughter's life."

Claire couldn't help but wonder if Vera somehow suffered because of her father's choice to keep her at arm's length in the view of others. She didn't think on it for long. Vera's words earlier were still heavy and prominent in her heart and thoughts.

Demyan loved his daughter. He just showed it to her differently.

For Claire, that made sense in more ways that the obvious ones, too. Demyan wasn't like every other man. He lived in a world where danger and threats were a constant. His life was ruled by crime and expectations. Some people considered his family a dynasty, and he was the heir. Of course, that walked hand in hand with fear. He experienced loss once because of it and wasn't willing to lose one more precious thing.

And Vera was so very precious.

"I think you're a good father," Claire said, wanting him to know.

"I didn't ask," Demyan murmured, watching her intently. "But thank you."

"Maybe I thought you needed to hear it."

"Sometimes I do." Demyan cleared his throat before adding, "I've done such a good job at distancing myself from my daughter in other's eyes. Even some of my family and her mother's believe there's not a loving bone in my body for her."

"That can't be true," Claire said, hurting inside just hearing it.

"Sadly, it is. I don't give them a reason to think otherwise."

"That's the problem though, isn't it? No one gets to see how much you truly adore her or the things you do for her."

"Rarely," Demyan admitted. "I keep her close."

"But everyone else perceives it differently."

"Because they don't look hard enough," he replied.

Claire did.

Demyan stood, fixing his dark slacks as he straightened. "It doesn't matter, Claire. I made it this way because otherwise, I'd live in a vortex of fear every single day thinking someone might hurt my daughter to get to me."

"Liam did all of this," she said, more to herself than Demyan.

To others, it might seem hard to believe that one man could cause such heartache and devastation, but not to Claire. She wasn't the least bit surprised. Liam Dolan had no feelings inside. He was dead—one human shaped block of ice dressed in good clothes with a charming smile. All sociopaths were charismatic, she knew. It was how they drew their prey in before they went straight for the kill.

"Well," Demyan drawled with a scowl, "... he certainly helped me along to get to this point. After all, he promised to take two things I loved away from me and he only took one. I won't give him the chance to take another. Not my child. I couldn't protect her mother and for a long time, I wondered if that was because I didn't love her enough to, in some fucked up way."

I'm a guilty man.

Those words rang like a loud bell in the back of Claire's mind.

"You still blame yourself for Gia's death."

"How could I not?" Demyan asked, widening his arms at his sides.

"Do other people blame you, too?"

"They've never said a thing." He twirled a finger at his temple. "That mess is all in here."

Monsters.

Demyan was finally showing her some of his.

"I have a favor to ask you," Demyan informed.

Claire wasn't sure why he dropped their conversation like it was a scalding pot when it had been going pretty decently for once, but she let him. If he didn't want to talk more on a topic that he clearly kept off-limits for good reason, she wouldn't push him.

"What's that?"

"I know it's probably not easy for you to stay under the Irish's radar when you're around us," he said.

"Easier than you think," Claire replied. "It's just my aunt and her husband, but they're never very interested in me or the things I'm doing. I always was forgettable to my family. I slip in and out without much muss or fuss for them."

Demyan's eyes flicked to hers. "You're anything but forgettable, Claire."

She wished he wouldn't say things like that. Every time he did, regardless if he meant the words or not, they stopped the goddamn air in her chest and made her heart beat so hard it hurt. Demyan didn't give off an affectionate or playful vibe, not even when they fucked. When he let statements like that escape, she found it hard to believe that kind of man wasn't hiding somewhere inside him.

Claire wanted to know that man.

"A favor, you said," Claire reminded him, needing to get out of her head and away from those risky thoughts.

"I could probably send Vera off with Ivan when he leaves—"

"He's not gone yet?" Claire asked. There wasn't a soul around and she hadn't seen Ivan or the man's wife for a while.

"I'm not the only one who wasted a lot of time and burned bridges the past four years."

Oh.

"He's with your dad."

"On and off. Sometimes Anton and Ivan look like they want to kill one another, my father's heartrate goes up, and Ivan takes a walk. They've left a lot of things unsaid for too long. Doesn't matter, though."

Claire smiled at the almost sentimental tone in Demyan's words. "Why?"

"Because they're always going to be best friends even when they fucking hate each other. Anyway, I could send Vera home with him or even one of her aunts, but I really don't want to. She has a schedule and it's important for her to keep it. I don't want Vera to see Anton until he doesn't look like he's been sitting in a hospital and just had a heart attack. I'm going to be here for another day or more."

"You shouldn't leave your father if you're not ready to."

"I'm not," he said. "And that's why I can't go home, but she needs to. She has her pre-k on Monday morning at nine. I already talked to a bull about picking her up then to take her, so you won't have to even leave my place or whatever."

Claire had a dinner she needed to attend at her aunt's place mid-week, but that was still far off.

"I'd really appreciate it," Demyan added quietly. "I can't see Ana leaving the hospital, never mind my mother, so she can't go with them. Vera likes you, and I know she wouldn't worry herself into a mess with you around. I wouldn't have to worry much, either."

Claire's heart stopped for a split second before kick-starting hard. He plainly admitted he trusted her with his daughter—had faith she would care properly for Vera. What did that really say about him and her?

She wouldn't pick it apart, but instead, take it for what it was.

"You can park your car inside the garage at my place. No one would see it. So, there's that, too."

"Don't worry. Sure, I'll watch Vera for you. I'd be happy to."

More than, even.

• • •

Demyan found Koldan gathering his jacket and Ana's things in the private family room situated beyond the locked doors of the ICU unit.

"You heading out?" Demyan asked.

Koldan nodded as he turned, tossing his jacket over his shoulder at the same time. "Ana's going to stay, though."

"I figured she would."

"Yeah, and apparently I'm an asshole for even asking if she would like to sleep in her own bed tonight."

167

Demyan tried not to laugh, but he couldn't help it. Trying to tear Ana away from her father right now would be pointless. She was always going to be Anton's princess, no matter what. "Are you surprised?"

"No, but I figured I should offer her the choice." Koldan shrugged. "I get it, though. Being in here makes me think of Adrik, too, and that just fucking kills me inside. I need to get out of here for five minutes, maybe down a half a bottle of vodka while I'm at it."

Yeah, Demyan supposed it would.

"So, I'm going to overlook the whole asshole comment," Koldan said, chuckling sadly. "Even if that kills me, too."

Ana loved Koldan to death and back and the guy loved her the same way. Demyan could see it and anyone with two brain cells to rub together would, too. The two rarely fought, were usually together in everything they did, and Demyan had never once seen Koldan treat Ana with anything less than the respect and honor she deserved.

It was one of the reasons why Demyan liked the guy. Some men in their business could be pricks about their women and how they acted toward them. Koldan was forward in his intentions and good in his heart. Well, toward Ana, in any case. Anyone else was fair fucking game. Demyan had been there to witness that nasty a time or two from Koldan, also. Despite his nice nature, Koldan had his dark side. It only flared when it needed to, like Demyan supposed the man was raised to do.

And only in business. Never to family.

That was the Russian way.

"How's your father doing?" Demyan asked.

"Kicking hard with no end in sight."

Demyan knew what that felt like and how easy it could be ripped away.

"And busting my goddamn balls about getting home to Jersey with Ana," Koldan added. "Preferably with a ring on her finger and her last name changed."

Christ.

"Don't mention that to Anton," Demyan warned. "He might die thinking you're going to move the wedding up sooner rather than later."

"I wouldn't. But seriously, is that man ever going to forgive me for loving and wanting to marry his daughter?"

"Probably not. You'd have to … I don't know, understand them."

"Actually, I think I'd have to understand him more than her. Her, I get. She's mine, Demyan. I get Ana. It's Anton I have the trouble with. Do you know when I asked him for her hand, he threatened to shove his fist down my throat and rip my heart out?"

Demyan wasn't surprised.

"Someday you might have a daughter, and then you can apologize to my father for taking Ana from him," Demyan said simply.

Koldan cocked an eyebrow at his friend. "Is that how you feel about Vera?"

Demyan felt his shoulders square, his automatic reaction to shut down any idea to outsiders that his daughter was his entire heart, soul, and world bubbling up from force of habit. For once, he decided to be honest. It was just Koldan, after all.

"That's exactly how I feel about Vera. And the man who takes her from me better be good and fucking ready for one hell of a fight. Anton let you off easy, believe me."

Koldan sighed. "I'll take your word for it. Although, I think that's the first time you've ever said something like that about Vera to me. I mean, I know you love her. Obviously, you love her. She's your daughter. But sometimes …"

"It's hard to tell," Demyan said, filling in the blanks.

"Yeah." Koldan cringed. "Sorry, I shouldn't have said that. It's not my place to question how you raise your daughter. I know how well you take care of her and that she's always your top priority. I apologize."

"That's the point."

"What?" Koldan asked, clearly confused.

"The point of why I let everyone think I keep my daughter at a distance. Because then, it's hard for them to tell how important she is to me. She is the only thing I have left that's worth keeping. No one will ever understand that, however. Not on my watch. I won't give them ammo to hurt me or her."

"I get it."

"Does Ana know you're leaving?" Demyan asked.

"Not yet. I was going to let her know, but I had to wait until Anton's room cleared of a guest."

The ICU had a strict policy on the number of visitors allowed in a patient's room at one time. Demyan suspected Anton was likely over his by at least one, considering Ivan was nowhere to be seen and Ana and Viviana had yet to leave the unit, as well.

"I'll send her out when I go in," Demyan said.

"Thanks."

Demyan left the private family room and made his way through the ICU. He met Ivan at the nurses' station that was located directly across from his father's room. While he and Ivan usually passed one another by with little conversation ever since Gia's death, Demyan figured this wasn't quite the same.

After all, the man had showed up and spent all day in this goddamn place. Just like family.

"Hey," Ivan said as Demyan leaned his back against the top of the station.

"Hey."

Out of the corner of his eyes, Demyan noted Ivan was going over paperwork and signing the bottom of each one.

"What is that?" Demyan asked.

"Legal shit for your father while he's in here," Ivan explained. "He doesn't need most of it, frankly, but it's good to have on file. Since Anton is so fucking stubborn about hospitals, doctors, and anything else medical-wise, it's best for me to get it done and in the system while I can. Unfortunate as it is that it had to be now and because of this."

Demyan's confusion climbed higher. "So, why isn't Ma handling it?"

"Because Viviana isn't Anton's lawyer, and if something were ever to happen in the future, worse than what happened today, she can't sign the power of attorney over to herself. Anton wants her to have it in that sort of circumstance, so that's just one of things I'm working out."

What?

It took Demyan longer than he wanted to admit to realize what Ivan was saying.

"You're still his lawyer?"

Ivan stiffened beside Demyan before he nodded once. "Of course, I am."

"But you two—"

"I blamed him for a long time," Ivan interjected so quietly

Demyan strained to hear the words. "For Gia's death and the circumstances. I thought if I had never aligned myself with that man, I wouldn't have put my daughter in this kind of world where she could be killed just for being alive."

Demyan got that, sort of. He didn't place blame on his father for Gia's murder, but he could empathize with why Ivan might.

"I burned every bridge between him and I as fast as I fucking could, and then I bolted for safety," Ivan continued, shrugging slightly. "And all the while, I knew the entire time the only thing I was doing in the end was pointing a finger to ignore the rest pointed back at me. I used my anger with Anton as a way to keep from blaming myself. We're the same, he and I. We're different, too, but still the same."

"I've never blamed my father," Demyan said before he could stop himself.

Ivan lifted a single brow as he regarded Demyan. "Oh?"

"Not once."

"No, I imagine you were too busy blaming yourself, huh?" Ivan asked.

"Blame," Demyan corrected. "No past tense. I've got no one to answer for that but me, Ivan. What happened to Gia—that's all on me. And I live with the punishment of it every single day."

And that punishment came in the form of memories that couldn't be erased and a little girl he had to raise alone.

"I don't think it's anyone's fault but the man who made the call, Demyan." Ivan dropped the pen down to the counter after he signed the final paper. "Should I blame you for doing everything my daughter asked? Gia loved you, but she didn't love the Bratva part of you and because of that, you only gave her the information she would want to know.

"Should I blame you for trying to keep her protected? Because you did, but she was the one who made the choice to leave that safe place. Who should really be liable in all this, Demyan? Who deserves my anger and my pain to be tossed onto them because I'm not man enough to look into the mirror?"

"Not her," he said quietly. "She was only human and I don't blame her for being that way."

"Not you, either." Ivan reached up and clapped Demyan lightly on the shoulder. "You're doing just fine, Demyan."

Strangely, he needed to hear that. Ivan didn't even say his

words were about the way Demyan was raising Vera or even how he was moving forward in his life without Gia. But he still needed those words.

"Do you still miss her?" Ivan asked softly.

"Do you?" he asked back.

"Often, but I have the best parts of her still living around me."

"Vera," Demyan said.

"And you. Because when I think of Gia, it leads me into memories of you, as well. I can't help but be happy though, even if this is hard for you and I imagine it must be."

Demyan didn't have the first clue what Ivan was talking about. "What do you mean?"

"Well, for the first six months after Gia died, every time I looked into your eyes, there was nothing there. Just a blackness staring back. Everybody talked about depression, and I suppose you were in that state, but it was ... blinding, deafening.

"Looking at you and not being able to understand because I was grieving too has been a huge regret for me. I thought you were so selfish because you got to hold a piece of her each day but when you did have that part of her, you were somewhere else entirely. I wish I could go back and see you again, understand you, Demyan, and tell you it was going to get better eventually."

"Sometimes it doesn't feel like it has."

"Maybe not," Ivan agreed, "but you're getting there and I'm sorry if it's hard to do."

"I still don't understand what you mean."

Ivan stared at Demyan in a way that made his nerves grow. "You really don't."

"No."

"Moving on, Demyan. Healing in a way, I suppose. Letting someone new—"

"There's no one new," Demyan interrupted firmly. He wanted to shut that fucking idea down before anyone else decided to jump on the bandwagon, too.

"Yes, there is. You know exactly who I am talking about whether you want to admit it or not. It started the moment she took Vera in, and you didn't stop it."

Demyan swallowed the thickness building in his throat, refusing to let it silence him. "There's nothing with Claire and me if

172

that's what you're dancing around."

"Oh, I'm not dancing around it. I'm outright stating it. I might not like where she comes from, but I like what she's doing for Vera."

Demyan glanced at the floor. "Me, too."

"And I sure as hell like what she's doing for you. Don't push that girl away, Demyan. You might not realize it, but you need her and she's good for you. No one else might see it, but I've known you from the first day you opened your eyes. I watched you grow up, stood on the sidelines and the frontlines of your life."

"Please don't," Demyan said, not wanting to hear anymore.

Apparently Ivan didn't care what Demyan wanted.

"Don't push that girl away because you're scared," Ivan repeated strongly.

Without another word, Ivan gathered the papers off the nurses' station, slid them into a waiting file, and left Demyan to stew in his thoughts as the man walked toward the exit of the unit. Demyan had no desire to let Ivan's words get inside his head and fuck around in there. He found them hard to ignore because in some ways, maybe Ivan was right.

The problem was, it didn't matter. Demyan just wasn't ready for that nonsense yet.

None of it.

CHAPTER THIRTEEN

Inside Anton's private unit, the space was dark and quiet but for the soft beeps of monitors and the steady hiss of oxygen. For having a massive heart attack, his father appeared better than he probably should. Demyan attributed that to how strong and healthy his father actually was despite his situation.

Really, it had scared Demyan. Straight to the fucking brink of insanity.

Anton Avdonin was not the kind of man to just lay down and die. He was the strongest man Demyan knew, so this was simply a bump in the road. Another one for his father to either climb the fuck over or move the hell around.

Ana sipped from a bottle of water where she sat in what looked like the most uncomfortable fucking chair ever, but she wasn't complaining. A quick glance at his mother and father sleeping on the hospital bed facing one another was enough for him to divert his gaze from their direction. Their fingers were interwoven together and they were so close, Viviana was tucked into Anton's chest.

Oddly, the two had always been like that. Only in the sanctity of their home and rarely when others were around, but it wasn't the first time Demyan witnessed something tender between the two. He knew how much his parents loved each other.

"Koldan is heading out for the night," Demyan informed Ana.

Nodding, Ana stood from the chair. "All right. How're you doing?"

"Fine."

Or as good as he was ever going to get for the moment.

"Vera?" Ana asked.

"Claire's taking her home to my place."

Ana's brow lifted in curiosity and for a long while, she simply stared at Demyan like she just *knew.* "I called your phone this morning."

Demyan arched a brow. "Oh?"

"Yep. Guess who picked up? Not you. You stayed over there last night."

It wasn't even a question.

"I'd tell you to mind your own damned business, but I know you won't."

"Nope," Ana replied, grinning.

"Does it bother you that she's around?" Demyan asked.

After all, Claire was a direct link to Ana's dead rapist. Demyan would understand if it did bother his sister a little.

"No. She's not her brother and she's not responsible for what he did to me. I actually like her from the few conversations we've had, and I know she's fond of Vera, too."

"You could say that," Demyan agreed.

"Spill."

"There's nothing to tell unless you want a play by play of my sex life."

Ana's mouth opened, but a quiet Viviana beat her to the punch, saying, "I sure don't."

Apparently his mother wasn't sleeping, after all.

"Fun sucker," Ana muttered low.

"Go say goodbye to your fiancé, Ana," Viviana ordered, never opening her eyes or turning in the bed. "And for God's sake, don't call that boy an asshole again for worrying about you."

"Agreed," Anton mumbled.

Demyan nearly choked on his shock. Had his father just defended Koldan? Christ. Neither one of them were sleeping.

Once Ana was gone, Anton groaned out, "Where is that bitch with the morphine?"

"Stop it," Viviana whispered. "You can't have another dose of that until morning at least. It's not good for your heartrate, Anton. It makes you antsy and aggravated."

"My shoulder feels like someone is fucking kicking it, Vine."

"Morning," she repeated softly. "I promise."

"When did he get a shot of morphine in the first place?" Demyan asked.

"A little while ago," Viviana answered.

"Why?"

"My goddamn shoulder," Anton said, his voice husky and dry. "Didn't you just hear what I said about someone kicking it?"

Viviana sighed. "No one is kicking it. Hush."

"But it—"

"Hush."

Anton grumbled but never once did he open his eyes.

"Since when has your shoulder been bothering you?" Demyan asked.

"Since I took a chunk of metal in it from a bomb nearly three decades ago."

Really, Demyan was pissed off his father hadn't mentioned his shoulder was causing him issues. "And you didn't tell me because …?"

"Because I get enough shit from your mother."

"Anton."

"S'true, baby," Anton mumbled. "I do. A lot. And I never say anything because I love you."

Demyan caught the slight smile curving his mother's mouth as she said, "Right. You say nothing. Ever."

"Sometimes in my head I do," Anton said.

Demyan chuckled. The morphine was obviously kicking in. "Anyway, are you supposed to be in bed with him, Ma? Or am I going to have to chase off another nurse?"

"They want him comfortable and when he's on his other side, his heartrate goes down. On this side, it's much better."

"So?"

"Hurts on this side," Anton said. "Bad shoulder and the nurses are bitches."

"Anton," Viviana chided again.

"They are, Vine."

Well, Demyan supposed that explained the morphine and his mother.

"I'm glad you took my advice," his father added.

Demyan's brow crinkled. "About what?"

"Claire."

"I don't know what you're talking about, Papa."

Anton smiled, though from where Demyan stood, it looked more like one hell of a smug smirk. Yeah, his father was going to be just fine. "Sure you don't, son."

"Anton?" Viviana asked.

"Yeah, baby?"

"You're supposed to be sleeping."

"I know."

"So sleep," Viviana ordered.

"But—"

"Sleep. And come tomorrow ..."

"Yeah?" Anton asked.

"I'm going to be really angry with you."

Anton said something under his breath, but it sounded a fuck lot like, "I figured."

• • •

"This is ridiculous," Anton said, waving at the IV attached to his wrist and the wires hooked to leads on his chest. "I am fine."

Viviana stood at the end of the hospital bed with her arms crossed and a frustrated expression drawing her features dark. "That's enough, Anton."

"What will they do for me here that can't be done at home?"

"Monitor your heart. You know, that thing in your chest that stopped beating for two entire minutes yesterday. The organ that keeps you alive, the one your son had to make beat for you until the ambulance arrived."

"Vine—"

"Yeah, the fucking thing that quit working and landed you in the ICU, Anton! No, they're not going to release you from the hospital the day after your heart attack just because you goddamn well say so. And if I have my say, you won't get out of here for a *month*!"

"Baby—"

"You lied to me yesterday morning, didn't you?"

Anton wouldn't look at his wife. "Stop it."

"You did, didn't you? Answer me."

Demyan stayed silent in the corner with Ana at his side. Neither of the two siblings wanted to get in-between their parents' argument. It never ended well before, not that Anton and Viviana did fight a lot. He could count on one hand all the times he had seen his parents' disagreements as he grew up under their roof. Usually, they kept their arguments quiet and behind closed doors.

Apparently, Viviana dropped that pretense with a mighty fuck you.

Demyan didn't blame his mother a bit.

She didn't lie the night before when she told her husband she was going to be very angry come the next day.

"Anton, I asked you a question," Viviana said, canting her head to the side like she just caught a prey in her sights.

"Wow, Ma's really pissed," Ana whispered.

Demyan pretended not to notice his sister wiping the wetness from her eyes. "For good reason. He nearly killed himself, Ana."

It also scared the living hell out of Demyan in the process. Losing his father … he couldn't possibly lose Anton.

Ana sniffed quietly. "I know. But he's …"

She couldn't finish her sentence. Demyan got the gist without her needing to. To them, even as grown adults well into their own lives, their father would always be a God to them. Invincible, deathless. Well, he had been before this whole shit show. This was a major wake-up call in more ways than one.

Demyan was walking a very thin line of control as he watched his mother crumble across the room.

Anton had barely made it out of his heart attack alive. What had Demyan done for the last four years? He wasted so much time trying to protect his father in his own way by keeping a distance and forcing Anton away. Demyan knew how much his father loved him, loved all of them. He didn't want Anton to suffer like everybody else did by being too close to Demyan and his … emptiness.

"He's never been sick before," Ana said. "Jesus, he doesn't even get colds, Demyan."

"Yeah, I know, Ana," Demyan replied too low for his still arguing parent's to hear.

"Vine, I really didn't—"

"I swear to *God*, Anton," Viviana hissed.

"Fine. Yes, I lied."

"And the night before, too, right?"

"Yes," Anton muttered under his breath. "Okay? Are you happy now? Yes, I fucking lied, Vine. I didn't want to worry you—"

"I already was worried and you knew I was!" Viviana's arms flew wide, her exasperation practically shrieking out of her. "I can't even believe you. The nerve of you, Anton Avdonin."

Demyan suddenly wished he could melt into the damn wall. His mother was crying, letting the tears fall freely and not wiping them away. When Viviana cried, shit usually went downhill from there, Demyan knew. Anton couldn't stand to see his wife in that state.

"I just ... I *can't* with you right now, Anton," Viviana said, shaking her head.

With that, Demyan watched in stunned silence as his mother turned on her heel and stormed out of the private hospital room. She didn't even bother to close the door on her way out.

"Ma!" Ana shouted.

"Go after her, Ana," Anton said, rubbing circles into his temples. "Get her something to eat ... a coffee, maybe."

Ana crossed her arms, glaring. "Has she even left your side?"

"No. So again, make sure she eats and calms down."

"Papa ..."

"I know, Ana," Anton said firmly but quietly. "And since one woman has already yelled at me enough today, can you at least wait until tomorrow before you start, too?"

Ana huffed. "I wasn't going to yell at you—"

"Yes, you were."

"—much," Ana finished, shrugging.

"Go find your mother, I'm fine today. Stable, or whatever. That's why they moved me from the ICU into this goddamn hell."

Ana nodded and left.

Once Demyan was alone with his father, he let out a loud sigh. One that voiced all of his anxiety, anger, and everything else that was tying his heart and soul up into a million and one little knots.

"You know, Nicoli died damn near on the spot where my heart stopped, too," Anton noted like he was talking to the air and not his son.

Demyan didn't know how to respond to that, so instead, he asked, "Oh?"

"Yeah, he did. I was downstairs counting money one of the brigadiers had brought in and didn't hear him call for me if he even did."

Demyan was aware how close his father had been to his step-grandfather, so he imagined that must have been hard for him to handle.

"Then, when I took his seat as boss, a lot of the guys thought I would give up that office in Seven Lights—it had a different name back then—but I couldn't. I might as well have grown up in that place. I probably learned how to walk on those floors. It was mine, too."

Anton kicked the stark white blankets off his legs, glowering at the sheets as if they might bite him. "This place isn't meant for men like me. Your mother doesn't understand. Being sick means having weaknesses—flaws in your body. I'm not a weak man."

"Well, your heart sure as hell is."

"My heart is fine."

"No, it isn't, Papa."

Anton eyed his son. "I'm not going to die."

"You almost did," Demyan murmured.

"I didn't die—"

"Your heart stopped beating, and guess what you can't live without if it doesn't work?" Demyan asked bitingly.

Anton acted as though he didn't hear his son. "Have Ivan call Trevor."

"Who?"

"Trevor, he's got a shop down on the boardwalk that's been there forever in the back of one of the old restaurants. He's done a lot of our work, most importantly, mine."

Demyan still didn't understand. "Work?"

"Tattoos, Demyan. I know you had that guy on the Coney do your rose and cross, but this is different. It's tradition and Trevor should finish your important ones while the fool is still alive."

"Tattoos," Demyan echoed.

Hesitance kept him from saying more. He didn't like what his father was implying without actually getting right to the point. Beyond that, it wasn't like Anton at all to dance around a subject. The man was known for his bluntness, painfully so.

"Time for some stars, I think," Anton said with a smirk that Demyan could damn near match with his own if he wanted. "Go with black, the blue ink fades too fast. The Bratva doesn't really give a shit what color the ink is anymore."

Demyan had admired his father's ink for as long as he could remember. And sure, he'd fought against the idea of the Bratva tradition of tattooing for a long time. Mostly because it would have been a very visual reminder for Gia of Demyan's chosen profession.

When Gia died, Demyan had his black rose done on his pec

since he really didn't have a reason not to. Plus, he basically immersed himself into the Bratva world for the following two years with little regard for anything or anyone else. The Russian Cyrillic lettering had come soon after. The cross between his forefinger and thumb was his favorite.

"Only a boss has stars, Papa," Demyan said.

Vors typically had roses done on the chest for initiation. Eight pointed stars on the chest was an option, too. But stars on the shoulder? No, only bosses had those.

Anton answered his son with a single nod. "They do."

"I'm not the boss, you are."

"What was it I told you yesterday morning before this whole nonsense went down?" Anton asked.

Demyan fists balled at his sides. "You told me it was too late."

"It still is." Anton gestured between them. "I'm not going to call myself old here, but you can bet your ass I won't be allowed to do very damned much with your mother on my back like she is. I can't be a boss from home, Demyan."

"I'm not—"

"Whatever you're going to say, don't," Anton ordered, his tone severe. "You are. You have always been. Get your stars done and take your seat before someone tries to steal it from you. The best kind of cowards have a way of weeding their way out of the woodwork at times like this."

"And what if someone objects to me as boss?" Demyan asked.

"I can't believe you even asked me that, son," Anton said, scoffing. "What do you think?"

"I've got a gun—use it."

"Exactly."

Demyan leaned back to the wall, still biting back his worry and heartache. He didn't want his father to see that from him, not right now. "What's Ivan got to do with it?"

"He was there with me when I went in and had mine done, plus he's good friends with the guy."

"Ivan's not in with the Bratva, Papa."

"He will for this," Anton said, unaffected. "Trust me. Christ, at least that awful burning in my chest is gone."

Right, because everybody wanted to suffer a heart attack just to relieve pain.

"How long was it bothering you?" Demyan asked.

"A couple days," Anton answered, shifting in the bed to be positioned higher. "I didn't think it was anything to be concerned about."

"Liar."

"All right, so I ignored it. I have shit to do and can't afford to be bedridden for God knows how long. You're not my doctor, Demyan, so back the fuck off."

"Jesus Christ. It's no wonder Ma wants to rip out your heart and pickle it."

Anton laughed, glancing up at the ceiling like he wished it would cave in on him. "Right now, that's a pretty damn apt description of her feelings."

"Speaking of doctors," came a voice from the doorway to the hospital room.

Demyan nodded to the man who stepped into the room wearing a lab coat with a stethoscope hanging around his neck and a file in hand. He knew the man as his father's private physician, Leland. Knowing how particular Anton could be, he probably had the hospital get the man in for a second opinion. Likely to appease Anton's grievance or shut him up.

Leland wasn't just Anton's doctor, either, but the entire Avdonin clan had been cared for by this graying, sharp-tongued man. In fact, Demyan could remember having his immunization needles in the man's private offices and then told to suck it up when he held back tears. He was also Vera's family doctor, although the man was a heck of a lot nicer to Demyan's daughter.

If nothing else, the family trusted him and Demyan was glad to see him at the hospital to firmly put Anton in his place.

"Anton, how've you been, old friend?"

"Go to hell, Leland."

The doctor chuckled. "Charming, as always."

"How do I look to you, asshole?"

"Exactly how I said you would if you didn't calm your nonsense down," the doctor replied tersely. "Do you want to go over the list again about why you were high risk for an eventual cardiac arrest?"

Demyan's respect for his father's doctor climbed a notch. Rarely did someone other than Viviana challenge Anton so blatantly. No doubt, that was exactly why Anton kept the man around as his physician.

"I know why," Anton said, waving a hand as if to dismiss the man. "I'm going on fifty-nine, so I don't need a damned lecture."

"Well, for old time's sake and a good ol' I-told-you-so moment, let's go over it again." Leland stepped further into the room, closing the door behind him. "Do you want your son to leave before I lay into you, or should he stay?"

"I'm not leaving," Demyan said before his father could kick him out.

"Yeah, I didn't suspect you would want to. You always were right under your father's boots, even as a boy. How've you been Demyan?"

"Terrible," he answered honestly.

"That's too bad," Leland said quietly. "How is Vera?"

"Perfect."

Leland smiled. "I'm happy to hear it. Now, Anton ..."

"Make these bastards release me," Anton barked. "I want to go home with my wife."

"Absolutely not. You're looking at another couple of weeks in here, at least. And if the chat I just had with your sweet wife is any indication, she's going to have them running every test they can on you. If something comes up there, well, you already know what she's going to do."

"This is insane. I am fine."

"How many times have you said that since you've been in here?" Leland asked.

"A few," Anton grumbled.

"Stop saying it. You're not fine."

"I need a new doctor."

"No, you need to listen to the one you have, Anton."

"Leland—"

"Shut up and listen to the man, Papa."

Anton stiffened in the hospital bed, turning to stare at Demyan. "What did you just say to me?"

"Shut up, listen to the doctor, and quit your fucking whining." Demyan shrugged, unaffected by the stinging glare his father sported. "You almost died yesterday because you're too stubborn for your own good. So yeah, stop acting like a child and let the man speak."

"Demyan—"

"That wasn't a request," Demyan stated simply.

Anton stared at Demyan like a second head had popped out of his neck all of the sudden.

Demyan waved at the doctor. "Please, continue."

Leland smiled at Anton a little sardonically. "I knew there was a reason you liked that mouthy kid so much."

"He picked that shit up from somebody, but I don't know where," Anton muttered. "Wish I did so I could smack the fuck out of them."

"He gets it honest," Leland quipped. "Spit right from your mouth, Anton."

"Stop patronizing me about my kid and lecture me again."

Leland laughed. "Will do because your wife wouldn't forgive me otherwise. I'd like to say yesterday was a minor arrest but since I've seen the ECGs, it wasn't. Cocaine and ecstasy abuse—"

"That was a long time ago," Anton interjected hotly. "And abuse is a strong word for recreational use, Leland."

"The damage remains, Anton. Sometimes it takes years to catch up, too."

"Smoking tobacco and marijuana, drinking alcohol, eating anything remotely decent," Anton shot right back. "Yeah, I know. I still exercise every fucking day, I don't sit around and do nothing—"

"And you're working in a very stressful environment. I have never judged you for your chosen profession, I simply treated you when you needed, as you asked."

Anton's mouth snapped shut audibly and Demyan swore he heard his father's teeth grind.

"As for that environment, you've worked in it for how many decades now?"

"Over four," Demyan said when his father wouldn't answer.

"A long time, old friend. We also have to take into account you don't have your biological grandfather's family history, but your mother's side had a few heart issues with the men. You were supposed to begin having twice yearly ECGs after you turned fifty, and you refused."

"Are you done yet?" Anton asked, barking out the words.

"Actually, yes. I am. No stress, drinking, smoking, your diet has to change, and that blood pressure of yours needs to remain stable. With the right meds, a better attitude, and some down time, this situation shouldn't happen again. I know you don't want to put your wife through the hell of burying you, so no more screwing around. It's time to relax, Anton."

"I don't know how to do that."

Demyan chuckled, despite nothing about their situation being funny. "I guess you need to learn, then."

CHAPTER FOURTEEN

Demyan stared at his reflection in the mirror, noting the artist sitting beside him and Ivan on the other side. In all his twenty-nine years on earth, he wasn't sure he had ever truly seen himself as clearly as he was now.

For so long, he'd been a boy in his father's shadow, always under Anton's feet learning, watching, and just ... being. Demyan liked it there, or at least, he remembered liking it. He remembered growing up and thinking he wanted to be just like his father one day. Strong, tall, commanding, and tough. He supposed he succeeded with that goal in one way.

In others, he'd failed.

Because Demyan Avdonin had long since stepped out of his father's shadow. There was a point in his life—some may have called it his fork in the road—when he began making his own footprints and stop trying to fill the ones Anton had made. Gia's death had been such a catalyst for so many things, Demyan couldn't count them all.

Becoming a man separate to who he was with her, who he had been before, and the person everyone thought they wanted him to be, had climbed out of that devastation.

Demyan decided he liked this man staring at him in the mirror. His eyes spoke of life, pain, and understanding. His body was grown, toughened with strength and perseverance. His mind was knowing and not disillusioned by the grandeur of love and false security.

He was real.

Demyan was real.

His father had been in the hospital for two days and it was only today that Demyan finally felt comfortable leaving Anton's side to do what the man asked of him.

So, as his shoulders burned and the tattoo gun buzzed, he felt.

He felt everything.

• • •

"Hey," Claire said, leaning against the doorjamb of the bathroom with crossed arms and a soft smile.

She didn't question him, shower him with useless chatter, or overwhelm him with nonsense to cloud his mind.

Demyan liked that about Claire. Well, he liked a lot of things about her, but the fact they could be quiet in a room together and neither needed noise to fill the silence was a huge thing for him. No one knew how to just *be* and enjoy it.

Claire did.

"Hey," Demyan replied.

He pulled off his jacket and tossed it over the sink before shrugging his shirt off. Claire looked his back over in the mirror, and he guessed she was taking inventory of the new bandages he sported over his shoulders beneath his surname in Cyrillic lettering.

"Vera asleep?" Demyan asked.

"Yeah, completely knocked out. It's been a long couple of days."

"I figured." Demyan twisted his neck, working out the stress kinking his muscles. "She seemed okay when I talked to her on the phone this morning."

A small shrug was all Claire offered back.

Demyan turned, using his hands to brace his body against the sink as he faced her. "What's up?"

"Nothing, really. She's just been asking for you a lot and she wants to see Anton. How do you explain to a little girl her father doesn't want her visiting her sick grandfather in the hospital without breaking her heart? I get you don't want her seeing him in a bad state, or whatever, but—"

"You never dumb it down for her, that's how," Demyan interrupted gently. "Vera is one of the most intuitive and understanding kids ever. Never dumb things down or try to soften the blow for her. She can take it and even if you think you're hiding it, trust that my little girl knows. She always does."

Claire sucked in a breath, shaking her head. "Yeah, I know. I adore her so much. She's a beautifully strange girl."

"She is. And I'm just going to take that as a compliment because it's how I would describe her, too."

Claire's grin grew. "She did miss you. I don't think the phone

187

calls helped a whole lot."

"I'll wake her up before I go to sleep so she knows I'm here."

"I think she'd really like that, Demyan." Claire laughed, but the sound came out shaky. "Also, she's in your bed and I hope you don't mind, but she practically demanded she sleep there."

Demyan shrugged. "Sometimes she does."

"Yeah, but she wanted me to sleep there with her. I figured now wasn't the time to argue."

Oh.

Well …

Demyan didn't really care. "Whatever."

"That's it?"

"Yeah. Is there a problem here or something?"

"Yes … well, no, but yes. We're not something, Demyan. That's what you said. Things like that can confuse a child, okay. I don't want her thinking we're in some kind of relationship if we're not."

Demyan cleared his throat. "Maybe I lied."

"Maybe?"

"Maybe we are something."

"Maybe?" Claire asked again, laughing.

"We are."

Claire smiled. "We definitely are."

"No promises," Demyan murmured.

"I'm okay with that."

"Good. Help me out here, would you?"

"With what?"

Demyan turned and waved at the bandages. He'd passed the hours he needed to keep them on, but he couldn't reach the damn things or he would have taken them off already. His shoulders itched like nothing else.

"Oh, sure," Claire said.

When her hands came in contact with his back, Demyan felt the stress he couldn't get rid of earlier suddenly wash away. Claire took notice of that and she ran her palms from the tops of his shoulders to the base of his spine.

"Fuck, that feels good," Demyan groaned.

"Your back feels like it's made of rocks," Claire noted.

"Tension."

"Probably. How's your father?"

"Better," Demyan answered truthfully. "He'll be discharged within a week and back to his usual routine."

Demyan flinched, knowing that wasn't entirely true.

Claire didn't miss it. "What?"

"Well, everything won't be entirely the same for him, I suppose."

"Why not?"

"Take the bandages off, Claire."

Claire didn't push him for more information and instead, did as he asked. Once his shoulders were free of the cellophane, gauze, and tape, and the mess had been thrown into the tiny trashcan, Demyan let Claire absorb the new stars on his shoulders.

"These are nice," Claire said, her fingers running along his skin. "Itchy, yet?"

"Very."

"The only downfall to tattoos, not that I would go out and get myself one."

"You're perfect the way you are, Claire."

It was true.

Claire's smile turned almost sensual as she met his stare in the mirror. "I do like yours a lot."

"Oh?"

"Mmhmm," she hummed, the sound traveling straight down to his cock.

"Good to know. We never stop getting them."

"We?"

"Russian mafia men—*Vors*," Demyan explained. "Our life, accomplishments, and deeds are commemorated by tattoos. So yeah, we never stop getting them, I guess."

Claire's fingers danced over his stars again. "And these are for what?"

"A boss wears stars on his shoulders to show rank," Demyan said quietly.

"So that means you're …?"

"Yes. Now, anyway. I thought maybe in a few more years when Anton didn't have a choice but to step down. I didn't think it would be now."

"I get that."

Demyan didn't understand how Claire wasn't the least bit

bothered by his new tattoos. Their significance meant he wasn't just involved with crime, he was the head of it. You couldn't get higher than he was or more hands-on than a boss.

Shocked would be an understatement. Especially considering how much she disliked her own connections.

"Aren't you disgusted with them?" Demyan asked.

Claire kept touching him. "No. Should I be?"

"I don't know."

Gia would have been, something whispered in his mind.

Demyan shook that thought away.

"Hey, where'd you go right there?" Claire asked.

"Huh?"

"You just blanked out and then came right back. What was that?"

Demyan swallowed the thickness building, knowing this conversation had been a long time coming when it came to Claire and his history with Gia. "Vera's mother would have hated this. If I had come home with stars on my shoulders, she might have either thrown a fit or ignored them completely. Gia despised the mafia, my connections to it, and anything even remotely pertaining to it. We just didn't discuss it. There came a point between us where that was how it had to be. We wanted each other, but she didn't want that. So, there you go."

Claire stayed silent for longer than Demyan liked, watching him in that knowing way of hers. "I'm sorry."

"For what?"

"That the woman you loved didn't love all the parts of you. Because this is you, right?" Claire's hands ghosted over his stars, making shivers course down his spine. "These are you, not just a part of you, but the parts that made you. A history, one that's shaped you. Not everything you do has to be something a woman likes, but she either accepts them or doesn't. If she doesn't, then she shouldn't keep trying to hold onto a man who can't be what she needs."

"A lot of people have tried to tell me the same thing and I ignored them. They didn't understand, I thought. How could they? Gia and I were something they couldn't see—meant to be, maybe. I was convinced of it. I wasn't hearing them, not what they were trying to say."

"Are you listening now?" Claire asked.

"Yes, but I don't know why."

"That's okay, too, Demyan."

He nodded.

"Taking over my father's spot means something else, too."

"What's that?" Claire asked.

"Taking control of his plans. I was trying to avoid it for so long, but I don't have a choice anymore."

"The Irish meeting, you mean?"

"Yeah."

Claire shifted from foot to foot, clearly uncomfortable. "There was something else, Demyan."

"Tell me," he said.

"Remember that girl I mentioned that my relatives had living with them?"

"The slave, you mean."

"Yes," Claire whispered.

Demyan sighed. "My father was going to help free her, I assume."

"Yes. I'd understand if—"

"I'll do it," he interjected quickly. "For you, I'll do it, Claire. Clearly, it's important to you. You've already put yourself in enough danger for all of this, you should at least get one thing from it."

Her lips pressed to the spot between his shoulder blades. "I'm getting more than you know, Demyan."

Something in the lilt of her tone caught his attention. "I haven't forgotten what you told me in that elevator."

"Oh?" she asked.

"No. Monsters, you said. We all have them. You're right. I'd like to know what yours are."

Claire didn't bat a lash at his question and he suspected that what she had to say was a long time coming for her, too. "While I was finishing up college, I lived with my parents instead of a dorm. It was easier and I could come and go as I pleased. Friends stayed with me in the guest house occasionally, but one friend, she basically lived with me."

"Her name?" Demyan asked, curious.

"Tess. We grew up together, went to the same schools, choose the same college. I knew what Cavan was like, but I never warned her because I didn't think he'd hurt someone that close.

And I knew saying something to anyone about him wouldn't make a difference—they never paid attention enough to care or they were too busy sweeping his issues under the rug.

"I should have warned her, though," Claire continued, her voice wavering. "I didn't and one night when I stayed with a boyfriend and she went back to the guest house alone, Cavan must have noticed and did the only thing he knew how to do."

"Attacked her," Demyan muttered.

"Yeah. She might have been okay after if they gave her what she needed. Help, care, professional attention. Instead, Liam paid her family off, the rest of us were told to pretend like it didn't happen and move on. How was she supposed to move on? I was her best friend and I knew, but I couldn't say a thing or help her. And if I had, it might not have happened."

"I'm sorry," Demyan said.

"Don't be. I don't deserve that and I knew it then. Tess committed suicide a couple of months after the attack by slitting her wrists in the bathroom of my guest house where Cavan raped her. Everyone was too busy trying to pretend like it hadn't happened and she was fine to realize … well, you know."

"That she wasn't."

"Her suicide brought a lot of attention to our family. Attention Liam didn't want or need. Tess was the attack that made Liam send Cavan to New York, Demyan. Maybe to cool down, or whatever, I don't know. But it was too close for comfort. And I felt like I was the one who walked her straight into his den. I hurt her. I failed her. That was me. Because he came here, he attacked Ana, too. I am sorry that I was too weak and stupid to do what I should have."

"Claire—"

"So, I don't do that anymore. I don't turn my cheek to what they've done and I won't be like them. Not again. That's why I'm doing this. I will never be like them again."

• • •

Claire didn't realize she was crying until Demyan turned to face her and began wiping the tears from her cheeks with the pads of his warm thumbs. She batted his hands away.

"Don't, Demyan."

"What?" he asked.

"Don't do that—give me sympathy I don't deserve."

"I'm not giving you sympathy. I don't pity you or think you're misunderstood, or any bullshit like that, Claire. I also don't think you want or need me to. You've got monsters, demons. Some people do. I get that. I get you, okay. I get you."

Claire stilled under his words and wandering hands, letting him wipe the remaining wetness from her face. "We're strange, you and me."

"Maybe a little, but I'm not here to ease your guilt," Demyan said quietly. "It's not my job. I just want you to know I understand. That's all."

Claire stared up into Demyan's heated, intense gaze and got lost. Because he did know and she needed that more than anything. She reached up and threaded her fingers into the hair at the nape of his neck pulling him down for a kiss that seared her from the inside out. She heard him slam the bathroom door behind her before he pushed her backward a few steps into it.

"You're going to be okay," Claire told him.

Demyan nipped at her bottom lip like she hadn't said a thing. His hands slipped under her shirt, traveling up to push the bra she wore off her breasts. His mouth crashed down harder on hers the second time, taking away the air in her lungs and the thoughts in her mind.

Her sex throbbed, her wetness dampening the cotton panties she wore. Already, her stomach was clenching with anticipation for Demyan, his body, and what was sure to come. Her nerves felt like they were crawling under her skin, begging for more of him.

Need. Want. Hunger.

They did this so well together.

"Want you," he mumbled against her mouth.

"Yes, please," Claire breathed.

Claire let him shed her clothes, baring her to his heady desire. Demyan always made her feel so beautiful when he stared at her and she didn't even think he knew the effect he had. She thoroughly enjoyed watching his body move as he stepped out of his own pants and shoved his boxer-briefs down, too.

"We're something, huh?" Claire asked as Demyan worked her panties down over her thighs and off her legs.

"Something," he agreed before licking her inner thigh and

standing again. "I'd love to feel you coming all over my fingers and mouth, babe, but I just really fucking need to be in you, taking you … anything else but the crazy shit I've had going on for the last few days."

Claire shivered when his hand slid between her thighs to spread her legs and cupped her hot sex. His fingers glided along the lips of her pussy, opening them and seeking, drawing her wetness around her entrance with talented circles before bringing his digits up to her clit.

"I do that for you?" she asked.

Demyan smiled the sexiest grin. "Always."

"You do that for me, too."

"*Hmm*, good. This is one thing I wouldn't want to be alone in."

Claire shuddered when two of his fingers plunged into her sex, spreading wide to stretch her sensitive tissues in a way that always made her shake. "Oh my God."

"Yeah, you're so fucking hot and wet. Christ, you're tight. You're already ready for me, Claire."

She whimpered at the loss of his fingers, feeling her juices smear from his hand to her naked stomach. Under his urging hands, she turned to face the door, letting him place her palms on the cool wood.

"Here, stand on this," Demyan murmured.

She stepped up on the small stool he dragged over with his foot. It put her at just the right height so she could feel his erection resting against the crack of her ass as he kissed a hot path over her neck and shoulders.

"You're shivering," he noted.

"I want you."

"Soon."

The promise washed over her body like silk.

Claire watched over her shoulder as Demyan turned to open the medicine cabinet and pulled out a box of unopened condoms. She waited as he broke the seal, pulled one out, and made quick work of opening the packet and rolling the latex down his length.

Her thighs tightened, desperate to relieve the pressure and ache building in her clit. Nothing helped. Her wetness smeared along her sex and Claire reached down between her legs to feel how soaked she was. Under her fingertips, she rubbed her pulsing clit in tiny circles, her breaths picking up speed when she noticed Demyan watching her with an arched brow and a sinful smirk.

"*Mmm*, I like seeing you do that," Demyan murmured. "Keep touching, Claire. Show me what you like, beautiful girl."

She didn't have to show him anything. The man knew.

Even so, she did as he asked, spreading her legs wider on the stool so he had a better view of her finger going back and forth between working her clit and then thrusting into her pussy. It never took her long to come when she was masturbating and this time was no exception.

Her body began to tremble as she added a second finger.

"I'm ... I'm going to—"

"Come," Demyan whispered.

Shit.

His smooth, dark tenor sent her over the precipice. A cry fought its way out of her clenching throat, her knees buckling as bliss raged.

Claire didn't have to worry about catching herself. Demyan was already there, his strong arm curling her waist while his other hand nudged hers out from between her thighs. The moment her fingers left her sex, she felt the crest of his cock pressing at her entrance. With one thrust, her tight channel took his length to the hilt. The power behind his body meeting hers sent Claire into the door.

Her second cry was broken, the sound forming his name, needing.

"Fuck, fuck, fuck," Demyan hissed, his hand finding her hip as his fingers dug in to hold her tight to his groin. "You are heaven around me. Fucking *heaven*."

Demyan slipped his arm under her leg and lifted it higher, widening her stance again, though she didn't feel off balance with only one foot on the stool. He didn't give her any warning before he started fucking her.

Each drive of his cock came a little harder than the last. Every one of her cries turned louder, more desperate. She met him for each one, begging and needing more. She could feel her juices coating his length, making the harshness of his thrusts easier, better.

Despite the roughness in their fucking, Demyan was so soft, too.

His mouth on her skin, kissing, tasting, and loving. Quiet, whispered words that caressed her senses closer and closer to a second orgasm. His fingers dancing over her shoulder, tangling into her hair to move the heavy strands from her eyes.

"God, you're so fucking beautiful," he said.

Just like that, Claire flew again.

• • •

"Everyone assumes my motivation is solely based on revenge," Demyan said.

Claire turned in the passenger seat to eye her usually quiet companion. His statement had been so random, but considering what they were doing, she supposed it wasn't.

Demyan grew silent again as he watched out the front window, surveying a restaurant that was apparently closed for regular business, but was slowly filling with men connected to the New York Irish syndicate. Two weeks had passed quicker than Claire thought they would. All the planning Anton Avdonin had done for this went off without a hitch, now it was time to wait for the bomb to blow. Literally.

"If not revenge, then why are you doing this?" Claire asked, honestly curious. "To see your father's plans out?"

Demyan chuckled a dark sound. It never failed to amaze Claire how the simplest of actions where Demyan was concerned spoke volumes on the things inside his heart and soul, never mind what it did to her.

She wasn't entirely sure what to make of how he affected her. Frankly, she had decided to just take it one step at a time.

"No, not for my father, either," Demyan murmured, never taking his eyes off the restaurant. "Vera, actually. This isn't me settling scores or feeding my anger for what happened to Gia. Believe it or not, but that's never been an issue for me. I loved that woman, but I said my goodbye. And I blamed no one but myself for it and I still don't. No, this isn't about revenge."

"Vera, you said."

Demyan nodded. "I need my daughter to be safe. The only way I can do that is by ridding the one person who could hurt her."

"There'll always be more people than just Liam, Demyan."

"Not today there isn't. He's the only one who wants to hurt

her by way of me, anyway."

Claire settled back into the seat with a sigh. Demyan's hand dropped from the steering wheel. Claire thought he was going to grab the cell phone sitting in the cup holder, but instead his hand found hers resting in her lap. She let the warmth of the feeling roll up her arm and travel through the rest of her body at the seemingly innocent action.

Because it was Demyan.

And it wasn't innocent.

"I thought I had you all figured out," Demyan said, still staring out the windshield. "I thought I knew exactly who you were and all the reasons why you were doing this, but I think I didn't really know a thing."

"Is that a good thing, or a bad thing?" Claire asked.

"Could be both, I suppose. I've lived the last four years with the prerogative it's never good to get too involved with someone. You didn't give me much of a choice."

Her?

"You're talking in riddles, Demyan."

He chuckled. "No, those are just my crazy ass thoughts coming out all at once. I don't know what to do with you anymore or where I go from here."

"You do realize this is the natural progression of life, right?"

"Moving on, yeah, I'm aware. It's been a long time coming."

Claire smiled, letting her thumb roll over his knuckles. "We could just … leave it alone and see where it takes us."

Demyan sighed, slanting his head just enough to eye her from the side. "Claire, it's already picked us up and gone somewhere. You and I both know it."

Yeah, it had certainly already picked her up.

"I don't mind," Claire said truthfully.

"You scare me a little bit," Demyan replied. "Because you're strong in an unassuming way, you're quiet like me, and you're not making your life out to be about pleasing everyone else. I like that. A lot."

Well, then …

The ringing of the cell phone interrupted their conversation.

Demyan let go of Claire's hand to answer it and she felt the loss of him everywhere.

"Yeah, Boss here," Demyan said as he put the phone to his

ear.

Claire could make out the hum of the voice on the other end, but she didn't understand whatever was being said.

"Good, perfect," Demyan said, a tight smile curving his mouth wickedly. "Call me for confirmation, though I'm sure I'll feel it … yes, later."

The phone was dropped to the cup holder again.

"Ready to help your friend?" Demyan asked.

Claire's brow furrowed. "Kissa?"

Demyan nodded.

Her heart exploded with love and gratitude. "You never said—"

"I wanted to make sure things would go off as planned before I broached that. I don't want people searching for her after today." Demyan leaned over and opened the glove box, exposing a file crammed in the space. "That's all she'll need right there."

Hesitantly, Claire pulled the file out, opened it up, and began flipping through it. There were instructions on how Kissa was to travel from spot to spot, bus tickets, a flight pass, road maps from there, a land and a car title, an entirely new identity and past, credit cards, and so much more.

"I don't think she knows how to drive or whatever."

"We've thought of that. There will be someone who meets us closer to your aunt's and will direct Kissa from point to point until she reaches her destination. In that time, I'm sure she'll be given a few lessons in driving and she can do with it what she wishes."

"Oh my God, this is amazing," Claire whispered.

"They will never find her, never hurt her again," he assured. His hand found hers again. "Ready?"

"So ready."

• • •

Demyan hadn't driven two minutes away from the restaurant where the Irish mob was gathering before he felt the first blow of pressure hit the back of his vehicle. Two more waves followed and Claire finally took notice.

"What was that sound?" she asked.

Demyan sighed, not knowing how she was going to take the news about the bomb successfully blowing. Being told it was going to happen was one thing, but realizing you had a huge hand in seeing it through was another altogether.

Claire was so good in her heart—beautiful, even. It was difficult for him to correlate violence and death with someone like her.

"The bomb," Demyan said, trying to keep his tone level for her benefit.

Claire stiffened. "Oh."

"Yeah, we had it rigged up so that most of the impact would come from the back of the building and less toward the front. That way, the possibility of innocents outside the building being hurt were lessened. It wasn't a for sure thing, though."

"That's part of the deal, right?" Claire asked weakly.

"Basically. Kill a few good guys to get a lot of bad guys. It's better if you don't justify it at all, Claire."

She nodded. "I won't."

Easier said than done, Demyan thought.

Claire chewed on her lower lip and twisted her hands in her lap. He could tell just by the look on her face, she was tallying numbers and wondering.

"Seriously, don't think about it," Demyan said softly.

"I'm trying."

"Hey …" Demyan used one hand to untangle Claire's fists, hoping it would help her. "I want you to stay the night with me and Vera tonight."

Claire's head jerked up. "Yeah?"

"Yeah, pretty girl. Everybody on your end is going to be way too distracted to know better and you'll have to stay away for a couple of weeks or so until things calm down again. Vera won't understand why you can't be around, but she'll miss you."

"What about you, Demyan?"

"I'll miss you, too." Demyan took a right turn, guessing they were maybe fifteen minutes away from Brian MacBride's home. "Your aunt will be getting a call soon that her husband has been in an accident, once she leaves the house, you have three minutes to get in and get Kissa out. Convince her or don't, Claire, but you only get the three minutes. Then, we leave. Understood?"

"Yes."

"You can't save them all," Demyan murmured, needing her to understand that every trafficked soul couldn't become her personal mission.

It was an impossible goal.

"But I can save her," Claire said firmly. "One is better than none, Demyan."

Maybe that was the thing about Claire he liked the most.

It scared him, too.

CHAPTER FIFTEEN

Claire slipped into the Avdonin family home. Hearing the laughter coming from what sounded like the kitchen, she called out, "Anybody home?"

"Back here!" Viviana yelled.

"Christ, baby, not so goddamn loud."

"Is your age getting to—"

"Finish that sentence and I will not leave this house today, Vine."

Viviana snickered as Claire came into view at the kitchen entryway.

"Everyone's up bright and early, I see," Claire noted.

"Big day," Viviana replied.

Anton scowled. "Yes, big."

Apparently Anton was still sour over his only daughter getting married.

"A little early for your attitude to start making an appearance, isn't it?" Claire asked, only half joking. "The wedding is in what, four hours?"

The man's frown only deepened. "*Vine.*"

"Claire, don't poke at him today. I might not get him to the wedding, otherwise."

Claire grinned. "Sorry."

"He loves her, Anton," Viviana said quietly, as if Claire wasn't even in the room.

"I know, baby."

"So do you," she continued.

"Exactly."

"He is so good to her. He worships her. He is everything you wanted for her to have in a husband. She picked the right man. It's time to let her go."

Anton sighed heavily. "I don't know how to do that, Vine."

"You have four hours to figure it out."

"Fucking perfect," Anton muttered. "I'll be lucky to make it through this day without my heart—"

"Okay, if you finish *that* sentence, I won't do that thing for you later. And you so like when I do it, Anton."

Anton's mouth snapped shut audibly, making Claire laugh out loud. She didn't even want to know what Viviana was suggesting she wouldn't do for her husband, but it didn't take a fucking genius to figure it out.

Claire had to admit, seeing Anton and Viviana Avdonin at their age, still totally in love, enamored, and attracted to one another gave her hope that one day, she would have the same thing. That maybe thirty years into her marriage—if that ever came along—her husband would still want her as much as this man wanted his wife.

It was painfully sweet.

Anton watched Claire as Viviana finished clipping the diamond cufflinks on his suit jacket. "I'm surprised to see you here today."

Claire shrugged. "It's been a rough couple of weeks."

"Three," Anton corrected. "It's been three weeks, sweetheart."

"Yeah, I know."

"I thought Demyan told you to keep your distance and let the smoke clear."

"I tried."

A ghost of a smile—knowing and sure—curved Anton's lips. "Tried, *hmm*?"

Yes, and then she woke up that morning alone in her bed, realizing it didn't smell like Demyan's spiced scent anymore. It took her all of three seconds after she opened her eyes to count the days that passed since she had seen him or Vera. Sure, she talked to them over the phone but it wasn't the same.

"Tried," Claire repeated. "And failed. So, here I am. The smoke isn't cleared, I have no information since my aunt is half-drunk all the time now and her husband is dead, and this is probably going to get me in shit."

Viviana cleared her throat. "But?"

"But, I figure Demyan needs a date for Ana's wedding, right?"

Anton chuckled. "He does, my dear. It'll be a nice surprise for him to see you show up there. You're right though, it's probably going to get you in trouble. There might be press because of Ana's status as my daughter, not to mention Koldan. I'm sure we'll be photographed."

Claire shifted on her feet, chewing on the inside of her cheek. "Are you ready for that, too? I mean, for them to know it was you who attacked them?"

"Well, I'm not the boss anymore and I technically didn't make the final call for it, but yes, I'd say Demyan is ready for Liam to know. Are you ready for them to know it was you?"

"I want to say yes," Claire said honestly.

Viviana smiled tenderly. "Fear is not a weakness."

"But it debilitates like one."

"Only if you let it," Anton replied. "It'll be fine, Claire. Trust Demyan to know what he's doing when the time comes."

"That's why I'm here."

Viviana looked Claire's clothing over. "Please tell me you're not wearing that."

"No, but I don't have anything appropriate."

The grin Viviana suddenly sported said she was going to fix that. "Well, it's a good thing I like to spend money on other people then, huh?"

"What?" Claire asked, confused.

Viviana waved the question off like it should have been obvious. "I took Ana shopping last week for last minute things and while I was out, decided to pick up a few things for you."

Claire was dumbfounded. "Seriously?"

"Of course. You're a part of our family, Claire. Why wouldn't I think of you?"

Was she?

"Oh," Claire said faintly.

Viviana lifted a single brow. "Does that surprise you?"

Claire wanted to say no. After everything, it shouldn't have been shocking.

Anton stood from his chair, asking, "You're in love with my son, aren't you?"

"Would it offend you if I said you're not the first person I feel should hear the answer to that?" Claire asked back.

Anton nodded. "No, I wouldn't. But, I have a feeling you didn't come to our home today because you suspected Demyan would be here. I think you knew he would be at his home with Vera and you wanted to get us alone. Why is that, Claire?"

Claire forced back her nervousness, knowing it wasn't the time for it. Anton was damned good at reading people and his assumptions were spot on.

"Claire?" he asked again.

"I know it's not the right time with the wedding being today and all … I can't help it anymore, and I can't ask him."

Without asking, she suspected both Viviana and Anton knew she was talking about Demyan.

"For you, we would do anything, Claire," Anton said. "What do you need?"

"I want to visit Gia."

• • •

Claire stepped up to the gravestone, noting the cleanliness of the black marble and the fresh flowers on the manicured grass. A framed photograph rested against the bottom of the marker face out for the world to see. The blonde in the picture was smiling widely, looking away from the person taking the photo at something off to the side that the photographer hadn't caught.

It was no wonder Demyan loved this woman as much as he had. She was incredibly beautiful and in the moment caught in the picture, she seemed carefree. With a life like Demyan's, Claire understood his need to have someone who felt unaffected by the things surrounding him.

Claire sucked in a hard breath, sitting down on the grass cross-legged. "You weren't unaffected though, were you, Gia?"

Of course, silence answered Claire's question. The dead didn't couldn't speak. It didn't matter. Claire hadn't come to the grave to hear a dead woman, she'd come to talk to her.

"He sees fault in you, now," Claire said, pulling her knees up to her chest. "And I don't say that to sound haughty or contrite, I just say it because it's true. I think it hurts him more because he does see fault and he'd rather remember you as perfect; remember how he loved you as flawless and untainted.

"Because he did, right? Everyone likes to believe love is unconditional, but for some people it isn't. Yours certainly wasn't, Gia. Not for Demyan. He loved you from the time he was two-years-old. He spent his entire life following behind you. Mostly he remembers trying to play catch up with your whims and at the same time, trying to be this man you wanted him to be, and then suddenly you were gone, just like that. So, here he was, thinking he failed the one thing in his life that was supposed to be his. I don't know if you ever were or if you both wanted to be."

Claire sighed, feeling a tear slip from the corner of her eye. She didn't wipe it away because emotion was good, even if it hurt. "You loved him, I'm sure you did. But you didn't love everything about him and I suppose in a way I get that, too. But the thing about love is that we don't get a choice and you don't get to pick and choose the parts of a person you want to love and ignore all the things you don't. That just puts them on a damned pedestal they'll eventually fall from. When they do, they break.

"In love, you have to be willing to be ruthless and brutal because there's not another game in life that's more dangerous. Demyan thought he lost with you. I think he was wrong. So yeah, he loved you totally and he broke into pieces for you when he fell. You made him feel unrepairable. Ruined. It wasn't the first time he felt like he had failed you though, was it?"

"Claire?"

Claire turned at Anton's call, gesturing for him to give her one more minute. He hadn't questioned her earlier when she asked for him to bring her here and he didn't say a single word when she asked him not to tell Demyan of her request. Some things needed to be done privately and this was one of them.

Demyan wouldn't understand.

Turning back to the gravestone, Claire felt a sadness sweep through her insides. "I've heard enough to know you loved him, but you hated the pieces of him that made up who he was. I'm so sorry you spent your life loving a man who couldn't be different for you, a man who let you hate those pieces of him and love only the ones you wanted.

"I'm going to say what he won't, now. He loved you the way you deserved—entirely. You didn't give him the same thing back, but I will. I sincerely hope you understand why."

Claire stood, putting two white calla lilies down beside the picture. She recalled Demyan telling her of how he'd brought the same flowers along the first and only time he visited the grave, so she thought it fitting she leave one for him and Vera, too.

"I'm taking him back, Gia. I'm taking him back from whatever hell he's been in for the last four and a half years. I'm going to make him live because this is his life and he's spent enough of it chasing after you, waiting for you to tell him he's finally caught up. I suppose that means Vera gets to come along for the ride. She's the reason I came here today ... well, mostly.

"I love her," Claire whispered. "Everybody says she's a lot like you but to me, she's just like him. She's strong like him, resilient, but she needs a mother. I want to be that for her. And he was so scared to let her love me because I might leave her someday like you did. So, I'm going to take her, too. They're mine, now. Let me have them."

Claire wiped off the bottom of her cream dress that had brushed along the ground when she squatted down. Her trip to this graveyard, to this woman's final resting place, was the last thing Claire needed to do for herself.

Things might not end well for her, not where her Irish family was concerned, but that didn't mean she wasn't going to fight to get to the final goal. Because that goal was a family, a man she loved, and a little girl who asked Claire to be hers.

She so wanted to be Vera's person.

A mother, if that's what she needed. A friend on days when she felt like she had none. The confidant to go to when the girl's father was being stubborn like he could be.

A *someone*. Vera's someone.

Strangely, Claire felt like to do that, she needed to tell Gia it was going to happen—it was happening. She thought the woman, even dead, was owed the knowledge someone would be filling the spot that should have been meant for her.

And then there was Demyan, too. But Claire didn't feel quite the same way about Gia's relationship with Demyan as she did for Vera. It wasn't the same thing, and despite saying she would be taking him for herself, Claire didn't think she needed Gia's permission or even acceptance, if it were possible, for it.

Standing there at that grave, Claire didn't feel like she had to compete with a dead woman for Demyan's love. There had been a brief moment when she considered it might happen. Of course, she would, given Demyan's past with Gia. The thought didn't stay long and she was quick to push it out of her mind.

The fact was, Claire knew there couldn't be a rivalry. A past could certainly shape a person, but the strongest people would leave theirs behind. Demyan was stronger than most and he had yet to fail in making Claire feel like she was one of the most important people to grace his presence, even with their strange circumstances and lack of titles on their relationship.

Claire *wasn't* Gia Lavrov. Demyan didn't try to make her like Gia, but at the same time, he didn't pretend like Gia had never existed. Claire didn't want him to, either. There was a little girl who was so much more important than they would ever be and Vera deserved to know where she came from and how she got on this earth. She didn't fault Demyan for keeping Gia alive in that way.

Claire would never be the woman in this grave, even if someday she ended up in the same kind of place for her choices in getting involved with the Avdonins.

Claire also didn't need Demyan to tell her he loved her because she already knew even if he didn't yet. It was there in the way he watched her silently. It was his hand slipping into hers when she least expected it to and the way his fingers wove with hers to squeeze tight. It was how he loved her in bed, the way she felt him long after he was gone, and the affection in his stare that he hid so well.

Because that man ... that man could hide everything he was from the world, but he couldn't hide a goddamn thing from her.

So yeah, she knew.

Claire just wondered if he knew it, too.

• • •

"Demyan?"

Demyan turned on his heel fast to face the person who had called his name in her familiar, sweetly soft tenor. Claire smiled wide.

"What are you doing here?" he asked.

Claire shrugged. "You're not really the wedding type, are you?"

"Is it that obvious?"

"To me," Claire murmured. "I thought you might like some adult company today besides family, you know. Might as well make this bearable for you."

Without even thinking about it, Demyan held out a hand. Claire took it without hesitating and he drew her into his embrace to hold her tight. For a quick moment—because he couldn't afford for more with so many people around to witness his open affection—he simply held Claire to his chest, soaking in the smell of perfume and the heat of her body.

Claire giggled in his hold. The sound was like sweet music to Demyan. "Missed me, huh?"

"Surprisingly, yes."

"Why is that surprising, Demyan?"

Because he loved her.

Demyan wasn't ready to say the words. He chose something else instead, hoping Claire could read between the lines. "Woke up this morning and realized it'd been a good couple of weeks since we spent any time together and it sucked like nothing else."

"Sorry, but you told me it wasn't safe until things calmed down after the whole bomb incident."

"I know and it wasn't. Still isn't, by the way," Demyan said, sighing. "You probably shouldn't be here."

He felt Claire's smile curve against his dress shirt. "True, but like I said, no need for you to suffer through this day alone, Demyan. I didn't want to stay away anymore. I missed you, too."

"Thank you."

Demyan let her go, not that he wanted to. His heart raced, beating a rhythm that demanded he bring her back as close to him as he could possibly get her.

No, he couldn't deny it. Not if he wanted to and not if he tried.

Demyan was in love with Claire and despite the way it seemed, she had been so easy to fall for. A perfect match for his soul with holes and wounds still fresh and needing repaired. But that was the best thing about his lover. Claire didn't try to fix him.

The woman took him for exactly who he was and loved him because of it.

"God, you look good," Demyan appraised, whistling under his breath as Claire did a little turn on the spot for him.

The cream dress she wore hugged her curves in the sexiest way, the skirt falling at her knees. The neckline plunged far enough to hint at her cleavage, but it wasn't enough to send Demyan's jealous tendencies rearing their ugly heads.

Good thing, he thought.

No need to ruin his sister's wedding, after all.

"I hoped you'd like it," Claire said.

Demyan leered, baring his teeth teasingly. "Oh, I like it."

"Cost a small fortune. You can thank your mother."

Yeah, probably not.

"Let's not mention my mother picking out clothes for you that I enjoy in ways that are anything but innocent, okay?"

Claire's brow furrowed. "Why?"

"Because it's fucking weird, that's why."

"Your mom is my friend, Demyan."

"Maybe, but she's still my goddamn mother."

Her laughter was the best balm to his aching heart.

Because fuck yeah, sometimes it still hurt.

Demyan didn't know how to tell her the truth about his feelings, not now. He knew too much about her and she knew way too much about him. It surely wasn't going to be easy, but he didn't think he could live without her, now.

There was still way too much surrounding them for love to take importance over the rest. Demyan wasn't ready for reality to catch back up to him and slam him into the ground once more. The first time he loved someone had been hard enough because he lost her.

So, maybe he was a little scared of it, too.

Wasn't he allowed to be?

After everything, couldn't he keep it private for just a little while longer?

"There's a lot of people here," Claire mused, glancing around at the people gathering inside the ballroom. Some were already taking their silk-lined seats while others stood in large groups chatting. Far too many were watching Demyan and Claire, but he did his best to ignore those people. "Where's Vera?"

"Getting ready with the girls, I guess."

"Demyan," Claire admonished.

"What?" he asked.

"She's a girl, Demyan!"

"Uh, yes?"

"Stop it. She might be little, but she still needs you to tell her she looks beautiful before she faces a whole bunch of people in her dress and makeup, Demyan."

Oh, well …

Hold the hell up.

"What fucking makeup?" he asked. "She's not even five, yet.

209

Vera doesn't need to be wearing that crap on her face."

The next thing he knew, his daughter would want her own vanity full of that shit. No way. Vera was perfect without it, a lot like Claire.

Claire shook her head. "Of course, she's going to have a little bit of makeup on. To make her feel grown up and pretty like her aunt and grandmother."

"I said no," Demyan replied swiftly.

"Hey, I'm just saying. Better prepare for it before you see her and when you do, don't be an asshole if she's got a little bit of lipstick and blush on."

Holy sweet baby Jesus, he would *kill*.

"You're not wearing makeup," Demyan said, his hand coming up so he could trace Claire's natural, pink lips with his thumb.

She caught his digit between her teeth, biting hard enough to wake his body up. Demyan forced back the groan building in his throat and pulled his hand away from her sinful mouth. Not the time, he reminded himself.

Not the goddamn time.

"You don't like it," Claire said as if that explained it all.

"Yeah, but—"

"So I went without," she finished quieter. "Besides, no one is supposed to be more beautiful than the bride, right?"

Demyan grunted his disapproval. "Still don't want my daughter looking like a little—"

"Oh my God, Demyan. Whatever you are about to say, don't."

"Yeah," he agreed. "Better not."

"Go find her, tell her she is beautiful before she walks down the aisle with her flower basket, and then come find me again. Remember, keep the asshole in check when you do see her. Sound good?"

Demyan knew arguing with Claire would get him absolutely nowhere, so he chose not to. "Sounds great, babe."

Claire winked. "By the way …"

"Hmm?"

"There's something sheer and lacy under this dress."

Demyan didn't bother to hold his groan back that time. "My kid is in this place, Claire. Do not tease me until I'm going fucking insane and then leave me hanging because of responsibilities. I know that's what's going to happen."

"Yep, but I heard she was spending the night with your parents tonight."

"She is."

"Yep," Claire repeated, letting the word pop from her lips as she waved a hand at her dress. "And it's all black, too."

Fuck.

Just the way he liked.

• • •

Demyan made his way to the back of the hall where the private rooms were. The woman who appeared from one of the rooms wearing a tight dress with her hair in curls was not the person he expected to see, but he shouldn't have been surprised. After all, Koldan was Sofia's brother. Of course, she would be here today.

Sofia stopped up short the moment the door closed. "Demyan."

"Sofia," he greeted.

Might as well be polite. They ended things amicably. There was no reason to be an asshole to the woman.

"What are you doing back here?" she asked.

"Finding my daughter before she dazzles the crowd."

"Oh." Sofia smiled, waving at the door a ways down from the one she had exited from. "Vera's in there with your mother, the other girls, and Ana. I saw her earlier in her dress. God, she's adorable."

Demyan couldn't help his growing grin. "Yeah, she's something else."

"She looks a lot like her mother, too," Sofia noted quietly.

"The older she gets, the more she reminds me of Gia."

It was the truth, but it didn't hurt as much as it used to. Demyan had decided to be grateful for the reminder his daughter was, not that he had ever felt resentment to her because she resembled her dead mother.

"She's a really sweet kid," Sofia added.

"Thanks, but she doesn't get that from me."

Sofia shifted in her heels, avoiding his stare. "We're good, right? No hard feelings and all that nonsense."

Demyan shrugged. "No hard feelings, Sofia. This is only awkward if you make it that way, huh?"

"I guess you're right and we never had issues before."

"No, that we didn't. No point in starting now."

Her laughter rung out in the hall, but it was nothing like Claire's. It didn't quite feel the same or hit him like his lover's did. Come to think of it, no one had ever made Demyan feel like he did when he was with Claire.

Sure, he'd loved Gia, but no love was the same.

Claire's was so amazingly, blindingly different. Because she wasn't the same and Demyan knew it. Everything about her screamed different and he needed that—needed her. What he didn't need was to replace someone he already had and Claire was her own beautifully unique soul. One that somehow, someway, managed to compliment his.

It was still fucking terrifying.

"By the way, you were right," Demyan said.

Sofia arched a brow high. "I usually am, but about what this time?"

"You said I would thank you someday and I am."

"That pretty brunette I noticed with you earlier?"

Demyan nodded. "Yes."

"You're welcome. You deserve it, Demyan."

• • •

Vera twirled for her father, the coral colored dress she wore spinning wide and shimmering. She smiled bightly. Demyan got down to his knees and held his hands out to meet Vera's palms with his own.

"Oh, you look so pretty, my *dushka*."

Vera bounced on the spot, making her black curls bob. "Yeah?"

"Yes, so pretty."

He could do without the rose tint on her cheeks and the pink lip gloss, but Demyan let it go. She was still goddamn gorgeous no matter what.

If her hair was blonde instead of jet black like his, she'd be a dead ringer for her mother at her age.

"You look so much like your mother," Demyan told her.

The movement at the other end of the room stopped as several pairs of eyes turned on Demyan and his daughter. Why it was such a surprise to others that he spoke to his daughter about her mother, Demyan didn't understand. Vera came from Gia and she would always be a part of their child. It didn't matter if she was there or not.

"Did she wear pretty dresses, too?" Vera asked.

"Every single day. Even when we played in the dirt."

"I like pink."

"She liked yellow."

Vera grinned. "I like yellow, too, but I like pink more."

"I know, baby girl. Guess who came today?" Demyan asked, squeezing Vera's warm hands in his own.

"Who?"

"Claire."

Somehow, Vera's features brightened even more. The sight only proved to Demyan that whatever choices he made with Claire, however he decided to move forward with her, it would be the right one.

"Really?" Vera asked.

"Yeah, and she's excited to see your dress, so you better stay clean, huh?"

"I don't like dirt, Papa." Vera smacked her lips and made a face. "My mouth is sticky."

"Sticky?"

She pursed her lips for her father to see. "Sticky with lip stuff and I don't like it."

Oh, thank fucking *God*.

"Want me to wash it off for you, *dushka*?"

Vera nodded. "Please."

"Papa would be glad to, Vera."

Demyan plucked his girl up and took her into the attached bathroom, kicking the door closed behind them. Setting Vera on the counter, Demyan found some paper towels before turning on the sink faucet. He wet the paper towel and began wiping the glossy mess off his daughter's mouth.

As he tossed the paper towel into a garbage can, Vera asked, "Do you like Claire, Papa?"

He didn't even have to think about it. "Yes."

"Yes, but do you like her like Grandpapa likes

Grandmamma?"

Demyan faced Vera, crossing his arms as he regarded his far too perceptive child. "And how does he like her, Vera?"

Vera shrugged. "A lot."

"Like I like you?" he asked.

"No, that's different."

"You're right, it is. Doesn't make it any less important or special, though."

"But … is that how you like her, Papa?" Vera asked quietly. "Like Grandpapa Anton and Grandmamma Vine?"

Demyan smiled, something he was learning to do more often. "Yeah, that's how I like her, *dushka.*"

"What's that mean, Papa?"

"What?"

"*Dushka.*"

It was the first time she ever asked what the endearment meant in Russian, but Demyan suspected that was because he had been using it for her whole life. She was used to it by now.

"In Russian, it means I think of you as my little soul. In English, it's the same thing as sweetheart."

"Huh," Vera mused.

There was also one other meaning for it. "It's also the nickname for a certain type of Russian made gun."

Vera giggled. "Bang, bang."

"Exactly. Good?"

Vera matched his smile with her own. "Good."

Checking his watch, Demyan noted the time was close to when the wedding was scheduled to start. "Almost time to show off your dress. Ready?"

Vera let her father lift her off the counter and she hugged him tight as he opened the bathroom door to face the room full of bridesmaids and family again. Instead, the sight that welcomed them back into the private room was not what he expected to see.

Everyone had left but for Ana and instead of Viviana standing with her like she had been before, now Anton was there. Demyan cursed inwardly, knowing he was intruding on a private moment between his father and sister. He didn't want to interrupt them, though.

Demyan had to admit his sister looked angelic and beautiful in her white gown fit for a princess. All grown up and ready for life though he supposed that had already stepped in and kicked both of them on their asses. Ana got through hers a lot better than he did.

He hoped she was happy, now.

"I love you, huh?" Anton said, his voice thick.

Ana nodded. "Yeah, I know."

"My beautiful girl, look at you."

"God, don't make me cry. It took them an hour to get this crap done."

Anton laughed, the sound strained with heavy laden emotions. "I'm sorry, but I'm not ready to do this, Ana."

"It's a little late to be having second thoughts, Daddy."

"No, I've just been watching you run ahead for a long time, Ana."

Ana's thumbs swept across Anton's cheek, but Demyan caught the sight of the wetness his sister wiped away.

"Don't cry," Ana whispered. "You'll make me cry."

"I can't help it. I'm so happy and I'm so sad."

"I'm going to be okay because you raised me, you know that."

"I love you," Anton repeated.

"I love you, too."

"Always, my *dushka*."

"Always."

Vera's arms around Demyan's neck tightened like she wasn't ever going to let go, but he knew … fathers had daughters just to give them away.

CHAPTER SIXTEEN

"Dance with me?" Demyan asked, offering his hand to Claire.

Claire took his palm in her own with a sensual grin. "Sure."

He led them to the dance floor, drawing her in close once they were swallowed by the crowd of dancing guests. The crooning slow song was more to his tastes when it came to dancing if he danced at all. Usually, the music Demyan preferred was not suitable for this kind of thing.

Claire's fingers wove with his, letting him lead in the dance. "It was a beautiful ceremony."

"It was," Demyan agreed, sighing. "I think Ana is glad to be over the stress and Koldan is just happy to have it done with."

Claire laughed. "And Anton?"

"Knew about his misgivings, did you?"

"He didn't seem very happy this morning."

"He's happy," Demyan assured, knowing it was true. "But he's close to Ana and she's never been more than a twenty-minute drive away. She's his one and only daughter, so I imagine today literally felt like he was setting her free."

"I think if I ever get married, it'll have to be quiet, private, and less than twenty guests."

Demyan hummed as he spun Claire out from him before bringing her close once more. "I agree. I'm not big on the show myself."

"What was your first wedding supposed to be like?" she asked.

"Do you really want to know?"

"I asked, Demyan. I'm curious."

"Exactly how Gia wanted it. Big, four-hundred guests, a three-course dinner service, and a never-ending party. We wanted to be married shortly after Vera was born, so the planning was crazy though I never did much because no one asked."

Claire frowned. "That kind of party doesn't sound like you at all."

"It wasn't, but Gia loved a good celebration and I was

ecstatic that she had finally agreed to marry me, so I let her have and plan whatever she wanted for the day. The size of the wedding and all the nonsense of the day wouldn't have bothered me in the end, I just wanted to marry her. I would have been happy with whatever she wanted as long as it ended with her as my wife."

"That's actually kind of sweet."

"Yeah, I try." Demyan blew out a puff of air, staring at his sister and new brother-in-law as they danced twenty feet away. "I don't like to think a lot about those kinds of things between Gia and me."

"Why not?"

"Because the more I do, the more I realize things weren't ever as perfect as I thought. The longer I think about us, the more time I have to pick things apart. Then, it almost feels like I'm painting her with a black brush. Or rather, painting what we were with it."

"It's okay to be imperfect, Demyan."

"Actually, I think we were comfortable. I think we were easy. I know I loved her for most of my life because I just did and she was the only thing I ever really went after. We split up several times as teens, I messed around with a couple of girls in a casual fashion during that time, and then we got back together. She almost married another man in an effort to prove to everyone that she could and would disconnect herself from the Bratva. I don't remember falling in love with Gia, not at all."

Claire pursed her lips and glanced away. "Why does that bother you so much? Not every love is going to be earth shattering, Demyan."

"My father," Demyan said quietly. At Claire's confused stare, he added, "My father used to tell me that the best moments in his life were when he fell in love with my mother all over again. And it wasn't that he'd fallen out of love, but rather, life came back around to force him to his knees with the feeling."

Claire's hand tightened in his. "You never felt that."

"Not with Gia. I did love her, though."

Just not like that.

"And the best kind of love is earth shattering, Claire."

"Yeah, I suppose it is." Resting her chin on his chest, Claire stared up at Demyan with amusement. He was grateful for her change in topic when she said, "You're too tall, Demyan."

217

"Do I make you feel short, *krasivyy*?"

"No, you make me feel safe. Like nobody can hurt me here."

"Nobody will."

"Well, not when I'm with you, anyway."

Something sweet and unexpected flooded Demyan with pure bliss, but at the same time, a heavier feeling pressed down on his shoulders. "I might not always be able to—"

"And that's okay, too."

Why did he suddenly feel like they were talking about more than what was on the surface?

"Papa!"

Claire stepped away from Demyan just in time for little Vera to fly in between them. Without even asking, she grabbed her father's hands and stepped up on his shiny leather shoes, scuffing them with her faux heels. He didn't mind.

"What, you want to dance with me again, *dushka*?"

She had managed to wrangle him out on the floor a good ten times already. Vera loved to dance.

Vera nodded. "One more, Papa."

"Are Grandmamma and Grandpapa leaving soon?" he asked.

"After Aunt Ana goes, they says."

"Said," Demyan corrected.

"After, they said," she mimicked.

It wasn't often he needed to correct her speech, but Vera looked exhausted. She spent most of the day smiling for pictures, amusing the crowd with her lovely little self, and running around with the kids of guests. No doubt, she was ready for a good sleep.

Demyan had plans to check up on a shipment coming in later, and his parents offered to take Vera for the night so he could get the work done. Claire's interruption had changed part of those plans, not that he minded. He'd check the shipment tomorrow and be grateful for the alone time.

"Dance, Papa!"

"You're supposed to ask if you can cut in when someone is already dancing with another person, Vera."

Vera's brow puckered as she glanced over her shoulder at Claire. "Can I dance with my Papa?"

Claire winked. "Of course."

"Thanks," Demyan said.

"I'm going to go say goodnight to the bride and groom."

SHATTERED

Demyan grinned. "Say one for me, too. I'm busy with something more important here."

After all, Vera wouldn't dance on his shoes forever.

• • •

Demyan didn't make it home with Claire.

No, he made it as far as the hotel across from the plaza where the wedding had been held. Claire didn't bother to ask questions when he took them there, booked a room, and shoved her into an empty elevator as fast as he possibly could.

Apparently the man was too damn impatient to wait and see what was sheer, black, and lacy under her dress. Not that she cared or complained.

This was good, too.

"Oh my God," Claire breathed.

Demyan's mouth trailed a hot path up her exposed collarbones and over her racing pulse point. Backed into the corner of the elevator with not a soul around to hear her begging cries, Claire writhed under his weight keeping her pinned to the wall. Skilled hands were already up her skirt and his fingers skimmed the lace of her panties between her thighs. She was already soaked, her sex clenching the moment his digits came in contact with her slit.

"Cameras ... there's a camera there."

Demyan laughed darkly, the sound sending shivers spinning through Claire's insides. "Don't give a single fuck."

"But—"

"You're fucking gorgeous when you come and as long as nobody else gets to make you do it, I don't care if they watch."

"Oh, Christ," Claire cursed softly. "You're so awful."

"I am and you want it. Scream for me, pretty girl."

Demyan's fingers spread the lips of her pussy. It was the only warning she got before two of his digits were knuckle deep inside her channel. His free hand came up to trap her wrists high above her head as his mouth descended on hers. Claire felt his fingers thrust deeper, harder, into her sex as his tongue speared against hers.

When the pads of his fingers pressed into her G-spot, she was lost—straight up spun in sensation and need. Claire didn't recognize the sound of her own voice as a whine of his name fell

219

from her trembling lips.

"Fuck yes," he ground out, punctuating the words with a nip to her bottom lip.

Pain from the bite mingled with the ecstasy coiling through Claire's body. She could feel the juices from her pussy soaking his hand and her panties. Every time his fingers plunged into her sex, her nerves clawed for release.

"Come on, Claire," Demyan murmured along the seam of her lips. "I want to feel you coming all over my hand and showing me how much you love this, babe."

Claire canted her hips into his hand with the rhythm of his thrusts, allowing his palm to work against her sensitive clit. She panted her way through an orgasm that all but blinded her with the intensity. Demyan's soothing tenor hummed softly in her ringing ears as the crushing waves subsided.

When the elevator dinged for their floor, he barely had her dress fixed before people slipped inside.

• • •

Claire leaned in the doorway, admiring the definition of muscles roping Demyan's naked back. His family name, tattooed in Cyrillic lettering across the back of his shoulders, moved with the black stars resting directly below. When he poured a glass of vodka, Claire fucking shivered.

The man was gorgeous and he couldn't possibly know the effect he had on her when he was doing the most mundane things.

"Demyan," Claire called.

Demyan turned to face her, his lips instantly curving into a wicked smirk that heated her up from the inside out. She got wet at the sight alone.

"Fuck, yeah I like that."

Claire winked. "Thought you would."

The lingerie slip she wore under her dress was all black, sheer with a lace trim along the top and bottom, and it fell just below her hips. It was tight around her frame, showcasing every curve and the color contrasted against her cream toned skin.

"I'm feeling overdressed," Demyan noted.

Claire eyed the dress pants and leather shoes he wore, wondering why he had taken off his shirt and tie. "I didn't know you were getting undressed yet. A little forward, aren't you?"

Demyan shrugged. "Just making it easier on you, babe."

"Oh, was that it?"

"Partly. Mostly I felt suffocated in that tie and I hate the color pink, but my mother demanded I match my daughter. So, there's that."

Claire laughed. "Cute."

"Actually, I'm starting to think you're the one who's overdressed, Claire."

"How can I possibly be overdressed in this, Demyan? You can *see* everything."

"Don't care." Demyan pointed a finger at her and make a circle. "Take it off."

Claire gaped. "What?"

"Take. It. Off."

"But—"

"I really, *really* like it," Demyan murmured thickly. "And if you come near me right now with it on, I'm liable to ruin the fuck out of it, Claire. Take it off so I can enjoy it again sometime."

Well, then.

Claire used her thumbs to tug the thin straps off her shoulders before she shimmied out of the slip. Once it hit the floor, she stepped out of the pile of fabric and a little closer to her lover. Demyan watched her every move in silence, wetting his lips under his tongue as she stood in nothing but skin and black heels. She'd taken her panties off earlier because she soaked them in the elevator.

"My God," he groaned.

There wasn't a lick of embarrassment flickering through Claire's emotions as Demyan raked his attention over her naked form. Demyan made her feel sexy, adored and wanted.

Always, always wanted.

Demyan twirled his finger again. "Spin for me, *krasivyy*."

Claire did a slow circle. His white teeth flashed as he whistled low.

"Yeah," he said, still smirking in that cocky way of his. "Fucking perfect. Come here … slowly, of course."

She did as he asked, knowing full well he was taking her in with every step. Once they were inches apart, Claire stood on the toes of her heels to press a quick but searing kiss to his lips. Even in her stilettos she was still inches shorter than him.

The coolness of the hotel room pebbled her nipples. Demyan's warm hands cupped her breasts, his thumbs rolling over the rosy buds with just enough roughness to make Claire shake. Goosebumps littered her flesh instantly.

"What do you want?" he asked.

Claire's mouth felt dry, her throat closing around the words forcing their way out. "You, Demyan."

"Be more specific, Claire."

There was one thing Claire loved to see Demyan do and that was lose control. The only time she had ever seen it was when she was on her knees sucking him off. She wanted to see it again.

"I want you in my mouth, I want to taste you."

Demyan released a noise that sounded a hell of a lot like a growl and washed over her body like a promise. "Please do."

When he leaned down to kiss her again, Claire used the distraction to work on undoing his belt, button, and pulling down the zipper on his pants. His tongue flicked against hers, the taste of vodka zipping over her taste buds. She pushed his pants and boxer-briefs down over his hips, freeing the weight of his erection from the confines.

Demyan held her face firmly in his hands, keeping Claire from dropping down to her goal. His cock rested against her naked stomach, the pulse in his shaft beating like the drum of her heart. Softly, he kissed her forehead, peppering a trail down to the tip of her nose. His thumbs grazed her cheekbones in a tender way as he watched her through a lust fueled haze. She caught the edge of his digit between her lips to kiss the pad of his thumb when it came close enough to her mouth.

"You are far too good for me," Demyan murmured. "And I am way too selfish of a creature to let you go."

"You don't have to let me go."

"Good, because I couldn't if I tried."

Claire knew without a doubt in that moment, even if he never said the words and she hadn't already known before, this man loved her.

"I'm yours," she whispered, wanting him to know.

Demyan nodded. "I know you are, but I will kill any man who touches you, has you like I do, or even tries, sweet girl. I will fucking *kill*."

That admission didn't even frighten her.

"I'm yours," Claire repeated.

His thumb swept along the seam of her lips before trailing her cheekbone once more. "And I'm yours."

"Do you want to fuck my mouth, Demyan?"

His grin turned sensual. "The only time your mouth gets dirty is during sex and I have to say, I like it a whole fucking lot."

"Is that a yes?"

"That's a yes, babe."

Claire didn't need to be told again. She lowered slowly, kissing a line between his pecs and down over the railroad path of his abdominal muscles until the base of his cock was in her palm and her lips were kissing the tip. Her tongue flicked out to taste the soft skin of his member.

Demyan was circumcised, and Claire swore the head of his dick was more sensitive because of it. The moment her wet tongue came in contact with his cock, his hips jerked backward, he groaned, and his fingers curled around the edge of the small end table filled with liquor bottles and glasses.

Claire smirked, watching him from below as she took the crown of his cock into her mouth and sucked hard, letting her teeth graze against his shaft while her tongue circled the tip.

"Shit, shit, shit," Demyan muttered. "You've got a beautiful fucking mouth and you have no idea how good you look when you suck me off, Claire."

Deliberate and unhurried, Claire took her time swallowing his cock down to where her hand stopped her from taking any more at the base. She let him feel her teeth as she drew back up, her hand beginning a slow rhythm that would match her mouth. The saltiness of his precum exploded across her tongue when she came back to the tip. Over and over she teased him like that until she could feel his body vibrate under her touch.

"God, you love this, don't you?" Demyan asked, his voice hoarse. "I'd love to feel how wet you are right now from sucking my dick."

Claire smiled around his shaft, lifting a single brow. It was the only response he was going to get. Demyan released his white-knuckle grip on the end table to fist Claire's hair. She stopped sucking, knowing damn well what he wanted to do.

"Let me fuck your mouth, sweet girl."

She relaxed her throat, flattened her tongue against the pulsing vein in his shaft, and let Demyan take over. He worked her mouth slowly at first, his hips pumping and his cock sliding in and out of her mouth. The harder his thrusts became, the more Claire loved it. His muscles were taut, his control slipping. There was a shake in his hands and a tremor vibrating over his thighs.

Without warning, Demyan pulled his cock from her mouth, let go of her hair, and tugged her up from the floor. His hands cupped her jaw and he bent down to kiss her hard enough to turn her body to nothing but moving limbs and jumbled thoughts. His kiss always felt like he owned her and was taking her just for him.

Claire found herself breathing fast when Demyan pulled away. His arm came to wrap around her waist before he picked her up, turned them around, and Claire was suddenly seated on the end table.

Bottles of bourbon, vodka, whiskey and rum crashed to the floor along with a pile of shot glasses and tumblers. Demyan didn't seem to give a fuck as his shoes crunched on glass and the end table shuddered from the sudden weight. He stepped back from her just long enough to dig in his pocket before shuffling his pants and boxer-briefs the rest of the way down and kicking them away.

Anticipation, lust, and need curled through Claire's bloodstream as Demyan opened the condom he'd taken from his pants pocket and rolled the latex down his length. Her chest heaved, heat traveling over her skin when he stepped forward between her spread thighs. Demyan opened her legs wider until the best fucking ache settled deep in her muscles.

Claire grabbed the edges of the end table, needing support as she leaned back to the wall. Like this, her pussy was bared for him totally, slick with arousal from sucking his cock. His fingers curled around her ankles with a firm grip and Claire found herself memorized by the way he took her in. His cock was thick and ready between them, promising. She needed him and soon.

"God, I've fucking missed you," Demyan said, a heady groan following. "I've dreamt about fucking you, woke up harder than steel, and already half-way out the door to go and find you, babe."

Claire licked her lips. "Fuck me, then."

"B`lyad', Claire. You have no idea. None."

"Show me, Demyan."

Demyan wrapped her one leg around his hip, pulling her to

the very edge of the table at the same time. His erection dug into her stomach, the delicious throbbing in his shaft waking up every nerve in her body. He lifted her other leg around his arm, keeping her spread wide open for him and her calf high. The heel of her stiletto bit into his arm but he didn't even blink.

"I want you screaming my name and feeling me for days, Claire." His fingers pressed roughly into her thigh as he growled out, "And I can promise by morning, you won't walk out of here the same way you walked in."

"Fuck, I love it when you talk like that." Claire swallowed audibly, the desire beating in her heart. "That better be a promise, Demyan."

"I don't make threats, Claire."

"Good."

Demyan released her thigh to grab the base of his cock. He rolled the latex covered head through the fleshy lips of her sex, spreading them apart and smearing her juices across her sensitive folds. Every time his cock came in contact with her slit, he pushed just far enough in to let her feel him begin to stretch her open. He repeated his motions over and over until Claire was trembling, her toes were curling in her pumps, and she couldn't breathe because she wanted him so badly.

Claire fucking burned.

"Demyan," she whimpered. "Don't tease me."

"Like you teased me?"

"*Please* fuck me."

He offered no notice before he slammed his cock balls deep inside her shuddering sex. Claire gasped in a lungful of air that stung inside her chest as her sensitive tissues flexed around his intrusion, taking him in all the way to the hilt. Claire's head hit the wall with a dull thud, surprise and bliss choking her silent.

"Fuck, yes," Demyan hissed. "Feel that, Claire. You take me so well, sweetheart."

She did ... she always fucking did. Her body was made for his. The perfect fit.

Demyan didn't give her a chance to recuperate or ready for his next thrust. No, he just pulled out and then took her again. Claire's shoulders hit the wall hard, along with the table. His rhythm was punishing and unforgiving.

Every single pound of his hips into her body sent her into

the wall, but she loved it. Demyan was the only man she would ever allow to use her, to fuck her like this. He was the only one who could do it and still make her feel like she was the one who had control over him. His hand between her legs grazed her clit, his thumb working her aching bundle of nerves in circles until she was shaking, flooding him with her come, and crying out his name.

Claire's teeth cut into her lips when the first orgasm she hadn't even felt until it was there subsided. Demyan's hand left her clit and found her throat, the scent of her sex on his skin driving her wild. Her eyes flew wide open, meeting his as he squeezing just hard enough to gain her attention.

"Harder," she demanded through the force of his thrusts.

"Whatever you want, babe," Demyan muttered through clenched teeth.

He obliged to her order, widening her thighs, his hand at her throat gripping just a little bit tighter, and his thrusts reaching even deeper. Her mind and body were reduced to nothingness—liquid and sensations.

She couldn't manage to form words, only sounds. Cattish cries that clawed their way from her raw throat and moans that originated from somewhere inside her chest. Her heart raced as her walls clamped down around him for the second time, milking him as he fucked her through another orgasm. Her muscles protested, her back was sore, and she knew come morning things were going to hurt.

Fuck, she didn't even care.

This was beautiful.

The waves of ecstasy hadn't finished before Demyan picked Claire up from the desk, walked them across the hotel room, and tossed her to the bed. Her fingers found the sheets, fisting them while her back arched off the bed.

Like the predator he was, Demyan crawled over her with the kind of grace only a hunter could have.

She would gladly be his prey.

Always.

CHAPTER SEVENTEEN

While Claire slept on his naked chest, Demyan plucked up the cell phone he sat on the bedside table earlier. He dialed a familiar number, putting the phone to his ear as the call went through.

"*Ello*, Demyan," his father greeted on the second ring.

"Hey. Sorry, I know it's late."

"It's no problem. We're just getting Vera to bed."

Demyan chanced a look at the clock, noting it was two hours after his parents had left the wedding. "What took so long to get her to sleep?"

"Excitement," Anton said like that explained it all.

Demyan guessed it kind of did. "She was tired at the reception."

"And she talked the whole way home."

"Yeah, she's good for filling the silence," Demyan said, chuckling.

"Why the call, son?" Anton asked, cutting straight to the point like always. It was one of the things Demyan appreciated most about his father, even if it had been a rough four years between them. "I would never ignore a call from you, of course, but I figured you'd be busy tonight, you know."

Demyan grinned. He'd never hidden things from his father growing up, including his enjoyment of women. There was no doubt in his mind that Anton knew exactly what Demyan had planned for him and Claire with a night away and Vera safe and sound at her grandparents.

"Oh, I got that worked out, too," Demyan murmured.

"I'm, sure you did. Pride where it counts," Anton replied, laughing deeply. "Wasn't that what you used to tell me?"

"It is. I learned it from somewhere, though."

"Not me, kid. You got that all on your own. Not that I don't have that kind of pride, mind you, but you never saw it."

"Yeah, well …"

"Maybe it's an Avdonin thing," his father mused.

"Maybe."

"Why the call, son?"

"A couple of reasons," Demyan replied quietly, running his free hand over Claire's mussed brown locks. The silkiness of her hair felt like heaven under his palms, kind of like how her body always molded so perfectly into his. Her quiet, gentle breaths huffing against his chest said she was still fast asleep. "Firstly, I wanted to apologize."

Anton cleared his throat, obviously surprised. "For what?"

"Everything. Me. How I've pushed you away. Some of the shit I've said and a lot of things I didn't say. For hurting you, because I know I did quite a few times these last few years. Failing you if I have in some way. Not being the son you raised. I'm sorry, Dad."

Anton was silent for longer than Demyan liked before his father said, "Demyan, you're exactly the man I raised. Because if you weren't, you wouldn't have said the things you just did, and I wouldn't have known you felt that way at all. And no, you haven't failed me, but you have made me incredibly proud in a lot of ways. I am sorry you've had such a rough go of it, though."

"Didn't you?" Demyan asked.

"For some things," his father answered quietly. "They usually revolved around your mother in some way. My attachment to her could have been my downfall several times over. She's also my cornerstone, so I guess you could call it a double edged sword."

"I have a feeling that's just the way love works."

"*Mmm*, it could be. I let you have your story like I had mine, and while I hoped yours was easier, sometimes the road less traveled is better than taking the beaten path. Something better usually comes from it. You're in love all over again, aren't you?"

Demyan smiled. His father knew him too well. "Yes, but in a completely different way."

"I'm listening."

"Fearlessly," Demyan said. "I love her fearlessly because I've already lost everything once and it won't happen again. I won't let it."

Anton chuckled. "Then you have one thing to your benefit already. Nothing can stop you unless you allow it to, Demyan."

"That's my hope, Papa." Claire shifted on Demyan, mumbling something he couldn't understand before settling again. He rubbed his hand up and down her arm as he went back to the phone call. "You don't know how many times I've stared at my phone and wanted to call you, but I couldn't. I know that sounds stupid because you've always been there for me when I needed you the most, but I couldn't let myself break apart again. I already had one foot in the door to being right back inside that black hole. I don't think I would have made it out a second time."

"Depression," Anton said, voicing the word Demyan hated to hear the most. "You can say it, son. You were depressed."

"For a while," Demyan admitted. "And then I just existed. She woke me up again."

"You said there was another reason for your call, what was it?"

"He's going to come, probably soon. I can practically feel it in my fucking bones."

"Liam," Anton said, filling in the obvious blank.

"Yes."

"You don't sound worried, son."

Demyan stared at the clock again, watching as the minute changed. Time was ticking down for him, but it wasn't proverbial anymore. It was real. "I'm not."

"I want to be surprised, but I can't say I am," his father noted. "Talk to me, Demyan. Tell me what you've done."

"A lot. I've done so much, Papa. I've been waiting four long years for this. I am not afraid of Liam Dolan."

"I always assumed you were frightened he would come back on you."

"For a while," Demyan replied. "And then I realized it was inevitable. Eventually, he would come back and try to finish what he started with me. I learned my lesson. I'm smarter this time around."

"You're being vague."

Demyan laughed, but even the sound was strained. "I'm different, but he's not. Liam is the same, he's unchangeable but for his age. He's always going to be cold and cruel. His main goal with me will always be to hurt me and to cause me pain because that's what he does best. The man is unfeeling and appealing to his sympathetic side is pointless as he has none.

"You know, when he told me that he considered Vera for the hit on Gia, I didn't realize it at the time, but he lied," Demyan said, propping his head up with a pillow carefully, as to not disturb

Claire. "He didn't consider my daughter at all. If he had, he would have known instant death for Gia didn't guarantee Vera's life would end, too. What was better for her, Dad, for Vera to die with her mother, or live an entire life without her? There was no considering there, none."

"I think I'd be more interested in why Liam has let Vera live all these years after his promise to take two from you, son."

Demyan nodded, though his father couldn't see it. "My point exactly. Because this is better for him, more pain he thinks. My child suffers, and therefore, I suffer. His circles are vicious, but mine are a little worse."

"He's still the same, you mentioned," Anton said. "What do you mean by that?"

"When everyone around him fucked up, he had to handle it himself. He had to come, he had to fix the issue, and he had to make all the calls. Liam has to have control, and given his sociopathic tendencies, I would guess he likes things to be the same. I thought it was arrogance when he had one of his men serve him, but I've had years to consider it, and I don't think that's it at all. I think he needs regularity, similarities, and schedules."

"Demyan—"

"When he comes down on me the second time, he's going to do the exact same thing, but this time, he'll do it himself."

"Because they fucked up with Gia," Anton said, finally getting it.

"Yeah. I can almost guess his every move from the moment he figures out it was Claire working with you. It'll be like Gia all over again."

"But you know this time." Anton blew out a heavy breath, saying, "What have you done?"

"Spent four years considering a man who tried to break me, found myself thinking like he would, seeing things the way he does, and waiting. And when Claire invited me in and gave me the chance, I took it. Then, I fell in love.

"At first I thought of my involvement with Claire as a way to get to Liam in the end," Demyan continued, unbothered. It was time to tell the truth, and explain just how little they all really knew about him and how far he was willing to go. "She woke me up and all that thinking and waiting I'd been doing suddenly made a lot more sense. Draw him out, give him another reason to come at me once more … even if a lot of people got hurt by it."

"And then you fell in love," Anton muttered. "God, Demyan."

"I know. I think this is better, though. The follow-through is the easy part here, it's getting her out alive that's going to be hard. I wouldn't have cared before, but I do now. You weren't the only one with plans, you know. I don't want to hurt her in the process, but …"

"It might be inevitable," his father finished.

"Liam feels no fear, not if he's like we believed he is. I can't make a man scared of me or death if he doesn't know how to feel it, Dad."

"Doesn't mean you can't make it hurt, Demyan."

That was the goal, wasn't it?

"I love her fearlessly," Demyan said, repeating his earlier words.

"Does that include letting her go, Demyan?"

Demyan wanted to say no, but doing so meant if he failed to keep her safe, he would lose who he was again. The shattered pieces of his soul Claire mended would fall and he'd no longer have one foot in the door walking toward the end, but be jumping for it.

Anton didn't need to know that.

Demyan changed the topic instead. "How long before you can get the jet into the air?"

Anton made a noise under his breath that sounded a fuck lot like a grumble. "Six hours off the tarmac, son."

The jet in question was a model his father had purchased a few years earlier after selling his older one. Old weapons charges still kept his father from being able to fly out of the country, but the private jet, hired pilot, and fake documents allowed Anton to do whatever the hell he wanted.

"Barbados is nice this time of year," Demyan said.

"Ana is on a plane for Paris currently."

"The wedding hadn't worked into the plans, but it's as good of a time as ever to get people away for a valid reason, I suppose. Ivan and Eva will gladly tag along for a vacation, I'm sure, Dad."

"And Vera?"

"In your safe at the club," Demyan replied. "I've thought about this for a while. She's got her pick of names, but I'm sure she'd like something pretty."

"All Russian?"

"Of course. She'll ask for me, want to call me, but it's better there's no contact just in case. Let her be sad if she needs to be and tell her I miss her and love her."

"I will. You'll be just fine, Demyan."

Yeah, he hoped so.

"And we'll stay away until it's safe again," his father added.

Because you always—*always*—handled family first.

Yeah, Demyan learned his fucking lesson the first time.

"Don't call me after tonight," Demyan said. "I'll call you when it's done."

If he could.

• • •

At some point in the night, Claire had managed to clamor her way onto Demyan's chest and stay snuggled there. Like a little bear cub, her face was buried into his body with her hands curled around her face in fists. He'd covered them with a heavier blanket and tucked it around her shoulders, but she didn't stir once. She slept soundly, unbothered by the things he knew would soon be happening around them.

She just slept.

He didn't move her, but he didn't sleep, either.

Instead, he watched her, felt the movement of her body in the dark, and heard her quiet breathing. It lulled him into the closest thing to sleep, but all he could do was think, consider, and plan.

Morning peeked through the crack in the drawn curtains, sending a single ray of sunlight casting across the room and over the bed. Spores of dust danced in the yellow stream, the color promising a beautiful day.

Demyan's one arm rested behind his head like a pillow while his other held tight to Claire's naked lower back. His thumb swept back and forth across the patch of skin above her backside, his body siphoning her softness and warmth like it was a drug. It was his own silent reminder that for the moment, she was here and okay.

So okay.

"*Mmm*, good morning."

Demyan smiled at the sound of Claire's groggy, tired voice. "Morning, sweetheart."

A feather light kiss pressed down to the spot above his heart. The erection he'd been ignoring for the better part of two hours made itself painfully known again at her innocent gesture by twitching against her stomach. She wiggled her lower half just enough for her body to rub along his hard length in a promising way.

"God, how long have you been up?"

"Never went to sleep," Demyan confessed, staring down at her green eyes surveying him.

It was only then she noticed her position. "I'm sorry, you could have told me to get the fuck off you, Demyan."

"I liked it."

"But—"

"I liked it."

Claire molded back into his chest with a contented sigh. "Still should have woke me up. And you must have gotten up sometime because you smell like peppermint."

"You rolled off me a little while ago and it gave me the chance to get up and do my thing. When I got back in here with you, you got right back on top of me again. It's been a while since I've had you in a bed," Demyan murmured, driving his hand up her spine and letting his fingers skip over her skin. "I like having you in a bed, you always want to be close and touching, like I'm a blanket or some nonsense. I don't mind, Claire."

"Oh."

"Yeah, best way I've spent a night in a while."

"A sleepless night," she muttered. "I am so comfortable right now but …"

Demyan laughed at the shimmy her lower half did. "Go, I'll be right here when you get back, *krasivyy*."

"You better be."

He felt the loss of her in the bed before she was even fully gone. She disappeared behind the bathroom door with a coy wink and giving him the best view of the swell of her ass. Five minutes later she crawled back on top of him, stretching out over his form with a soft mewl that sounded a hell of a lot like a kitten waking up, smelling like peppermint and him.

"Thank God for mini mouthwashes and toothpaste, although

233

I could do without using my finger to clean my teeth," Claire informed before pressing her lips to his.

The kiss started out slow and sweet with every brush of her mouth to his but quickly deepened the moment her lips parted to allow him in. Demyan groaned her name as her tongue struck hard against his and her lower half rolled gloriously along the length of his cock. With her legs straddling his hips and her knees pushing into the mattress, she was in the perfect position for her pussy to grind his dick. He could already feel the wetness of her sex slicking him up with every cant of her hips.

Claire pulled away from the kiss far too soon for his liking, resting her forehead to his. "Yeah, it's a really good morning. Sex and a shower sounds perfect."

Demyan laughed but sobered quickly, realizing something important. "I don't have any more condoms, Claire. I only keep the one on me just in case. I didn't know you were coming last night. I mean, I don't really care because it's you, but you—"

"Don't care, either," Claire mumbled, her mouth finding his again.

Demyan was lost the moment those words left her pretty lips. He drove his hands between their bodies, spread her thighs further, and positioning his cock at her entrance while she kept kissing him. Sliding into her hot, tight core bared and aching was the best thing Demyan could ever remember feeling. Her channel hugged every inch of his cock, soaking him with her tart smelling juices and taking him deep.

Claire sunk down his length, her body shuddering while he filled her. Demyan's hands found her ass, his fingers digging into the supple flesh to hold her tight and lift her off his length before slamming right back in. Claire's head fell back, her hair tickling his skin.

"Christ, you are so fucking wet for me. Always ready for me, babe."

"God, yeah," Claire breathed, her green eyes glittering with approval and desire. "I love this, feeling you."

With another thrust that was hard enough to send her sprawling over his chest, Claire's face contorted with absolute bliss. Her cry was loud and beautiful, like fucking music to his ears. Her fingernails clawed against his shoulder and neck, throwing him straight into insanity. Her teeth cut into her bottom lip, but it did little to muffle her second cry when he lowered her roughly on his cock again.

What control he had left was gone with the sight of her above him, so willing to be taken and marked by him. Demyan fucked her harder, needing to feel her come undone all around him, wanting all her cries swallowed by his kisses while he found her deepest, darkest ecstasies. The harsher their sex turned, the more she begged.

Demyan rolled them over so she was on her back and he was above her. Claire's head tilted back into the pillow, desperation crawling out with her whimpers as her teeth clenched. Her pussy clamped around him, the sounds of their fucking driving him to take her harder still.

She was so, so close.

He just wanted to feel it.

Claire's fingers weaved into his hair, tugging at the stands. His teeth found her shoulder, biting in and giving her the sting of pain right back. She tasted like sex, him, sunlight and life on his tongue.

Nothing was better than this.

Nothing.

• • •

"Probably not the best time to say this, but I miss Vera."

Claire laughed, poking Demyan's side under the blanket. "Why wouldn't it be a good time? I miss her, too."

"We're naked and … yeah."

"Oh, well, that's life."

Demyan snorted under his breath. "I guess. I do, though."

"Want to get up and go? Check out is probably soon. We'll have a goddamn maid knocking on the door and kicking us out before we know it."

"No, I booked the room for a couple of nights just in case."

Had he? Claire couldn't remember. The night before was just a blur of them, bodies tangled together, sweat beading down her skin, and bliss in her blood.

"We could still go and pick her up early from your parents."

"Can't," Demyan replied.

"Why not?"

"Currently, she's twenty-thousand feet in the air, sitting in a private jet, on her way to play on a white sand beach in one of the most beautiful and safest places she could ever be. Her name won't be Vera, no one knows she's even gone, but it was the best thing to do for her right now."

Claire was frozen in place. "You sent her away."

"I did, just in case. It was a last minute thing. Don't worry about it, babe."

She didn't know if she could do that.

"You hungry?" Demyan asked.

Claire shrugged in his warm, strong hold. "Getting there."

"Fucking you is a workout. I'm starving."

She didn't even bother to hide her smirk. "Thanks."

"You're welcome. It was a compliment."

"Oh, I know."

Demyan's hand on her ass tightened, his fingers digging in harshly to her sensitive skin. Claire sighed her pleasure at the selfish touch. "And how do you know that?"

"Because you told me so."

"No one else touches you, Claire. No one but me."

"I didn't forget what you told me." She kissed his pec. "Just you, I promise."

Claire didn't mind his demanding, possessive tendencies about her, even if they weren't labeled with proper titles and all the nonsense that came along with it. She had long ago decided she wanted to be his, anyway.

"You know, that does nothing but turn me on, right?" Claire asked, cocking a brow. "It's not very scary, Demyan."

"For you, it shouldn't be frightening." Demyan flashed his white teeth in a sneer. "For a man, it might make him piss himself. You're mine, that's all there is to it."

"Yours."

"He's going to come for you," Demyan informed.

Claire shivered, but it wasn't from the words. She already knew what Demyan meant and who he was talking about. No, she shivered from the feeling of his fingertip drawing soothing, loving circles over her shoulder. She felt his lips press to her mussed hair as his other ghosted down her side. With barely any prodding at all, he'd woken up her lust all over again.

Christ, they spent half the morning in bed fucking,

whispering, needing—*feeling*. She wanted a shower, but that meant washing the smell of their sex and him from her body and she wasn't ready for that.

The world didn't exist for the moment. Only they did.

Claire leaned up to find his kiss, letting him burn her all over. "I don't want to talk about that right now."

"We need to," Demyan replied simply, his tone offering no chance for argument.

Sighing, Claire tucked herself back into his side. "A buzz kill."

"*Hmm?*"

"That's what you are, a goddamn buzz kill."

"Claire, stop."

"Well," she grumbled half-heartedly. "You are. We were having such a good morning and you just had to go and—"

"Bring us back to reality, babe. Because eventually we have to leave this room and I need for you to know what's going to happen."

Claire pushed away from him, grabbing the blanket to take with her and hold to her chest. He let her go, thankfully. She needed the space. "You can't possibly know what's going to happen and frankly, I think it might be better if I didn't wonder, Demyan. If I do, I'll be terrified. Is that what you want, for me to be scared?"

"No, I want you to be prepared and not living in some delusion that you're untouchable," he said, seemingly unaffected by her irritation. "You are not untouchable, you are human. You should know what might happen and why."

"Liam will kill me if he gets his hands on me, that's what's going to happen. I think it's pretty self-explanatory, Demyan."

"You're wrong. So wrong."

Claire felt pinned in place. "What do you mean?"

"Liam's main goal is to hurt me as much as possible. I have no doubt he's kept tabs on my family over the years, just to see how our family is or might have been growing. He's odd like that, but he's smart, too. I bet for him, it's a way of picking out the weaknesses."

"Your point?"

"Ana's wedding was highly publicized because of the couple's status. Those pictures will have made the rounds by this morning.

He'll have them—he'll see us. Anyone with any sense would know just by looking at a picture of me with you that I am so in love with you, even if I hide it well.

"My father worships my mother, but he was always careful about showing affection to her in public," Demyan continued like he hadn't just blurted out seven words that Claire couldn't forget. "It wasn't hard to see that he loved her, though. It was just difficult to distinguish how much or how deep his love really went for her. I think I'm like him in that way, or that's where I learned it from."

I am so in love with you.

"Those pictures of us will be out there," Demyan repeated. "Liam will know and because of that, no, he won't kill you."

I am so in love with you.

"Demyan—"

"Listen to me, please. Not immediately, anyway. He won't kill you the moment he catches you … and he will catch you, sweetheart. Not his men, but him. His men fucked up the first time with me, they didn't do what he needed them to do which was take two lives from me. When he comes this time, it'll just be him to do the job."

Her heart ached.

I.

Am.

So.

In.

Love.

With.

You.

How could he not see how those words affected her? Separately, they meant nothing. Together, from him, they were everything. Of course, she knew. Hearing him say it was something else entirely.

A confirmation.

A need.

A shelter.

"Not immediately," she heard herself echo.

"No, because he'll want me to hurt; he'll want me to be terrorized again; he'll want me panicked. Liam will need for this to feel like Gia all over again. He might take you from your apartment or even the hospital. Anywhere you frequent, somewhere in the open to show his power and control as if it were a way to tease me."

"And he will catch me," she whispered.

Demyan nodded. "I have to let him because if I run, he'll follow. Men like him always do."

"What else?"

His hand found her thigh, squeezing gently. The tender action grounded Claire instantly, giving her affection she didn't even know she needed until he offered it.

"Liam thinks lowly of women," Demyan said, sighing heavily. "He's proved it in his business, in the way he treats his family, and hell, he's even said it. How did he treat you before this?"

"Like I didn't exist most times," Claire admitted. "Other times when he had no choice but to see me, he dismissed me because I wasn't Cavan, I wasn't important. I didn't mind, you know."

"I get that. This won't be the same."

Claire's heart found her throat. "I didn't think so."

"You will literally be proof to him in his mind of how worthless women really are. To him, you've betrayed him, the life, and the mob—those things are most important to Liam and you've pissed all over them. He is not going to be even remotely respectful; he'll call you names, he'll taunt and threaten you with your family, maybe me, or possibly the things he'll do to you. They will hurt, they will scare you, and you'll want to bolt if you think you have a chance, but know that no matter what, he is not the kind of man who will give you an opening to run, even if it seems like it. Do not run."

"Why not?" she asked.

"Because he is like an animal, especially in his anger. Like any animal, if you force him into a corner, he will bite back. Don't fight, don't run, and try to the best of your ability to keep him calm and pleased. If you somehow force him into a situation where he feels there is no other choice, he will end you, even if it means losing the prize of hurting me. Don't show arrogance or rudeness. Respect what he believes is his position."

"Okay," Claire said. "I don't understand how you know any of this."

"I've had a long time to pick that man apart. A long, long

time, Claire. Do you want me to keep going?" Demyan asked.

Claire nodded, but she couldn't speak again.

"Always do as he says, even if everything inside is screaming for you not to. He might hurt you, hit you, but he won't kill you if he doesn't have to because he'll want me to see that. Don't be surprised if he thinks of you like nothing more than a dog, one he can abuse however he sees fit. It's just his mindset and the best thing you can do is be compliant, soft-spoken, and well-behaved. He likes weaknesses, he thrives on manipulating them, so try not to cry and don't beg. Never let him see those things. Never *give* him those things to hurt you with."

"I'm not very good at hiding when I'm scared," Claire said.

"Fear is not the same thing. Fear will remind you about these things. Fear will keep you alive."

"What about you?"

Demyan smiled, but it was laced with sadness. "I'm going to try and save you."

"Don't try to save me. Do. Because I love you, too."

"I know you do. Don't panic when it happens."

"Because it will happen," she said.

"It will happen," Demyan replied.

CHAPTER EIGHTEEN

After saying her goodbyes to her last patient, Claire gathered her things from the nurses' station, clocked out, and changed out of her scrubs like she usually would. Once she was inside the elevator going down to the ground floor, she pulled out her cell phone to call Demyan.

He answered on the first ring. "Hey, babe. How was work?"

No fear or worry edged his voice, not even a shake. Claire wasn't surprised. It had been two weeks since the wedding and there hadn't been a single incident to say Liam was coming for her. Demyan didn't talk about it, but he assured her there were bulls keeping a close eye on her. Claire never noticed one of them.

She had simply decided to go on with life and her days as she normally would. What difference would it make? Claire was happy. Demyan made her that way. She trusted him. But she still worried all the same. It was impossible not to.

"Work was good."

"Did you want to meet up for supper?" Demyan asked.

"God, yes. I'm starving. How about the Georgian place on Brighton Avenue, does that sound all right?"

"Sounds perfect."

"In what, thirty?" Claire asked.

"Sure. I'm finishing some things up and I'll head over. My place or yours tonight?"

"Yours," Claire said instantly. "I miss Vera, so …"

"Yeah, I know. Feels like she's there sometimes. Love you, huh?"

Claire smiled, because yeah, she knew. And it was so fucking good to know it. "Love you, too."

"See you in thirty, babe."

Claire shoved her cell phone into her messenger bag as the elevator doors opened to the bottom floor. She pushed her way through the evening crowd of last minute visitors to the hospital to get to the second set of elevators for the car park. Employees of the hospital had the top four levels for personal parking, but it was a bitch to have to go down one elevator only to take another all the way back up again.

She didn't make it to the second set of elevators.

A familiar figure leaned against a corridor wall that lead to the back end of the hospital's ER. He stood three feet away, close enough for her to smell the scent of his cologne and whatever smoke he'd had. His cool, cold demeanor never changed as he regarded Claire through icy green eyes that burned her skin. Liam Dolan twirled a thick, snuffed cigar between his fingers while the rest of his body was a stone statue, totally unmoving.

Dead.

Death.

She could feel it radiating off him from a mile away.

Claire chanced a glance around, noting the people milling about, oblivious to the sudden panic threatening to suffocate her. The grip she held on her bag tightened, her hand itching to reach for the cell phone inside.

Something said she shouldn't.

Run, her mind whispered.

Demyan's voice was louder: He will catch you … Don't run.

"Please don't make a scene," Liam said, his voice coming out almost bored. "It's a damn shame when I have to clean those kinds of messes for little bitches like you."

Claire refused to grace his diatribe with a response.

"While I don't truly care, I would like to know why you did this, Claire."

"Tess," Claire said instantly. "I did it for Tess. And Jen Troy, Lilian Casen, and Ana Avdonin. I did it for every woman you let Cavan get away with hurting, all those girls you brushed off and overlooked. I did it for them."

"Cunts," Liam murmured in the most unaffected fashion Claire had ever seen someone speak with. "Useless, utterly insignificant cunts, the lot of them."

"To you. Not to me."

"Women have no value in this world but for the wetness between their thighs and their ability to spread them when told to do so. Your brother understood that. You, on the other hand, are fucking worthless, just like your goddamn mother, Claire. I should have put her down when Dylan first started bringing her around, a lot like I'm going to do to you … and then she managed to produce Cavan, the only thing she was good for, so I gave her a pass."

He'll call you names, he'll taunt and threaten you … They will hurt.

Claire didn't even blink when Liam added, "There will be no pass for you, my dear."

Liam pushed off the wall with the grace of a cat jumping from a high tree limb. Before Claire could even considering turning to run, her uncle's hand had caught her upper arm, squeezing as roughly as he could. The shocking pain of Liam's fingers digging into her muscle was enough to make her want to scream.

"Make a sound and I will slit your tongue down the middle and let you choke on your own blood until I have to put you out of your misery," Liam warned.

Claire fought against her instinct to flee.

Don't fight. Don't run.

"Can you walk like a proper lady on your own two feet without making a fuss, or shall I force you to move?" Liam asked.

Demyan was still there talking in her mind, pushing down her fear.

Always do as he says … be soft-spoken.

"I can walk," Claire whispered.

"Good, you are making this much easier than I assumed it would be." Liam moved forward into the crowd of people behind them and Claire followed quietly at his side. Low enough so no one would hear, Liam said, "They were beautiful wedding pictures the papers printed. I imagine Anton is quite proud of his daughter though you would probably know more than I."

"He was pleased," Claire replied.

"And his son, what of his boy?"

Claire tensed, feeling Liam's hand on her arm tighten again. Her knees nearly buckled from the ache. She didn't want to talk about her lover with Liam; she didn't want to give him that opening to hurt her. "I—"

"What of his boy, whore?" Liam asked again. "I saw the pictures of you two, and even one with you holding his little girl. Does he love you?"

"He's happy," Claire said honestly, refusing to answer the second question.

Liam did the closest thing to a smile that Claire thought he could, which was nothing more than a fucking sneer. "I hoped so. I have waited a long time to finish my job with him. It'll be good to have this nonsense over and done with finally. Perhaps I will get the pleasure of seeing him break. I missed it the last time."

Sickness welled in Claire's stomach as bile spilled on the back of her tongue.

"You digust—"

Immediately, Claire found herself somehow tripping over her own two feet. She knew without a doubt that wasn't actually the case, as the strong grip Liam had on her turned into a violent shove. Claire's knee hit the tiled floor as the side of her head bounced off the cement wall.

She couldn't stop herself from crying out that time. Pain spread like a blooming flower through her temple. The nausea rolled harder. Her vision blurred as she tried to steady her swaying and get up from the floor, but she couldn't move. Her messenger bag slipped from her shoulder to the floor with a thud.

Maybe she would have thought it lucky that Liam had turned violent in front of so many people … maybe, if he weren't Liam.

"Oh my gosh, are you okay?" Claire heard someone ask.

"Don't worry," Liam responded to whoever stopped to help. Claire could almost see the charming smile her sociopathic uncle wore to lull the good samaritan into believing his lies. "She's perfectly fine, my dear. Simply tripped over her feet. She's clumsy sometimes."

"If you're sure …"

"I am. You're fine, aren't you, Claire?"

Claire would have screamed her denial for the world to hear, except Liam had leaned down and was holding her hand in what appeared to be an innocent gesture to help her from the floor. It wasn't innocent at all. His fingernails bit into her palm deep enough to force her to her feel even through the dizziness she was experiencing.

"Ready to leave, Claire?" Liam asked.

Claire nodded.

Apparently, the bystander had moved on, satisfied with Liam's lies.

"My bag," Claire managed to say.

"Leave it. You won't be needing it after today."

Don't fight.

Feeling unsteady on her feet from the pain in her head, Claire let Liam lead her through the hospital. She could barely see as they exited the building's revolving doors at the main entrance from the blinding sunlight. Still, she peered around desperately trying to see anything in the small emergency parking lot that might help her. There was a bit of traffic, both from vehicles and people.

Maybe, if she could shake off the dizziness, she could make a run for it. Surely Liam wouldn't make a scene in front of a bunch of people and run the risk of getting himself in trouble. Right?

No matter what, he is not the kind of man who will give you an opening to run, even if it seems like it. Do not run.

The moment those words passed Claire's mind, Liam's hand found its way to the back of her neck. Like a suffocating noose, he grabbed tight, forcing her to stand straight and stare at him again.

"Beautiful day for killing, isn't it?" her uncle asked.

"Beautiful," Claire echoed.

"Try not to be difficult and make me chase you, Claire. I have plans and I don't wish for them to be ruined by your petty nonsense."

I have to let him catch you.

Don't try to save me. Do.

"Follow me," Liam ordered.

Claire did as she was told.

Liam weaved in and out of the cars in the main parking lot. Claire couldn't help but wonder why her uncle had run the risk of getting a ticket by parking in the emergency parking lot instead of the car port like he should have, not that it was important. She supposed her mind had a funny way of coping with stress if those were the things she considered walking to her death.

As Liam stopped beside an unfamiliar dark sedan, Claire did another sweep of the parking lot with her eyes, but came up with nothing. Before she had turned back to her uncle, Liam's hand snapped up and cracked across her face, sending her flying to the ground beside the car.

Pain and blood saturated her mouth. Claire spit red saliva to the pavement, tears welling in her eyes. Liam stood above her looking down, coldness radiating off his entire form as he turned unmoving and crueler in a blink.

"No cameras sweep this part of the parking lot, my dear," Liam informed. "I've been watching you for a week and this was an interesting and easy way for me to take you from him. Funnily enough, I couldn't help but notice how the rest of Demyan Avdonin's family has suddenly up and disappeared from the state, yet you remained. Why is that?"

I have to let him catch you.

Claire swallowed back the fear threatening to silence her.

Fear will keep you alive.

"I wouldn't go with them," she lied.

Liam's gaze narrowed. "So, he knew I would be coming, then."

"He's been waiting for it."

"To your knees, girl," Liam demanded with a dismissive wave.

"Wh—"

The toe of his leather shoe landed on her ribs, taking away her breath and ability to speak. Her cry lodged in her throat and she realized her position and the cars surrounding them kept her from view. No one could help her.

"To your knees, girl," Liam said again. "If there is one particular thing I despise the most about the female gender, above all else, it's the constant need to have me waste my breath with useless chatter and reminders. I will not repeat myself again and you will do well to remember that. Your life has an expiration date, but I certainly don't mind throwing you out before it arrives, Claire. Do you understand what I'm telling you?"

She nodded.

"Good. Now, what did I say?"

"To my knees."

She got up, the pavement scratching her exposed skin as the dress she changed into after work fell above her knee line and her leather boots weren't high enough to use as a buffer. Below him like she was, Claire almost felt like she had just put herself into the most vulnerable position of them all. She did not want to be at this man's mercy in any way.

Liam reached out with a single finger to touch her face, his nail digging into her cheek. There was nothing about the action that felt tender or well-intended. As his finger found the spot under her chin, Liam dug a little harder, forcing Claire to look upward. She could taste blood on her lips and she was positive Liam thoroughly enjoyed seeing her as she was.

Evil.

He was so fucking evil.

"You're in the proper position, now," Liam said. "All bitches should be on their knees, waiting to serve or be struck. Which would you prefer?"

Don't be surprised if he thinks of you like nothing more than a dog ... the best thing you can do is be compliant, soft-spoken, and well-behaved.

"Neither."

"There are only two things I will accept coming out of your mouth from this point on, Claire," Liam said.

Respect what he believes is his position.

Liam tapped his finger under her chin and it felt a hell of a lot like a warning. "Those things are *yes* and *I'm sorry.*"

Claire shivered but hid it well enough. "O—"

His palm slapped under her chin hard. More blood spilled over her tongue.

"Yes," Claire forced out.

"And?" Liam asked.

"I'm sorry, Uncle Liam."

Liam dropped his hand, reaching over to open the back door of the sedan. "That will have to do for now. Remember those words and this will be a much more pleasant trip."

Trip?

"Get in," he said, nodding at the back seat.

Claire hesitated even though she knew better than to do so. One sharp look from above sent her scrambling to her feet and rushing to get inside the vehicle that felt a hell of a lot like a prison once the door was closed.

She didn't want to earn herself another slap, after all.

Liam climbed into the driver's seat and turned on the engine. In that unnerving way of his, he watched her from the rear-view mirror as he buckled his seat belt. "Be quiet, don't demand answers from me, sit still, and perhaps I'll give you something to knock you out during the flight."

Oh, God.

Flight?

Flight.

Demyan said nothing about Liam possibly taking her out of state. He didn't prepare her for this and Claire didn't know how to react or respond. How would Demyan know?

No, no, no, no.

Panic and terror saturated her from the inside out. The sick feeling pounding at her stomach returned with a vengeance while pain still clawed at her temple and her mouth. A blurriness still remained at the edges of her vision and her thoughts were slower than usual. She couldn't help but wonder if a concussion was the culprit from smacking the wall.

Claire bit down on her tongue to force herself to remain calm and well-behaved like she needed to be. Neither of the things she was allowed to say or the things she wanted to scream appropriate responses, so Claire kept her mouth screwed shut. It hurt to do it, though, and every instinct she had fought against it.

Liam noticed that, the edge of his mouth curving into a wicked smirk as he put the car into reverse and began backing up. "You're shaking, girl."

"Yes."

"Fear has a lovely smell, Claire."

Fear will keep you alive.

"Do you love him?" Liam asked.

Demyan's voice was still in Claire's head like a record on repeat that she couldn't stop. Not that she wanted it to. At the moment, thinking of him was the only thing that helped her.

He likes weaknesses, he thrives on manipulating them.

Demyan was definitely one of Claire's weaknesses. Seeing him hurt, or even considering him in a situation where he could be was one of the last things she wanted. Liam would surely use that to his sick advantage if he could.

Still, Claire couldn't lie about her feelings. "Yes."

"Fantastic. This should prove to be interesting." Sighing with a roll of his eyes, Liam added, "While I am sure you think yourself in love with the Russian, I can assure you it's far from the truth. Love is merely a concept—it's nothing more than an infatuation weaker people allow themselves to believe in for the sake of feeling closer to someone else. As if humans need the intimacy a notion as ridiculous as love could provide. It doesn't exist. Convincing you of that fact would be a waste of my time so I won't bother trying, but it's true, nonetheless."

"To you," Claire said before she could stop herself.

Liam was incapable of love, he wouldn't know the emotion if it slapped him in the face. It wasn't a surprise that he didn't believe the feeling could literally wrap itself around a person's entire heart and soul to fit two people together in a way that permanently bound them to one another.

"That's one, Claire," Liam said, putting the car in drive and hitting the gas hard.

Claire didn't ask what he meant, but it probably wasn't something good.

It never was with Liam Dolan.

"For every time you speak out of turn or answer me with anything less than what I told you to, you will earn yourself another mark. Each mark is a lash, girl."

Claire blinked, unsure if she'd heard him correctly. "A lash?"

"Two," Liam murmured.

Claire straightened, her spine turning ramrod straight in the backseat as fear trickled through her bloodstream like a poison. Her brain finally caught up with her goddamn mouth. "I'm sorry, Liam."

"Well, you certainly will be. As I said, a lash for each one. So far, you've earned yourself two, Claire. You'll meet death, to be sure, but I will make certain you are wishing for it long before your maker comes, girl."

Panic held Claire in its choking grip. She couldn't catch her breath as anxiety overloaded her senses. Down at her sides, her hands balled into tight fists. Her fingernails cut into her palms, the pain keeping her from reaching for the door handle to open it and jump out of the moving vehicle. She wanted to be as far away from this man as humanly possible.

Something said she wouldn't get far.

He was going to beat her. Like a fucking animal.

The sad thing was, Claire couldn't find it in herself to be surprised.

"And," Liam continued, unbothered by Claire's panic attack in the backseat, "… it'll do you perfectly well to suffer for what you've done. You deserve it. I'm going to enjoy delivering it while you wait for your Russian to save you."

Claire didn't care about the possibility of earning herself another lash later on when she asked, "How do you know he's going to try and save me? He'd be better off to let you kill me."

Liam smiled. It was the most sinister sight Claire ever witnessed, but it was there. She was pretty sure it was the only time she ever saw him do it, too.

"Oh, he'll try, girl. He couldn't save the other one, and I would be willing to bet the guilt has all but killed him inside. I'm sure others will pity his poor daughter once I make her an orphan for good this time, but I think it's rightfully deserved."

"My God, for what?"

"Being a girl isn't enough?" Liam asked seriously.

Claire wanted to vomit. "You are ...."

Awful. Vile. Disgusting.

"The word you're looking for is heartless, Claire. I do not feel for anyone, and certainly not for a tiny Russian girl who will grow up to be nothing more than a useless Russian whore."

Oh, Vera ...

"And that's five," Liam said. "Continue if it pleases you. I didn't realize you had a taste for pain."

You will literally be proof to him in his mind of how worthless women really are ... try to the best of your ability to keep him calm and pleased.

Claire checked herself. She needed to get back in the right frame of mind and not a combative one that might possibly send Liam into a fit where he could hurt her or worse.

Trust, trust, trust.

Her mind chanted it.

"I'm sorry, Liam."

"As I said, you surely will be."

Liam fell silent as he drove through the parking lot. As he came to the spot where he had to drive past the exit of the car park, their vehicle slowed down. There was a row of parked cars on Liam's side, all patients or visitors, Claire suspected.

One, in particular, caught her eye. It was a dark cherry colored Chevrolet truck. A newer model with chrome all the way around. The windows were tinted so dark she was sure they were illegal. Even so, Claire had the distinct feeling she had seen that truck before.

Liam rolled his window down a few inches at the same time his car slowed to almost a stop in front of the truck. Before Claire could comprehend what was happening, Liam had a gun with a long silencer pointing out his window directly into the truck's front windshield.

Claire's scream was muffled into her palm as three pops followed one after the other in quick succession. The bullets shattered the front windshield of the truck, exposing the body of a man slumped over the steering wheel. Blood had splattered all over the back windshield. Calmly, Liam hid his gun from sight, rolled up his window, and the car moved forward. Claire didn't even know if anyone had noticed.

"Why—"

"Six," Liam interrupted.

Claire flinched.

Liam answered her unfinished question, anyway. "That was one of the two fools who have been following you for the last week. The other stays inside the car port and when your vehicle leaves, he follows, and then that man I just killed follows him. They're predictable."

Questions burned on the tip of Claire's tongue, but she wasn't looking forward to earning herself more strikes than she already had.

"I have to leave him something to find, after all," Liam said quietly.

Claire didn't want to hear one more thing. She had a feeling she wouldn't get the choice.

• • •

The ringing cell phone resting in the middle console of Demyan's SUV drew his attention away from the road. Keeping one hand on the wheel, he reached over and hit the speaker button to answer the call.

"Avdonin speaking," Demyan said.

"Boss, we've got a problem."

Ice slipped through Demyan's veins, dread filling him to the brim. He wasn't surprised. This wasn't a shock and honestly, he'd been waiting for this call.

In fact, he'd waited four long years for it. Maybe not for the call to be about Claire, but someone—anyone—he loved. Plans were in place, of course. A smart man always planned. A patient man waited silently while he did.

Demyan was a patient man, one who had learned from the very best.

So yeah, he knew and he didn't need to ask, but he did anyway.

"What kind of problem?" Demyan asked calmly.

251

"Alik's dead," the bull answered. "Cops are thick as fuck in the area, Claire's car hasn't left, and her shift ended twenty minutes ago."

Demyan took the news in silence, letting his heart and thoughts absorb what the bull was telling him. While fear would keep Claire alive, it would do nothing but debilitate Demyan. He couldn't afford to get lost inside his head.

Not right now.

Instead, he steeled his nerves for what would surely be the most difficult thing he ever had to do.

"In my office at the club there's a key in the top right drawer," Demyan informed the bull. "It's my house key. Chances are, once the officials figure out Alik was Russian mafia, they'll come knocking on my door. As always, the bastards know Anton is no longer head of the Avdonin Bratva, so they'll look to me. Someone needs to be there to deflect my absence."

"Absence?" the bull asked.

Demyan wasn't stupid and neither was Liam. Brooklyn— really, New York as a whole—wasn't Liam's territory. He didn't have enough Irish in the state to have an impact or fight a decent war against the Russians. If it came down to it, even the Italians would probably chase Liam the fuck out of town.

Nobody wanted a piece of that man's mess.

Nonetheless, Demyan figured that made Liam predictable in the end. Hopefully to a fault. Liam would not stay in New York, he just wouldn't. Liam was liable to get Claire to a place he felt he had the upper hand on Demyan in. Detroit.

It made the situation all the more dangerous and particular, to be sure, but Demyan was thorough. He'd considered this—he'd considered everything.

"Boss?"

"Someone needs to be there to deflect my absence," Demyan repeated, not wanting to go into details about what he knew and his plans. The fewer people involved, the less their mouths would run and speculate. He didn't want to take the risk of it somehow getting back to Liam, not that it was likely. "This might take a few days."

• • •

Demyan walked across the private tarmac, offering a nod to the men standing at the bottom of a jet's reclined stairs.

"Boss," Boris greeted.

"Prince," Rory followed with a grin.

"Evening," Demyan replied, coming to a stop at the stairs and glancing up. He'd had this jet on standby for ten days and paid a mighty fucking price to have the pilot and crew on twenty-four-hour call, waiting for his signal.

Today was the day.

"How long's it been?" Boris asked.

Demyan didn't even check his watch. "Forty-five minutes since I got the news."

"Chances are, he's not in the air yet," Rory noted. "Last time he came in on a privately chartered flight and he had to wait to be approved for a last minute flight again when he left. Maybe today was just the right circumstances to grab Claire and he didn't have time to schedule another flight time."

"That's my hope," Demyan said. "I'd like to land before he does. Detroit is his, but I just have to piss in a few choice spots to make it mine. Anyone answer up there?"

Boris nodded. "It's not a big Bratva there, though."

"Are they willing to help?" Demyan asked.

"They're willing to make a diversion if you need it, but only if it's absolutely necessary."

"That's helping."

"It is," Boris agreed. "They have to consider the backlash they might face after, too. We'll get it done either way, Boss."

Boris was the kind of man who had fuck all to lose in life and didn't fear giving up what he did have. Rory was loyal to a fault when it came to the Avdonin family and always would be. If Demyan was going to pick any men to help him, even if it meant losing them in the end, these were the men he wanted to have at his side.

"Everybody on board?" Demyan asked.

"The one you asked for," Rory replied.

"And?"

"They're agreeable so long as they don't have to be involved with anything that might get them in trouble."

"Well, not until after, anyway." Demyan chuckled though the sound came out hollow. "If I do this right, he's not going to know what hit him."

Rory smirked. "How long have you been planning this?"

"Years—"

"God willing, the poor girl doesn't get herself killed in the process," Boris muttered.

"—but she gave me the chance to get close enough to finish it," Demyan said, not missing a beat. "I want to be in the air in less than ten minutes. Let's go."

• • •

"There will only be so much I can do with what I have and our current situation, Demyan," the doctor informed.

"You're a last resort," Demyan replied dryly.

Leland sighed, rubbing at his forehead. "What are you expecting?"

Demyan didn't want to answer that because it meant thinking about it, too. Between the time Liam got his hands on Claire to the point when, or if, Demyan got her back, it was hard to say what the man would put her through.

Horrible things, maybe.

Things that could kill Demyan.

"Demyan?" Leland asked.

"Violence," Demyan answered. "I expect him to be violent."

"With this ... Claire."

"Yes."

"And—"

"I expect her to need care," Demyan interrupted sharply, wanting to end the conversation. His mind had better things to do than ponder the sort of abuse Liam could be leveling on Demyan's lover. "I expect her to be hurt. That's why you're here."

Demyan watched the darkening horizon glitter with lights below as the plane reached proper altitude. His ears ached from popping, but that was the least of his worries. Far too many things rolled around in his head for him to settle on just one thing. Instead of trying to shove them down, he allowed them to take over.

The numbness would surely come back—he needed it to survive and do what he had to do. For now, Demyan needed to feel and let his heart settle the war with his mind before he could go back to the cold place that wouldn't rule him through this.

He missed his daughter and her sweet laughter first thing in the morning when she crawled into bed and woke him up. He missed their nighttime chats, her childish smile, and the dozen and one books she always had to read before going to sleep. He missed how she smelled like sunshine and home.

Demyan wished he had told his father more things the last time they spoke. Stuff he hadn't said over the last four years that Anton probably deserved to know, like the fact Demyan couldn't possibly be who he was now if he hadn't seen how strong and determined his father was.

All the parts of him that made Demyan a good man and boss came from Anton Avdonin.

Every single one of them.

Demyan thought of his mother, too. Viviana had been a quiet, supportive cornerstone for Demyan growing up. Probably in more ways than she knew. His mother had never voiced displeasure about her son's choices or the person he strived to be, she simply let him grow and follow the path he wanted to take. She was beautiful inside her soul—light, love, and life his father always said. He figured he understood that, now.

He wished he had taken the time to see Ana and Koldan off on the night of the couple's wedding. Or at least, took the time to say goodbye. He regretted not dancing with his sister at her reception because he couldn't remember a time when he had danced with Ana.

The house he had never felt like calling his home was in the back of his mind, too. Strangely, he missed the hallways and floors he hadn't connected with safety and security before now. He missed his bed, especially when a green-eyed brunette was filling the empty space beside his.

Claire.

Claire, Claire, *Claire*.

Her name was present, a constant in his mind and unrelenting in its quest to take center stage for the moment. Demyan let it.

Everyone else would be perfectly fine, if not a little heartbroken for a while, if he didn't return. They would eventually heal from whatever might happen to him—life would move forward because that's what it did.

But Claire didn't have that gift or the ability to do any of those things if he failed.

One foot in the door, Demyan thought.

He was right there again, standing inside that precipice between wanting to stay and needing to leave. The last time he stared into that black abyss, Vera pulled him back in and kept him with her. Despite thinking someday he might resent her for it, Demyan never did.

Vera wouldn't pull him back a second time.

One foot in the door.

If he didn't succeed, he'd jump the fuck through it.

So yeah, he thought about Claire.

CHAPTER NINETEEN

Claire's knees ached and her eyes stung. She felt disoriented and confused, but the sensations didn't last long. A sharp pain radiated through the left side of her face, making her snap fully awake.

Liam sat a foot away, his elbows resting on his knees as he regarded her with a blank stare. He shook his hand, and the burn in her cheek confirmed her suspicions that he must have slapped her. "Ah, she's awake."

Well, I am now, Claire thought.

She barely remembered being stuck with a needle before Liam and another man shuffled her onto a waiting plane. Apparently being given a sedative—or whatever the hell that had been—didn't mean Claire was off the hook when it came to Liam's twisted punishment for what he considered to be her disloyalty. The moment the plane had reached the desired altitude, Liam made Claire get out of her seat and forced her to her knees between a set of plush leather seats and told her to stay there.

"We're ten minutes to descent, girl," Liam informed. "Sit and buckle up, or the pilot will have a proper fit. I would hate to kill the man for being annoying and then have to explain it later."

Claire blinked, uncertainty filling her to the brim. Her thoughts felt sluggish and trying to move only added to the mess her mind was.

Before Claire could attempt to move again, Liam struck out and slapped her hard. The force behind the hit sent her flying to the carpeted floor with a sob she couldn't hold back. Dark chuckles echoed from the man sitting across from Liam as he watched Claire struggle to regain her breath and will on the floor.

Don't fight.

Respect ...

The words screaming in her head, warning her to keep quiet, didn't stop her rush of anger.

"Bastard," Claire hissed, feeling her lip begin to swell around the throbbing cut it now sported.

"Eleven," Liam said like he was talking about the weather.

What? Eleven?

Claire glared up at him, not even bothering to hide her hatred. "I haven't—"

"Twelve. And you talk in your sleep."

She spat blood to the floor.

"Fuck you."

Liam's expression didn't change. "Thirteen."

Demyan's whispers became louder.

Claire listened. "I'm sorry."

"You will be."

• • •

The Bratva isn't about you, Demyan. It's more than you. There is no one man, there is every man. You are not going to like every goddamn man, but you need them. Manage it, son, or figure out what in the hell you want to do in life other than this because you'll never make it as a boss.

Demyan blinked out of the memory, the scent of a city that wasn't his filling his lungs as he stepped up to the exit door of the plane.

"You good, Boss?" Rory asked.

"Am I?"

Rory's brow crinkled. "What?"

"Boss," Demyan clarified. "Am I one?"

He was, of course. That didn't mean he currently felt like one.

Had he earned it? Was he made for this? Did he do the right thing?

Would any other man make the choices he had? Would they have let a man like Liam Dolan take their very heart and soul just for the chance of getting a piece of theirs that had been lost back?

Monsters, his father once said. Love made them one.

"What the fuck is this all about?" Rory asked.

Demyan wet his lips, knowing he'd thought about that particular memory for a reason. "I hit Alik once and he never fought back. Do you remember that?"

"You were sixteen, stupid, and had one hell of a temper when people talked and you didn't like what they had to say. Yeah, I remember it. A lot of guys in the Bratva probably do, Prince."

"Interesting way to put it," Demyan murmured.

"You're not the first fool to lose his temper, Boss. Trust me."

No, probably not.

"Anyway, I was thinking how I hit him and he never came back on me for it, not once. He always respected my position, never defied me, and he had every reason to dislike me after that. I don't know, I suppose it makes me feel low, knowing he died today doing a job I asked him to."

"Prince, take a fucking look around," Rory said, laughing darkly. "I'd say you're sitting pretty high at the moment."

Second-guessing yourself was a bitch, Demyan knew. One he didn't need on his back. The flight had gone quicker and easier than he expected it to, but that didn't mean shit. He had a long way to go and the more time he spent away from Claire, the worse his doubts became.

"Did he have a family or anything?" Demyan asked.

"Couple of kids, two different mothers, no wife," Rory informed.

Demyan filed that info away for later. Those kids were going to need to be financially provided for in the future.

"Hey," Rory said, drawing Demyan from his thoughts.

"Yeah?"

Christ, why did his throat feel so raw and tight?

"Whatever that is right there," Rory said, waving a finger in Demyan's face, "… let it go, Demyan. Shake it off, get out of that headspace, and leave it at the fucking door. Whatever you need to do so we can get started, do it."

Leave it at the door.

Demyan glanced at the exit of the plane, figuring it kind of fit with the analogy. "I can do that."

"Good. You are good, right?"

Well, he'd really like to talk to his father, but that wasn't an option. Demyan chose the next best thing. Nothingness. Numbness bled into his nervous system slowly, feeding him the drug he craved.

"Perfect," Demyan replied. Noting the workers fueling up the plane, he added, "See how much cash they need shoved in their pocket to get us a couple of jugs of that shit, would you?"

Rory arched a brow. "Jet fuel?"

"Yeah, jet fuel."

• • •

Claire's teeth cut into her lip as Liam fisted her hair and forced her across the tarmac. Every inch of her demanded she fight back, screamed at her to hit him, hurt him … just do something to show him she wasn't the weak, worthless female he thought she was. She had never felt more like dirt on the ground than she did at that moment.

"Move faster, girl, or I will kick you the rest of the way," Liam warned.

Defiance bubbled through Claire, promising to get her in even more trouble than she already was.

Not considering the consequences, and knowing what Demyan had told her about running, Claire slapped at Liam's face, her fingernails clawing into his cheek to draw blood. Her compliance through the trip must have lulled the man into the idea that she wouldn't fight back at all, because he instantly released her hair with a hissed curse.

"Fucking bitch," Liam growled.

Claire took the opportunity the second she had it. Unsteady on her feet, she bolted toward the rows of private hangars. She didn't make it very far before all the blood in her body froze. The door of the closest hangar opened, exposing a row of men standing side by side and staring straight at her.

Oh, God.

What were the chances those men had nothing to do with Liam?

Likely nil.

Sickness rolled through her gut. Panic waged a war in her mind.

"You couldn't help yourself, could you?" Liam asked dully, coming up behind her. "You stupid whore, this could have been easy."

Claire heard the swing of his arm before she felt something hard land at the base of her skull. Blackness took hold of her vision as she hit the ground.

• • •

SHATTERED

Claire blinked awake with a groan. Agony played a mean game of ping pong in her head, side, and back. It took her a while to realize she had been resting on something far too cold and hard to be a bed. Something awful banged in the back of her skull, like she'd taken a hit to the head.

That had to be bad.

"Get up, you lazy girl," she heard someone order.

Why did that voice sound so familiar?

The demand was shouted at her again, closer the second time. Still confused and feeling like she was two seconds away from losing her lunch, Claire tried to do as she was told. At first, she rolled to her knees, using her palms as a source of support on the cold floor.

A hardwood floor, she realized as her vision started to clear.

The dark, cherry wood color was familiar.

"Up, I said!"

"Demyan ..."

It was the only thing Claire could think of to say and the one person she wanted. He would help her, whatever it was that she had gotten herself into. Surely he would help her.

"Demyan!" Claire called louder.

Where was he?

"Christ, you fool," came a bark from the side. "He is not coming to help you. Get up, girl, or I swear you will taste the heel of my boot between your teeth."

It was the only warning Claire received before someone's foot landed into her ribs. The already sore spot bloomed with an absolute pain like she'd never felt before. She heard the telltale snap of bone as her air cut past her lips in a scream. Every breath she tried to take after that only added to the raw throbbing in her ribs.

"Stop, please stop," Claire pleaded. "Please, please stop."

Don't beg, a voice whispered.

Don't fight, don't run ... don't beg.

He thrives on weaknesses.

He will hit you.

Don't beg.

Demyan.

All of the memories Claire had lost of the last several hours—or was it days?—came rushing back in a wave of hurt, fear, and panic.

Liam's face clouded her vision, his breath foul and hot in her face as he yanked her to her knees by her hair. Claire didn't shout the second time and she definitely didn't beg. She refused to give him anymore power over her than he already had.

"Are you going to cry now, girl?" Liam asked sadistically.

Claire sucked in an aching breath. "No."

"Twenty," Liam stated. "And it's time for you to earn those lashes out, girl."

Pressure filled Claire's head and chest the moment Liam released her hair from his painful grip. She nearly fell forward to the floor in her dizzied state, but somehow, she remained upright. Something in the corner of her eye caught her attention and she chanced a glance in that direction.

Men—at least a dozen of them—stood against a wall.

Claire didn't want to know what they were there for, she didn't even want to consider it ... she couldn't help it. Her mind went straight to the worst place possible, knowing what her uncle was like and the things he enjoyed, especially when it came to hurting women.

Another quick look around the space through her daze told Claire she was in an office, one she knew because she'd been in it before. It was the one Liam used in his home.

Liam darkened the spot in front of Claire again, gaining her attention with the tap of his boot to her sore knee. Three items rested in his hands and all of them made her want to vomit.

A studded belt, a leather whip, and a three-foot long by two-inch thick metal pole.

"This will be the equivalent of picking your switch, girl," Liam explained. "While you choose, feel free to explain to these men why you're being beat and why you know you deserve such punishment."

Claire swallowed the disgusting taste in her mouth, unsure of what to do. The belt with sharp metal studs would rip her skin to shreds and the leather whip was liable to do the same. The metal pole, on the other hand, was probably strong enough to do serious damage to her already hurt ribs, maybe even worse.

"The whip," Claire managed to say.

Welts, bruises, and pain she could manage.

Sure she could.

Fuck, Claire wished she could believe that.

Liam tossed the pole and belt behind him, the items landing to the floor with a thud. Someone stepped up behind Claire, not giving her the slightest chance to fight back before her dress was ripped open all the way down her spine.

Cold air crawled over her skin as shock took over. Claire found a spot to stare at on the wall as Liam walked behind her, the whip uncoiling to the floor in his firm, sure grasp.

"Explain," Liam demanded.

Claire stayed silent.

The first strike of the whip whistled in the room before it landed across her back. Instead of hurting only the place it hit, the bite of the whip rained pain over her entire body. She couldn't breathe, couldn't think. The second strike came harder and tears spilled without permission from her eyes.

Claire recoiled, her hands hitting the floor in front of her as bile spilled into her mouth and splashed to the floor. The smell of her sickness only caused her to retch more.

"Explain!"

Claire gasped, every breath hurting because of her ribs. Her body craved the oxygen through her panic. She waited for the third hit to land and tried to prepare for it.

It didn't help when it did come.

"Girl, if I have to repeat myself one more time …"

"I fell in love," Claire whispered.

Because she had.

And that was exactly the reason why she was there.

Liam could take it or fucking leave it.

"Count them out," Liam stated.

The whip whistled again.

Her skin bled.

Claire let the tears fall.

"Four …"

• • •

Demyan's silence was deafening in the stolen car. The engine was running, but he'd cut all the lights to keep from being noticed by the men down the road.

"She was walking, Boss," Boris said.

"Stumbling," Demyan corrected.

Claire had been stumbling, struggling for air, and a mess of dried blood and bruises when Demyan watched Liam and his men force her from a car, through a gated entrance, and into his home twenty minutes earlier.

She hadn't been fighting, crying, or screaming, though.

"She looked out of it," Rory noted quietly.

Yes, that, too.

Demyan had to wonder if Claire was even lucid enough when the car delivered her to hell to realize what was happening.

"What do you want to do now?" Boris asked.

"Wait," Demyan answered. "We have to wait."

"And while we do?" Rory asked.

"Talk to the Russians here, set up a spot, and let Liam do the rest of the work."

"Sounds easy enough," Boris muttered.

Demyan seriously doubted it would be. What was happening to his lover in that house? He couldn't allow himself to think about it. His anxiety and anger would overload him. Demyan went numb again.

"Let's go find us an Irishman," Demyan murmured.

"Why?"

Demyan shrugged. "I want to know what the inside of that house looks like before I make my way into it. I figure if we find the right one, he might even get us inside."

Boris smirked. "Snakes in every man's grass."

"Precisely."

• • •

Claire stayed cowered in the corner, her home for three days, as fury filled shouts echoed from across the room. She knew better than to move after the last time, and she certainly wasn't about to speak again.

Not that she was sure she could. Her mouth ached and her teeth throbbed. Liam had no issue with hitting Claire for the smallest infraction he could think of. Even looking at the man could earn her a punch to the head. Blood had become a permanent taste in her mouth.

God, she felt like she was dying.

Where was Demyan?

Where was *he*?

"What do you fucking mean he didn't come back?" Liam growled.

"Just what I said, Boss. Court didn't show back up after the first night like he said he would to check in. It's like he fucking disappeared out of thin air or something. Can't even find his goddamn car and his wife is having—"

"I don't give a single fuck about that whore," Liam spat.

While Claire knew her uncle to be well-spoken and generally emotionless in all aspects of life, his anger was finally starting to show. He yelled, cussed, and acted like he was losing control bit by bit. It was a side of him she had never been privy to before.

It also terrified the living fuck out of her.

"Liam, they've got a brand new baby," the man said, his frustration coloring his words sharp. "And three older boys, too."

"Not my problem. Get back out there and find that fucking fool. You better hope he's not alive because if he is, I'll kill him myself for pulling this nonsense when I have better things to attend to."

"Boss—"

"Get out!"

The slamming door had Claire cringing. Pain ricocheted through her pounding head from the noise level. She didn't even have time to crack her eyes open and find where Liam now was in the room before something made of glass shattered against the wall directly above her head. Shards rained down over her shaking form.

"And you!" Liam shouted.

Claire blinked, trying to focus through her fear as Liam came to stand at her feet. His fist found her hair, a particular thing he favored with her, before he dragged her to the middle of the office. She wanted to fight, craved strength, but her energy was gone and she had no desire to earn another beating.

Liam forced her to her knees in front of his desk before a gun was pulled from inside his suit jacket. Claire didn't flinch at the sight of the weapon. She was close enough to death as it was and a bullet would be nothing less than merciful.

But did she want to die?

Liam shoved the gun under her chin, making her stare up at

265

him as he cocked the hammer back. "Is he coming, or not?"

Claire stayed silent. She knew as much as Liam did, so asking her anything was pointless.

"Is he coming, or not?" Liam asked, more forcefully the second time. The barrel of the gun bit into her throat.

Love.

Love, her mind whispered.

Demyan loved her, so he would come. Whatever he was waiting for, Claire didn't know and she didn't care.

He would come.

Only two answers were acceptable to Liam.

"Yes," Claire whispered.

Liam sneered. "Good."

He should have known better.

Liam shouldn't want Demyan there at all.

Claire smiled right back through the pain. "I'm sorry."

• • •

"Look at this, Boss," Boris muttered, dragging a bound but fighting man into the entrance of the warehouse. The shaggy-haired man was gagged, but his shouts could still be heard. "Noticed this fool coming out of Liam's earlier and thought I might follow him for a bit."

Boris tossed the guy like he was a ragdoll toward his boss. Demyan didn't move from his spot on the shabby couch beside Rory. The Irishman landed on his stomach, staring up at the men with wide eyes and likely knowing what was about to happen to him.

"And?" Demyan asked Boris.

"He headed over to the other guy's house we hit a couple days ago, stayed there for a bit, then left. I picked him up before he even got back inside his car."

"Well done," Demyan murmured. "*Ello.*"

The Irishman glared back at Demyan's quiet greeting.

Demyan didn't really mind.

"Did you get him to talk any on the way over here?" Rory asked.

Boris shook his head. "Nope, but I think he's going to be a fun one."

Rory laughed. "Why is that?"

"The tough ones always are."

"Very true." Demyan pushed off the couch, standing straight. "Let's get to work."

Fifty minutes later, Demyan rested against the far wall with his arms crossed as he watched Boris wake the Irishman up again. The man's kneecaps were blown out, beaten in by a hammer. He'd sustained six broken fingers, three broken toes, and lost one of his ears. Slices from a knife crisscrossed in a bloody pattern over his jean covered thighs.

They'd finally gotten his name before he passed out the third time: Terry.

Boris was right. The tough ones were always fun.

The older brigadier tapped the sharp end of a knife under Terry's chin as Rory tossed a bucket of ice water over the man from behind. If he hadn't woken up fully before, he was now. Terry jerked in the chair, spluttering out water and gasping for air. A dozen words flew from his mouth in a language Demyan didn't care to learn.

Water mixed with blood on the floor, diluting the heavy red to a pink as it trickled into a nearby drain. Demyan made a mental note to thank the Detroit Bratva for letting them use this particular building. It was perfect.

"Fucking worthless Russian scum," the man shouted in English.

Demyan laughed deeply, wondering if that word was supposed to hurt him. "Try again, Terry. Maybe the next one will get the desired effect and we'll kill you."

"I doubt it," Boris added with a chuckle. "I'd cut your other ear off, but then you won't understand us very well. How's your mouth feeling?"

"Why?" Terry asked, teeth chattering and body shivering.

"Curious."

Boris flipped the knife around in his hand so the blunt metal hilt was facing outwards. Then, he hit Terry straight in the mouth with it. Demyan was positive he heard teeth break from twenty feet away.

Yeah, that shit hurt, too.

Finally, the moment Demyan had been waiting for came. Terry sobbed as he spit blood and teeth from his broken mouth.

His words were a garbled, mumbled mess of things, but one statement in particular stood out as the man kept repeating it.

That fucking bastard.

Demyan suspected if Terry was talking about Boris, he would have used a different phrasing. "Liam?"

Terry laughed, choking on his own spit at the same time.

"Christ," Rory muttered. "He pissed himself."

"Give him some credit," Boris replied. "He took a lot before it happened."

Demyan sighed, stepping away from the wall. Clearly they hadn't heard him or the Irishman speak. That, or they weren't listening. "Shut up you two."

Boris and Rory stilled.

"Terry," Demyan said sharply, gaining the swollen, bleeding man's attention, dazed as it was. "Liam?"

"That fucking bastard," Terry repeated.

Demyan grinned. "Is he pissed, wondering about me, taking it out on his men—is he losing control?"

It was everything Demyan hoped would happen. He wanted Liam second-guessing, having doubts, and looking over his shoulder. He wanted the ever-calm, unfeeling man to question his men, unaware of the things happening around him, and possibly even worried about when, or if, Demyan would show up.

It was a risk. It meant Demyan had to keep his distance, not show himself, and let the human nature take over for Liam, even if the man didn't act like he had anything normal going on inside him.

All the while, Demyan died a little more inside. The longer he waited this out and let Liam's carefully constructed walls break down, the more time his lover spent with the insane man.

"Is he losing control?" Demyan asked again.

"Fuck you," Terry spat.

Demyan didn't need to know more about Liam. Terry's refusal to answer was enough. His actions before Boris had picked him up were even more telling.

"That other man we killed, was he your friend?"

Well, Demyan imagined the Irish assumed their comrade was dead.

Terry sucked in air through broken teeth, his chest heaving. "What does it matter to you?"

268

"Curious."

"He was," Terry mumbled.

"And you cared enough about his family to go check up on his wife and kids, I suspect. Knowing Liam, he probably didn't care a bit ... not about the man's family, anyway."

Terry wouldn't meet Demyan's eyes.

"What about the girl?" Demyan asked.

"W-what girl?"

"Claire."

Terry laughed again, more blood spewing from his mouth. "She's a lost cause, Russian. Already got a foot in the fucking grave, so give that shit up."

No, Demyan didn't think so.

Passing by Boris, Demyan took the knife from his brigadier.

"She's not dead," Demyan said. "He won't kill her."

"Pretty fucking close to it," Terry said.

"But she isn't dead, yet."

Demyan swung the knife upward from his side, the blade catching Terry directly under his chin in his throat. The ten inch blade sunk into the man's head, going up through his mouth and straight into his brain.

Letting go of the knife's handle, Demyan stepped back to watch the man's body jerk through his final moments of life. Terry's eyes rolled back, blood spilled from his gaping mouth, and the scent of urine saturated the air again.

"I am not cleaning that shit up," Rory said. "I don't do piss, Boss."

"Doesn't matter," Demyan replied.

"Huh?"

"Liam is hours away from a breakdown. Once this fool doesn't show up to wherever he was supposed to be tonight and Liam gets the call for that, he's going to figure it out. One man could be explained, but two is not a coincidence. I want to be there when his meltdown happens."

"Tonight, then?" Boris asked.

"Have to hit him at a bad time, you know," Demyan explained. "We know he's got men inside his house and outside. Claire is the most important thing and I don't want distractions with her inside the house, so I'll be the only one going in."

Demyan waved at the building they were in. "Burn it the fuck down and call the Russians to let them know we'll be needing that diversion. It's time."

CHAPTER TWENTY

A loud bang jerked Claire awake. She didn't have time to focus on where the sound had come from before she was being yanked up from the floor by her arm. Liam shook her until her teeth rattled. With her wrists and ankles bound by duct tape, any fight she had left was futile. Every inch of her body protested from the harsh treatment.

She was already disoriented and in pain as it was, but Liam didn't relent.

"Did you not hear me, girl?" Liam asked, his tone cutting into her nerves like a blade.

"No," Claire whispered.

"Why hasn't he come? Why did another one of my men disappear tonight? Where is he, girl?"

Claire swallowed back her sob as more agony ripped across her tender, raw back when Liam tossed her to the floor like a ragdoll. She didn't have answers for him. She didn't know any of Demyan's plans or what he was going to do.

"I don't know!" Claire cried. "I don't!"

"You must," Liam hissed. "You will tell me or I will beat it out of you, girl."

"I don't know!"

Claire's protests fell on deaf ears. The telltale swoosh of a belt being pulled out from belt loops echoed in the quiet office.

"No, no, no," Claire begged.

"Tell me," Liam demanded.

"I don't know, I don't!"

Claire managed to miss the first whip from the belt, rolling just in time for it to smack against the hardwood floor with a crack.

"Keep moving, girl, and the next one will—"

Liam's words were cut off by the frantic, loud shouts ringing through the house from outside the office. Claire barely understood what the people were yelling and she didn't realize there had been that many men in the home to begin with.

Fire, she heard.

Get out, someone else had yelled.

"What in the fu—"

"Boss, petrol bombs," came an anxious voice from the office doorway.

Liam stiffened. "Where in the hell have you been, Court? Who allowed you in and where is Terry?"

Court shrugged. "I've been around, but I don't know where he is."

"You haven't been around!" Liam shouted.

"The front of the fucking house is going up in flames, Boss. Do you really want to argue with me about who I've been fucking for the last couple of days?"

Liam ground his teeth. "A Molotov cocktail?"

"Yeah, front and back. And they're lighting up like crazy. It's not normal gas, Boss."

Claire did her best to crawl away from Liam while he was distracted, but being bound made it more difficult and excruciating.

"Open the gates! Open the fucking gates!" someone shouted outside in the halls.

Liam exploded, rushing to the door and disappearing into the hall. "Do not open the gates!"

Claire rolled to her knees, meeting the gaze of Court. She stared at him unabashed and unafraid, knowing exactly what was happening. Demyan was coming. Claire didn't understand why, but the man walked over to her, drew a pocket knife from his jeans, and cut the tape from her wrists and ankles.

"Run," he murmured.

Claire froze. Her arms and legs ached. It burrowed so deep into her bones she was pretty sure it would be impossible for her to run. "W-what?"

"Every man can be bought for the right price," Court said. "Especially if he's got something to protect, you know. It's not going to take Liam long to realize I was the one who let the gas bombs go in his foyer and that nothing is burning in the back like I said. So you need to get up and run."

Was he saying what she thought he was saying? She recognized his name. The man from earlier ... Terry ... had said Court was missing. Yet, here he was, letting her go.

"Demyan?" Claire asked.

Court nodded. "Run, girl."

Claire stood on shaky legs, her hands waving in front of still blurry eyes to steady her swaying body with nothing but air. "Where?"

"Toward the back. You know the house."

Claire ran.

But it wasn't long before she heard shouts and gunfire ringing out behind her.

• • •

Demyan slipped over the back fence as rapid assault fire echoed from the front property of the mansion. He knew given the size of the land the house was on and the privacy the surrounding trees provided, they had a good twenty minutes before the cops would show.

Turning, he waved at Rory, who was still driving the stolen vehicle. It was Rory's signal to give his boss ten minutes of headway time before he made his way in, too. If Demyan could get it done on his own, even better. Boris was in the front of the property with two other Russian men from the Detroit family. He was keeping focus where Demyan needed it to be and not in the back where he hoped he'd find Claire. If Court did his job, she'd be there waiting for him.

Demyan broke into a jog, knowing what was coming. Two sharp barks resounded before a pair of the nastiest looking Rottweiler's appeared out of fucking thin air. Court's words about the dogs flooded Demyan's mind. They weren't afraid of guns, they would attack if you breathed, and they always went for the throat—*always*.

A good two-hundred-fifty-million dollars' worth of Demyan's family's fortune was going to be transferred over into an offshore bank account for Court's wife and children. Demyan didn't regret paying the man off for a minute. Court had been fucking invaluable. Even if he was a goddamn rat. Court just didn't want to be in the lifestyle anymore, but the problem was, the only way out was death. Demyan supposed they were lucky that the man they grabbed the first night was the right one for the job.

"Here, puppies," Demyan said, waving his magnum toward the dogs.

He didn't believe in killing animals, but these things were

273

fucking beasts. And if he didn't put them down, they would sure as shit put him down. The second the dogs lunged at Demyan, he fired off two rounds in a quick succession. The black bodies of the dogs fell with two yelps, dead before they even hit the ground.

Demyan had two acres of land to cover before he'd come up on the back of the house. He could see the bright lights of the jet fuel Molotov cocktails doing their job from his position at the end of the property. He also had a water bottle full of that shit in his jacket pocket, too.

Breaking into a fast sprint, Demyan crossed the property in record time.

The backdoor where the large deck leads to is never unlocked because no one would ever get past the dogs, Court had said.

Demyan pulled the large one-liter bottle full of jet fuel from his pocket and untwisted the cover, tossing it to the ground. He started a trail from the bottom of the deck's stairs all the way to the back door, making sure to splash the stinky shit all the way around it.

Liam was not a stupid man when it came to his house. He was like any fucking mafia man. The fewer entrances and exits, the better. It was also going to be his downfall considering Court had barricaded the only other entrance there was with fire. Jet fuel burned hotter and faster than any kind of gas a regular person could get their hands on. It was dangerous shit.

Demyan kicked the door in, not wanting to get the jet fuel on his hands, and came face to face with a sight he hadn't expected and didn't want to see.

• • •

Liam's boot landed between Claire's shoulder blades as he fisted her hair in his hand and yanked her head back. Her knees hit the floor hard, a cry shattering what relief she had felt at seeing the back door of the mansion.

She almost made it.

Almost.

She barely rounded the last hallway corner when Liam caught up to her.

"You foolish whore," Liam spat.

The pain in Claire's back from being beaten by the whip days ago intensified.

Something hard pressed to the back of her head and she knew exactly what it was: a gun.

"I shouldn't have bothered waiting for the Russian," Liam muttered. "I should have killed you right there in the parking lot of that hospital and waited to see what he looked like when he found you dead like her."

"You can see me now, Liam."

Love, fear, liberation, and need washed through Claire's senses at the sound of Demyan's voice. But he sounded so cold and nothing like the man who she had last seen. No, now his voice reminded her of the Demyan she first knew.

Icy on the outside and nothing on the inside.

She searched for her lover, finding him standing in the back doorway. A bottle of oddly colored liquid was in his right hand while a gun rested in his left.

"You can see me now," Demyan repeated.

Liam chuckled, pulling on Claire's hair again. She cried out, her body shuddering from pain and exhaustion. "Look at her, boy, not me."

"I don't have to look at her to know what you've done," Demyan replied.

Claire released a shaky breath, wondering who this man was standing only twenty feet away. Demyan didn't grace her with the least bit of his attention—it was like she didn't exist.

He loves you, her mind whispered.

"Look at her!" Liam shouted.

Demyan didn't even blink. "You know how I did this, Liam?"

Claire winced when Liam pushed the barrel of his gun harder into her head. She squeezed her eyes shut, not wanting to see anything else. The smell of fire and fuel saturated the air. She could still hear gunshots ringing out from somewhere behind her. Liam heaved with his anger and panted through his rage like an animal.

She wasn't scared, though.

Somehow, that debilitating emotion bled its way out of her system.

Claire opened her eyes again, finally seeing Demyan. He was cold all over, his posture rigid and his expression uncaring and dismissive. His eyes, though … she knew those eyes.

I love you, she mouthed.

And it was so okay if he failed. Because she did love him and that was enough for her. He'd shown her a dozen times over his own love and gave her access to a part of his life that she would always cherish.

Demyan's attention flicked from Claire back to Liam. "I was able to do all of this because you were right, Liam."

"What—"

"I learned my lesson the first time, the one you wanted to teach me. I learned it so well, you can't possibly understand. Learning it meant I knew you were predictable and you wrongly assumed that the second time we met, I would be predictable, too."

Demyan barked out a bitter laugh. "Yeah, I fucking learned that lesson. And now I think it's time for you to learn one, too."

Claire heard Liam cock back the hammer on his gun at the same time she watched Demyan raise his. Her heart stopped in her chest as she felt Liam's gun press into her skull while Demyan's barrel aimed straight at her face.

"Do you know what my father taught me, Liam?"

"Watch me kill her like I did to the other one, boy," Liam taunted.

Demyan didn't look away from Claire's face as he said, "My father taught me to make sure when I had to take a shot, I knew exactly what I was shooting for."

Claire remained frozen on her knees in a prone position as smoke blistered from Demyan's gun. She could have sworn she was able to watch the bullet cut through the air, going straight for her head.

Several things happened, then. But her life flashing before her eyes was not one of them.

A stinging burn seared across her cheek. Liam shouted, the sound filled with shock and pain before he released his hold on Claire. She hit the ground at the same time Demyan's gun fired a second round.

Liam's gun went flying to the floor as he staggered further away from Claire.

"*Move*," she heard Demyan bark.

Claire gasped in as much air as she could take, scrambling to get away from the cussing, angry man behind her. Demyan was already moving forward. She turned around in just enough time to

276

see Demyan's gun aim again. Smoke and light billowed from the weapon with two more bangs. Claire felt the vomit rise in her throat as Liam's kneecaps exploded when the bullets tore into them. Her uncle hit the ground, falling to his back.

Demyan started waving the bottle he held, splashing the foul smelling liquid all over the floor and Liam's cursing form. Blood poured from the man's wounds. Demyan added two more bullets to both of Liam's hands before he tossed his gun off to the side.

"Demyan ..." Claire's voice came out softer than a whisper.

It's okay, she wanted to tell him. *I'm fine.*

"Look at her," Demyan snarled, his emotions finally starting to show. "Look at what *you* did to her!"

The sound of fire crackled through the house. Claire wondered how long the front had been burning and how bad it really was.

"Fucking bastard," Liam said through clenched teeth, his hands and knees bleeding as he grappled at the injuries.

He couldn't walk or hold a gun. He couldn't hurt them, now.

"You couldn't possibly make this the same as before," Demyan said quietly. "Because she isn't the same as the woman you killed and I am no longer that naive man. This is going to hurt, Liam. Burning alive will do that, you know."

With those words, Demyan turned on his heel. He picked up a shaking Claire without a word, cradling her in his arms. He continued drizzling what bit of fluid was left in the bottle all the way to the opened back door before he tossed it back inside.

"Can you stand?" Demyan asked.

Claire nodded.

"Can you run, *krasivyy*?"

"Yes."

"Run for the fence," Demyan ordered.

With a single squeeze of his hand around hers, he let her go and she did what he asked. Claire glanced over her shoulder just in time to see Demyan coming down the deck stairs with a lit Zippo lighter in his hands. Once he stepped off the stairs, he tossed the Zippo behind him without even looking.

The back of the house went up in flames in less than a second.

• • •

Rory's voice in Demyan's ear was a harsh reminder things had not gone entirely to plan in Detroit. "Boris didn't make it, Boss."

Demyan let the rush of sadness fill his body, knowing the news had been inevitable. Boris took three bullets to the chest and he was lucky to make it to the hospital. What Demyan didn't want to do was think about how badly it would hurt his father to learn one of his oldest and most trusted friends had lost his life.

The plane kept climbing, the pressure building in the cabin.

"Make sure they know we'll want his body transferred back to New York," Demyan heard himself say though he didn't feel quite in the moment. "Deflect whatever you can on the official side of things. We do not want to get mixed up in that shit. We were lucky to get through it as unscathed and unnoticed as we did."

"Will do," Rory replied. "How's Claire?"

"Better."

At least that was the truth, as far as Demyan knew.

"I'll keep you informed," Rory said.

"Thanks."

Demyan ended the call and immediately dialed another number. It was the house phone to the Barbados home his mother and father owned. On the fourth ring, his father picked up, instantly knowing who was on the other end.

"Demyan," Anton said.

"Dad, hey."

Just like that, Demyan felt as though he was a little boy who needed his father all over again.

"Christ, son …"

"Yeah, I know, you were worried. It's good. I'm good."

"Claire?" his father asked.

"Alive."

"Alive," Anton echoed quietly. "And the rest?"

"The worst is gone, we'll say."

"The worst had a whole army behind him, son."

"They have their own mess to clean. Bring my daughter home, please."

Anton laughed. "God, she's been asking for you nonstop."

"Bring her home to me."

"All right, son. I'm proud of you, Demyan."

"Don't be," Demyan replied before ending the call.

Once the plane reached altitude and the pilot announced it was safe for the few passengers to leave their seats, Demyan made his way to the private room in the back as fast as he could. The doctor was just getting Claire into the king-sized bed.

"Wait," he heard Claire mumble.

"Sweetheart, I need to look at these ribs of yours. You're badly bruised and swollen, there's likely a break. I'll need to wrap them at least until we land and I can get you to my clinic."

"But—"

"And your back is covered in welts and cuts. Let me roll you onto your stomach. I have to see the damage to your back," Leland attempted to explain.

"No, wait," Claire said, more forcefully the second time.

Leland wasn't having it. "Claire—"

Claire's voice was dry and hoarse, and her pain was clear to hear when she spoke again. "I want Demyan, please. I want him."

Demyan stepped into the room the moment she said his name, wanting her to know he was there. "Claire, let him do what he needs to."

His heart was aching. It was breaking in ways he couldn't explain. Every mark on her beautiful body was because of him. All of her pain had been caused by his choices.

Demyan knew this wasn't going to be easy, and Claire was the kind of woman who could handle what Liam had put her through, but that didn't ease his guilt. Did the end result work out? Sure, but that didn't make it any easier. Nothing would or could ever ease his guilt.

Claire's water-filled gaze met his and the tears spilled down her cheeks. "You came."

The lingering tension straightening Demyan's spine released. "Yeah, I'm here. Of course, I am, *krasivyy*."

Claire shook her head in a frantic motion, her brown hair sticking to her tears. "No, I mean ... you did it, you came and saved me."

Don't try to save me. Do.

"Yes," Demyan said, unsure of what she needed from him.

"Oh my God, that hurts," Claire whispered, pressing her palm to her side.

"How many times did he hit you there?" Leland asked, going right back to doctor mode.

"Three or four. Kicks, not hits," Claire said.

Demyan flinched, something invisible keeping him from going any further.

Leland examined Claire through the mess of her dress, muttering under his breath about broken ribs and infection.

"An IV would help," Claire said.

"Most certainly," Leland replied. "Especially for the infection breeding in those injuries on your back. I can ready one, but I won't have a good enough antibiotic concoction to add until I have access to my clinic. I do have a light antibiotic to add, but it won't be enough to really do the job with the IV."

Claire nodded. "And the open wounds on my back?"

Leland shot Demyan a look, frowning. The worry on the man's face said a lot.

"Whatever you can," Demyan said.

"I have gauze, antibiotic creams, alcohol and sterilized water," Leland said softly, giving Claire his attention again. "It's the best we have to work with for now."

"It's going to hurt," Claire said, more tears spilling.

"It will, but they need to be cleaned and I can't support that broken rib you've got without covering your back injuries. I need to clean them first. I also need to seal that cut on your cheek."

Demyan thanked whatever God was up above watching over them that Claire didn't even flinch at the mention of her bullet graze that came from his gun.

"I also have morphine, sweetheart."

"I don't want—"

"Give it to her," Demyan interrupted Claire.

Claire heaved a breath, gritting her teeth. "I don't need morphine, Demyan."

"It will help, Claire."

"No, it won't," she shot back. "It will make me dazed, make me feel slow and confused, but it will not dull the pain all that much. I know. I don't want to be high, Demyan."

Leland sighed. "She has a point."

Demyan didn't want to argue with Claire. She didn't need more stress.

"Whatever she wants," Demyan said.

"I'll be fine," Claire assured though the constant grimace and never-ending flood of tears said differently.

"She will be," Leland agreed.

That didn't help the guilt Demyan felt, either.

• • •

Claire woke surrounded by the softest sheets and to the sound of a quiet beep of a machine. Before falling asleep in Demyan's bed, the doctor explained the medications he was delivering through her IV. She remembered her lover's form in bed with her, holding her.

Where was he now?

The bed was empty and Claire felt cold without Demyan.

"Claire!"

The happy, joyfully familiar voice made Claire turn to find the person it belonged to. Vera climbed onto the bed without prompting, snuggling into Claire's chest and open arms, being mindful of the tube coming from her left hand.

"Vera," Claire breathed.

"I missed you, Claire," Vera mumbled. "I missed you so much. I came home because Grandpapa said we could, but I don't like the plane. I don't like it at all."

Christ.

How long had she been asleep?

Claire sniffed back the tears threatening to fall again.

Hadn't she cried enough?

She was safe, Vera was safe, and Demyan was safe.

They were so good. Claire didn't care about the rest, or the bruises she sported and the soreness spreading over her body … no, she didn't care a bit with Vera hugging her tight.

"Papa said I couldn't wake you up," Vera explained.

"Because she needed to rest, Vera."

Demyan's voice came from the doorway. Claire turned to find him, but every inch of her desperately wanted to reach out to him and have him close to her, too.

"Demyan."

"Hey, babe," he murmured. "How're you feeling?"

"Fine. Come here."

Demyan didn't move. "You must be—"

"I am fine, Demyan, because you're here. *We're* here. I am fine," she repeated.

Something inside said he needed to hear that.

Demyan crossed the space between the doorway and the bed in three long strides. Once he was in bed with her and Vera, she relaxed into his body holding her tight from behind.

"I'm sorry," Demyan whispered.

"Don't be. We're okay."

"Do you need something?" he asked. "Tell me what you want, Claire."

Claire blinked rapidly, wetness gathering along her lashes. "I want you."

"I'm here, babe."

"Yeah, I know. Don't leave me again."

"I won't."

CHAPTER TWENTY-ONE

"Wake up, sweet girl," Claire heard in the background of her dream.

And good God, her dream was wonderful. Something wicked was teasing her senses, making her nerves twist and snap like live wires ready to light the earth on fire. Her muscles clenched at that blissful, cloying feeling, craving more.

When she felt the pads of Demyan's warm hands push her thighs further apart, she knew. Christ, did she ever know. His tongue found her slit, teasing the entrance of her pussy through her panties with quick strikes as his nose nuzzled along her throbbing clit.

Sparks of pleasure flashed behind her closed eyelids.

"Look at me, *krasivyy*," Demyan demanded. "I want to taste you coming on my tongue, but you're not going to get that if you don't watch me fuck you with my mouth."

The loss of his mouth from her sex had Claire's eyes flying wide.

"Don't stop."

Demyan's hands left her thighs just long enough to fist her panties and yank them down over her legs. Claire arched off the bed as his attention went right back to where she wanted him the most. His teeth scraped along the sensitive folds of her pussy while his fingers dug deeper into her thighs. She didn't know how it was possible, but she was already climbing a fast peak to heaven and he had barely done a damn thing.

"Oh, God," Claire moaned.

Demyan grinned a sinful sight, kissing up her sex as he murmured, "Fuck, you taste like honey, babe. And you're so goddamn good in the morning, getting wet and mumbling my name in your sleep. I had to wake you up for this. Beg me, Claire, and I'll give you just what you want."

Claire burned under his heavy stare. "Please fuck me with your mouth."

"Anything else, beautiful?"

"Everything … God, *everything*, Demyan."

Demyan's mouth encased her pussy before she could say another thing. Claire's eyes locked on him as his tongue dipped into her core, tasting her fluids. The second his fingers slid along her folds, his tongue flicked up to her clit. He fucked her blindingly fast with his fingers and tongue, giving her no time to breathe or think.

Claire's orgasm came strong and swift, sweeping her under the current while a heated blue gaze watched her drown from down below. He didn't relent as the waves of sin and need coursed through her bloodstream. His tongue lapped at her juices while his fingers took her to the finish.

God, it was glorious.

"*Demyan!*"

He answered her call by removing his fingers and mouth, making Claire whine to have him back. His body covered hers and his lips dotted down over and over to her jaw line. Claire felt his hand slip under her knee, lifting her leg over his shoulder.

The hard ridge of Demyan's cock was all she felt pressing at her wet, tender sex before he entered her. Claire's gasp echoed in the quiet room while her body reveled in the feeling of him filling her so full of him and taking her like only he could. There was no resistance in their fucking, no hesitance or fear.

Like he always did, Demyan loved her beautifully. He made her crazy with every stroke of his cock. He drove her insane with the explorations of his fingers across her hyperaware flesh. And he took her to the brink of insanity when his hands cupped her jaw and he forced her head back so he could stare at her before his kiss swallowed every cry of his name.

When she begged for more, he fucked her harder but never let her go.

This was how they loved best, she decided.

On early mornings, in sheets that smelled like them, with sunlight dancing on naked skin.

Yeah, the very best.

• • •

A knock on the bathroom door broke Claire from her confused daze.

"Claire?"

Claire scrambled off the floor, flushed the toilet, and grabbed the air freshener off the cabinet before spraying the artificial strawberry smelling mist into the room. She unlocked the bathroom door and turned to the sink where her toothbrush and toothpaste were waiting.

Demyan opened the door a few inches and poked his head through the crack. "You okay?"

Claire shoved her toothbrush in her mouth. "Fine," she mumbled.

"Sure?"

"Yeah. I'm kind of busy, though."

The words came out as a garbled mess around her toothbrush, but Demyan understood well enough.

"Vera wants you to drop her off a pre-k. She's pretty insistent that you take her today. I don't know why."

Claire shrugged. "Sure, okay."

"Thanks." Demyan opened the door further, coming inside just far enough to lean in and kiss Claire on the cheek. "Love you, huh?"

"Love you, too."

"I've got shit to do on the east side today, but I'll pick her up and bring her home. Are you going to be around for supper?"

Was he really asking that?

For the last three months, Claire practically lived with Demyan and Vera. Most of her wardrobe had somehow made its way into Demyan's dressers and closet. She had her own seat at the dinner table. Vera climbed into Claire's side of the bed every morning instead of her father's.

Nothing felt like home at her apartment and since she stayed far away from anything even remotely related to the Irish, Demyan's place felt safer.

It was home.

She didn't understand why he didn't already know that.

"Yeah," Claire finally said.

"And I meant to ask …"

Pulling the toothbrush out, Claire rid the paste in her mouth and rinsed with water, not wanting to have a conversation looking like a rabid human. "What?"

"Is the lease on your apartment almost finished for this

year?" he asked.

"In two months."

"Are you going to sign another one?"

Claire stilled. "Do you want me to?"

Demyan's hand found hers, squeezing tight. "You know I don't."

"Good, because the landlord asked if I'd be willing to let him break the lease for a new tenant to move in next month."

"Why didn't you tell me?" Demyan asked.

"Just got the message yesterday when I picked up some things after work."

Demyan grinned. "So ... you're all mine, now, right?"

Claire laughed, but nervousness prickled at her insides. "Yeah, Demyan, I'm all yours."

• • •

"No work today?" Viviana asked as Caire came up to the counter.

"No, I took a couple of days off, actually, but I wasn't working today anyway."

Viviana cocked a brow. "Why the days off?"

Claire shrugged, anxiety eating away at her insides. "I just ... need some time to think and whatnot, so I called the hospital earlier and used a couple of sick days for the rest of the week."

"Wow, you're not usually this vague and strange, Claire."

"Sorry," she muttered.

"What's wrong?"

"Nothing, in a way."

"Something in another way?" Viviana asked, sounding as confused as Claire felt.

"Basically."

"Claire—"

Claire lifted the convenience store bag in her hand up for Viviana to see, and then promptly turned it over to dump the contents across the countertop. Viviana's eyes widened at the pink and white box, sitting there unopened and waiting to be used.

"Oh my God," Viviana said, an excited grin forming.

"Um ... so I took Vera to school today for Demyan and then I went to the store and bought this."

"You came here to do it?" Viviana asked.

Claire felt so awkward it wasn't even funny. "I don't have friends, Vine."

"Hey, I'm your friend."

"You are, so I came here. You don't mind, right?"

Viviana shook her head, her smile turning almost conspiring in nature. "Does he know?"

"No."

"Why not, Claire?"

"Because I'm scared and if I'm scared, he'll really be freaked out. This is soon ... maybe too soon for him. We've only been together officially for a few months, so it's soon. Okay? It's soon and this would be a huge change."

Claire was rambling, but she couldn't stop. Thankfully, Viviana took it in stride.

"Listen, time doesn't equate to a whole hell of a lot when it comes to love. It took one week for me to change everything I thought I wanted in life. Just one week on a white sand beach with a man who only needed to look at me and I loved him. As long as your love is real to you and you know his is honest and true for you, nobody and nothing else matters. Absolutely nothing. No one's opinion bears any importance to what you already know."

"The last time he went through this—"

"Was with a completely different person and under circumstances that would never, ever happen again," Viviana interrupted firmly. "My son loves you—adores you, Claire. And do you know how he fell in love with you?"

Claire nodded because Demyan had told her. "Sure. Because I loved him without strings and I took all of him as he was."

"Exactly. Time doesn't matter. You are so loved by that man."

"He's going to freak out."

"Maybe at first because memories are a bitch to kill, but he'll come back. Give him a chance."

Claire knew Viviana was right. "He always does."

• • •

"Demyan?" Claire called before the front door closed.

"In the kitchen, babe," Demyan said.

Vera shoved another potato under the stream of water to

wash for her father. "Like this, Papa?"

"Just like that, *dushka*."

"Hey," Claire said.

Demyan grinned at the sight of her in the kitchen entryway. "Hey."

"Can I talk to you for a minute?" Claire tilted her head to the side as if to silently ask for privacy. "You know, somewhere else."

"Uh, sure." Demyan replaced the cover on the paring knife before putting it on the counter. "No cutting, Vera."

"Okay."

Demyan left his daughter alone in the kitchen and followed an unusually quiet Claire through the home, up to the second floor, and finally into the room they shared. Well, he supposed they shared it now. He closed the door behind them, turning to watch Claire wring her hands together as she stared at the wall.

"I have to tell you something."

Demyan didn't like the sound of that at all. "Am I not going to like it, *krasivyy*?"

"Maybe," she whispered. "I don't really know."

"That's not a great way to start this out, babe."

Claire nodded, wetting her lips under her tongue before blowing out a shaky breath. "I love you."

"I know."

He loved her, too. Demyan didn't think he had to say it all of the time; she certainly didn't ask him to. Sometimes actions spoke louder than words and Demyan was big on doing things more so than speaking. It was just easier for him to do it that way.

Claire got that—she understood him.

"Are you ever going to marry me?" Claire asked suddenly.

Demyan stiffened. "Excuse me?"

"I just … Listen, I don't mean to say you need to drop down on one knee today and ask for my hand, okay. That's not what I'm saying. But I want to know if we're ever going to be more than this."

Demyan cleared his throat, noting how she avoided looking at him. "Is what we are not enough for you?"

"It's enough and I am so happy with us," she replied instantly. "I just want to know if we're going to be more, or if you're going to let me be more to Vera and—"

"What, like a mother?" Demyan interrupted.

"Yes, exactly like that."

"That's not really up to me," he said quietly.

Claire stared at him, confusion drawing her lips into a frown. "You're her father."

"Sure, but Vera is her own little person. If she wants to see you as her mother because that's how you feel to her, I don't get a say."

"So, if she started calling me Mom—"

"She'd call you Ma, probably. That's just what she's heard mostly."

"You'd be okay with that?"

"Being a mother is more than sharing a last name and DNA, Claire." Demyan shrugged, adding, "And you're the closest thing to a mother she's ever had, so I don't see the problem."

"You did before."

"No, my issue was you leaving and her being hurt. I've hurt enough for the both of us. Vera didn't even understand what she didn't have and what she wouldn't ever get to have because of Gia's murder. I always knew. I kept thinking I couldn't give her what she needed because Gia was irreplaceable."

"Is she?"

"You're not Gia," Demyan said.

Wasn't it obvious?

Claire was irreplaceable, too.

His. Beautiful. Life and love when he touched her.

"I want to be me. I don't want to replace a dead woman, Demyan."

"You're not. Not to Vera or I, anyway. You've made your own place and in the end, it has very little to do with Gia."

"Good," Claire said softly. "I needed to hear you say that."

"I thought you already knew," he admitted. "I'm sorry if you've felt any other way standing beside me. You're ..."

"What, Demyan?"

Yeah, actions spoke louder than words, but sometimes Demyan forgot Claire wasn't like him in that way. She needed him to speak, too.

"You're everything to me, Claire."

"Not everything. I can't be everything, Demyan. Don't turn me into some infallible, perfect being I can't possibly strive to become."

"I don't see you like that. You're just human to me. Honest and mine."

"Then how can I be everything?"

"Because everything to me is the most important things," he said simply. "The kinds of things that make me happy and keep me here."

"I don't know if I should be responsible for that, either," Claire murmured.

"Too late." Demyan sighed, wondering how this crazy beautiful girl felt anything less than loved by him. Maybe he was still too guarded. Maybe he would always be. "Have I done something to make you think I didn't want you here, now?"

"No."

"Then what's going on, babe?"

"You've never made me feel like I was replacing Gia, and I don't want you to think that you have. But today, I wondered when I came home and told you what I had to say, would you look at me like I was her? I don't want you to be scared of forever."

"With you, I'm not."

"And I don't want you to think it's going to happen again," she said.

"That what will happen again?"

Nothing she was saying made a hell of a lot of sense to Demyan. He figured she must have had some insane nonsense running wild inside that head of hers, so he wanted to slow it down. She did that for him, always. Gave him quiet in chaos. Loved him through pain.

Yeah, she might not want him to see her that way, but she was still everything to him. All the things that made the difference. Those little pieces of him that had shattered, the ones he thought were gone for good, she fixed them and was still putting him back together.

"I'm going to ask you to marry me," Demyan said, wanting her to know. "I don't know when, but someday when it feels right."

Claire smiled, laughing. "I'll say yes."

"I know you will."

Because she was fucking *his*.

Demyan reached out to snag Claire's hand in his own. The warmth of her skin soaked into his like a drug instantly, washing his senses with her and love. It was the best fucking feeling and he craved it. Outside of his home, Demyan had to be a lot of things. The persona of the Bratva boss, the Russian mafia prince who was not allowed to have weaknesses and couldn't afford for his cracks to show. He had so many to hide. Claire reminded him he didn't have to keep anything from her.

"I don't want you to see me like her," Claire repeated. "Not for this, please."

Claire was nothing like Gia. But he refused to see either woman as better than the other. Seeing it like that would be a disgrace to Gia's memory and a shame to the things he felt for Claire, now. Memories were all he had left of one, but he had an entire lifetime of memories to make with the other. So yeah, he was going to start on making as many of those as he could and soon. Claire deserved so much more than to be compared to someone she wasn't because he loved her in an entirely different way than how he loved before.

Demyan loved her in a way that understood life and loss a hell of a lot better than most, yet he still *loved*. He would say it was fearless but without the emotionless vortex sucking him in. Claire didn't have to be someone else. Demyan didn't want her to be. *Words*, he reminded himself.

Demyan tugged her into his chest, wrapping her in a tight embrace as he rested his lips to the crown of her head. "I only see you, Claire."

Some people only got the chance to love once. Demyan was lucky enough to have it happen twice. But with Claire, it was different. Hers was the kind of unconditional, all-consuming love that swept a person off their feet and swallowed them whole for life. It was sort of like drowning the way it took someone under, but it was right all the same.

"Don't be scared, okay?" Claire said again.

"I told you I'm not."

"I'm pregnant."

CHAPTER TWENTY-TWO

The words were quickly said and muffled against his chest as if to make them disappear. They couldn't, though. He heard them and there was no taking it back.

Demyan understood her previous warnings immediately. Just like how his inner reaction was to flinch away from the words and reality of that statement; to get as far away from the abrupt rush of memories and the fear that accompanied it.

It should have been a good thing. It shouldn't have made a sickness well in his gut or stop the breath in his lungs. The new stars on his shoulders itched, reminding of who he was and the dangerous nature of his lifestyle. A dull pain settled somewhere in the middle of his chest because Demyan couldn't help but *consider* ...

"It's not going to happen again," he heard Claire say.

He wanted to agree.

Wanted to so badly.

Momentarily, his embrace holding Claire tightened. "Can you help Vera with the rest of those potatoes for supper?"

Claire stared up at him, her jade eyes dimming, but an understanding still dawned. Of course, she knew. He loved her more because of it.

"Sure. How long are you going to be?"

"Not long," Demyan said. "Maybe an hour or so. I just ..."

"Need time to breathe."

"Yeah."

And think. Christ, he needed to think, too.

"I'll be here."

She always would be, he suspected.

• • •

"She's pregnant, then?" Anton asked quietly.

Demyan didn't bother to question his father on how he could possibly know that. Anton Avdonin always had a knack for drawing the right conclusions about people and situations. That, or his mother somehow knew and told his father.

After Demyan showed up at his parents' home a half hour earlier with nothing to say and no real reason to be there, Anton had taken his son out to the backyard with a beer in hand. Well, beer for Demyan. Anton wasn't allowed to drink what with his heart attack.

Demyan didn't know how to tell his father that life terrified him, that everything they were was not guaranteed. When he saw his father, he remembered being a little boy again and believing his father was king of the world. Because to a younger Demyan, Anton had been.

"We're not the same, are we?" Demyan asked instead of answering.

"You and me?"

"Yes."

"No. We're two entirely different men, even if we look a lot alike and share a few interests."

Demyan chuckled. "I meant the way we used to be. It's not the same."

"Well, it's not all that different at times," Anton replied. "I like it better this way. You don't see me like a God anymore. Instead, I'm just a man, your father. It took me a long time to see my own father that way, too. Believe me, this is much better."

"How did you manage watching your father waste away for years, knowing he was going to die eventually and there wasn't any way around it?"

"Most times, awfully. I hid it well," Anton admitted with a sigh. "But when he did die, I crumbled under the weight of everything I had been keeping locked up. Next to thinking your mother was going to leave me once, I don't think I ever cried that hard."

Demyan remembered his father's tears at Ana's wedding in private. Knowing his father the way he did, Anton likely wouldn't want Demyan to bring that moment up. Not directly, anyway. "I can't think of a time you cried in front of people."

"I've never but for Viviana. She is an exception to the rule and only because I trust and love her inexplicably. Any other time, which is far and few in-between, was out of my control."

"It always comes down to control, doesn't it?"

"For me, absolutely. You're not me, Demyan."

Demyan raked his fingers through his hair, feeling the pressure from earlier build in his chest again. "She is pregnant."

"I figured. How'd that happen?"

"How does it usually happen?"

Anton laughed darkly. "When you don't intend for it to."

"Well, there you go."

"It's not going to happen again, Demyan," Anton said softly. "What happened to Vera and Gia was born from entirely different circumstances that won't occur a second time and you know it."

"You're not supposed to find a second soulmate, either, but I did."

"I think you wanted Gia to be the perfect fit for you more than she actually was. I think comfort and security drew both of you together and kept you that way. You spent nearly as many years apart as you did together and when you were, you had to be a completely different man with her than who you actually were outside of your home. I'm not saying you didn't love that girl with everything you were, but I don't think it would have been a forever kind of thing."

Anger swelled in Demyan, even though he knew what his father was saying had merit and truth. He just didn't like when other people felt it was okay for them to point it out. "How can you say that?"

"She was all you ever knew and all you ever wanted to know." Anton shrugged, leaning forward in his chair to rest his clasped hands between his knees. "I say it because I only had to tell you once not to try and change who Gia was, but she never stopped trying to change parts of you."

Demyan sucked in a hard breath, willing his annoyance to leave. "I didn't come here for you to paint my past with a black brush."

"Then perhaps you should start leaving the past where it belongs, son."

"I want to."

"It won't happen again, Demyan," Anton repeated.

"Claire said that, too."

Anton smiled. "She's right. I like her, she's a good fit for you and Vera."

"Love is about more than being a good fit."

"It is," his father agreed. "I'm happy you see it now because you sure as fuck didn't before."

• • •

Demyan found Claire snuggled on the couch with a sleeping Vera tucked into her side. An hour away had turned into three before he realized it. He took the drive home slower than he usually would to give him even more time to think.

What he needed was to get his thoughts in order and his feelings settled. Claire deserved more than a reaction stained with his fear and shock. She was pregnant with his child and that was a beautiful thing. It was something he wouldn't allow to be taken away from him or her.

Demyan was allowed to be a little scared of it, too. After everything, sure he was.

Bending down, he scooped Vera out of Claire's sleepy embrace, cradling his daughter close as his lover blinked awake with tired eyes.

"Hey," she whispered.

Demyan smiled. "Hey, babe."

Claire glanced at the clock on the wall. She didn't say a thing about the time, though. "Good visit with Anton?"

Why wasn't he surprised that she knew where he had gone?

Claire understood him. She didn't have to spend her entire life growing up at his side to have the knowledge, either.

"Perfect." Demyan leaned further down, being mindful not to wake Vera up, to drag his nose along Claire's cheekbone. Silently, he took in her softness and smell so close to him. "Sorry I missed dinner."

"It's okay. I made you a plate."

Demyan made a face. "I'm not all that hungry for food."

"Good, because I screwed up on the roast."

"You're not that good of a cook."

"I'm not," Claire replied, laughing quietly.

"Except for breakfast."

"I am the queen of breakfast."

"So long as you have pickles on the table, everything is great."

"Pickles for breakfast is still disgusting," Claire said, sticking her tongue out.

Grinning, Demyan kissed Claire, soaking in her life and love. "I'm sorry I had to leave."

"We managed."

"Meet me in bed after I put her down to sleep?" Demyan asked.

"Like you even have to ask."

As much as he didn't want to, Demyan left Claire to take Vera up to her room. It was only when he placed his daughter in her frilly pink bed did he notice her groggy blue eyes watching him in that quiet way of hers.

Children had a way about them, Demyan knew. Seemingly simple questions often didn't feel as innocent as they were. By the look on Vera's face, she was about to ask her father one of those questions.

"Is Claire my ma?" Vera asked.

Demyan mulled over his answer as he tucked Vera in under her blankets. "Gia was your mother. She died shortly after you were born, but she loved you for every single minute she knew you were there."

Well, Gia died the day of Vera's birth given her brain activity never returned, but officially on paper, it wasn't until a few days later when they took her off the respirator.

"I know that, Papa."

"Then you know Claire isn't your mother in that way. Not in the way that she made you."

"She's like a ma," his daughter pressed.

Demyan stood, crossing his arms. This was all on Vera to decide as far as he was concerned. He wouldn't sway her opinion either way. If she wanted to see Claire as the motherly figure in her life, that was her choice.

"What's a mother to you, *dushka?*"

Vera shrugged under her blankets. "I don't know."

"Well, what do you think a mother should do for you?"

"You're my papa," Vera stated like Demyan should already know the answer she hadn't even given yet.

"Of course, I am, baby."

"So she should love me like you love me."

Demyan stilled in place, not expecting that. "You're right, she should."

"And you do love me, don't you, Papa?"

"With everything I am, my *dushka*."

He'd do absolutely anything to keep her safe and happy, too.

Vera's hand snuck out from under the blanket and caught her father's silently. Demyan let her hold his hand until she dropped it just as quietly and it disappeared back under the blanket. That, like it would always be, was his girl's way of saying she knew he loved her.

Demyan had never forgot how that NICU nurse told him that the best love for a child, even if a person didn't know how to verbally express it, was to show them.

"Do you have an answer for me about what a mother should be?" Demyan asked.

Vera smiled, turning in her bed to face the wall. "Claire."

"*Hmm?*"

"My ma should be like Claire."

• • •

Demyan's hands instantly found Claire's the second he slipped into bed. Without a word his lover rolled to her back on the soft sheets, letting him go with her. He fit between her spread thighs, pulling the tank top she wore over her head as his mouth made a quick descent down the toned contour of her stomach. The sweet smell of her skin saturated into his senses like a drug.

More, he always wanted more of her.

"God," Claire breathed, her legs falling open further the lower Demyan went. "I didn't think you were going to be in the damn mood for—"

"I am always in the mood for you." Demyan chuckled darkly, his fingers curling around the edges of Claire's cotton panties. "And I think you're lying because if you crawled in bed wearing nothing but these, you knew exactly what you were asking for, babe."

"Maybe I did. Are you going to follow though?"

"Oh, I always follow through."

And he figured ending his day the same way he started it out was a pretty good choice to make.

Demyan moved up to let Claire close her legs so he could pull the panties off her body. The moment they were gone, he was right back in place between the heaven that was her thighs. His hands roamed up to the curve in her waist, yanking her flat to the bed as his mouth encased her sex.

"*Shit.*"

Claire was hot and tart on his tongue. Her juices flooding his mouth was the best fucking thing he ever tasted. Her hips lifted to his lips when his tongue swept through her fleshy folds up to her clit. Demyan didn't waste time teasing Claire. He wanted her soaked and ready for him, begging him like he knew she could.

Fast strikes of his tongue urged her to a swift peak. Claire's hands found his shoulder and hair, gripping tight as her leg tossed over his shoulder. When she started shaking and her body twisted under his hands into the bed, Demyan knew she was close. Demyan released her waist with one hand, still keeping her pinned to the bed with his other. While he fucked her with his mouth, his fingers joined at the entrance of her sex, sliding into her core. The rhythm of his digits matched the beat of his tongue.

"There," Claire mumbled, the word melting into a low moan. "Christ, *there.*"

A low hum built in the depths of Demyan's chest, hard and deep. Curling his fingers at the same time he drew her sensitive clit between his teeth, he knew she was gone. Claire flew off the edge with his name in her mouth, shouting it so loudly the sound bounced off the walls.

Pleasure crawled through Demyan's veins. She was so fucking beautiful when she came. The way her bottom lip trembled and her air stuttered at the crown of her bliss. Lapping at the arousal he smeared up to her clit with his fingers, Demyan kept staring at Claire, taking in the sight of her under his want.

"More," she groaned.

"That's what I like to hear," Demyan murmured as he lifted himself over her body again.

Demyan's clothes took the same paths hers had, lost somewhere to the blankets and floor. Claire's fingers wove with his, pressing into the pillows above her head as he took her slow. Like she always did, her body sunk into the bed as his cock filled her full. Satisfaction sighed from her parted lips, the sound ghosting along his cheek before it disappeared.

She shuddered around his length, her legs tangling with his in the sheets. His pace was frantic, needing to find his safe relief with her like he knew he could. Her cloying sounds washing over his skin were quiet the faster he moved.

Claire's lips found the underside of his jaw and her hands in his squeezed. "Fuck, fuck, fuck," she whimpered.

Demyan couldn't speak at all. Not surrounded by her like he was in a tight, searing velvet, slick bliss.

When Claire came undone around him a second time, Demyan rolled them to their side. His hands found her face, bringing in her close enough for his lips to crush down on hers in the best way as her orgasm raged through. While the waves of her pleasure subsided, their limbs tangled, bodies moved and he let the pressure build.

"Love you," Demyan said thickly.

Claire kissed him softly. "I know."

"I'm not going to be perfect."

"I don't want perfect, Demyan."

Demyan's release came swift and harsh, numbing his fingertips digging into her jaw as his moan was swallowed by another one of her tender kisses. His cock pulsed, emptying his come as deep as he could manage into her sex as he held her firm to his body.

"*Shhh*," Claire soothed, running the pad of her finger under his eye. The touch was so affectionate in its intent that Demyan's chest hurt from the intensity of his heartbeat. "You look so good when you come."

Demyan laughed. "Do I?"

"It's the only time you're ever really … completely bared, I think."

"Maybe you're right."

"There's no maybe about it, Demyan." Claire scoffed playfully, her hand smacking his chest lightly. "I'm always right."

"Even when you're wrong, huh?"

"Even then," Claire agreed.

Crazy girl.

"When did you find out?" Demyan asked quietly.

Claire didn't need prompting as to what he meant. "This morning. I wasn't feeling well, I was late, and I just … knew."

"I'm terrified," Demyan confessed.

"Me, too."

"Probably not for the same reasons."

"Probably not," Claire said. "I don't know how to be somebody's mom."

"Vera thinks you're pretty damn good at being hers."

The way his lover's face lit up at those words sent joy spiraling through Demyan all over again.

"Yeah?" Claire asked, barely above a breath.

"Yeah, baby."

"Huh."

Demyan brushed a stray lock of hair from Claire's forehead. "I don't remember much of the first six months after bringing Vera home."

"Nothing at all?"

"It's like a blank space." Demyan shrugged. "I don't ever want to do that again, Claire."

"It's just us, right? He's gone, now."

Demyan appreciated the fact she didn't verbalize her uncle's name more than Claire could possibly understand. But she was right ... he was gone.

"He is," Demyan said.

Claire snuggled in close to his chest, like she was a kitten taking in his warmth. "And that family is happy he's ... gone."

"I'd say so."

"Then, we have nothing to worry about," Claire said.

Even if they did, Demyan wouldn't think twice before slaughtering anyone who came near Claire or his daughter. He would never take another chance that might cost those he loved their lives. Ever.

Demyan kissed the apple of Claire's cheek before pulling away.

"Thank you."

Claire watched him under thick lashes, her green eyes glimmering with lust and love. "For what?"

"For making me live."

• • •

Roman Anton made his way into the world on a cold March morning, straight into his father's waiting arms. He was cleaned while he cried on his mother's chest before his little body was wrapped in a fluffy blue blanket to warm his brand new skin.

SHATTERED

Demyan traced the features of his child, as he rested beside Claire on the bed, taking in every little amazing inch of the life he helped create. Two people milled around them in silence, cleaning what needed cleaned and clearing the room of what noise there was. Demyan barely noticed them at all.

Claire was adamant about birthing at home in the privacy and comfort of her own bed and Demyan couldn't argue with her to save his life.

What his girl wanted, she got.

Well, his wife, now.

They had married just a month before their son's birth in a quiet ceremony with little guests and no fuss. Private, like they were. Loving, like their life was.

Claire wanted a home birth with a midwife, low lighting and quiet music. Demyan didn't leave her side for a second, and seeing as how Vera's birth—one he didn't get to be a part of at all—was stained with awful memories, he let Roman's replace them with something better.

Claire was amazing, but when wasn't she?

Roman was the third generation of an Avdonin boy to be born with the signature jet black hair and blue eyes, just like his father and grandpapa before him.

Demyan had already decided he didn't want more children and luckily, Claire agreed. They had their boy and their girl, but there wasn't very damned much that was white-picket about them.

"He's perfect," Claire said, running her fingers over the sleeping baby's hair.

"Of course, he is." Demyan grinned. "He's an Avdonin."

"Yes, stubborn, particular, moody, possessive, and a little bit crazy."

Demyan laughed. "Damn, you have us nailed, babe."

Claire shifted to her side in the bed under the blankets, effortlessly moving the newborn to her other arm. She continued cradling Roman without waking him up. "How are you doing?"

Christ, why was she asking him that right now? It wasn't Demyan who had birthed an eight pound baby boy an hour ago.

Really, he wasn't surprised. Claire knew him too well.

"I'm okay," he said honestly. "So okay."

The midwife Claire had carefully chosen to attend her birth and the woman's assistant came to stand by the bed, waiting until the couple had finished fawning over the baby.

"Claire, we'd like to get you up and moving," the woman said. "See how you feel on your feet and maybe take a shower if you're up to it."

Demyan sighed at the sight of his lover's frown. Without even needing to ask, Demyan knew she didn't want to part with her son just yet. "I promise I won't let him go until you're done, sweetheart."

"Yeah?"

"Not for a second," Demyan assured.

"There's at least five people downstairs waiting to meet him."

Five people for now, anyway. The boss's son had been born, so the Bratva would surely follow. Tradition was what it was, even if Claire and Demyan would prefer to have their privacy for as long as possible, sometimes it just couldn't be helped.

"They're going to want to hold him," Claire added.

"And they can meet him from my arms. I won't let him go."

Claire smiled tiredly. "Okay."

Demyan took his sleeping son from his wife's arms, tucking the child in close to his chest. He swore he could feel the heartbeat of the baby match his own as he stared down at the peaceful, contented child.

"I'm just a shout away," Demyan told Claire.

She waved him off. "I'll be fine."

Well, she did pretty damn good so far.

Still ... "Claire, I'm just a shout away, babe."

Claire nodded. "Always, I know."

Demyan slipped out of the bedroom once he knew Claire was good. Downstairs, he found his family waiting in the kitchen where a meal was being prepared. Even more surprising, was that Ivan and Eva were also sitting together at the table. Ivan chatted quietly with Anton. Both men wore smiles. Demyan figured the two had a way to go before they would mend the bridges burned, but this was a start. A good one.

Standing in the entryway, Demyan watched his family move around one another, unknowing of his presence. Koldan had Ana sitting on his lap while she picked from a plate of fruit, a hand resting on her rounded stomach. It hadn't taken those two long to start their own family. A boy, Ana had told Demyan the last time they spoke.

Another Avdonin child, even if he wouldn't carry the last name.

"Oh!"

Demyan smiled widely at his mother's exclamation. Every head in the room turned in Demyan's direction, joy lighting up faces. Viviana crossed the room with a wide embrace, instantly closing it around her son and new grandchild. Her hands fluttered over the swaddled baby.

"He's so beautiful. Look at his tiny nose." Viviana all but gushed her happiness. "Anton, come see him. He looks just like Demyan did when he was brand new."

"Still Roman?" Anton asked, coming to stand behind his wife.

"Roman Anton," Demyan said.

"Chrissy took Ivan, anyway," Ivan put in, joining his old friends as he regarded the sleeping baby. "Anton is a better fit for this little man, I think."

Anton smirked. "Anything with my name is perfect."

"To you," Ivan joked. Then, he gave Demyan a nod. "Congratulations."

"Thank you," Demyan murmured. "For coming, too."

Eva shrugged at her husband's side. "Oh, we couldn't miss this, Demyan. We've waited so long to see you happy again."

"We have," Ivan echoed.

"Move aside so the pregnant one can see the baby," Ana ordered.

His sister would never change. Demyan didn't want her to.

Ana and Koldan had made the trip to Little Odessa from Jersey without question the moment Demyan called to say Claire had gone into labor. Despite the two beginning their own life, and Koldan stepping into the role as his father's right-hand man for the Jersey Bratva, Demyan would miss them both.

Ana, of course.

Koldan for entirely different reasons. Without really meaning to, the guy had been Demyan's closest friend and confidant for years. They were family, now. Business partners in some aspects, too.

They were also rivals.

That couldn't ever be forgotten.

At least family and friendship gave them a reason to always

keep things clean.

Koldan rested his chin on Ana's shoulder as the two whispered over the sleeping baby still snug in Demyan's arms. He promised Claire, so Roman wasn't leaving him until the baby's mother could take him back.

"He's gorgeous, Demyan," Ana said, smiling down at her new nephew.

"He is," Koldan agreed.

"Can I see? Can I? Please? Let me see him, Papa! *He's mine, too!*"

Laughter rang out from nearly everyone at Vera's furious exclamation at having been excluded from the group. The family dispersed to let her through and Demyan squatted down to eye-level with his daughter.

"He's mine, too," Vera repeated fiercely.

"He absolutely is," Demyan replied.

Vera peered over her brother with interest and a tiny, beaming smile. "He looks like you."

"Does he?"

"Yes, and like Ma."

It didn't matter how many times Demyan heard Vera call Claire that, it still had the same insane effect on his soul every time. Like his sweet girl had everything she needed to be happy in her life. So did he.

"I look like Ma," Vera added quieter. "Mine, I mean. That's what people say to me."

If the room hadn't been silent before, it sure as fuck was now.

Demyan glanced up, noting the uncomfortable expressions his family sported.

"You do look like Gia," Demyan said, reaching out to hold Vera's hand tightly in his own. "And a little like me, too."

Vera bounced on her heels, the excitement back in a blink. "Can I play with him?"

"He's not a doll, *dushka.*"

"Can I feed him?" she asked.

Demyan chuckled. "Maybe Ma can explain to you later how he eats and why you can't help."

Vera huffed. "Can I hold him, then?"

"Soon."

Vera wasn't pleased at her father's answer. "But, Papa, he's *mine*, too."

"Let her hold him, Demyan," came a soft, sweet voice from behind him.

Demyan stood, turning to face his wife who had dressed in a robe and didn't appear as tired as she had before. "I thought you were busy."

"I was missing the excitement and I can shower later," Claire said with a shrug. "Vera, let's go sit on the couch and you can hold baby brother Roman."

"Okay!"

Vera skipped past her father and mother as fast as she could go, running before flinging her little self over the arm of the couch with a breathless giggle.

"Christ, she reminds me of—" Ivan's words cut off as he winced.

"Gia," Claire said, filling in the obvious blank. "You can talk about her; it doesn't bother any of us and certainly not me. We don't hide her name in this house. Vera knows where she came from. She also knows she can talk or ask as much about her mother as she wants. Doesn't she, Demyan?"

"She does," Demyan replied with a smile.

And he was so grateful to have Claire in his and Vera's life because not all women would be as secure and confident in her place, their home and the love they shared as she was.

"Thank you," Eva whispered.

Demyan followed Claire to the couch where Vera was tittering in her excitement.

"You have to be still and careful," Claire explained.

"I will, Ma."

"Don't hold him too tight," Demyan added.

"I know."

"And—"

"Please let me hold him!"

Demyan shook his head with a laugh, bending down to situate Roman in Vera's tiny arms. He stayed low to keep one hand on the baby, just to be safe, though he didn't think Vera would drop Roman.

"Look, his eyes are open," Vera said, leaning over her brother to meet his hazy, confused stare. "Hi, baby."

The rest of their family had gathered around the back of the couch, watching the scene unfold.

"What do you think, Vera?" Demyan asked, jokingly. "Should we keep him?"

"Yes." Vera grinned down at her brother. "I think you're going to like it here, Roman."

EPILOGUE

Anton Avdonin had spent the majority of his life striving to reach one goal: happiness. It was something he learned he had to wait for, like most things … well, anything worth having.

There were surely people who would scoff at the truth, for whatever reason, but he didn't much care for those people or their opinions. Maybe some would be quick to point out his beautiful home, the success he held strong in his business, his healthy, lively wife and grown children, or even his amassed wealth and ask how he could be anything but happy.

Anton wouldn't be able to answer those people because truthfully, there would never be a proper answer. Not one they could be satisfied with, anyway.

Happiness came in many forms. It was more than just one entity and it couldn't simply be defined by many things, either. For Anton, happiness was life.

It was the bright smile his wife still wore in the morning and her face tucked into his chest at night. It was growing older and having the pleasure and luck of being able to watch those around him grow, too. It was the pride where it counted and his blood continuing on.

Because he wouldn't. Not forever, in any case.

Anton also knew pain. He knew his own and he knew his family's. He felt it crack through all the bones in his body, infect his blood and poison his soul. But that was okay, too. Eventually, the pain passed on, even if it took a lot to work through it and the agony of the grief lasted for longer than a person thought was possible. There was no happiness in life if there was no pain. There could be no growth, otherwise.

Experiencing and surviving hardships had little to do with being a Bratva man and everything to do with being human.

It took Anton a long time to realize that. Longer than he wanted to admit, actually.

The brightness of the sun was shadowed as Viviana came to stand in front of her husband, a knowing smile edging the corner of her lips upwards. Even in her sixties, with the world aging her gracefully like it always did, she was still the most beautiful woman he had ever seen.

She was still life and love to Anton.

Her eyes never changed. Familiar. Home. Warmth.

Vine was everything to him.

"Roman is this close to making you toss a baseball with him," Viviana said, holding her forefinger and thumb an inch apart.

Anton sighed, not wanting to admit his shoulder was bothering him again. Because really, he couldn't deny his grandson a damn thing. It was kind of terrible, actually. Roman was spoiled rotten and when anyone asked why, everybody pointed at Anton.

They weren't wrong.

"Yeah?" he asked.

Viviana nodded. "Demyan offered the football and you know how that went down."

"Roman can't throw a football."

"Nope."

But he could throw a baseball like nobody's fucking business.

Anton took all the props for that shit.

"Vera here, yet?" Anton asked his wife.

"Demyan said Claire was just driving her back from dance. They're coming."

Ballet, actually.

Vera, at ten-years-old, was quite the dancer. Anton wasn't sure where that interest of hers had come from, but Demyan couldn't deny his daughter anything. She started dancing at five and a half of a decade later, she was already ranked at the top of her age category for the state and in her studio. Vera was undefeated in every competition she had ever attended. She spent four hours a day, five days a week at dance school.

Anton only asked Demyan how he felt about that once. Did his son feel like Vera was missing out on being a kid, or was her attention too focused on posture instead of books? Demyan shrugged, said it was what Vera wanted, and that was it.

Because what Vera wanted, Demyan gave.

Simple as that.

Someday, that fucking kid was going to be a star. Maybe it'd be Broadway or some dance company traveling the world, but Anton would bet everything he had that Vera's name would be the one in lights.

To Anton, she already was a star. Vera still reminded him a lot of her dead mother, especially in her features, but she was also her own little person. A beautiful, happy in her heart and innocent in her soul little person. He suspected they could give a little bit of thanks to her father for that, and a hell of a lot of respect to her adoptive mother, too.

Grateful didn't adequately describe Anton's feelings toward Claire Avdonin. When no one else could pull Demyan back from drowning in the blackness of his life, she had. God knew Anton tried over and over to reach his son somehow, but he couldn't. Claire did and in a way, she gave Demyan back to Anton.

So yeah, he kind of loved that girl, too.

And she was so good for Demyan.

"Grandpapa!"

"I is here, too, Grandpapa!"

Viviana moved out of the way just in time to miss being caught in the crossfire of her grandsons' stampede. Five-year-old Adrik and three-year-old Daniil didn't care that their grandfather was resting back in a gently swinging hammock.

No, the two clamored up with Anton, nearly causing the damn thing to turn over in the process. Ana's two boys were little monsters, to be sure, but he loved that, too. The Vasin family was known to be laidback and quiet while the Avdonin clan raised hell when they could. Clearly the two black-haired, blue-eyed brothers took more of Ana's genes than they did their father's.

It had taken a while, but Anton didn't get as aggravated over Ana's marriage as he once did. People might think him silly for it, but they weren't him and Ana wasn't theirs. He adored his daughter and giving her away to someone else was one of the hardest things he ever needed to do.

Again, life moving forward.

"Grandpapa, guess what Papa brought?" Adrik asked, bouncing on one side of his grandfather while little Daniil snuggled into the other side.

"What?" Anton asked.

"Water guns."

"And he's gonna soak Uncle Demyan's ass," little Daniil put in.

Anton tried hard to keep the laughter at bay and failed

miserably. He shouldn't have laughed at all because he was trying this new thing where he didn't swear in front of the kids. Making light of Daniil cussing probably wasn't what Ana wanted him to do.

Oh, well.

It didn't matter. Like always, Viviana stepped in to save the day.

"Daniil Koldan," Viviana chided.

"Yeah?" Daniil asked, squirming on the hammock and making it rock dangerously again.

Anton held back chuckles at his grandson's attitude to his grandmother's chiding. If Ana wouldn't like Anton making light of Daniil's bad language, Viviana definitely wouldn't.

"That's a bad word, Daniil. You know better than to say those words."

"That's right, little man," Anton agreed.

"What word?" Daniil asked, his little brow crinkling.

"Ass," Adrik whispered.

"Adrik!"

"Papa says ass," Daniil stated very matter-of-fact. "He says he's gonna soak Uncle Demyan's a—"

"Yes, Daniil, we got that," Anton interrupted, his body shaking with silent laughter.

"Yeah, 'cause Uncle Demyan pushed him in the pool, remember?" Adrik asked, looking up at Viviana with all the seriousness the kid could muster. "And then he called him a bas—"

"We remember," Anton said, stopping the kid before he got himself in more trouble.

Viviana stared helplessly at her husband. Anton wasn't offering any opinions this time. Sometimes, with Ana's boys, it was better just to let them go off and do their own thing. Bad language included.

After all, Koldan was raising his boys the way he wanted. Respect was at the forefront, of course, but so was the Bratva. They followed under their father's feet nonstop. Koldan didn't complain and Anton admired the man for it. It took a hell of a lot to raise your sons into the kind of man you were. Anton knew it better than most.

"Ouch," Anton grumbled when a little elbow jabbed into his rib. "Christ, Adrik, that fucking hurts."

"Bad words," Daniil said, glancing at Viviana like his grandfather's slip got him off the hook, too. "See, bad words, Grandmamma."

"My God," Viviana groaned. "Anton—"

"Sorry, baby."

"I'm sure you are," Viviana replied, rolling her pretty brown eyes. "All right, let's go get some popsicles and juice, huh?"

"Okay," the two boys shouted together.

Anton barely managed to brace himself on the hammock as Adrik and Daniil scrambled off in a mess of waving limbs. Viviana leaned down and Anton caught his wife's smiling lips with his own, taking his sweet time to kiss her before letting her go again. She tossed him a coy wink before waving to the two boys to follow her into the house. Not two minutes after they were gone, another form darkened the sun shining down.

"Hey, princess," Anton murmured.

"Hey." Anton reached up to snag his daughter's hand in his, soaking in Ana's smile above him. "What are you doing, Papa?"

"Relaxing."

That was all he ever did now. Once Anton learned how to sit back, enjoy his life, and ignore all the bullshit, everything else came easily. The only thing that would have made it better was a glass of vodka and a blunt, but the doctor was clear on that what with his heart attack all those years ago. No sense in aggravating the organ he needed to live, after all.

Besides, Viviana was clearer on her position and Anton didn't like to piss his wife off much.

Ana pressed the heel of her father's hand to the side of her slightly rounded stomach. Something nudged his palm gently and Anton grinned at the feeling of his fifth grandchild's movement. At five and a half months along in her pregnancy, Ana wasn't quite as a big as she'd been with her previous two. Anton wondered if that was a sign that perhaps the gender wouldn't be the same this time around.

Her next words confirmed his suspicions.

"We found out yesterday for sure. Definitely a girl."

"And you're so goddamn happy and smug," Anton said.

"You're damn right," Ana muttered. "Mr. I'm-going-to-have-all-boys is going to learn how to pour pretend tea and maybe play dress up, too."

Anton flat out died on the hammock with laughter. "Good God, take pictures, Ana. Please."

Because it didn't matter how old Anton was, blackmail was the best fucking pastime. Especially if it involved his son-in-law.

"Ma never did for you."

"She did. I burned them one day when I found them hidden in her bookshelf." Anton sighed, eyeing his sweet girl. She'd grown up in a lot of ways. Ana wasn't as spoiled now as she once had been and beyond that, she reminded him a lot of her mother at her age. It was bittersweet. "How many more babies are you going to make with Jersey, anyway?"

"Papa!"

"Kidding," Anton mumbled, waving Ana's dirty look off. "I like him, you know I do."

"How hard is it for you to admit that, Papa?" Ana asked.

Well, it took at least one grandchild but Anton really burned that bridge after two, he supposed. Koldan was a good man and he loved Ana. That's what was most important to Anton.

"It's not hard at all, *dushka*," Anton admitted honestly. "But seriously, how many more?"

"None. Three is my limit."

"You're a good mother, you know."

And he was mighty fucking proud to have a hand in that as her father.

Ana shrugged. "Yeah, well, I learned from some pretty great people."

Anton grinned. "We think so, too."

"I'm still not giving you more grandbabies, though. Look at what you did to Roman."

"Hey, that kid is perfect."

Because he was just like his grandpapa.

"You'd do well to let me teach Adrik and Daniil a thing or two," Anton added. "Still willing to buy you a house in Odessa, *dushka*."

"Cute, Daddy," his daughter drawled. Ana leaned down and kissed her father on the cheek. "I make sure to come home at least twice a month and you know it. Anyway, Ma said dinner is almost ready and I'm starving."

"Yeah, go feed my grandbaby."

Ana left her father still swinging in the hammock. The silence and peace didn't last long. Anton heard the familiar footsteps of his son long before Demyan's large shadow covered the hammock.

"You're looking mighty fucking smug about something," Demyan noted. "Not that it's anything new for you. What did I miss out on this time?"

"Ana's having a girl. I knew it."

"Poor Koldan."

"Best payback ever, Demyan."

Demyan sighed quietly. "Yeah, well, I still have my own daughter to give away eventually, so. I can't say much."

Anton figured that was going to be pretty damn hard for Demyan to do, too, even if he still had quite a few more years to go before Vera would take that step.

"Roman wants to toss the baseball with you," Demyan said after a moment.

"I know. I'm teaching him patience."

And soaking in as much sun as he could while he was at it. It was never sunny enough in New York. Anton needed to take his wife on another trip to Barbados and soon.

Demyan laughed. "Isn't that my job?"

"You need a village, son. That's how you raise a kid like Roman. A village, quiet love, and time."

"I'm thinking maybe we could take him out to Vermont in a month or so, let him get a feel for a gun, you know. He's sniffing around shit and I just … want to make sure he understands. Like you and me way back, huh?"

Anton eyed his boy from the side, taking in Demyan's stony features. Despite having finally found his peace and happiness in a green-eyed girl who was nothing like what he loved before, Anton was aware his son still found it difficult to show emotions. Maybe not to Claire, Anton couldn't really say, but to everyone else, Demyan was as cold as ice.

Well, mostly.

Anton didn't judge his son as far as that went. It was Demyan's choice to keep everyone at arm's length. Anton suspected, because he'd been given the honor of seeing it with his own two eyes, that when the doors closed in Demyan's home, he was an entirely different man.

Loving, protective, and soft at heart.

A good man.

Anton would always—*always*—give Demyan the credit for that, but he hoped his son thought his father had a lot to do with it, too. After all, they were a little different, but they were alike all the same.

And like Anton knew he would be, Demyan was one hell of a Bratva boss. Fierce, frightening, and ruthless. The Avdonins were still a force to be reckoned with, only now they had a new boss to answer to.

Maybe even a better one.

"You know I love you, yeah?" Anton asked.

"Yeah, Papa. I know."

"And I'm proud of you, Demyan."

Demyan's shoulders loosened, but the man didn't give a single thing away otherwise. "In what case?"

"Every single one," Anton answered honestly.

"I learned from the best, didn't I?"

Anton put his arms behind his head to use as a pillow. "So the rumor goes."

"I fucked up, Dad."

Well, Anton didn't expect to hear that. "With what?"

"Vera. She's got this goddamn competition next week that she needs to fly out for."

"Oh?"

That wasn't anything new. "What's the issue and how did you make it worse?"

"It's in Detroit and she can't go with her studio like she usually would for other things."

"Shit," Anton muttered.

"Yeah. And I am the worst father that ever existed apparently. She also told me she hated me and slammed her door. She never does that. It's like a damn knife to the heart. Even Claire can't get her to sit down and talk to me and that woman can get anyone to do anything. I don't know what to do."

"She can't go to Detroit alone."

"No, and at her age, we can't exactly explain why, right? So, yeah, horrible father. Ruining her life. You know the deal."

"She's only ten, Demyan. You've got another eight years of this sort of thing."

Demyan snorted under his breath. "Thanks for the fucking support."

"Hey, just giving you a heads up."

"I know it's important to her," Demyan said. "And getting a spot in the competition itself is huge for her age and everything. A win would be massive for her portfolio. She's worked hard for this, which was something else she screamed at me."

Anton shrugged. "She can't go to Detroit alone."

"You already said that."

"Exactly, alone, Demyan. Besides, you might be making too big of a deal out of it, anyway. It's been years and Claire cut her ties with the Irish. You keep a good watch on them to make sure no one is planning anything."

"They're not. We're amicable, now."

"So, set up a couple of bulls. Take a few days off. Keep a low profile. Take your daughter to Detroit." Bracing his leg to the ground, Anton pushed the hammock again to make it swing before saying, "It's not all that dangerous if you plan for it. Make sure she understands why you won't be gallivanting around the city or whatever. She's a good, smart kid. If you explain, she will be fine. I think you need to give her a bit more credit."

"She doesn't even know what I am, not really."

Anton scoffed. "Yes, she does. Trust me. I thought Ana didn't for a long time, too. She knew from the time she was five that her daddy was different from other daddies. She figured it out when she realized she had a bodyguard and nobody else did when they went to the park. Vera fucking knows, Demyan."

"All right, so we don't talk about it then."

"Maybe it's time to."

"Maybe," Demyan echoed. "And I suppose that'll lead into Gia again."

"Hmm, and for once, Vera will fully understand all the circumstances of her life and what her mother gave for her. You, too."

"Will she hate me for that, too?"

"Of course, not. You gave her something beautiful, too. A family, love ... Claire." Anton thought about what he told Ana earlier. Demyan deserved the same. "You're a good father, Demyan."

"Sometimes I wonder."

"Don't ever wonder about that. Your children are the proof. It took me a long time to learn that. By the time I did, you were already walking away, son."

"Sorry about that."

Anton laughed low and deep. "No, don't be. That's life. We raise you just to let you go."

Demyan cleared his throat. "Thanks."

"It's what I do," Anton replied. "When will Claire and Vera get here? I'm hungry."

"Another twenty minutes, or so."

"Great. Now, go get me a coffee."

"I beg your pardon?" Demyan asked.

"Go get me a coffee, son. I'm not in the mood to move."

"You take this relaxing thing far too seriously."

"Not according to your mother," Anton retorted. "Coffee, remember?"

"Asshole," Demyan muttered as he turned on his heel and stalked toward the house.

Ten minutes later, Ivan was the one who brought the coffee out to Anton. Both men were silent as Ivan rested into a lawn chair set up by the hammock. Unwilling to sit up and drink his coffee, Anton took the pillows Ivan offered to prop him up in the hammock.

Sipping from the hot, bitter liquid, Anton smiled, soaking in the remainder of the summer day.

Ivan matched it the smile with his own. "At least you still manage to wrangle your kids in at least twice a month for dinner. I rarely get my girls at the same time."

"And when you do, they fight."

"Truth," Ivan muttered. "Some things never change."

No, but a lot still did.

Kind of like Anton and Ivan. Theirs was a friendship, an old one that had been tried and tested more times than Anton cared to count. It had failed them more than once, too, a long time ago. But, like the old souls they were, the two men couldn't help but eventually make their way back to one another for the friendship that always came so easily for both of them.

Even if that meant a hell of a lot of yelling would be involved to fix the burned bridges and heal the wounds that never really faded. God knew Anton and Ivan had cut a lot of scars into one another over the years.

Anton knew for a long time Ivan blamed him for what

happened to Gia. Hell, for a long fucking time Anton blamed himself, too. Some things were unavoidable; Anton was fully convinced Gia's unfortunate death was just one of those things.

Something that had taught them all a lesson or two. Not that each person's lesson was the same one, to be sure, because they weren't. It affected them all in different ways; none of them were the same humans, after all.

"Heard Ana's having a girl," Ivan said, a knowing grin forming.

"I like Koldan, Ivan."

"I know you do."

"I like him a whole lot more now that I know he's going to learn what it feels like to raise a little queen and then hand her over, hoping he's the right one."

"Koldan was the right one, Anton," Ivan said.

Anton nodded. "Still snuck up on me."

"Yeah, they always do." Ivan pushed out of the chair to stand, saying, "You good out here?"

"Perfect. Send Roman out once he's done annoying his father, would you?"

Ivan laughed. "How'd you know he's pestering Demyan?"

"Because it's Roman and he's his father all over again."

"Ah, very true. I'll send him out."

"Thanks."

Once again, Anton's peaceful silence didn't last long after Ivan left to make his way back into the house for dinner. Anton heard the sound of a familiar car's engine before two doors slammed shut. He figured Vera and Claire would go in the house first like they usually would, but his granddaughter surprised him by making her way around to the back.

Vera, in all her nearly eleven-year-old glory and with as much attitude as his little ballerina could muster, stood with her arms crossed. She flung herself into the same chair Ivan had vacated earlier.

"Expecting someone else, princess?" Anton asked.

"No," Vera said shortly.

"Yes, you were. I bet you thought your father was out here."

Vera didn't answer, but the look on her face said enough.

"Were you going to apologize for acting nasty to your father?" Anton asked. "Because I heard about that stunt you pulled."

"No, I wasn't."

"Liar, liar. You were because you can't stand for your daddy to be angry with you."

Vera rolled her eyes, but the girl might as well have been cellophane to Anton. Completely see through. "Maybe I was going to say sorry, but he's not out here, is he?"

No, but he usually would be. Demyan didn't like crowds and he preferred to be alone unless it was his kids or Claire, even if it was a family dinner.

"You can still apologize when you see him. And for the record, doing nonsense like that isn't going to get you anywhere with your father. Demyan deals with men a hell of a lot more difficult than you, princess. He's not going to roll over and give into your whims just because you stomp your feet and scream bloody murder."

Vera made a face. "So?"

"So," Anton drawled, pointing a finger at his granddaughter. "You're better than acting like a spoiled brat, Vera Avdonin, and you know it. You weren't raised like that, kiddo. Cut your father some slack. He loves you more than you can possibly understand."

Well, more than any of them understood, really.

"Yeah, I know," Vera mumbled sadly.

"How was dance?"

Vera frowned, refusing to meet her grandfather's stare. "Not that good."

That was surprising. Vera rarely, if ever, said a bad word about ballet.

"Why?" Anton asked.

"Couldn't concentrate."

Anton didn't need Vera to say anymore. Again, the girl was see through.

"Apparently hurting your father doesn't just leave him in a shitty mood, does it?"

Vera shrugged. "No."

Knowing how strict her teachers were at that goddamn studio, Anton was willing to bet they didn't let her lack of focus slide, either. It was another thing Anton disliked about the whole dancing shebang, but Vera was adamant about the school and her drive. She likely needed her father and fast if the wetness welling at the corners of her eyes was any indication.

"Go find your daddy, Vera."

"Yeah, okay, Grandpapa." Despite her agreeing with him, Vera didn't move from the chair. "Is he really angry with me?"

"That man doesn't know how to be angry with you, princess. A little disappointed, but never angry."

"Just as bad."

Yes, it certainly was, and it was also a far more effective discipline than anger, too. Especially when it was a child like Vera who adored her father with her entire heart and soul. Anton wasn't going to keep his granddaughter away from Demyan any longer so she could sit and stew in her own personal hell.

"Go find your father," Anton repeated.

Vera didn't need to be told a second time.

Knowing damn well once Vera got Demyan in her sights, Roman would make his way outside to find his grandfather, Anton closed his eyes and stilled on the hammock, pretending to be asleep. Sure enough, what sounded like a stampede of a tiny elephant's feet echoed across the quiet backyard before the porch doors had even closed fully.

Roman was not a quiet child. He was a hell raiser, loud to the extreme, quite opinionated for a five-year-old, and goddamn, he reminded Anton so much of Demyan at that age it was ridiculous. Anton wouldn't take the kid any other way. It was like watching his own son grow up all over again.

"Grandpapa!" Anton didn't open his eyes as Roman came to a stop beside the hammock. A tiny hand reached out and poked Anton's side. "Wake up, Grandpapa. Wake up, wake up, wake up!"

Sweet Jesus, the kid was relentless.

Quietly, Anton said, "What did I tell you about waking people up, Roman?"

"Not to."

Anton tried not to let his amusement show and failed miserably. Cracking open one eye, he turned to see the wide smile his grandson sported. "I was taking a nap."

"Oh." Roman's happiness fell, but only briefly. "Can I nap with you, too?"

"Someone said you wanted to play baseball, little man."

Roman lifted a shoulder like it didn't make a difference. "Nah, I'll just welax with you."

"We-lax?" Anton asked, drawing the word out slowly.

"Yeah, that's what Grandmamma says you're doing. Welaxing."

"*Relaxing*," Anton corrected.

"That's what I said."

Anton chuffed under his breath before rolling over in the hammock enough to let Roman climb on. Big, familiar blue eyes surveyed him in silence as the kid snuggled in contently to his grandfather's side. While Roman was mostly hyperactive and always on the go of some sort, when Anton told him it was time to be quiet, he did just that.

Roman's chin rested on Anton's chest. "Why do you relax?"

"Because I can," Anton murmured.

"But why?"

"Because it's nice to not worry."

"I don't worry," Roman informed.

Not yet, anyway. Someday, he would.

"When you're big like your father, you'll have lots of worries and little time to relax," Anton explained.

Roman cocked a brow almost challengingly. "Like you, too."

"Hmm?"

"When I'm big like you, too."

"Yeah, like me, too," Anton replied.

Roman tucked himself back into Anton's side without another word, his arms curling around his grandfather to hold tight. It was moments like these Anton cherished the most in his life. Quiet moments that were rarely duplicated but so important to his memories. And he did have a lot of them between his beautiful wife, his daughter and son, and now his grandchildren.

Yes, he had surely been given the best life.

"Grandpapa?" Roman asked.

"Yes?"

"What's patience?"

Anton chuckled. Clearly someone had told the kid his grandfather was making him wait to play baseball and that word must have been tossed out there. "Why?"

"Papa says I need more patience."

"You do."

"Why?" Roman asked.

"Because."

"Because *why*?"

"Because a good man needs to know how to wait, Roman."

"Why?"

"You ask too many questions."

And it was a damn good thing he did, too.

"You said I should," Roman pointed out.

"I did."

"Why's a man need to wait, then?"

"A good man," Anton said. "Not just any man."

"Okay, but why?"

"Because, little man, good men wait. They just do."

"Did you?" Roman asked.

"I sure did."

"For what?"

Anton didn't even have to think about it. "For everything."

Happiness was everything, after all.

And it was all worth it.

ABOUT THE AUTHOR

Bethany-Kris is a Canadian author, lover of much, and mother to three very young sons, one cat, and two dogs. A small town in Eastern Canada where she was born and raised is where she has always called home. With her boys under her feet, a snuggling cat, barking dogs, and a spouse calling over his shoulder, she is nearly always writing something ... when she can find the time.

Find Bethany-Kris at:
Her website www.bethanykris.com,
or on Facebook at www.facebook.com/bethanykriswrites,
on her blog at www.bethanykris.blogspot.ca,
or on Twitter - @BethanyKris.

Sign up to Bethany-Kris's New Release Newsletter here:
http://eepurl.com/bf9lzD

MORE BY BETHANY-KRIS

Watch for more at www.bethanykris.com.

www.ingramcontent.com/pod-product-compliance
Lightning Source LLC
Chambersburg PA
CBHW051100030726
47504CB00006B/1719